Remembrance Day
THE SQUIRE QUARTET

Brian Aldiss, OBE, is a fiction and science fiction writer, poet, playwright, critic, memoirist and artist. He was born in Norfolk in 1925. After leaving the army, Aldiss worked as a bookseller, which provided the setting for his first book, *The Brightfount Diaries* (1955). His first published science fiction work was the story 'Criminal Record', which appeared in *Science Fantasy* in 1954. Since then he has written nearly 100 books and over 300 short stories, many of which are being reissued as part of The Brian Aldiss Collection.

Several of Aldiss' books have been adapted for the cinema; his story 'Supertoys Last All Summer Long' was adapted and released as the film *AI* in 2001. Besides his own writing, Brian has edited numerous anthologies of science fiction and fantasy stories, as well as the magazine *SF Horizons*.

Aldiss is a vice-president of the international H. G. Wells Society and in 2000 was given the Damon Knight Memorial Grand Master Award by the Science Fiction Writers of America. Aldiss was awarded the OBE for services to literature in 2005. He now lives in Oxford, the city in which his bookselling career began in 1947.

THE SQUIRE QUARTET

BRIAN ALDISS
Remembrance Day

The Friday Project
An imprint of HarperCollins
77-85 Fulham Palace Road
Hammersmith, London W6 8JB

www.thefridayproject.co.uk
www.harpercollins.co.uk

First published in Great Britain in 1993 by HarperCollins
This edition published by The Friday Project in 2012

ISBN 978-0-00-746118-9

Set in Minion by Palimpsest Book Production Limited,
Falkirk, Stirlingshire

for
Doris Lessing
a bad terrorist
with love

Contents

Introduction

This third volume in the Squire Quartet is probably the most complex, and least popular of the four. It may have too many characters in it for a lazy reader. Yet the critics liked it.

The Daily Express described it as, 'a crisply philosophical novel on the topic of disaster.'

The Daily Telegraph called it, 'an enjoyable companion piece to *Forgotten Life.*'

Unlike the earlier novels in the Quartet, in *Remembrance Day* we meet the rural poor: Ray Tebbutt and his missus, Ruby.

Ruby has a goat she loves, and raspberries she picks. Memories of their childhoods during wartime intrude on their lives. Peace is still troubled; better perhaps to live in a backwater.

They are getting by, living frugally. Ray has acquired a credit card; the card is used only for identification purposes. They never pay for anything with the card in case they fall into debt. But Ray is browbeaten into lending a considerable amount of money on his card, and has problems in getting it back from a more prosperous neighbour.

Both Thomas Squire and Clement Winter, protagonists of the earlier novels, put in appearances. Ruby and Ray Tebbutt live not far from Squire – who is now past his days of fame – in deepest Norfolk. There comes a prolonged supper of rabbit pie, at which the squires and the Tebbutts sit and discuss the current state of play. Squire remarks - giving their current spate of IRA bombing as an example – that when underdogs seize power they rule no more wisely than those they supersede. (Power is also a leading subject in the fourth volume of this series.)

The great going world is buzzing with actions and ideas. The IRA is active in England. Learning and ignorance advance cheek by jowl, as usual.

Eventually, Ray Tebbutt gets his money back. So Ray and Ruby decide to go for a stay in a quiet little hotel called the Dianoya, in Yarmouth.

I once came across a gravestone in a Yarmouth graveyard bearing the name of Embry, and this story ends with an American professor called Hengist Morton Embry – a man who seeks advancement, one way or another. He has prepared a report on a bomb outrage at the Dianoya Hotel where several people have died. He is going to see Professor Stern, the principal of Anglia University. The people killed in the explosion, and their moratoriums, fortify Embry's theory that misery attracts more misery. He claims it is time for a new understanding of life.

Stern is left alone to think and decide. The TV is on in his room. It is Remembrance Day, with the ceremony at the Cenotaph. He reflects on the endemic wars being commemorated. England is a good peaceful place. But some things need changing . . .

Brian Aldiss
Oxford, 2012

Those who constantly recall their history are doomed to repeat it.

Hengist M. Embry

It is difficult to say to what extent a deeper understanding of the mystery of personality would ensure that these tragedies did not arise, since the still deeper problem of destiny itself is involved. We cannot say with any certainty whether it is, in the deeper sense, inevitable that certain persons should meet a certain time, and with certain results. A lifelong study of such mysteries indeed inclines to such belief.

The Nature of Genius
Dallas Kenmare

1

A Visionary

Professor Hengist Morton Embry was at the wheel, gliding along through Fort Lauderdale, pointing out the sights to his English visitor.

'This is the place if you want to eat fish. Absolutely first rate. I was there two – three nights ago, with Bobby Strawson and her crowd. Try the dolphin. Not the mammal, the fish. Go upstairs for better service. There's a waitress without a bra, and they serve a good Australian Shiraz.'

Gordon Levine was impressed. He would not have expected such information, so crisply delivered, from an English professor of Stochastic Sociology – even if there was such a thing – in an English town. Embry had facts spilling from his fingertips.

Fort Lauderdale slid by, malls, slummy bits, houses of the wealthy situated on well-tended canals. Levine was paying his first visit to Florida, and liking it. The month was March, the temperature was warm. He had already taken a swim in the hotel pool and exchanged a few words with the influential Bobby Strawson, organizer of the ASSA conference. He was impressed by the air of efficiency and glamour exuded by la Strawson. Equally, he was impressed by the charisma of this important professor, who had taken time out to show a stranger the town.

Embry was the sort of scholar referred to as outgoing, though

1

Levine had glimpsed a more thoughtful person beneath the surface. He had already given Levine some insights into other members of the ASSA, the American Stochastic Sociology Association.

Embry was an untidy man, moderately massive, given to large ties which hung over one shoulder of his cotton jacket like the tongues of wolfhounds. Academically, he was considered brilliant; yet he could schedule a neat eight-stream conference in a matter of moments, totting up all the scholars involved, friend and foe, like columns of figures. So why was this paragon accepting a sabbatical year in England at the Anglia University of Norwich, opening a new department? This was the question Levine put to his companion as they surveyed Fort Lauderdale.

'This mansion with the laburnums we're coming to, that's the Florida home of Jeff Stackpine, the Stackpine Trucks man. You think I'm side-tracking my career trajectory by taking off for a year? I don't read it that way. The US needs a breathing space from me. I can do wonderful things in England. They'll name the department after me.' He ground to a belated halt at a red. 'Traffic lights always see me coming. When did I last get a green? It's nature's way of telling me to slow down, I guess.

'Now we're heading for Mount Lauderdale. Have you heard of Mount Lauderdale? It's the highest point in the city, snow on it in the winter. Coaches lose their way and have to be dragged out.'

Levine expressed surprise. But, just as the Americans had their own views of what English weather was like, he had his views on the extremes of the American climate.

They turned into a less elegant road and were passing the Everglades Motel, faced with fake logs. The sign was supported by two fibreglass alligators.

'There you see the real unreal America, Gordy,' said Embry, gesturing. 'The wish to get on, the wish to get off, the longing to have you on, the longing to have it off. See how one of those gators is female – mammal female, with boobs and blond hair? It represents some sort of displacement in time as well as space. You clear the Everglades, then you fake 'em to get 'em back. Consider the diversity of mentalities in these so-called United States, the sheer diversity of mentalities. Some of us are living, or attempting to live, in the next century, and face up to the demographic conundrums ahead. Others – don't construe this as an ethnic remark in any way, Gordy, but some of us are still living and thinking last century, and the centuries before that, way back to primitive times, when tribes first wandered into North America.' He knocked significantly at his forehead.

As Embry exchanged an unscholarly word with a driver proceeding in the opposite direction, Levine said, by way of agreement, 'I saw in a recent poll that fifty-five per cent of the population believe the sun goes round the earth, rather than vice versa.'

Embry shot Levine a glance, half-smiling, one eyebrow crooked. 'You mean the other way round, surely? The earth going round the sun?'

'Fifty-five per cent believe it's the other way about. Maybe it was sixty-five.'

'You mean the sun going round the earth?'

'That's what fifty-five per cent believe.'

Embry gave a snort and concentrated on the traffic ahead. Levine saw a muscle in his cheek working, one of the muscles he used for talking; maybe it never rested, even when no speech was forthcoming.

Levine experienced a pang of doubt, sudden as toothache. Could it be that Hengist Morton Embry, founder, president, of the ASSA, was himself one of that fifty-five per cent? Or sixty-five? It couldn't be. Could it?

'Astronomy was never a subject I specialized in,' Embry said. 'But I do know that one American in seven carries a gun in his or her car.'

Levine wanted to explain to him that you did not have to go to university to learn that the earth went round the sun, taking a year to make a complete orbit, because this was one of the known facts you imbibed with your mother's elderberry wine, if not her milk. That there was a whole raft of things, a skein, a web, a map, a safety

3

net, you absorbed like your native language itself, if you were normal, by the time you made your first date, and that that safety net was an indispensable component of – well, of Western culture. Yet here was this professor of a distinguished Illinois university – a whole lot of them managed to get down to Florida in March – who appeared to have doubts regarding a cardinal fact known to ancient Greeks. Levine had on his safety belt in the Toyota; but in the other world, that great nexus of circumstance we call life, there was no safety belt. He was sitting next to an eminent academic who believed the sun was in orbit about the earth.

'Right, Gordy,' Embry said, 'here's Mount Lauderdale coming up.'

He gestured grandly and chuckled. The car was heading up a slight incline. There were trees on either side of the road, expensive properties, a neat waterway, and the slight rise in the road.

'Mount Lauderdale. How d'you like it? All of eighteen feet above sea level. We're a great country for making mountains out of molehills.'

'I see.'

Embry chuckled again. 'Just kidding you before, Gordy. Exercising your British sense of humour . . . We'd best head back to the conference.'

Embry was a Happy American. It was easy to appear Happy. It was patriotic to be Happy. It was also good business to be Happy. Good business and patriotism went together, and their lubricant was the kind of good humour in which Professor Embry specialized.

Returning to the conference, he drove Levine past The Fronds, a gigantic shopping mall built on adventurous lines, with undulating façades and interior waterfalls. It had been standing half a year, and was due to be pulled down, Embry said, in eighteen months. The carpark beside it was full of cars. Embry took it in with a gesture.

'See that? The Fronds. A fad of yesteryear, but still making millions for a guy I used to know. Sold wallpaper in Denver. We were talking about people wandering into North America thousands of years ago. That's what they came for – the shopping.'

He told Levine you could eat a good hotdog in The Fronds. Hotdogs went with the good business and the patriotism; hotdogs marked a guy out as a good, average joe, even if he was a professor and president of ASSA.

Levine asked himself why he was thinking in this vein on this Florida afternoon, when palms waved their leaves against the ever-enfolding walls of commerce. Didn't I eat hotdogs myself and without being self-conscious about it? Didn't I succumb to the unconscious pressure of society and present a cheerful demeanour? Wasn't it true that that demeanour became more and more my real self?

Punching a tape into the radio-cassette player, Embry filled the car with quadrophonic sound. Male voices sang: stately, assured, harmonious.

'Recognize it?' Embry asked. 'My passion! Medieval French Gregorian chant. Latin, as you know. *A capella*. I bought fifty tapes of the stuff when I taught a semester at Toulouse University, France. Can't get enough of it. They say the world lost something when instrumental music was introduced into churches, and I believe 'em. Listen to this "*Veni, Redemptor*" now . . .'

Levine listened. He knew nothing of the subject, had never specialized in it.

They were back at the Hilton in time for the cocktail reception. Traffic was moving steadily up and down Highway One. Planes were landing on time, bars were doing good trade, yachts were docking in expensive marinas. Barbecues were sizzling in yards, evening soaps bubbling on TV screens. Day's end was calm, but alert with promise all over the Sunshine State, even in the senior citizens' condos: time for fun unobtainable in England: the sort of evening you feel you deserve, with the sun skiing through a sky containing only one decorative cloud, positioned so as to grow more golden as the hour slipped by. Happy Hour. Most of the delegates to the conference were already gathering in the pool area, where a quartet discreetly played Mozart and drinks were served by lynx-eyed Hispanic barmen.

Palm trees, music, warmth, light-coloured clothes, Hilton service. No hassle.

Embry was greeted on all sides. A lot of shaking hands and embracing went on. You couldn't tell when people were not glad to see each other. Levine went along with Embry some way, moving into the heart of the crowd with a glass in his hand, exhilarated. Crazy to exchange all this for England! Here were people he knew, if only by reputation, creative people, alienists, scholars, fermenters of society, men and women, involved in one branch or another of stochastics and/or education.

Hi there to Dale Marsh, plump and genial, wearing only a T-shirt above gaudy shorts, though most of the guests had adopted more formal attire. The legend on Marsh's T-shirt said 'Squint when you look at me lest you be blinded by my beauty'. Marsh was English, but had lived eight years in the States, teaching Urban Relationships in an Eastern seaboard university.

Levine was not all that enthusiastic about meeting another Englishman, but stood to chat politely for a minute or two. With Marsh was a pretty blonde woman called something like Polly Ester – Levine did not catch the name and, unlike Americans, was afraid to ask for it to be repeated.

'Funny Hen Embry should elect to spend a year in Norwich at AUN,' he said.

'Is that anywhere near London?' Polly Ester asked.

'Not really.'

'A year out at pasture and he'll come rushing back Stateside into a government post at zillions per month salary,' said Marsh, in a lordly way. 'That's how it works. That's how the system works.'

'Besides,' said Polly, lowering her voice and sliding a bare arm through Levine's, 'Hen's got big trouble brewing here with the ASSA. It pays him to make himself scarce a while.' In response to Levine's surprised look, she whispered into his ear. 'Cooking the books.'

The phrase, he thought, was like some secret sexual signal, releasing a flush of testosterone through his arteries as he felt her warm aromatic breath in his ear. That sod Dale Marsh had always been known as 'Lucky' Marsh. He knew how to pick the birds.

After the reception came dinner. They drove out, a dozen of them in hired cars, to a seafood restaurant someone had recommended up the coast in Boca Raton, where stone crabs were the juiciest.

Embry was in good form throughout the meal, drinking heartily, expounding a blueprint for a better world.

Levine, as a hard-pressed administrator at a university increasingly under financial pressure, did not believe in better worlds. He turned to Marsh, who happened to be sitting next to him, to express his cynicism, expecting Marsh as a fellow Englishman to respond similarly to Embry's plans.

'Things are different in the States, Levine,' Marsh said, condescendingly. 'In London, psychotics are guys who have discovered how life really is. Over here, that bit of luck goes to mountebanks. They can capitalize on their discoveries in ways valuable not only to themselves but to the public at large.'

'Embry?'

Marsh sucked on a crab claw. 'You should read Embry's book on transpsychic reality – and not just because it's sold a million. Basically, what he says – I'm wedging his argument into a nutshell – is that the nature of self, and hence of our perceived world, is – or can be – up for grabs. He says everyone has visions, sees ghosts, or whatever. Parapsychic phenomena . . . Such things are dismissed as childish – which they may be – or disgraceful in our Western societies, and so are repressed or misinterpreted . . . well, something like that. But actually such so-called delusions are pleas from an inner self for change. Urgent communications. We must all change.'

'Nothing very new there.'

'OK. That's no objection, is it? But Embry states that our early experiences can cause us to fix on a mental model of the world which we may need to junk. Like some disaster early in life can set us on disaster courses later. "Circumstance-chain" is his phrase. Pass along the pitcher, "old chap".' He put his mode of addressing Levine in humorous quotes, as if recalling a phase of life he had jettisoned.

Marsh's friend, Polly Ester, sitting on his far side, had hitherto contented herself with reading the legend on Marsh's T-shirt over and over. She bestirred herself to lean forward and say smiling to

Levine, 'Dale's forgotten the part of the argument I like best. It's not just individuals whose memories of disaster can lead them to further disaster later in life. There's a brilliant chapter on how the individual is a microcosm of the nation. Hen shows how certain countries are ruled by – ruined by – memories of disaster.'

Several places away, engaged in argument, Hengist Embry nevertheless caught the mention of his own name and roared down the table, 'Alpha for you, Polly. Examples include Georgia, Serbia, many Latin American countries, maybe China, and, of course, Ireland.'

Marsh formed a circle of thumb and forefinger and made Embry a cheerful 'spot-on' sign as the latter plunged back into his own noisy conversation.

'Whether all that's true or not . . .' Deciding against completing the sentence, Levine returned to his platter of crab.

Rather to Levine's surprise, Embry paid him renewed attention as the group left the restaurant. In the carpark, he took Levine's arm in a friendly way and led him apart from the crowd, his mind evidently still full of his dinner conversation.

'Remember that lovely *"Veni, Redemptor"*? Well, man has to be his own Redemptor, to my way of thinking – but fast.'

'Most human plans for improvement come to grief.'

'There opinions differ. Look what the US has become. This was all wilderness two centuries ago.'

While Levine was feeling ashamed of his English remark, Embry deftly changed the subject. 'As a successful man, I have my enemies here, Gordy,' he said. 'Some are not above spreading lies about me. You find the same kind of thing in every community. Now, let's get to the crunch. I'm a visionary but I'm also a practical man. I was hoping you could maybe give me a few introductions back in England, to ease my path in the new post.'

Levine said he did not entirely understand what line of work Embry was planning for the AUN.

'Gordy, I will be more than happy to inform you. What I mainly require from you is a warm personal intro to Sir Alastair Stern, principal of AUN. He's your uncle, right?'

'Father-in-law, actually.'

'How I relish that British "actually". I didn't know you were still using it.'

'I've heard the word on American lips.'

'Now, in a few sentences, I'll explain the project I have up my sleeve. It's a real beaut. I am eager to be working in Norwich. It's the capital of the County of Norfolk, right? See, I have some Norfolk blood in my veins. My great-grandfather sailed over to New England from Norfolk, back in the 1830s. That was a terrible time for the poor. The legend in the family is that the last great-grandfather saw of England was a line of hayricks burning on the horizon.

'My proposed project involves the analysis of an incident which occurred in the Norfolk port of Great Yarmouth. Do you know Great Yarmouth, Gordy?'

'Yarmouth. Yes, I've been there more than once. It's a seaside resort.'

'It so happens that there are Embrys buried in Great Yarmouth cemetery.'

'Quite a coincidence.'

Embry stopped his strolling and looked hard at Levine. 'A coincidence – or something more? Is it not what I term a circum-stance chain? Is the universe of human affairs random – stochastic – or pre-ordained, or ruled by God? Or what? That is precisely the question I mean to research. It's a big question, with large implications.'

Looking as if for inspiration towards the distant neon sign proclaiming JUMBO STONE CRABS, Embry began to recite. '"What of the Immanent Will and its designs? It weaves unconsciously as here-tofore Eternal artistries of circumstance, Whose visions – wrought in wrapt aesthetic rote – Seem in themselves its single listless aim, And not their consequence." Thus the poet . . . Well, we are going to diagnose those artistries of circumstance for the first time. Ingenuity lavished on space technology will now confront Fate. Pardon the expression.'

The wine had somewhat clouded Levine's perceptions. He felt they

9

should drive back to the Hilton, where he could lie down, or perhaps have another drink.

'I don't follow. A diagram of circumstance? I mean, couldn't you pursue such research more effectively in the US? Why Yarmouth, for heaven's sake?'

'It so happens that Great Yarmouth presents us with precisely the contained situation required, the kind of laboratory test case.' He smiled benignly. 'I'm an optimist, Gordy, and, what's more, I have the future good of humanity in mind. I see – I do believe I see – a way in which poor suffering mankind might be made happier, safer. And I'm not talking about SDI or anything like that.

'Ask yourself why we are always running towards disaster. Just when you might think affairs were straightening out, along comes a fresh crisis. It happens in individual life, it happens in international affairs. I can remember back to the aftermath of World War II. Just when we were sorting out the peace and trying to put everything together, along came the threat from the Soviet Union, and the Cold War descended upon us, warping millions of lives for decades.'

'That may be so, but it doesn't have much to do with Yarmouth.' He should have known that such a remark would not have ended the discussion.

A sagacious finger was wagged at him. 'I hope it has everything to do with Yarmouth,' Embry said. 'There I shall test out my hypothesis of transpsychic reality . . .' He repeated the phrase thoughtfully, as if more for his benefit than his listener's. 'Transpsychic reality . . . If I'm right, then a new epoch in human relationships will dawn. I shall father a revolution in how we view the physical world around us . . .' He took a deep breath and then said, suddenly, 'I should have gone to the john before we left the restaurant.'

'We'd better get back to the hotel.'

The bladder problem evidently wasn't too serious. Embry dismissed it with a grand gesture. The physical world was going to have to wait.

They had come to the end of the carpark. Beyond some smart new plastic warehousing, masts of dinghies could be seen. Music of the swing era could be heard.

'I may as well admit it, Gordy. It's an ambitious plan, and it will need a whole heap of moral support from Sir Alastair Stern, not least because of the depressed state of the British economy in 1990. I want your father-in-law on my side.'

He outlined the circumstances of the case as clearly as if he was lecturing a class.

One of the depressants afflicting British life was the situation in Northern Ireland, which cost the British taxpayer many millions of pounds sterling a year. The Irish Republican Army, the IRA, although not politically effective, existed as a disruptive force in social life. In the mid-eighties, it had attempted a major coup when it planned a series of bomb outrages in English seaside towns during the holiday season.

Scotland Yard had got wind of the plan. Bombs of Czech-made Semtex were detected and defused in six towns along the South Coast. Three men had been arrested, including a high-ranking IRA officer. Unfortunately, one bomb had escaped detection. It exploded in a small hotel in Yarmouth.

'Four people were killed in the Great Yarmouth explosion,' Embry said as they climbed into his car. 'I am not concerned with the IRA. Though I may say parenthetically I do not approve of American support for the IRA. They can be described only as terrorists, killing and maiming innocent people. My AUN unit will investigate the lives lost.

'Who were those four persons killed that day? What were their lives like? What brought them to that hotel on that date? Was their presence merely stochastic, or had it to do with, say, economic conditions?'

'Or the hand of God?' hinted Levine, smiling.

'We are open-minded. We rule nothing out. Not even the Immanent Will. "*Veni, Redemptor*". I do not go into this project with preconceived

11

ideas, Gordy. I want to establish whether the random was at work, or were those deaths circumstance-chain deaths – with submerged social causation of the same kind that draws me back to ancestral ground?

'It's going to be an original and epoch-making sociological field exercise. Who exactly were the four who died that day in the Hotel Dianoya in Great Yarmouth?'

2

Displaced

Midsummer 1986

The car was an orange Hillman which had seen better days. Ray Tebbutt drove it with the kind of care he devoted to most matters, slowing to corner, braking gently to stop, signalling whenever humanly possible. He left the main Fakenham–Cromer road and turned north in third gear. Although the side road was empty of traffic this summer evening, he handled the wheel as cautiously as if in one of the city traffic jams to which he had previously been accustomed.

Clamp Lane was a narrow strip between high banks. History had split it open to the sun like a walnut. Within living memory, the lane had been shaded by elms, their woody topknots havens for birds. The trees were all that remained of extensive forest which had once choked this region of Norfolk before the Enclosures Acts of the previous century had begun a process of denudation. Then Dutch Elm Disease, spread through the importation of cheap foreign timber, had wiped out the last grand sentinels. Three summers and they were gone, and the birds they sheltered gone with them. Clamp Lane was now bathed in impartial summer sun, banal, no longer secret, me-andering between unfrequented wheat fields, easy going for orange Hillmans.

Tebbutt slowed still further where the road sloped into a depression which provided some shelter from the wind for two cottages, solitary in the landscape. Like the landscape, these two Victorian cottages, close yet apart, built for farm labourers, were dominated by the socio-economics of their time. Machinery had superseded the labourers; they and their families were gone long ago, as the birds had gone.

The cottages contemplated each other across the roadway. The building on the left, No. 1, never distinguished for its beauty, was tumbledown, many of its windows broken; it had remained empty for some years, a little too distant from the coast to attract speculative builders. The garden had run riot in a tangle of weeds, while clawed arms of bramble reached up to the bedroom windowsills. Ivy had gained the chimney pot. On the front bank, a wattle fence had collapsed, but marigolds still flowered there, year after year.

The opposite cottage, No. 2, to the right of the lane as Tebbutt approached, presented a more cheerful aspect. Though its original denizens had been packed off, and it had endured years of emptiness, it was now occupied and maintained. Its windows, which were open, shone brightly; all paintwork and guttering were spick and span. Its rather poky aspect had been improved by a small front porch. Its neat little garden, with stone garden seat, was planted out with flowering annuals, while the gravel drive leading to a lean-to garage was weeded and lined with box.

A small black and white cat sat alertly on the sill of one of the upper windows, as if anticipating its master's arrival.

Turning in at the white gate, Tebbutt brought the car to a gingerly halt in order not to disturb the gravel, and tooted the horn.

A comfortable-looking woman came bustling immediately round the side of the house. Her hair was dyed brown. Over her thin form she wore a handwoven red blouse, jeans, and a pair of sandals, country garb which did not entirely disguise her look of being a displaced townee.

Removing her spectacles from her nose, she kissed Tebbutt on the lips as he emerged from the car.

'Hello, Ruby love, how's the day been?' he asked, squeezing her narrow bottom as he embraced her.

'Naughty Bolivar caught another bird this morning,' she said, glancing up accusingly at the cat on the sill. 'A poor little corpse was waiting for me on the back doorstep when I got home.'

'Little devil,' said Tebbutt indulgently. 'Not another thrush? Bolivar must have killed every thrush in Norfolk by now.'

'A robin this time,' replied his wife, linking her arm in his. 'I warned him that one day a dirty great eagle would fly down and carry him off to be fed to baby eagles.'

'That should have a tonic effect on his morals.'

Laughing, they went together by the narrow way between fence and garage, and turned in at the back porch.

The porch was built of breezeblock topped by insecure rustic work. It had been added to the main structure by previous occupants of No. 2 Clamp Lane. The Tebbutts had camouflaged the crude wall by nailing a trellis to it and growing a Russian vine up the trellis. The vine had threatened to cover the entire cottage until Ruby took shears to it; now it was regularly clipped.

The kitchen which they entered stretched across the rear of the building, and overlooked farmland. The view from Ruby's sink was pleasant, but curtailed by rising ground, above which could be seen a line of treetops and one chimney, belonging to the Manor Farm in Field Dalling. The ground floor of the dwelling consisted of kitchen, toilet, a passage doubling as hall, and a front room. This living-room had once been two rooms, a tiny parlour and a smaller dining-room. When newly installed in the cottage, soon after Ray had lost his Birmingham job and they were still optimistic, the Tebbutts had removed a rusty solid-fuel stove and knocked the two rooms into one. The stove they sold for five pounds to a scrap dealer from Swaffham.

'Cup of tea, love?' Ruby asked, continuing without awaiting an answer, since she knew what it would be. 'You look a bit tired.'

Ray sank down on one of the two chairs they had managed to cram in the kitchen beside the small table where most of their meals were eaten. He was a small wiry man in his early fifties. What remained of his hair was dyed black. His bullet-head gave him an aggressive aspect, though the expression on his red-tanned face was amiable. His large feet were crammed into boots which he now proceeded to remove, sighing heavily as he did so. He dropped them on the matting on the floor, paused, then arranged them under the table.

'That bugger Greg made me dig the upper field all afternoon,' he said. 'He'll never grow anything on it when it's dug. It's far too dry under the shade of that line of poplars.'

'He should get a thingy on it.' She was four years younger than her husband, but occasionally forgot the names of objects. 'A mechanical digger.'

'It's full of couch-grass. You can't make any progress.'

Tut-tutting in agreement, she passed him his mug of tea. As he thanked her, she nodded and pointed with elaborate pantomime in the direction of the front room, while silently mouthing the word 'Mother'.

Tebbutt nodded and smiled and mouthed the words 'I'm going' in return. After a noisy sip at his tea, the mug of which carried a picture of a sheep wearing spectacles and the legend 'I've been fleeced', he rose to his stockinged feet and padded dutifully into the front room.

His mother-in-law sat in a big wicker chair, her chin resting on her chest. A wisp of scanty white hair had fallen over her face. She was a small frail woman in her seventy-fifth year, retaining her position in the chair only by dint of four large colourful cushions which, like sandbags round a beleaguered building, served to bolster her morale.

Although Agnes Silcock gave every appearance of being asleep, she spoke distinctly as Tebbutt approached. 'Early tonight then, are we?'

'Excuse my stinking feet, Ma. It's gone seven. Usual time, thereabouts.'

'So it is. I must have been wool-gathering.' She raised her head to observe the clock with the loud tick, an old wind-up relic from better days standing on the mantelpiece, and then let it fall again.

He told her the events of his day, while Ruby stood behind him, listening, in the doorway.

Tebbutt knew that both Agnes and her daughter had a passion for small detail; Agnes had been a jigsaw addict before her eyes had failed her: the accretion of the small pieces, each to be accommodated in one place only in the whole picture, had greatly satisfied her. Ruby had shared this hobby.

But for Tebbutt it was precisely the small accretion of incident which pained him. His day, like all days now, had been passed in manual labour at Yarker's garden centre. Though he liked to please his mother-in-law, it was with no great pleasure that he recalled its details for her. But to see her listening thirstily to the details of the outer world was rewarding. And it pleased Ruby.

His boss, Greg Yarker, had driven to Hunstanton to collect a consignment of plants, leaving Ray in charge of the centre until noon. Yes, he'd been quite busy. Despite the hot weather and the recession, people were still buying plants. He had sold four nice tamarisks to a woman who said she was from South Creake. Never seen her before. Some people still had money to spend.

'Don't know where it comes from,' Agnes said, with a cackle.

Pauline Yarker had issued forth from her caravan and brought him a coffee at about noon. He had chatted with her for a while.

'Awful woman,' Ruby said.

Then he'd shifted bags of peat. Yarker had returned with the plants. He had done a deal over some furniture with some people in Hunstanton who were having to sell up. Yarker was more interested in furniture than plants; he would sell up the centre if anyone would buy. He had brought Tebbutt a pasty for lunch from a new bakery in Hunstanton. So Tebbutt had saved Ruby's sandwiches and brought them home again. She could fry them up for his supper and that would save the rest of the ham for tomorrow.

'Raspberries and cream for seconds,' Ruby promised.

He plodded on with an account of his banal day. The old woman was now fairly lively, her wrinkled face turned to Tebbutt's. Ruby, smiling, polished her spectacles and adjusted Agnes's cushions.

'I need a new pair of corsets,' Agnes announced, before Tebbutt's account was done. 'Can you buy me a pair in Sweeting's next time you're over there?'

'You don't need corsets, Ma,' Ruby said from behind the wicker chair. 'Besides, you've only had that pair you've got on six months. We can't afford another pair when it isn't necessary.'

'Corsets help my poor old back,' Agnes said. 'Ray knows, don't you, Ray?'

Tebbutt laughed. 'Corsets aren't my speciality, Ma. Excuse me, I'm going to get my slippers on and milk the goat. Then it'll be supper and your bedtime.'

The goat, Tess, was tethered in the back garden in her own enclosure. She had not been the money-saver the Tebbutts had hoped when they had bought her on their arrival at No. 2 Clamp Lane. She needed supplementary feeding over the winter. But it was reassuring not to have to buy milk from a supermarket, and they were fond of the animal. Tebbutt talked soothingly to her as he milked her into a bowl, his capable hands moving gently on her teats.

Ruby Tebbutt never wasted a drop of Tess's milk. If the milk ever went sour, she would make cheese of it and serve litle round pats of the cheese, grilled, on toast with a sprig of parsley. It was one of her husband's favourite dishes.

Any surplus milk Ruby took to Fakenham market to sell. Having bought the cottage when house prices were high, even in a relatively cheap region like Norfolk, they now put aside every penny they could to restore their fortunes.

After supper, when Ray had eaten his fried sandwiches, followed by raspberries from the garden, and drunk a mug of tea, Ruby got her mother upstairs to bed. The old lady had all but lost the use of her legs. Fortunately, she was light and amenable, ready to be tucked up between the clean sheets. As yet, she was not incontinent every night. Ray went up in his socks and kissed her goodnight. It was nine o'clock and almost dark in her little room with its sloping roof. By her bedside she had a photograph in a silver frame of her dead husband and her two daughters when they were small.

Downstairs, Ruby and Ray sat together on the sofa, holding hands a little and watching an hour of television. They could not afford a daily newspaper. Wine was one of their luxuries, and they sipped half a tumbler each while watching some news and the weather forecast. At ten, they switched off to prepare for bed. Tebbutt had to rise at six in the morning. Matters had been rather different before he lost his job as a printer. In the mid-eighties, many people were losing their jobs, as he often said, consoling himself.

'Perhaps we could get Ma a medical corset on the National Health,' Ruby said, as they were washing up their supper dishes.

'We'll ask Dr Fowler on Monday. I'll see if Bolivar wants to come in.'

Ray looked about the garden, but the cat was nowhere to be seen. The animal could always sleep in the garage.

The stairs were shut off from the living-room, cottage-style, by a door with a latch. Ruby and Ray were about to go upstairs when the phone rang. Ruby's foot was on the lowest step. She withdrew it, hastily closing the stair door so that her mother would not be roused by the ringing.

'Who can it be at this time of night?' she asked.

'Fuck knows,' Ray said.

For the Tebbutts, the telephone was a silent, baleful instrument. Certainly, they sometimes received calls from their daughter Jennifer or, even more infrequently, from Ruby's sister Joyce. But by and large the instrument was used only for emergencies. For reasons of economy, it was rare for the Tebbutts to phone out. And to receive a call at this time of night could only mean bad news of some kind.

Ray crossed to the window where the phone lay on the windowsill. As he lifted the receiver to his ear, he looked out over the garden to the lane and beyond it to the forlorn façade of the cottage opposite, just visible in the light from the living-room.

'It's Jean here, Ray,' said a female voice in his ear, continuing without pause, 'and I have a little favour to ask you. Mike can't – you know how he is. I'm sure you won't mind, and it's only a little thing, but it's about the car . . .' Her voice trailed away.

'Has it gone wrong again?' Ray asked, signalling with his left hand to Ruby, who stood anxiously by, that everything was all-right-ish. 'Jean Linwood,' he whispered, momentarily covering the mouthpiece.

'It broke down on the A148 and it's in Stanton's garage – you know Joe Stanton, I expect.' The Linwoods always assumed other people knew things.

'No, I don't. We always take the Hillman to the garage in Fakenham, where we—'

'Anyhow, as I was saying, Stanton phoned a couple of hours ago to say the Chrysler's repaired, and Michael was wondering if you'd kindly drive him over to Melton Constable in the morning on your way to work so that he can pick it up.'

'Er – well, Jean . . . I mean, Melton isn't really on my way to work. In fact it's in the opposite direction.'

'It's not far.'

Silence on the line. Then he said, 'Er, Jean, what about Mike's father? Wouldn't he drive him over?'

He heard the anger in her voice. 'Noel? We never ask *him* for anything, not the slightest thing. We'd never hear the end of it. I thought you understood our situation, and how difficult it was.'

'But in this case . . .'

'Oh, OK, Ray, forget it, then. Never mind. We knew you lived near Melton. I just thought you might like to do a friend a favour, but please forget all about it. Poor Michael will just have to go on his bike and it'll take all morning.'

Ray pulled a face at his wife as he said, 'Yes, yes, I see that. It's just that I've got to – well, never mind that, of course I'll drive him over to Melton. Be glad to. You know I'm an early riser – in fact Ruby and I were just going to bed – but I'll be over to pick Mike up, tell him, at seven thirty. Don't worry.'

Jean's voice, which a moment earlier had brimmed with

indignation, sounded a note of dismay. 'Couldn't make it eight, could you? We aren't early birds like you and Ruby. Eight or half-past would be better. More civilized.' Tebbutt had heard her laying down the law on what was civilized before.

Another face to Ruby, who waved her hands in silent mime of caution. Ray scratched the back of his head. 'Look, Jean, you see, I promised Yarker I'd be there early tomorrow. I want to get on with my work before it's too bloody hot. I hope you understand?'

The tone of her voice told him she did not entirely understand. 'There's no point in leaving at seven thirty, Ray, dear, because Stanton doesn't open up the garage till nine, if then.'

'I'm a slow driver, as Mike knows of old.'

'I wouldn't have asked, Ray, if I'd thought it was going to be such a hassle.' Her tone was that of a woman dealing with a difficult man. 'He'd take a taxi but you know things are a bit tight at present. The boys need new school clothes. Mike's Auntie April needs looking after. As for Noel – he's not too well. He's still looking for a house. Or so he says. Meanwhile we're stuck with him. So make it eight o'clock then, all right?'

'I'll be there,' Ray said, and put the phone down. 'Manipulative female,' he said. Then, 'Still, I suppose we do owe them a favour.'

Though they would never admit it to each other, the Tebbutts felt disadvantaged by the Linwoods. Michael and Jean Linwood behaved as if they were slightly above everyone else; yet their situation was similar to that of the Tebbutts. Both couples had met with financial misfortune in a cold economic climate; both were struggling to make ends meet; both had an elderly parent living with them. Whereas the Tebbutts had only one daughter, currently working as a public relations officer with a technical development company in Slough, the Linwoods had three youngsters still at home.

'Trust them to use a garage so far away from their place,' said Ruby, feelingly. She was well aware of Ray's warmth for Jean.

There was one considerable difference between the two families, thought Ray Tebbutt at seven fifty-five the next morning, as he drove to Hartisham and turned cautiously into the drive of St Giles House: the Linwoods, for all their poverty, lived in a grand if tumbledown home.

He drew up neatly in front of the substantial brick building, hearing, as he switched off the engine, the Linwood dog bark somewhere at the rear of the house. Then silence fell. Curtains were drawn across the windows of the upper front rooms, where lived Mike Linwood's rather terrifying father, Noel.

St Giles House had once belonged to Pippet Hall, the manor house of Hartisham. In the difficult days following the Second World War, the Squire family of Pippet Hall had sold it off in dilapidated condition. Successive private owners had patched things up as best they could, but the value of the property had declined. By the early eighties, the house had deteriorated to a point where Michael Linwood was able to afford it – probably with a grudging loan from his father. Tebbutt knew that he was hoping to make a profit by selling off a parcel of land at the rear, thus enabling him to repair the leaky roof, and was engaged in lengthy and so far unsuccessful negotiations to that end with the local council.

When his watch read eight o'clock, Tebbutt got out of the car. The driver's door needed a good slam to make it shut properly; he left it hanging open in order not to wake anyone. He walked about, biting his lip. He was dressed in what he called his Working-Class Gear, with a denim jacket, bought at a car boot sale, worn over a dark blue shirt. His trousers were of thick donkey-coloured corduroy. As he often remarked to Ruby, he was 'got up to look like a character from Hardy – one of his minor novels'.

At five past eight, he went round to the Linwoods' back door. Various pieces of junk Mike had collected lay about in long grass. Washing had remained hanging on a line overnight in their weed-choked garden. In Mike's old Toyota truck, long defunct, were stored his paints and other necessities of an occasional decorator's trade.

Both Tebbutt and Linwood, after their displacement to Norfolk, had been forced to take up odd-jobbing. Tebbutt had some small success, and was hoping to save enough to buy into Yarker's garden business. Linwood was less able to adapt to reduced circumstances; he barely scratched a living working for Sir Thomas and Lady Teresa Squire, the owners of Pippet Hall, or doing part-time jobs for the religious community in Little Walsingham.

Tebbutt knocked quietly, starting the dog barking again. After an interval, the battered door was opened by Alf, smallest of the three Linwood boys. He let Tebbutt in without a word.

The scent of the house hit Tebbutt. He had tried to analyse it before when he and Ruby had been here. Damp dishrags, watercress, and woodlice, with perhaps a hint of the cheap perfume Jean used. Not unexciting.

The house, standing in an exposed position, had for years withstood the cold winds blowing in from the coast. About its interior was a feel of erosion; the draughts of winter, even when copper strips had been tacked round all the doors, had licked at corners, scoured floors, and whistled into every last nook with a flavour of salt.

The six-year-old had been sitting alone in the dark, antiquated kitchen, into which Tebbutt now followed him, looking round hopefully as he did so. The room, as previously, was in utter disarray. He spared a second glance only for a pair of panties hung up to dry on a line. Jean's, no doubt of it. He thought of what they usually contained.

A heavy black retriever came bounding up, thrusting its blunt nose into Tebbutt's crotch. 'Down, Felonious,' Tebbutt said, pushing the brute away. He refused to pronounce the animal's real name, which was Thelonius. Too pretentious to be spoken.

And who had named the dog Thelonius? The same person who, on the insubstantial grounds that it would provide them with a good start in life, had insisted on the three boys being christened Alaric, Aldred, and Alfric, overwhelming the boys' parents, presenting them with such a puzzle of nomenclature that they addressed their own sons as Aye, Bee and Alf respectively: none other than Mike's father, Noel Roderick Linwood, retired arms dealer with connections in the Middle East.

The scantiness of the kitchen furnishing was emphasized by an oil painting of a younger Noel Roderick Linwood, hanging above the unlit grate. Bearded he stood, stern and bushy of eyebrow, in a double-breasted suit, regarding a palm tree and a much smaller mosque. He clutched a diagram of a fighter plane, an emblem of his profession. A heavy gold frame surrounded him.

This was the presiding spirit of St Giles House, old Noel – at once the saviour and ruination of his son Michael and Michael's wife and their three boys. Battening on to his progeny, he had more than once saved them from destitution by selling off a painting or a Persian miniature.

Alf observed Tebbutt's gaze on the portrait. 'Wanna buy it? That's Gramps.'

'I know. I've met him.'

The lad snorted. 'He's mad. So's Auntie April. Barking mad. Madness runs in our family. I expect to be round the twist myself before next term.'

'You shouldn't think things like that.'

The boy hauled his right leg up on his chair and bit his knee. 'Do you think loonies are generally religious? Was Christ bonkers, for instance?'

Shortly after the Linwoods had acquired the old house, Noel Roderick Linwood had descended upon them. He was in transit, he said, seeking a house of his own. He would not be staying. He regretted the inconvenience. But if he could borrow the top floor for his treasures, that would be splendid. Couldn't the boys sleep all together in the breakfast room? Two years later, old Noel, well into his cantankerous seventies, was still searching the county for a house for himself, still burdening Mike and Jean with his presence, his conversation, his complaints.

Ray had heard Jean's monologues on this subject. Noel had gradually spread like a cancer through the house, taking over attics as well as top floor, and then, in a coup, a little study on the ground floor. He had even entertained old colleagues for days on end in his quarters.

Jean had raged. Mike had withdrawn into his shell. Noel had sailed on, untroubled.

In an endeavour to persuade the old man to move, Mike and Jean had arranged a dinner for him the previous month; Ray and Ruby had been invited, together with a local estate agent. Jean had opened up the unused dining-room. Although the ploy had not worked and Noel stayed put in St Giles House, plenty of Bulgarian wine had been served.

Before the meal, Jean had taken Ray's hand and whispered to him aside, 'Do be charming to the old blighter. He can be so difficult.'

The old blighter had set himself out to enthral. Tucked into the open neck of Noel's white flannel shirt was a cerise cravat. That and his untidy white hair gave him a theatrical air. He kissed the hands of the women guests.

With calculating eye, he surveyed the other people gathered round the oak table (since sold). He splashed his soup and grumbled about the beef and discountenanced Jean. But what he did mainly, in a rather argumentative way, frequently resting his left elbow on the table and waving his fork accusingly at Ruby, who sat next to him, or Ray who sat opposite him, was to dilate on his successful career as a military advisor to the Shah of Persia – a fine man by his account – before the disastrous turn of events which had ended in the expulsion of the Shah, leaving him to wander homeless on the face of the earth, while his country was taken over by a bunch of religious Muslim maniacs.

Noel swallowed down wine before repeating the last phrase in case someone had missed it. 'Religious Muslim maniacs.

'Not much fun for estate agents,' he said, braying with laughter, gesturing at the local specimen of the breed.

Ray's unease during this long discourse, which drove all other conversation from the table, was considerable. He knew little of Iran, and did not greatly like what he knew, but he understood that Noel Roderick Linwood was presenting a prejudiced view of events – the view in fact of a parasite, who had self-confessedly made a fortune selling arms to a despotic leader, at the expense of the leader's people. That there had been a violent reaction against the Shah's materialism was hardly surprising.

Since no one round the Linwood table had ever come within dreaming distance of the fortune Noel Linwood had accumulated, everyone listened to his tirade with varying degrees of respect or patience, some nodding or smiling in agreement. Not understanding the situation in Iran, they accepted his boasting for truth. No one disputed that the Ayatollah Khomeini, who had replaced the Shah, represented the greater of two evils. Noel's claim that Muslim fundamentalism was a threat to the West met with no argument round the table. Instead, the men reached solemnly for their wine glasses. The wine came from the Suhindol region of Bulgaria; they knew no harm of it. The estate agent said he drank it by the crate at home.

Ruby appeared to be enjoying the glimpse of the world beyond Norfolk provided by Noel. To Ray's mortification, she showed an unexpected understanding of Iran's internal affairs. 'They chop off people's hands in Tehran,' she said.

'They amputate the hands of thieves,' Noel Linwood elaborated, in a schoolmasterly tone, as if correcting a pupil. 'At the wrist.' He did not fail to demonstrate the action on himself, smiling fiercely at the company as he did so, showing his too-white teeth. 'The work is done by a criminal élite who were, under the late Shah, respectable surgeons, many of them trained here in England, at Bart's and elsewhere.'

Guests expressed their disgust and said it should not be allowed.

'It's barbaric!' exclaimed Ruby, gazing admiringly at her neighbour's wrist, which he still clutched as if in agony.

Prodding her under the table with his foot, Ray said, 'Better to have a surgeon do it than a butcher.'

A dessert spoon was pointed across the table in his direction.

'They're butchers. You have to understand that, if you're to under-stand the first principles of the present intolerable regime. Let me repeat – Muslim extremism, and there's no other word for it, Muslim extremism has ruined many a good honest English businessman. I tell you, I transferred to Iraq. Saddam Hussein is a man who understands the West.'

Ray, who had had to listen to his daughter's arguments on the subject, was against the armaments trade; he said no more, recalling Jean's caution earlier.

At the end of the meal, following coffee, the estate agent was already rising unsteadily from the table. At that juncture, Noel turned beaming to Ruby. Laying a hand on her arm, he said, 'You and your husband must come and stay with me in my little eyrie for a few days. I could show you some of my treasures from the East, since these two' – indicating his son and daughter-in-law – 'aren't much interested.'

Ray read a look of horror on Mike's face at this summons and a look of bemused delight on Ruby's. Before there was any chance of Ruby's fatal acceptance, before he could stop himself, he leaned across the table and said, 'Oh, I don't think you'd like us at close quarters, Mr Linwood. You see – Ruby and I have no manners.'

The old man turned to him, thrusting his neck forward as if to make sure he was hearing correctly. 'You're not a barbarian, man, are you?'

'Our table manners are very obnoxious,' Ray continued. 'And we're dirty. I'm sorry to have to admit it, but we're dirty. Ruby especially.'

'Ray!' she exclaimed, but he pressed on as excitement welled in him. The other guests, about to leave the room, turned to listen in fascination.

'You see, a few months back we decided to become Muslims, so we'd never agree with your views as expressed this evening . . . It's Mecca five times a day. We're not fanatics – we just hate Christians.' He rushed on. 'And in my case – it's shaming to admit this, Mr Linwood, but in my case it's a medical problem – an intestinal incontinence. And if I forget to take my pills – help, help, an attack coming on! Goodness, oh – excuse me—'

And with that he rushed from the room, Ruby following.

Outside the house, he had collapsed over the car bonnet, helpless with mirth, while she clouted him about the head, calling him a drunken brute.

'You stupid bloody liar!' she yelled.

Thinking over that occasion now, Ray could not repress a smile. The tyrannical old man had steered clear of him since. Mike and Jean, too, had been a while before they saw the joke. After a short stand-off period, Jean had congratulated him on confounding her father-in-law.

Turning his back on Noel's brooding portrait, Ray checked his watch, vexed that Mike had not put in an appearance.

Alf had returned to a piled bowl of cereal. The boy sat at a bare scrubbed pinewood table, doing major work with both elbows as he spooned the food into his mouth. Near to his hand stood a small radio, transmitting what Tebbutt assumed to be Radio One. Above its blare, Tebbutt asked the lad where his father was.

'Upstairs, of course. Praying or something boring.'

'Go and tell him I'm here, will you?' As he spoke, he leaned forward almost unthinkingly to switch off the noisy radio.

'Hey, leave that alone, bugger you!' the boy yelled, with unexpected vigour, and snatched the instrument out of Tebbutt's reach.

'Well, bloody well go and tell your father I'm here and waiting for him.'

Taking a look at Tebbutt's face, Alf slid down from his chair. He went off complaining, carrying cereal bowl and spoon with him. The dog followed, claws clicking on the bare flagstones. After thinking things over for a minute, contemplating the panties, inspecting the unwashed dishes piled in the sink, Tebbutt went to wait outside and stood and breathed in the morning air, gazing towards the roofs of Hartisham.

'Muslims,' he said aloud, and laughed. 'It would make a change . . .'

Only a few minutes later, Michael Linwood appeared, struggling into a jacket, breathing hard, his eyebrows arched with effort.

'I thought it was half-past eight,' he said, whether by way of apology or explanation Tebbutt could not determine.

As they went round to the front of the house to the car, Tebbutt leading, he said, 'Hop in, Mike, and I'll try to make up for lost time.'

'I know what a scorcher you are, Ray.'

Michael Linwood was ten years younger than Tebbutt. He was a small, broad-shouldered man, to whose evident strength was married an incongruous uncertainty of manner. In his well-tanned face, under a pair of furry dark eyebrows, was set a pair of round blue eyes, whose appearance of innocence was not entirely illusory.

He was dressed today in an old shiny suit, about which Tebbutt refrained from making comment.

'It's good of you to pick me up,' Mike said. 'Charity begins at home. I thought you were very rude to my father when you and Ruby last came round for supper. What did you mean by telling him you were a Muslim?'

'Let's not get into that. I was drunk. How's the work going?'

Mike was silent before answering. 'I dislike people who make fun of religion, Ray. Please don't do it again, eh? My father was quite deceived by what you said. It was very hurtful to all concerned.'

'For fuck's sake!' Ray exclaimed.

'There's another thing I object to,' said Mike, eyebrows beginning to work, but he refrained from naming it. Instead, he said, 'I'm at a spiritual turning point in my life, Ray. Light is dawning. We live in a wicked world . . . I'm cutting down on my work for Sir Thomas Squire at Pippet Hall. I'm going to work two days a week for the Fathers at the Abbey in Little Walsingham. They need reliable help, which I believe I'm in a position to provide.'

Tebbutt found it difficult to keep his attention on the road. 'But Tom Squire pays well, over the odds? He's a generous employer.'

'Sir Thomas Squire is a very worldly man. Just because the market is difficult, he's closing down part of the estate – not that that affects me . . . Doubtless you recall the words of the poet, "The world is too much with us, late and soon". I prefer the reverential world of the Abbey to Squire's privileged life.'

'But will it pay, man?'

In a voice of utter calm, as if he were addressing an aspidistra,

Linwood said, 'You have saved me half a day's work by playing the Good Samaritan on this journey, and don't think I'm not grateful. There's little enough gratitude in the world. We have been friends in adversity ... There are considerations other than the material. At the Abbey, I shall clear up after the pilgrims and do whatever else I am called upon to do. I shall assist Father Herbert, who is getting a bit doddery, poor dear fellow. "Groundsman": that will be my rank and station. "Groundsman". I appreciate that. It's a sign. "The man who looks after the ground". To my ear it has a Biblical sound about it.'

'So does "pauper".' He saw the round blue eyes upon him and regretted his hasty tongue, softening the remark by adding, 'We're both paupers, Mike, old lad. We have to earn a crust where we can. I'd have thought Pippet Hall was a good place to work. Better than Yarker's lousy nursery.'

Tebbutt and Linwood had met at Pippet Hall, the big house in Hartisham, a few miles west of the Walsinghams. Both had been employed by Sir Thomas Squire, redecorating and restoring farm cottages on the estate which the Squires intended to let out to the holiday trade. Even then, he remembered, Mike had undertaken odd jobs without pay for the religious community in Little Walsingham.

As if catching his thoughts, Linwood added, 'Of course, the salary isn't much. I don't know what we'll do over the winter, but no doubt the Lord will provide. Day by day I become ever more aware of His goodness.'

The reluctant provider in the Linwood household, as far as the Tebbutts were aware, was Mike's crusty old father, acting as combined saviour and *bête noire*.

Tebbutt had heard Linwood's history while working with him at Pippet Hall. Indeed, had heard it more than once.

Like his grandfather and uncles before him, Michael Linwood had started adult life as a modestly prosperous farmer, taking over the farm at an early age when his father suddenly disappeared to do something more exciting. The Linwood farm was near the Rollrights in Oxfordshire. Headstones in the local churchyard displayed many vanished Linwood names.

Mike's marriage to Jean Lazenby caused a row in both Linwood and Lazenby families. Mike had recounted this part of his story with morbid relish.

The Lazenbys were no farmers. Their money came from sugar. Despite its associations with slavery on West Indian plantations and caries in the teeth of children, sugar had brought a rise in social class for past Lazenby generations. Farming was a little below them.

Jean's parents had refused to attend the wedding.

Jean had been philosophical. 'Renegade father, weak mother – what do you expect?' and the remark had been quoted with pride. Mike's parents shared not dissimilar qualities.

The Linwood farm at Middle Rollright was comfortable enough. Jean enjoyed playing the role of farmer's wife. Mike had watched approvingly as his new wife took to baking her own bread and carrying cider to the men who worked on the land with Mike. She tolerated mud. She bottle-fed piglets. She shopped locally. She dressed the part in scarf and wellies by day, and was popular in chintzy frocks at Young Farmers' parties in the evenings.

'A dream world for us both,' Mike had commented, with bitterness.

In the golden haze, he had bought more land. He made deals with a leading fertilizer company which took much of the burden of actual crop-growing off his shoulders. He bought the adjoining run-down Base Bottom Farm for cattle, for what he regarded as a bargain price, although the pasturage was poor and sour. During the seventies, generous subsidies were available for beef farmers.

Disaster came knocking with the eighties. As unemployment mounted, inflation rose, the price of mortgages climbed. EEC agricultural policies ran counter to Mike's expectations. When he realized how serious were his financial problems, the fertilizer company proved unhelpful. They were closing down one of their factories outside Sheffield. They were off-loading commitments. They wrote threatening letters.

'Seemed God had it in for me,' Linwood commented, carelessly enough, as he and Tebbutt slapped emulsion on the cottage walls.

The bank gave him a loan at stiff interest rates which he soon found himself unable to pay off. Smart accountants took to visiting him in smart cars. Someone was making money.

That winter was a bad one. He lost some stock. The bank foreclosed. He sold off Base Bottom Farm at a loss to a London insurance company. Came the following summer and drought, and he threw in his hand. Jean urged him to hang on, but at the last he was even relieved to see the old place go.

At the time the Linwoods were packing up and leaving their ancestors to moulder in the local churchyard, trouble also visited the Lazenbys.

Jean's father, 'Artful' Archie Lazenby, died of a stroke over dinner in his London club. His will presented the family with some unpleasant surprises. Not only had Artful Archie lost most of the last of the sugar money gambling in the Peccadillo, a Mayfair club, but what sums remained were in generous part bestowed on a hitherto unsuspected Miss Dolly Spicer, of Camberwell Villas, London, SE5.

Jean's mother went into sheltered housing and died of influenza within eight months.

'How did Jean take all that?' Tebbutt had asked.

'Like a trooper. Not a word of mourning. Bit unfeeling, really.'

With no option but to farm again, Michael Linwood moved with trooper-like wife and sons to somewhere where land was cheaper. He settled on Norfolk.

The acres he bought proved difficult to work and were liable to flooding. His heart had gone out of the business. Again he got his sums wrong. Within a twelve-month, he was forced to sell to a scoundrel who swindled him and turned the land into a caravan park.

The shipwrecked family had moved into St Giles House and Linwood had taken up odd-jobbery. Jean had worked in a local dairy until that was taken over by a larger company.

You can't blame the poor sod for being a bit difficult, Tebbutt thought, mentally reviewing his friend's history, as they headed for Stanton's garage.

They had driven in silence for some miles before he dared to ask about the progress of the Linwood boys. Their sons seemed always more a source of anxiety than pleasure to Mike and Jean.

Instead of answering his friend's question, Mike said, 'In all our misfortunes, I have surely seen the guiding hand of Our Lord, directing me into His paths. After constant prayer, I can at last see a way to clarify our lives. This is confidential as yet, Ray, but I am thinking of joining the Church of Rome as a lay preacher.'

On reflection, Tebbutt realized he might have thought of something more tactful to say than the question he now blurted out. 'What did Jean say when you broke the news to her? Crikey, Mike, you can't earn a living as a lay preacher. You've got three kids to support.'

'Jean said more or less the same thing.' The blue eyes gazed serenely at the road ahead.

'I bet she did,' Tebbutt said. 'And your father?'

Mike clasped his hands together and trapped them tightly between his knees. 'We're not on speaking terms just now, Noel and I. My father is a heathen. When Jean ran upstairs and told him the news, he rushed out of the house roaring profanities. Jean wouldn't speak to me.'

'Where did your father go?'

'Oh, over to my dotty Auntie April in Blakeney, of course. If only he'd stay there . . .'

'I don't want to interfere, Mike, but how are you all going to eat if you . . . well, I mean, if you decide to go into the Church?'

'The Lord will decide, the Lord will provide.'

Tebbutt felt driven to say something in Jean's defence. He spoke cautiously. 'The Lord provides best for those who help themselves. Jean must be very anxious as to where the money's going to come from. I know Ruby would be.'

'Jean will eventually see the light. We shall manage,' Linwood said, with infuriating calm. An awful inflexibility in his voice silenced Tebbutt.

It was ten to nine. They were nearing Melton Constable. Tebbutt drove more and more slowly, feeling anger and despair welling up inside him. He stopped the car. Linwood looked at him curiously, raising one of the neat furry eyebrows, saying nothing as Tebbutt turned to him.

'Mike, the country's gone down the tubes. You are I are both hard put to earn a crust. But times are bound to get better. Maybe if we clubbed together we could buy out Yarker and make a go of the garden centre. What do you say?'

The reply was slow in coming. Gazing out at the placid countryside, Linwood said, 'You might like to know I nearly did away with myself when I lost my land here. God intervened through Jean. I knew then I was in sin. In sin, you understand? I no longer wish to operate within an economic system I consider wicked. It's as simple as that.'

Tebbutt closed his eyes. 'But you can't possibly dream of going into the Church with a wife and three kids to support. You must be fucking mad to think of it.'

Linwood's face grew red. Making a solemn moue which would not have looked out of place above a dog collar, he slowly shook his head and said, 'You sound just like the rest of them, my friend. I know you mean well. But there is such a thing as conscience, and I am bound to obey mine. We live in a sinful world, but our obligations to God must never be forgotten.'

'There's also such a thing as an obligation to your fucking family.'

'Swearing will do no one any good. I'm not angry with you, Mike, but please will you drive on to the garage. I can't sit here all day.'

Bottling up his fury, Tebbutt threw the Hillman into first gear and they jerked violently forward. Five minutes later, they rolled into the forecourt of Joe Stanton's garage. A CLOSED sign swung idly by the pumps and the large double doors of the service station were padlocked. An old blue car stood forlornly on the forecourt with a FOR SALE notice stuck under its windscreen wiper.

'That's funny,' Linwood remarked. 'I had anticipated seeing the

Chrysler standing ready for me out the front. Wait here a minute, will you, Ray?'

He got out of the car and stood about indecisively on the forecourt, arms hanging by his side. Tebbutt was tempted to drive away. Later, he regretted he had not done so. But a feeling of loyalty to his friend kept him where he was, tapping the fingers of his right hand on the steering wheel. After a moment, he tried the radio, hopefully, but it had not functioned for some months.

Joe Stanton's garage did not inspire confidence in a discerning motorist. First impressions suggested that many cars rolling in here never left. Most had been cannibalized and their wheels removed. Rust, weather, and hooliganism had reduced them to a kind of auto Stalingrad. Long-defunct Stantons had worked a forge on the site. The ramshackle old building had been converted by Stanton's wife, Marigold, into a shop for the sale of newspapers, bread, milk, Mars bars, and other necessities. But the shop was either too near to or too far out of Melton for it to flourish. It had died by slow degrees, until the 'Out to Lunch' sign in the door window became an informal funeral notice. The concrete of the more modern filling station was crumbling in sympathy. The whole place, Tebbutt considered, would qualify for a picture on a 'Quaint Norfolk' calendar. November, probably.

Marigold Stanton had retreated to the bungalow behind the garage, where she kept geese in considerable squalor. A handwritten notice on the Four Star pump advertised 'Gooce Eggs'.

After walking about the forecourt for some while, Linwood made his way through the automobile skeletons to the bungalow. The geese roused a hullabaloo as he disappeared from Tebbutt's sight.

Tebbutt sat at the wheel of his car, staring at a tin advert for Pratt's High Test, remembering how life used to be. He watched bees tumbling among the trumpets of a bindweed growing up a telegraph pole. Ruby would be at work by now. She caught the bus into Fakenham every weekday to do a summer job in Mrs Bligh's cake shop. Agnes would be safe at home with the cat for company.

Ray got out of his car and pottered about the forecourt. He took a look at the car offered for sale. It was a model unknown to him, a Zastava Caribbean, with an Oxfordshire number plate. A faded sticker on the rear window said, 'I Love Cheri'. On the FOR SALE notice, under the price, Stanton had written WON ONER.

Melancholy increased, Ray went back to sit in his car.

When Linwood reappeared round the side of the old forge, he was accompanied by Stanton. The two men were arguing. Stanton was an untidy, straggling kind of man who walked with a limp and a decided list to starboard. He wore boots, a pair of dungarees and an incongruous checked cap. His chest was bare. He shook his head in time with his rapid slanting walk. Beside Linwood's rather boneless figure, Stanton appeared an embodiment of energy.

Crossing to the double doors of his shed, he unlocked the padlock, wrenched the doors a few inches open, and elbowed his way inside, to leave Linwood on the forecourt. Linwood appeared to be studying the cracked concrete at his feet.

After looking at his watch, Tebbutt leaned out of the car window and called, 'Any problems, Mike? Is it repaired?'

His friend looked round slowly, as if previously unaware of Tebbutt's presence, and said, nodding his head, 'Hang on a minute, Ray.' It was not a satisfying response.

A small builder's lorry drew up at the pumps and tooted. As Stanton emerged from his fortress, the driver of the lorry, leaving his engine running, jumped down from the cab and stretched. He appeared to be on good terms with Stanton, who momentarily stopped scowling.

While Stanton filled the lorry's tank with Four Star, the driver nonchalantly lit a cigarette, flinging the match down on the ground. Tebbutt watched the two men talking, Stanton gesturing jerkily in the direction of Linwood. Linwood, taking advantage of this diversion, walked rapidly into the garage.

''Ere, come on out of there, you!' Stanton bawled.

Linwood reappeared, looking embarrassed, thrusting his hands into his pockets and immediately pulling them out again.

When the lorry drove off, Stanton walked rather threateningly towards Linwood, gesticulating loosely with both hands, as if he was trying to toss them over either shoulder. Both men went into the garage. Tebbutt sat tight, sighing. Silence reigned on the forecourt.

Very shortly, Linwood emerged again, clutching a piece of paper.

He walked over to the Hillman with an expression of unconcern, to lean through the driver's window so that his nose was only a few inches from Tebbutt's.

'We've got a bit of a problem here, Ray. It's old Joe Stanton, cutting up a bit rough.'

'I'd gathered that.'

'Yes. Poor chap used to be pretty trusting. Caught him in a bad mood this morning. He's repaired the car and it's fine – good for another eighteen months, he says. He's had to do more work on it than anticipated. He said something about the rear shock-absorbers, I believe. Replacements needed.'

He showed Tebbutt the piece of paper in his hand, on which a number of items were scrawled in Biro.

'It's a bill for three hundred pounds, Ray. Bit of a shock.' He cleared his throat.

'Is the car worth it?'

Linwood looked very serious, withdrew the paper, and straightened to tuck it into his pocket, so that when he spoke again Tebbutt could not see his face for the roof of the Hillman.

'Of course the car's worth it, Ray. You don't understand the situation. The problem is, as I say, Stanton's not in his usual trusting mood. He refuses to allow me credit this time. That wife of his was frankly abusive. I can't have the car back, he says, until I've paid the bill. It makes things rather difficult.'

After considering the situation for a moment, and in particular debating what he should say next, Tebbutt folded his arms behind the wheel and asked, 'So how do you intend to resolve this dilemma, Mike? Prayer?'

He still could not see Linwood's head and shoulders from where he sat, but he heard his reply distinctly enough. 'Unfortunately, I forgot to bring my cheque book along. I was wondering if you'd be kind enough to write him one of your cheques, and I'll repay you when we get home.'

Opening the car door, Tebbutt climbed slowly out into the sunshine, so that he could look Linwood in the eye. 'I'm in no position to lend anyone money. I don't have my cheque book on me, either.'

Smiling, Linwood said, 'But you do carry a credit card, Ray, I believe?'

Stanton had emerged into the light to stand before his barely opened doors, fists on hips and legs apart, as if prepared to repel all boarders.

'I ent taking a penny less, neither,' he shouted. 'Three hundred quid I want.'

'Well, you can see it from Stanton's point of view, in a way,' Linwood said.

'Stanton evidently doesn't expect the Lord to provide,' Tebbutt said, feelingly.

'I doubt that he and the Lord are on speaking terms.' Linwood mitigated the humour with a miserable look, adding, 'If you could pay with your credit card, Ray, just to get us out of this mess ... We can't stand here all day. I'd be immensely grateful and can repay you within the next couple of days.'

They stood regarding each other until Tebbutt lowered his gaze. Unable to think of a convincing lie, he decided on the truth.

'Mike, you see Ruby and I have a Visa card just to identify ourselves – for identification of cheques and so on. Nothing else. We never ever charge anything to the account. It's our rule. That way we don't get into debt. You know how it is.'

'Well, charge this sum up now, and I'll repay you before the end of the month. That's how those things work, isn't it? They won't sting you for interest. Then you stand no chance of "getting into debt", as you put it. That's not asking much, is it? We can't stand here all day.'

Tebbutt pulled an awful face. 'Well, it is asking quite a lot, to be honest. As I say, we have never had anything on credit. That's how we live.'

Linwood turned away. 'I'm sorry. You don't mind a friend asking you a favour, do you? Very Christian, I must say. I don't know what to do. I'll have to phone Jean. I'll walk into Melton and find a phone, don't worry. This means another terrible family row . . . But you'd better get back to work. Thanks for the lift, anyway.'

As he made off towards the road, Stanton called, ''Ere, what about my bloody money? I'll sell your bloody junk heap else.'

It was not in Tebbutt's nature to let a friend down. 'Hold on,' he called. 'All right, I'll charge it on my card. You will pay me back at once, won't you? Otherwise we'll be in the shit.'

Turning briskly back, Linwood said, 'Thanks. I'll let you have the money by the end of the week at the latest. Perhaps you'd like to cope with Stanton – he seems a bit miffed with me this morning.'

While Linwood stood about in the sunshine, Tebbutt penetrated the gloom of the garage and completed the transaction with Stanton, who muttered darkly as he processed the credit card. 'That there bugger never pay up. Must think as I'm a millionaire. I can't do the work for narthin', can I now? 'Sides, these old Chryslers, time they was off the road.'

'Thank you very much, Mr Stanton,' said Tebbutt, retrieving his card and pocketing the Visa slip the man gave him. He stood aside as Stanton rolled the garage doors back and drove the car out to the forecourt.

'Don't come a-bothering me again,' Stanton told Linwood, shaking his fist. Linwood, ignoring him, asked Tebbutt for the slip. Tebbutt hung on to it; it was his transaction. Frowning, Linwood jumped into his car and drove off without another word.

'You got a right one there,' Stanton said, laughing at Tebbutt's discomfiture. 'I notice as you don't trust him further than what you can throw him, neither.'

'He's thinking of entering the Church.'

'And a fucking good place for him,' Stanton shouted, as Tebbutt drove away.

On Wednesday, Tebbutt went to work with Yarker as usual. As he rolled into the garden centre, he could see both Yarker and his wife.

Greg Yarker was a big, ill-proportioned man in his mid-thirties, vain, uncertain of temper but, in the words of those around, 'not a bad sort'. 'Ole Yarker'll do you a favour,' his drinking buddies in the Bluebell would say.

At present, Yarker was doing himself a favour, standing in the doorway of his mobile home half-dressed, savouring the morning sun and biting into a huge bread roll from which pieces of bacon dangled. He took both hands to the job. There was little half-hearted about Greg Yarker.

Meanwhile, Pauline Yarker – 'Ah, she'll do you a favour too,' they said, and cackled – was trundling down the pathway between the clematis section and the roses, hugging to herself a plush-covered armchair almost as rotund as she was. Pauline was a big old gel, as they said, strong, and quite a match for her husband. She was carrying the armchair down to the black-painted store where their better furniture was kept. The Yarkers' trade in secondhand furniture supplemented their income from the garden centre.

Half-way along the path, Pauline set the chair down and subsided into it for a breather. As he locked the Hillman, Tebbutt heard Yarker shout something at his wife. She shouted back. They both burst into raucous laughter. Yarker crammed the rest of his bacon roll into his mouth with the flat of his hand.

'Morning, Greg.'

'Look at her,' Yarker said, with a derisive gesture, by way of response. His eyes, dark and in-dwelling – almost as if he had some sense, thought Tebbutt – were set in a knobbly face blue with shaving and crimson with exposure to the elements and alcohol. His hair, cut by his wife, stood out here and there in tufts, giving him a ferocious appearance which his manner did not belie. 'Lazy as they come, our Pauline.'

'What do you want me to do today?'

'I tell you what, Ray,' Yarker said, stepping down from his perch and taking up a blue and white banded mug of tea in one fist. 'When I thinks of how that little bugger Clenchwarden . . . Well, I could kill him. And her.' He took a drag of tea before repeating, 'Little bugger . . .'

'He was a little bugger,' Tebbutt agreed. 'Still, it's over now – I wouldn't think about it.' The little bugger referred to was Georgie Clenchwarden, the previous occupant of Ray's job, who had been caught making advances to Mrs Yarker, or possibly vice versa. Ray took the frequent references to Georgie as a personal warning, as though Yarker believed his wife's virtue, if any remained, was under constant threat. He had no intention of trespassing.

Yarker ordered him to get on preparing the rough ground under a line of poplars marking the northern boundary of the property. After a while, he came over with a second spade to help with the work. Hiring a mechanical digger did not appeal to his pocket.

The dark uncordial Norfolk soil yielded flinty stone and bricks cozened so long under the earth they emerged like rough old fossil tongues. These the men chucked aside into a metal wheelbarrow. Their work was punctuated by a succession of clangs, bangs, and tinkles as the debris hit the target on the path behind them, at which they often aimed without looking. But the biggest obstacle was the roots of the tall poplars, which sometimes had to be attacked with a little tree-saw kept handy for the purpose. Grubbing and digging went by turns.

Greg Yarker straightened up, making his spade bite down into the earth to give him a little support as he rested on it.

'My back ent so good today,' he said. 'I'll leave you to it, Ray. I've got to go see a lady about some furniture Dereham way.'

As he stalked off, Tebbutt returned to the digging, working more slowly now, at his own pace. Although he had heard about Yarker's back before, he held no brief against the man; he was grateful for the job. Five minutes later, he looked round at the sound of an engine, in time to see Yarker driving off in his old van in the direction of Dereham.

Within minutes, the door of the mobile home opened, and Pauline Yarker emerged into the light of day, smoking a cigarette, resplendent in a pink candlewick dressing-gown. Tebbutt straightened up and eased his back as she approached. He smiled and bade her good morning.

'Don't know what's good about it,' she said. 'I'm having trouble opening a tin of peaches, Ray. Would you give me a hand a moment?'

'Which hand do you want?'

She looked at him straight. 'You can use both hands if you fancy it,' she said. Then she smiled. They both laughed as he followed her to the caravan. He thought to himself, she may not be very lovely, but she's willing. Luckily I can control myself.

The mobile home was an ancient model, once yellow, now patched with white flowers of damp. A toilet stood like a sentry box near the front step. Since it was situated in the middle of the garden centre, privacy had been attempted; a square trellis surrounded caravan and thunderbox, up which several varieties of clematis grew. Bees tumbled and buzzed amid the blossom. A dog kennel, now empty, stood to one side of the step. An irregularly shaped nameplate had been tacked against the door, evidence of Pauline Yarker's sense of humour: 'Fakenham Castle'.

'Come on in, love,' she said to Tebbutt. The whole caravan creaked as she grasped both sides of the doorway and heaved herself in, large and jolly. He looked with some awe at her rear view as he followed. She had a well-developed bosom which she knew no harm in displaying. Born shortly after the end of the war, she had recently taken to dyeing her hair. 'You're as young as you act, that's what I say,' she was fond of repeating, and the male customers of the Bluebell, where they met on most Saturday evenings, agreed vociferously.

'Ah, and I'm going to act as young as I feel,' she'd add, with an arch look at her husband. Many of the men fancied her, with her big tits and her complaisant humour.

But Tebbutt took the tin-opener and opened her can of peaches without being molested. They understood one another. She liked flirting with her husband's new employee, but it went no further; the flirtation was a part of her humour; it would be difficult to determine whether she knew another way to behave towards men.

Her little radio was playing music of a dated kind to be heard only during mid-morning on a local station.

'Have a beer while you're about it, while the old bugger's away,' she said, patting a patch of bunk beside her, encouraging him much as she might have encouraged a dog. He showed her his soil-stained hands as warning and sank down gratefully beside her.

'Those bloody roots . . .' he said.

The beer, which he drank from the can, was produced from her little fridge. The chill of it trickled luxuriously down his throat. 'Not a lot is ever going to grow in that ground even when we've cleared it,' he told her. 'It's too near the trees. I told Greg as much.'

'He never listens to a thing you say, he don't. Where are you going for your holiday this year?' Plainly she was not interested in her husband's business.

'I don't reckon we can afford a holiday this summer, Pauline. We're broke. I've got to renovate the back porch.'

'I may go to Yarmouth on me own. I know a nice little hotel on the front, ever so posh, has a Jacuzzi and everything.' Her plump arms briefly sketched the shape of a Jacuzzi for the benefit of those who had never visited Great Yarmouth. 'Why don't you come with me?'

'Don't think Ruby would like it.'

'She hasn't got much meat on her, though, your missus.'

When he was getting ready to go, he gave her a light kiss. Pauline did not attempt to follow it up, though she made grateful cooing noises. At heart, she was a decent woman and he did, after a fashion, owe his job to her.

She pinched his buttocks and gave him a juicy wink. He nodded and went back to his digging.

Arriving home tired after seven that evening, his first question to Ruby was whether Mike Linwood had come round with the money.

Ruby said no, and looked rather tight about the lips. She had heard the whole story from her husband the evening before, and secretly blamed him for being weak enough to lend money to anyone. Her moods being transparent to him, he perceived this without her uttering a word.

'You'll have to go to Hartisham to get it back,' she said now, lighting one of her rare cigarettes. 'You've got us in a real doo-dah. Supposing he refuses to pay us back?'

'Don't be silly. 'Course he'll pay us back. Mike's no crook. Besides, you know how that household works. Difficult though his father is, he bales them out in a crisis. Jean told me once that he's got a heap of loot stashed away in those rooms of his – stuff he acquired in the Middle East. Every now and again he flogs something off in the London auctions.'

'When did Jean tell you that?'

'Ages ago. She told you, too.'

'No, she didn't. I don't remember.'

'You're getting forgetful.'

The evening passed rather silently. Like the silence, the sum of money owed seemed to grow and smother them. It was a sin, a squandering. It represented the amount they might hope to set aside for Christmas for themselves and Jenny, Ray's wages for three weeks, earned by the sweat dripping into Yarker's arid soil. He could no longer believe he had been credulous enough to pay Stanton's repair bill.

That night, he lay next to Ruby in the double bed, listening to her quiet breathing, wondering what he should do. Ruby always slept well. Owls cried about the chimney tops of the ruinous cottage opposite, a partridge croaked in the hedgerow. Still she slept. From across the landing came the downy snore of his mother-in-law; they never closed her door at night in case she should need something.

Agnes in her little wooden room became woven into his anxieties. Fond though he was of the old lady, who represented herself as having had a fairly dashing past, she was in her present decrepitude a burden, one more factor requiring attention every day, like a goat with no yield. Yet, meanly, they made a tiny increment of money from her: Agnes wanted little, corsets apart – another of her sudden whims, easily deflected – and a tithe of her old-age pension flowed weekly into the shallow family coffers.

He tried to shut the stale thoughts out. Come on, cocker, Mike's a friend and he's got a job. He'll pay up. Sure to. Jean will insist, won't she?

After a while, Ray sat up in bed, staring at the dim curtained square of their window. He hated to think that he, in his fifties, should be dependent on a few coppers from his mother-in-law's pension; that he and Ruby now lived so near penury they could not afford a daily paper; that she should have to work part-time in a shop, leaving her old ma alone in the cottage; and, above all, that he should be worth so little on the labour market.

They were caught in the poverty trap. They had come to Norfolk from Birmingham because property was cheap in East Anglia, not realizing that jobs would also be scarce, and wages in consequence low.

In only a few hours he would be obliged to get up and go back to those bloody poplars.

Perhaps he had always been a failure. His thoughts trailed back to the palmy days in Birmingham with the Parchment Printing Company. Parchment had been founded by his uncle, Allen Tebbutt. When Allen had died prematurely, Ray had taken over, and greatly extended the company, which had gone public. He had then lost control of the company in a famous boardroom battle, but stayed on in an executive post. The company had weathered technological change well, installing new plant in 1979, mainly because of impressive new orders from one firm, Summpools. Summpools was a rapidly expanding firm of swimming-pool installers. They owned a subsidiary, Summserve, specializing in conservatories and house extensions. Both companies wanted expensive coloured literature. It all looked fine at a time when conservatories were suddenly fashionable.

Both Summpools and Summserve were owned by a man called Cracknell Summerfield, known familiarly as Charlie. Charlie was Ray's contact, which greatly improved his standing with Parchment. Charlie owned a large manor house near Iver and Heathrow, which Ray Tebbutt once visited for a conference. He was impressed by what he saw. Only weeks later, Cracknell Summerfield went bankrupt with debts totalling £24 million, almost £6 million of which was owed to the Parchment Printing Company. With unemployment mounting and the country undergoing one of its regular recessions, Parchment was forced into liquidation. Ray and many others were thrown out of work.

Cracknell Summerfield sold up his manor house to a yuppie from the city, one of a new breed. After his wife left him for a sacked Summpools salesman, he started up other companies, selling double-glazing and replacement windows. Ruby stayed with Ray when they too were forced to sell up their home; taking their daughter Jennifer, they moved to Norfolk. Ray often asked himself why hadn't he joined that rascal Charlie? He could have been rich by now.

Born to sink. Born to be a sucker . . .

When greyness seeped like dust round the bedroom curtains, he rose and crept barefoot downstairs. He had been one of three million unemployed. In a way he was lucky to find a job; they did get by and, after all, the countryside was lovely, at least in summer.

That lie about being a Muslim . . . well, it would make a change . . .

He sneaked carefully through the door closing off the stairwell, in case the cunning Bolivar was on the other side, awaiting a chance to rush upstairs and jump on Agnes's bed. But the cat was nowhere to be seen.

He stood in the kitchen. Could he afford an extra cup of tea at this early hour? Don't be self-indulgent, he told himself, letting himself out into the garden. The honeysuckle by the back door smelt like something from a picturebook childhood. He wandered up the path and went to see Tess, grazing peacefully. She looked up, shook her ears, and went back to her nibbling.

He returned to the cottage, and to an aroma of last night's fried potatoes lingering in the passageway. In the front room, he stretched out wearily on the sofa, and was immediately asleep. Then Bolivar jumped up on his stomach.

Ruby went to work as usual on the Wednesday morning. Her habit was to cycle from home an hour later than her husband, after she

46

had organized her mother. She concealed her bicycle in a hedge near the main road, caught the bus on the main road, and was in Mrs Bligh's cake shop by nine fifteen, in time to pull down the awning over the shop window and put the wooden sign saying CAKES out on the pavement.

Mrs Bligh herself turned up laden with two heavy wicker baskets shortly after half-past nine, before the baker delivered. She set them down on the counter, gasping. 'Heaven helps them as helps themselves but not all that bloody much,' she said.

Bridget Bligh was a self-contained lady in her forties, generally to be seen in a black Guernsey sweater and denim skirt.

The cake shop specialized in a line of Cornish pasties and sausage rolls which sold briskly at this hour. As Mrs Bligh said on numerous occasions, 'Fakenham folk are funny eaters.' The lady herself retired into a back room to prepare a range of sandwiches which would be on sale from ten thirty onwards.

Ruby had always liked Bridget for her sense of humour. Once when she had asked her why she had left the North of England to come to Fakenham, of all places, Bridget had pressed hands to bosom and said it was to forget.

'To forget what?' Ruby asked.

'I've forgotten,' Bridget said. Ruby had often repeated the joke, even when she suspected Bridget had borrowed it from a TV comedy. Perhaps the joke also expressed something unconfiding in Mrs Bligh's nature. She had a grown-up son, Teddy, who worked in the shop on occasions, but nothing was ever heard of husbands or lovers. For this reserve, Ruby had much respect.

At ten minutes to eleven, about the time when Bridget produced cups of coffee, Ruby glanced out of the window and saw, further down the street, a man she recognized. It was Noel Linwood, white hair stirring in a slight breeze. He had climbed slowly from his ancient car and was gesticulating to someone sitting in the passenger seat; Ruby could just make out a female with a shock of black hair.

Whatever Noel Linwood's exhortations, they failed, for he slammed the car door and began to walk, shoulders hunched, along the street towards the shop. The sight of that curious mottled face brought a feeling of panic to Ruby and she rushed into the back kitchen, clutching Mrs Bligh.

'It's that old chap, Noel Linwood. I think he's coming in here. Please go and serve in the shop – I can't face him. Ray told him we were Muslims . . .'

Bridget surveyed her coolly. 'You look as if you've seen a relation, dear.' But she went into the shop as requested.

A minute later, the door opened, the bell tinged, and Noel Linwood marched in, showing his large teeth in a smile.

'Good morning, Mr Linwood, and what can I do you for? Cream horns are nice today.' Ruby cowered behind the refrigerator as she heard Bridget's pert voice. Most of the traders in Fakenham knew the elder Linwood, and his reputation for being in the money; although there were dissenters who, having seen the dilapidated house in Hartisham, claimed he hadn't two brass farthings to rub together.

Noel looked about him short-sightedly, came to some sort of decision, and said, 'I've got my sister in the car. Give me a dozen cream horns. Got to feed the bitch.'

When Bridget had arranged the cream horns in a cake-box and he was paying, he said in a sharp tone, 'So where is Mrs Tebbutt? I understood she worked here. Is my information correct?'

'No, dear,' Bridget said, handing over his change. 'There's no such person works here. Oh, hang about, though. Would it be Ruby Tebbutt you're asking after? Rum-looking little woman? Yes, she did used to work here, that's true. Not no more. Can I pass on a message for you?'

'Certainly not.' He stood by the door, nursing his box of cream horns. A female assistant from the nearby chemist came in, bought a sandwich and left. Still Noel Linwood hesitated on the threshold.

Bridget leaned over the counter and spoke in a confidential way. 'I don't know if this Ruby Tebbutt is a friend of yours? Tell you what, frankly it was men. Men all over the show, like nobody's business . . . Once she turned Muslim there was no stopping her. I mean, you'd think at her age . . . Well, what was I to do? I'm sorry, but if you keep a cake shop, you've a reputation to keep up, so it was Off she went . . .'

The elder Linwood regarded her with some distrust. 'I met such cases during a long career in the Middle East. However . . .'

Giving her a savage frown, he left, slamming the shop door behind him. From the vantage point of her window, Mrs Bligh watched him return to his venerable car, parked on double yellow lines. It appeared that as he climbed into the driver's seat, he and his passenger started an energetic dispute. Then the car pulled away in a series of jerks.

Ruby burst forth from the kitchen, stifling her laughter in a handkerchief.

'How dare you?! "Rum-looking" – look who's talking. As for my reputation . . . You're as bad as Ray.'

The two women had a good laugh together, controlling themselves only when the next customer entered the shop.

'Wonder what on earth he wanted,' Ruby said later, over their cups of coffee. 'But you didn't have to make up that crazy story . . .'

And the more Ruby thought about it, the more she worried. The mere sight of Noel's approach had triggered all the fears awakened by Ray's problem at the garage two days ago. Her first notion was that he had been coming to complain – perhaps to say that they should not have lent his irresponsible son money.

On reflection, and increasingly as the morning wore on, she cursed herself for hiding from him. Who knows, perhaps Noel had come in to repay the debt. It was not inconceivable that the old boy would regard it as a social slur to be beholden to people like the Tebbutts.

Or he might have intended to drop in a message from Jean. Jean counted as a kind of friend. The Tebbutts had few enough friends in their exile in this strange part of the world. Possibly Jean was angry with Mike for imposing on Ray; it seemed likely.

And another thing. Bridget's joking deception might have unpleasant repercussions. If Jean were told that she, Ruby, had been sacked because of affairs with men, that rather strait-laced lady might not wish to associate with the Tebbutts any more – might, indeed, even use this false knowledge as an excuse not to pay back the three hundred pounds.

It was a worried Ruby who caught the bus and dragged her old bicycle out of the hedge that evening. As she cycled home to put the kettle on, she said aloud, free-wheeling down the lane, 'Ray's going to be mad at me.'

Their back garden was one of her refuges. After she had dealt with her mother, Ruby went out into the sunshine.

July was almost over and the raspberries were coming on so fast she could not resist, as she passed along the row of canes, reaching under the netting to pick a few fruits. In case the overripe ones, cushiony crimson under sheltering leaves, fell at a touch into the grass and spoiled, she kept her other hand cupped below the clusters. As the fruits eased away, they left little mottled white noses behind on their stems.

Savouring the sweet fruit, she unlatched the gate into the goat's enclosure. She was bringing the animal the tribute of a stale slice of bread. Tess had a soothing effect on her jangled nerves. She loved the lines of the nanny, its bumps, its curves, its sharp angles. She stroked its white coat lovingly. The goat looked interestedly at her with its inhuman eyes. It knew Ruby meant well.

As she entered the back porch, the phone rang.

She thought immediately that Ray must have run into trouble. But it was their daughter Jennifer on the line.

Jennifer's voice was always a delight to Ruby, so clear was it, so calm and untroubled, so – what was the word Jenny would have used? – *together*. Today there was a trace of excitement in that clear voice. Jenny was driving up to Norfolk for the weekend with a young man.

'Oh, that's lovely,' Ruby said, looking hastily round the living-room and thinking how shabby it was. Bolivar had sharpened his claws on everything in sight. 'What's his name?'

'Don't worry, I'll introduce him when we meet, Mum,' said the clear voice, possibly with a trace of mockery. 'He happens to be foreign.'

'Coloured?' Ruby asked, and could have kicked herself for letting the word slip out. So unsophisticated of her.

'Not very coloured. He's a Czech – from Prague, you know? We are going to stay on the coast, so we shan't be a burden to you, but we'll look in for tea on Sunday on our way, if that suits. How's Father?'

'Well, Jenny, he's very upset just at present—'

'I am sorry, give him my love. See you Sunday.' And the clear voice was replaced by a dismal whirring tone. Ruby put the receiver down, frowning.

Czech? She'd have to give the cottage a bloody good clean before Sunday. Czech. Presumably he would speak a bit of English since, as far as she knew, Jennifer spoke no Czech. If only the window-cleaner would buck up and come. She'd have to get in another pint of milk. Chocolate biscuits, of course. Perhaps she should bake a cake.

Ruby started to go round in circles, slowly, lighting a ciggy as she did so.

Czech? What on earth did Czechs eat on Sunday afternoons? Ginger biscuits? Something savoury? Perhaps she could ask Bridget Bligh, whose sister had once been married to a Finn. She didn't want to let her daughter down. It wasn't as if they saw her all that often these days.

'I shall get the palpitations,' she told herself. She went out to the garden to finish her cigarette in the company of Tess and Bolivar.

Friday came. The hot anti-cyclonic weather continued. Ray Tebbutt was working as usual in the garden centre. At lunchtime, he sat under the poplars, resting in their shade and eating a pasty from Mrs Bligh's shop which Ruby had provided for him.

Gregory Yarker came over, grinning under the brim of his hat, his deep-set eyes in shadow. He was wearing Wellington boots, jeans, and a tattered old multi-coloured pullover his wife had knitted. 'His looks are against him,' Tebbutt always loyally proclaimed.

Yarker plonked himself down on the bank beside Tebbutt, saying, 'How're you going on? You've got something on your mind, that I know. Your wife hasn't left you, has she?'

'Nothing like that,' said Tebbutt, laughing at the idea.

''Cos if so, I've got a nice piece of crumpet lined up over in Swaffham.'

'No, no. Thanks all the same.'

'I shall have to see to her myself, no doubt of it. What's up with you, then, Ray? It's nothing catching, I hope.'

Ray took a swig from his can of Vimto. 'It's nothing catching, Greg. It's just I've been a bloody fool. I lent someone some money and he isn't inclined to give it back.'

'Ah.' A pause. 'Perhaps we could creep up on him one dark night and sort of incline him.'

'It's an idea.'

'Do I happen to know this fly gent?'

Letting a little more of the liquid run down his throat, Tebbutt decided to tell his boss everything. Yarker listened intently, sucking a long grass from the hedge behind him.

'Pity you was carrying that credit card,' he commented, when Tebbutt finished. 'They're a trick of the banks to get you in their power. If you've got money, carry it round in fivers. If you haven't got money, go round with empty pockets. You're a townee, that's your problem.'

'I love the way you blunt countrymen see everything in black and white. What if you've got too much money?'

'Get married.'

'Or buy a pig?'

'I'd like to see this bugger Linwood's eye in black and white. He got you over a barrel proper, didn't he? Tell you what, go and confront him tomorrer, that's Saturday, demand your rightful money back, and tell him if he don't hand it over by Monday we'll beat him up. That's straightforward, isn't it? He should understand that.'

He stretched himself out on the dry ground, hands clasped at the back of his head, satisfied with his own plan.

Tebbutt tried to explain his latest thoughts. 'I'm afraid the poor sod may not have the three hundred to give back. That's what I'm afraid of. Having worked with him, I know his problems. If I press him, it may only get him in trouble with his father. I was wondering if it wasn't better to go and have a word with his bank manager. I know he banks—'

'What? I must have been falling into a light doze here. I thought for a moment as you uttered the dreadful words "bank manager". No, you've got to have it out with the bugger straight. No other party involved.'

'I suppose you're right.'

''Corse I am, boy, and don't you never doubt it. Now, time's up. I ent paying you to lie about drinking Coke. See if you can make an impression on this here soil, and I'll give some thought to your problem.'

'Thank you, Uncle Greg.' He sat where he was for a moment, listening to the second-rate music issuing from Pauline's radio before returning to his work.

On Saturday mornings in season, Ruby worked and Ray did not. He drove her into Fakenham to the cake shop, keeping the car to a crawl, to the annoyance of other drivers, so that they could talk over anew the problem of the debt. He had hoped for a cheque from Linwood in the morning's post. It had not arrived.

'You'll have to go over to Hartisham and confront him,' Ruby said. 'It's our money. We've got every right to get it back. But keep that goon Yarker out of this. You don't want to be had up for GBH.' She laughed.

'Supposing he's even now preparing to drive over to us and return the money. He did say he'd pay it back by the weekend. Then he'd be offended if I showed up there this morning. It would look as if we didn't trust him.'

'We don't trust him.'

Agnes had been let in on their problem over breakfast since they could not keep it to themselves. Agnes had her own indignant opinion.

'What you should do, Ray, is get on to your bank and cancel the payment. Don't let it go through. Three hundred pounds is three hundred pounds, I mean to say. It was a year's wages when I was a young girl.'

He frowned. 'Forget about Victorian times. This is now.'

Agnes said no more, withdrawing hurt from the discussion.

It's no fun stuck in this chair. He ought to understand that. Your bottom goes numb after a bit. Of course I hark back to the old days. I was properly alive then. It's very rude of him. I reckon it was because of his way of behaving that Jenny ran off and joined the CND. She couldn't stand her father any more.

Still, all families have their differences, I suppose. I was lucky. Good husband, nice couple of girls, Ruby and Joyce. Well, Joyce was nice till she married that builder. All through the war, I was terrified Bill was going to be killed, him being at sea, but he came through safely. Never torpedoed.

First thing I ever remember was the war. I'd be, let's see, about seven. That was the Great War . . . And I was asleep when there was this terrific bang. I remember sitting up in bed. We were living down in Southampton then, of course. I got up and went through to Mum's room and the far wall was missing. There was the sky and our garden where the wall used to be, and the early morning sun shining in. Mum and Dad were sitting up in bed looking surprised. And what I thought was . . . sounds silly now . . . 'How beautiful!' I was clutching my golliwog.

So we went to live with Auntie Flo down the road from us. Poor old Auntie Flo, I liked her. She was fun. It would be 1917. Yes, that's it, because she had lost Uncle Herbert the year before, fighting in France, so there was plenty of room in her house. I was as proud as punch, telling the kids at school as we'd been bombed out.

Years later, perhaps that was after I married Bill, Mum heard me telling someone we'd been bombed out when I was a kid, and she corrected me, saying it was a gas main blew up and not a German bomb at all. But I always somehow connected it with the Germans. The entire wall, gone like that, and the sun shining in, lighting up the room . . .

Bill and I had a lot of fun . . . Purser on a P & O liner, so he was away a lot of the time, and I pretty well brought up Ruby and Joyce on my own. But when he came home, well, we always had parties and presents. The thirties . . . Looking back, I reckon they were the best time of my life. Somehow, after the war, the second one, Bill wasn't quite the same. He used to be very depressed at times . . . I suppose we were getting older by then . . .

Ruby was always our pet. We ought to have made more of Joyce, but she was more difficult. I suppose she's paying us back now by never having me to stay with her and her husband in their posh house in Norwich . . . Still, things could be worse. It's quite nice here, and Ray really isn't such a bad chap. At least Ruby likes him, and that's half the battle . . .

Although Ray had dismissed Agnes's remark over breakfast, he took her advice and went to his bank.

He always felt apologetic in the bank. Even the modest Fakenham branch oppressed him with its pretence that money was easy to acquire, easy to spend. He looked at the posters on the wall, offering him huge loans so that he could buy a new car or house, or take a holiday in Bermuda; immune to such seductions, Ray nevertheless felt that he was the only man banking here who could not afford to take advantage of such offers.

It had to be said, however, that none of the other customers looked particularly rich, though some wore suits and ties. I'm glad that someone's keeping up the country's standards, he told himself and, slightly amused, went up to one of the girls behind the counter. She explained to him in some detail why it was impossible for the manager to interfere with any credit card transaction, which did not go through the bank but through a central accounting system in Northampton.

Was she sympathetic or condescending? he asked himself, returning to the comfortable anonymity of the streets. The little bitch had probably just come off a training course in Purley or somewhere.

He drove slowly out of town and along the road to Hartisham but stopped before reaching East Barsham. Other traffic roared by as he pulled up in the gateway to a field.

By the side of the road a phone-booth stood knee-deep in cowparsley and alexanders. From it he could ring Mike. It would save him the embarrassment of a personal encounter. He sat for a while, thinking over what he would say. As he walked back to the booth, he could hear Mike's voice clearly in his head. Oh, hello, Ray. I'm sorry you had to ring me. Jean and I were just going to pop over to see you and Ruby – you know Jean has always had a bit of a crush on you. Yes, I've got the money, of course. I had a slight problem or I'd have been in touch sooner. We'll be over in about an hour, and I can't tell you how grateful I am to you for getting me out of a hole. You know what an awkward cuss Joe Stanton is – trusts no one.

The Linwood number was ringing. It was Jean who answered.

Immediately she spoke, the sound of her voice, the intonations she used, conjured up her face, her figure, and the way she stood. Ray saw in inner vision her dark old kitchen with the portrait of her father-in-law above the grate, and Jean with her dark hair about her cheeks. He also heard the change in her voice when he announced himself.

'Oh, Jean, hello. How are you? Could I speak to Mike?'

'Mike's still over at Pippet Hall. What exactly do you want?'

'Well, it's something really between the two of us.'

Her tone was unyielding. 'It's about the money, is it?'

'Jean, it's about the three hundred quid I lent Mike at the beginning of the week, and I didn't want to bother you—'

'I've got quite enough problems here, Ray, thanks very much, without being pestered for money just now.'

'Look, Jean, it's not a case of—'

In the same undisturbed voice, she cut in, saying, 'Michael will repay you that money next week, OK? Does that satisfy you, because right now we're involved with the suicide at Pippet Hall. Goodbye.'

Suicide? Tebbutt said to himself, as he replaced the receiver. What was the cheeky woman on about? Inventing excuses not to pay, rather as he had invented excuses not to stay with Noel Linwood; but at least he'd been drunk on that occasion. What a misery! She was lying – well, forced to lie, of course, because the Linwoods were dirt poor and still keeping up a middle-class façade. Bloody suicide, indeed: 'bankruptcy' was the word she was looking for.

Ray took a walk in the field to try and calm down. The sheep moved grudgingly out of his way, as if, he thought, they too had borrowed money from him.

He could write a book about being poor, except that it would be so awful that no one would read it. The poor would not read it. They could not afford to read, they had an increasing contempt for reading, being slaves to the video machine; in any case, they knew all about the miserable subject. The rich would not read it. Why? Because being rich they did not want to know. And why should they?

Every day, almost every hour, brought a humiliation unknown to solvency. He did not want to have that conversation with Jean. Moreover, looked at coolly, the situation was such that she probably did not want to have that conversation with him. She liked him, and maybe more than that, though not a word on the subject had ever passed between them. She too was in bad financial straits, poor dear.

He did not want to be walking about this field, trudging through sheep shit. He did not want to be wearing these clothes – in particular, not these boots and these trousers. He did not want to be wearing his patched underclothes. He would not want to eat whatever it was he was going to have to eat for lunch (nor did he want to call it 'dinner', as did most of the people with whom he associated). He did not want his poor wife to work in a cake shop, a sign of genteel poverty if ever there was one.

This evening, he would most probably go out and get pissed at the Bluebell. He did not particularly want to do that, but there was little else to do in North Norfolk on a Saturday night if you had not got two pence to rub together.

When he had walked round the field three times, he went back to his car. He did not want to be driving this clapped-out old Hillman.

What he really wanted was a brand-spanking-new red BMW from the dealer in Norwich. He would whizz over in his sporting clothes to see the Linwoods in their eroded old house in Hartisham. Mike would be out, taking holy orders or something they could laugh about. Noel and the boys would be out of sight. Jean would be there on her own. And he'd say, as he put his arm round her waist, Sorry about this morning. Just testing. Look, forget about that three hundred. Have it as a present. And now you and I are going to scud down to Brighton for a dirty weekend.

That Saturday evening he went as usual to get pissed at the Bluebell. As he left home, Ruby kissed him tenderly and said at the gate, 'Don't have too many, darling. Remember Jenny's coming with her Czech boyfriend tomorrow, and we've got lots to do to get ready.'

He always left the car at home and walked to the Bluebell. It was four miles to Langham, but he preferred to walk both ways rather than drive after he had downed a few pints. His mood was cheerful. You generally had a laugh in the Bluebell. True, the company was not exactly out of the top drawer, but they often had good raunchy tales to tell. The incidence of adultery and grosser sexual offences must be higher in Norfolk than anywhere, if the tales they told were to be believed.

As he came to the crossroads and turned right, he overtook old Charlie Craske hobbling in the same direction.

'Rain's holding off still,' Tebbutt said.

Charlie squinted up at him. 'What you think about Tom Squire's fruit-packing business failing, then?' he asked, more in the way of a statement than a question. 'It's a bugger, ent it?'

'What's that then?'

'Well, it's a bugger, ent it?'

Entering the Bluebell, where several drinkers had already gathered, Tebbutt found that the same state of gloom, and the same opinion that it was a bugger, prevailed. They were eager enough to divulge the bad news to Tebbutt, on the principle that there was always enough misery to be shared.

Sir Thomas Squire at Hartisham had an orchard and a fruit-packing business on his grounds. It had rated as a small local success in the late seventies, to be written up in the local papers, shown on Anglian TV. Squire had extended the business and packed for a number of Norfolk fruit-growers. There was even a rumour at one time that he might build a private rail-link from Pippet Hall to Norwich Thorpe BR station. But imports of fruit from the European Community had cut into the trade. Local growers were undersold by the French, Spanish, and Italians.

After losing money for two years, Squire had closed the enterprise down. Ten men had lost their jobs.

A man named Burton, who sometimes brought tame ferrets to the pub, said, 'That weren't no reason for young Lamb to go and hang himself, to my mind. Blokes have been kicked out of jobs before this.' He laughed. 'It's always happening to the likes of us.'

'Very like being sacked crushed his hopes,' someone remarked. 'Don't forget young Lamb were on the verge of matrimony.'

'Which is a form of suicide,' old Wilkes remarked slyly. Everyone laughed.

'What's this about suicide?' Tebbutt asked, suddenly recalling Jean Linwood's remark over the phone.

'They say Tom Squire found him himself, barely cold, hanging there from a metal beam in the store, among all the crates. Just this morning, it was. A terrible thing to do to yourself, and this young girl he was about to marry from over North Walsham way.'

They all put on solemn Sunday faces and shook their heads before taking another drink.

The landlady, who had been polishing glasses and listening behind the bar, said in her smoky voice, 'You gentlemen want to get your story straight. As I was told by someone who knows, Mr Billy Lamb did not kill himself because he lost his job. He didn't even know he was to be declared redundant.'

Her statement was immediately challenged, but she went on unperturbed, resting her fists on her counter as if prepared to take them all on in physical combat if necessary. 'Reason he done what he did was because the girl, Margy Sulston, who once worked for my cousin at the Ostrich, threw him over. Margy's quite a decent girl – no chicken, mind you – and as I understand it she couldn't put up with some of Mr Lamb's obnoxious habits.'

'Such as?' Craske asked.

'I'm not one to gossip,' said the landlady with finality, turning away to polish another glass.

To ease himself into the company, which had not yet settled down properly, Tebbutt went over to the counter and bought everyone a round of bitter. They all drank it, except for old Craske, who was reckoned strange for sticking to cider, and Georgie Clenchwarden, who preferred ginger beer shandy.

Swallowing their pints, the company cheered up and began to tell stories of the unfortunate Billy Lamb. The only man there who knew him at all was Pete Norton, a dark-complexioned brickie and plasterer in his forties who worked for a Fakenham builder. He was soon holding them spellbound with details of Lamb's sex life.

'There's a girl works in Boots as I took out a time or two. She'd been with Billy Lamb when he was working in the DIY. She reckoned as he had a problem. Some problem it was too. Seemed Billy was keen enough to get it in but he couldn't stand the sight of women.'

They all roared with laughter, agreeing he certainly had a problem.

'So what he done, he borrowed a sheet of hardboard out the DIY, and he'd stick that between them, so's he could just see her legs and twot, and the rest of her was covered. Bit like screwing a fence, if you ask me.'

This revelation caused much discussion, some debating how long a girl would put up with such treatment, others dismissing the story as a complete fabrication, though later agreeing that nothing to do with sex could be either believed or disbelieved. Only Georgie Clenchwarden, reputed lover of Pauline Yarker, said nothing, sitting back on his bench with his shandy, smiling and listening over the top of his glass.

The Bluebell was a curious pub, with a collection of ornamental shoes on display upstairs. Tebbutt felt himself to be something of a curio in this company, displaced rather like the old shoes.

He took a certain interest in the hollow-chested young Georgie Clenchwarden, whose reported exploits with Mrs Yarker had earned him the sack. This crestfallen lad, who squirmed when he caught

Tebbutt's eye on him, lived over in Saxlingham with a decrepit aunt.

Tebbutt had wondered idly how so insignificant a youth as Georgie could bear a resonant name like Clenchwarden, guessing the family had come down in the world, much as he had himself; this he later found to be the case. In the eighteenth century, the Clenchwardens had owned a large house and estate the other side of Hartisham. Captain Toby Clenchwarden had been a compulsive gambler. One night, playing cards with a group of cronies that included a novelist and pamphleteer, he had staked his mansion on a hand at brag – and lost. The novelist won.

After which, Clenchwarden had ridden his mare back to Hartisham at dawn and roused his wife – so it was reported – with the cheering words, 'Get up, you sloven, it's the poorhouse for you today!'

The novelist had taken over on the following morning. The two men, so the story went, shook hands at the gates, one going, one coming.

Since then, it seemed, the Clenchwardens had never lived more than a stone's throw from the poorhouse.

The company at the Bluebell was three or four pints along the way when in came Yarker with Pauline. Yarker had abandoned his Wellingtons for a pair of trainers – his way of smartening up. Pauline dressed in a common way, in a tight red satin dress which the men admired; as the men often agreed among themselves, she was welcome as the lone female in their group because she had good big tits on her. Pinned over these assets was a white carnation from the garden centre. She wore large bronze earrings made in an obscure country which rattled when she laughed.

Yarker bought them all a round of beer and sat down next to Tebbutt. Clenchwarden sank back on his bench, unwilling to catch his ex-employee's eye, and tried to drown himself in his shandy.

'I done well this afternoon,' Yarker told his employee, genially. 'Bought a whole load of furniture off of an old girl Dereham way who didn't know no better. Drove it round to a mate of mine in

61

King's Lynn and sold it all for ten times as much. Well, eight or nine. Not bad for one afternoon, hey, bor?'

'Who was that then, Greg?' asked Burton.

'Woman name of Fox, whistles when she talks, looks at you out of one eye, keeps an old dog who smells like a bit of used toilet paper.'

The ferret man laughed heartily. 'That's my missus's aunt, Dot Fox. Funny thing happened to her some years back when she was married. She used to live over Happisburgh way, woke up one morning and found her back garden had fallen over the cliff. Apparently she'd been drinking so heavy the night before, she slept through one of the worst storms on the coast for twenty years. What was funny, was her husband Bert had gone out in his nightshirt to see to the chickens, what they kept in the garden shed, and he went over the cliff edge with the rest of 'em. Three in the morning, it was.'

Everyone present roared with laughter. The ferret man followed up his success with a postscript. 'They found Bert washed up on Mundesley beach a week later, they did, still wearing his nightshirt. Old Dot Fox kept that nightshirt for years as a souvenir. She's probably still got it, 'less you bought it off her, Greg.'

More laughter, and more drink called for.

Yarker said to Tebbutt, when they were comfortable, 'You know that line of poplars where you been digging this week? Me and Pauline been thinking. They're getting on a bit, must be ninety year old, and poplars don't last that long. We reckon they best come down.'

Tebbutt frowned. 'They look all right to me. They aren't that old, are they?'

'Ah, I can see the notion ent very *poplar* with you,' Pauline said, leaning revealingly forward and bursting with laughter at her pun. Soon the whole table was laughing and making puns about trees. I knew a gell but she was a bit of a beech. I ent going to die yet 'cause I ent made no willow.

It was quite an uproarious evening. The suicide was soon forgotten.

Old Craske was unfolding a familiar tale about how, when he was a lad, he had seen a naked woman run through the village with a dog on a lead, and maybe it was a ghost or maybe it wasn't.

Tebbutt felt an impulse like lust blossom in him. 'I'll tell you something,' he announced to the company. 'When I was in Birmingham, I knew a man by the name of Cracknell Summerfield. A real rough diamond. He made a packet of money at one time or another. I used to go down to this place near London, near Heathrow, where he gave lavish dinners for his clients.

'Cracknell dealt in swimming pools in a big way. Mind, this was before the Obnoxious Eighties. This time I was down at his place, he was negotiating a deal with some Kuwaitis. There were three of them to dinner, very polite in lounge suits. They were going to finance hotels, Cracknell was going to build the pools and do the landscaping. I was going to print all the prospectuses and brochures. There was also a pretty young duchess there.'

'Now comes the sexy bit,' said Yarker, winking.

'The duchess had a contract to supply all the internal decor of these Kuwaiti hotels. Worth millions. She'd begun the evening very off-hand with everyone, but we'd all had a lot of champagne. She was on Cracknell's right. His wife was on his other side.'

Am I to go on with this lie? Tebbutt asked himself, but already he heard his own voice continuing the tale.

'At the end of the meal, Cracknell suddenly turns to the duchess and says, "Show us your quim", just like that. Instead, she jumps up, pulls off her clothes, every last stitch, and climbs up on the table. There she dances a fandango among the plates, naked as the day she was born, and a sight more attractive.'

Mutterings all round from the company, until Pauline asked, 'What did the Kuwaitis do?'

'Oh, they all thought it was a normal part of English home life.'

'You Brummies had a rare old time,' Yarker said, enviously.

After closing time, the drinkers staggered into the night air. Langham lay about them, quiet and serious, with the great stone shoulder of the church looming darkly nearby. They stood outside the pub, in no hurry to say goodnight to each other.

Offering to give Tebbutt a lift home, Yarker flung a heavy arm round his shoulders and propelled him in the direction of his car.

He ignored Tebbutt's protestations that he preferred to walk. As soon as her husband's back was turned, Pauline Yarker grabbed young Georgie Clenchwarden and planted a big kiss on his lips.

The drink had given the lad courage. Returning the kiss, he grabbed as much of her as he could. Someone cheered. In the dark, lit only by the light from the pub windows, in the middle of the road, the two danced slowly together. The others made way for them, muttering encouragingly. 'Git in there, Georgie boy, it's yer birthday!' Slowly they gyrated, while Pauline sang 'I am Sailing' into Clenchwarden's ear.

Turning at the car, Yarker saw what was happening. A kind of war cry escaped him. He rushed forward. Warned by the roar, Clenchwarden let go of Pauline and started to run in the direction of Blakeney, yelling for help as he did so. Burton, the ferret man, with a wit quicker than anyone would have attributed to him, started up his stinking motorbike and ran it between Yarker and his quarry. A swearing match started. The landlady appeared and begged them to be quiet. Tebbutt took the opportunity to escape.

He marched home in a cheerful frame of mind. Though darkness had fallen, the ambience of a summer's sunset lingered, with a legacy of honeysuckle fragrance. Bats wheeled about the church where, in a few hours, a congregation would be gathering. A harmony of slight noises rose everywhere, from farm and field, comprising the orchestral silence of a Norfolk night. By the entrance to a lane, he halted to urinate under a tree, listening to a leaf fall within the circumference of the branches. He plucked another leaf, pricking himself in so doing. Holding it woozily before his eyes, he made out its sharp outline, with a green heart rimmed by yellow; without being able to determine the colours, he could distinguish their difference. It was a leaf of variegated holly.

'That's right, that's the ticket,' he said aloud, ponderously. 'That's life right enough. Variegated. Very variegated.'

He was impressed by his own wit, and sober enough to stand for a minute listening to the night about him. Even at this distance from the coast, the presence of the sea could be felt, calming, chastening.

That story of the dancing duchess, he reflected, had been an invention to make his past life seem more exciting than it was – to others, but to himself above all. The truth was, Parchment had always been a slog. His uncle had seen to it he was underpaid. He knew Cracknell Summerfield, but no dancing duchesses. Well, you had to make what you could of the moment, and no harm had been done.

Truth was, he rather despised the company in the Bluebell, and despised himself for going there so regularly.

When you think about it, they're always running down women. What's the matter with them? Is that just an English thing? Or maybe none of them have had my luck in finding a Ruby in their lives.

It's impossible to see how things will get better for us. I'm not likely to find a better job. Not at my age.

But at least I've got Ruby . . .

I suppose some would say I've made a mess of my life, seeing the family business go bankrupt; the economic climate was mainly to blame for that, but I realize I shouldn't have trusted the word of a liar and a crook. There were danger signs. I ignored them. I was dazzled by all his money . . .

Perhaps I'm attracted to liars. I hated being told always to tell the truth when I was a kid because I could see even then how adults were terrible liars and dissemblers.

Still, you can't say life's a complete cock-up, he told himself complacently as he slouched down the country road, listening to the echo of his own steps. I had the savvy to marry Ruby.

Shows I know what's what. First time I set eyes on her. That day she came into the works I was in a bad temper – can't remember what about now. She brought those samples over from Dickinson's. I hardly glanced at her and made some crappy remark about the colours. And she answered me so nicely, not at all put out.

So then I looked up. There she was. Neat and bright and slender. So slender, and with a playful air I still catch in her sometimes. You couldn't really say it was love at first sight, but certainly I took a shine to her there and then. Escorted her to the door, in fact. She was wearing sandals. Watched her going down Bridge Street, thought – oh, what a real darling of a girl she was. I remember it so well, standing at that door. It had been raining; the pavements shone.

Those first impressions have never left me, never have. I was going with Peggy Barnes at the time – let's see, of course that was the year I traded in my old Triumph for my first car – but I slung her up. In a rather rotten way, sad to tell. Unfeeling sod, I was. It was Ruby awoke tender feelings in me. Maybe the blokes at the Bluebell never had anything like that.

By ringing Ruby's firm, I got her name. Ruby Silcock. She was engaged to a chap in the tax office, what was his name?, but she agreed to have a milk shake with me in the lunch hour.

Time I'd got to the bottom of that glass, I knew I was mad about her – I didn't tell her so, of course. Not then. Didn't want to scare her.

He peered back into the past, recalling how he'd been late back to work that afternoon, so that his uncle had grumbled.

Then we were meeting again. Then she let me take her to the Saturday hop. Oh, to feel that body against mine, to look into her eyes, to move with her!

There was always something restrained about Ruby. Withdrawn, do I mean? Not sexually, mentally. Still is. Not a chatterbox, a blab-berer, not like Peggy Barnes, thank God. A girl who can keep a confidence.

Nearly home. You did well then, matey. Not such a ditherer in that instance.

I walked on a sea of thistledown when I found she had a little warmth for me. Happy in a hundred ways. My mind and heart were full of her like being crammed with flowers. Oh, yes, Ruby, darling . . . how you haunted me, possessed me!

She rang me one day – we'd known each other about three weeks – to say she'd broken off her engagement. Alex was his name. She never told me then how she did it or what happened. It was just off.

Oh, the passion of those days! Me, whose idea of foreplay was to drag my pants down – I was a fast learner. You could never feel that way twice in a lifetime, could you? I sometimes think it's all gone, then back it comes. We lived in a dream, didn't know ourselves.

Amazing how it's lasted. Oh, when I saw her naked . . . I could have eaten scrambled egg out of her darling armpits.

Well. Ruby, love, pissed though I am, I have to say you make my life worth while. You're my religion. The Bible.

It wasn't all lovey-dovey. Christ, was I a fool! When I first met her younger sister, Joyce, I kidded myself I fancied her more. Some kind of madness, just because she was the snappy dresser. Silly bugger. Ruby caught me kissing her. What a row we had! She gave me such a clout! Naturally I was all bull and rubbish, all the time thinking I'd shat on my chips as far as she was concerned. Women know how to stage-manage these things.

That's long enough ago. We soon made it up. Then when Jenny was coming along, we decided we'd better get married. Just as well. Without a contract, she'd have left me, the way Cracknell Summerfield's wife left him . . .

What'm I saying? 'S balls. She'd never do anything like that. Too loyal – it's part of not being a blabbermouth. She's a good 'un, is Ruby, a real good 'un. Better missus than any of that lot have got. I don't think I could face life without her.

I wonder how long it is since we went to a dance? 'Softly, Softly, Come to Me' – that was our tune.

He attempted to sing the song aloud, but had forgotten the words, could only remember '. . . and open up my heart.'

An owl called as he passed Field Dalling church. He recognized its cry as that of a barn owl. Tebbutt reeled slightly from side to side as he walked. There was no traffic on the road, apart from a cyclist without lights, who shouted a goodnight as he passed. The cyclist too was unsteady.

Tebbutt turned off Clamp Lane and in at his own gate. He tapped on the living-room window, the curtains of which were drawn, and sang 'Come into the garden, Maud', before letting himself in at the front door. The door was unlocked, awaiting his return.

The cosiness of the living-room registered on him as he marched in. It was lit by a lamp on the side table where the *Radio Times* lay. The electric fire, with one bar blazing, set a tongue of crimson on all the shiny surfaces of the room, on Ruby's jugs, on the glazing of various framed pictures, and on the doors of the bookcase which housed their green-bound John Galsworthy novels and copies of the *National Geographic*. In front of the fire the cat lazed.

Ruby sprawled in the bigger of their two armchairs in her night-dress and dressing-gown. Beside her was her mending. She had been patching one of her husband's shirts. The work-basket which stood open had been her mother's until Agnes could use it no more. The delicate sewing scissors, with their Sheffield mark, probably dated from the turn of the century. Work done or abandoned, she was watching a movie on TV. A car was driving in pursuit of another car in a North American city with plenty of narrow side-alleys. Luckily, no pedestrians were involved.

'We've seen this one before,' Ruby said, switching off and removing her glasses. 'So I believe.' Setting the cat down on the hearthrug, she rose and surveyed her husband for damage, smiling, shaking her head, and making slight clucking noises like a hen.

Tebbutt sat down heavily and pulled his boots off. 'Usual crowd,' he said. 'That little bugger Clenchwarden was snogging with Pauline.'

'You drunken lot of country bums . . .'

'Bumpkins,' he said, 'variegated bumpkins,' as his wife went through into the kitchen to boil a kettle for him. Bolivar followed her out, hoping for a last snack.

'Tom Squire was on the telly news earlier,' Ruby called from the kitchen.

'He's always on telly.' Ray was feeling distinctly dozy, and had no inclination to talk.

'He looked very nice, I thought.'

He stirred himself, asking between yawns, 'What was he on about, then?'

From the kitchen came the chink of a spoon in a mug as Ruby replied. 'It was something about paintings and computers, I don't know. Oh yes, something he'd been up to in Russia, in the Soviet Union. I didn't quite understand. Someone or other is threatening to shoot him. I wasn't listening.'

'It's about his fruit. Everyone's fed up . . .' He had some difficulty in getting the words out.

He heard her laugh. 'You want to lay off the booze, old duck.' She began to talk to the cat in a manner at once scolding and caressing; it was her nightly address to her pet. 'Fruit . . . fruit . . . What's he on about, then, Bolivar? You don't know, do you? No more do I.'

Ray drank with gratitude the tea she brought him, grasping the mug in both his calloused hands. They shut Bolivar downstairs and proceeded up the creaking stair to bed. Ruby went ahead, carrying her slippers. He reached up and grasped her bottom.

On the landing, they could hear Agnes's soft snores emerging from her poky bedroom at the rear of the house. The hesitant noise filtered through her door, ajar as always.

Once in their own bedroom, Ray and Ruby threw off their clothes and climbed naked into bed. Ray began feeling his wife at once. He never ceased to relish the way in which she lay with her legs wide during their love-making, as if doing the splits. On occasions, she made a little humming noise at the back of her throat, when it was particularly pleasant for her.

'You're so smashed you can't get it up, my honey lamb,' she whispered teasingly.

But he could.

Tebbutt sat at the counter in the kitchen next morning, sipping coffee while Ruby was in the garden tending the goat. Only then, thinking vaguely over the night before, did he recall the suicide of Billy Lamb.

When Ruby reappeared and he started to tell her the news, she said she knew about it; Bridget had phoned her. Ruby then repeated word for word what she had heard of the matter.

When she got to the end of the story, Ray said, 'It wasn't quite like that. The way I heard it, Lamb hanged himself in the packing shed at Pippet Hall.'

'That's not what I was told. Bridget has a customer lives in Hartisham. She heard he hung himself with his clothesline in his own home, in the garden, from the branch of an apple tree. No, perhaps it was a pear.'

'We can probably get the details from the paper tomorrow. Pity we can't ask Mike – he works at Pippet Hall, after all.'

She started to clear the breakfast things. 'It's nothing to do with us, fortunately. It was rotten for him, though, poor chap. He was in his forties – not much chance of another job.'

'I thought he was in his twenties.'

'You'd better get properly dressed, my lad. There's a lot to do with Jenny coming this afternoon, and I must finish the ironing before they arrive, her and her Czech.'

I can just imagine the flap Mother's in. Of course she always gets excited when I'm about to show up – no wonder I don't show up very often. And turning up with a foreign chap . . . It's bound to be embarrassing.

All I hope is that Father won't start to argue with Jarry. There's a bizarre streak in my father. I don't understand it. Funny, he always says he doesn't understand me. When I think back to when I was a teenager, I really hated him. Really really hated him. Anything I liked, he was against it. Music, hairdos, boyfriends, clothes – every one of them, he had to sound off about. And of course the money . . . Old miser. What a pain. What a bummer. Did he have to make me feel so bad? Bad enough as it was, stuck in that miserable dump with old gran going on about this and that, eating in that disgusting way of hers.

They seem happy enough there, I'll say that for them. Jennifer, you must swear you'll be cheerful and nice, even to bloody old gran.

Running off. Of course it was a shock for them. I suppose I was a bit thoughtless. I wanted to get back at them.

I never planned to leave home like that, as I remember . . . It was when I went over to Norwich on that chap's bike. Derek? We got involved with the CND march. He didn't want to know. He supported Norwich City. I stopped to listen, can't think why. That woman who spoke, Joan Ruddock. It was as if for the first time a real live thought about something other than myself entered my head.

That was it. Suddenly, I saw I could live outside myself, live for something else other than a new pair of shoes. All right, a cause. The sort of thing they laugh about in the office, just as I do nowadays.

But – why, it was a burning issue! A conversion, almost religious. One moment I was just a selfish bitchy little teenager, the next moment I was a crusader with a blazing desire to get rid of nuclear weapons, defying the mad male world. Although it seems silly to me now I'm older, I still miss something – that pure sense of conviction, I suppose. Nothing else mattered, only that. All the issues were clear. Funny how you change.

I went and joined the women picketing the Lakenheath base.

The excitement of it! I can see why blokes want to go to war. It's a way of booting up your life. There was this bloody great airforce base, loaded with Cruise missiles, right in the middle of peaceful old Norfolk, enough of them to blow the world to bits. And there we were, almost a hundred women at one time, camping among the pines and bracken. Oh, how wonderful the camp looked and smelt and felt. Just women. Very funny that. Just women. I wouldn't like it now, but of course I was a virgin then, practically.

Of course I'd always heard how Grandad and Grandma Tebbutt had been killed by bombs, but that was just a piece of the family's lousy luck, like Dad's printers going bust. It didn't touch me. I mean, it wasn't the reason why I got the hots for nuclear disarmament. Nor had I ever bothered my head about nuclear war – too ig. for that, Jenny girl. It was the older women worried themselves sick about that kind of thing.

Many of them had deserted their husbands. Some left families behind, just up and quit. They were really nice to me, perhaps because I ran about doing what I was told. They didn't see it all as fun like I did. They used to try and organize themselves like men, like soldiers, keeping sentry duty and all that. It was just fun for me. Like nipping off somewhere and shitting in the bracken.

Even being filthy, stinking . . . Now I'm so neat, so pernickety. Quite different. One day, I picked up a sheet of newspaper by the roadside and read it. Sitting under a tree. It sounds daft now, but that was really the first time I realized that the other side – the Russians, and the Warsaw Pact countries, to which this sleeping hunk of Czech belongs – had a great arsenal of nuclear weapons too, and were quite capable of using them against us. And that nobody in their countries was allowed to protest about the situation, as we were.

That nagged at me. I brought up the subject in camp. Some women said that I'd got hold of a bit of propaganda. Others said that if we gave up nuclear weapons – the USA and England, that is – then the other side would give them up too. They got really angry with me and called me Tory and Fascist and the rest of it. However hard I tried, I couldn't believe their arguments. I kept thinking of those Russian missiles pointing at England.

Jarry says under this new Russian President things are going to be different. Gorby – is that his name? I wonder if that's really so. There must be someone knows the truth of such matters.

There was a woman in the camp called Maeve, a nice Irish woman in her forties. She told me – this was between ourselves, she said – that she hoped the government wouldn't disarm. She had had to knock her old man cold with a poker because he offered her violence. That was her argument. Keep a poker handy. She said nations no more than individuals saw reason. Why was she at Lakenheath? She said she liked it there, camping out without her kids, and she knew we were safe with the air force nearby to protect us.

Although I thought Maeve was probably right, I said nothing to anyone. Everyone was so dedicated.

I stayed in the camp – how long was it? All that summer. Then the autumn. It was so lovely, the nip in the air, the freshness, those sunsets, the sense of the year drawing in. Four or five months, I suppose. Suppressing my doubts. In all that time, I'd only once phoned Mum at Bligh's cake shop, just to say I was OK. I wouldn't tell her where I was. I rang off quickly. It really wasn't very fair to her, I suppose, poor dear.

Then one day I caught a cold from nowhere. I still can picture it. Three of the older women who lived under a big tarpaulin were having a row, and suddenly I wanted – oh, all the home comforts . . . A decent bed and a hot-water bottle at my feet. Mum to look after me like she used to. I got homesick. I started to cry. Perhaps what they say is true, and we are a decadent generation. I believe it. I remember so clearly that I stood there in the clearing longing for a clean handkerchief to blow my nose on, one that Mum had ironed. It was the thought of her ironing, all those years she'd ironed all my gear since I was born, never complaining . . . Not only that. Also the feeling, quite unexpected, that I'd been living in a foreign country among a foreign tribe. Wouldn't it be lovely to be in bed with a real man, his arms around me, forget the cold and the hot-water bottle . . .

So that was the end of my idealistic phase. Here I am, snuggled up beside this Jarry guy. I quite love him. I must say he's well hung and knows how to go about it. Can't count the number of girls he's had in Prague, the bastard . . . There's something sinister about him, too, which I rather enjoy, different from the wets in our office. Won't tell me what he does for a living, though he makes out that you can't live decently there without doing something not strictly legal.

To be honest, I'm not sure I'm not a bit in love with Jarry. He talks so gently to me and makes Prague sound so romantic. He says why don't I go out there with him when he goes back. Ten days' time. What'll I do? He's got such a sweet face.

It remains to be seen what Father will make of him – or him of Father, come to that. Still, we won't stay long. Jarry has plenty of money to spend, so he must be a bit of a wheeler-dealer. After a cup of Mum's home brew, we'll buzz off to the coast – Yarmouth or somewhere.

It's a bit boring lying here. Men sleep so much. Let's wake him in a nice erotic way, stick a fanny in his face. That should bring him back to life.

By two thirty on the Sunday afternoon, they considered the cottage was clean enough, and all vases well enough stuffed with flowers from the garden. Ruby was good at flower arrangement; cabbage leaves went well with cornflowers. Agnes was settled comfortably in her favourite chair in one corner of the front room, where she was instructed to watch for Jennifer's car. Ray and Ruby sat down in the kitchen with an early cup of tea, to await the arrival of daughter and Czech boyfriend.

Ruby was wearing her brown dress with a halter neck, preserved from better days. Ray had on a suit of denim, another souvenir from the past, and a white shirt, one of a pair bought at a closing-down sale in Wells. Both looked slightly uncomfortable.

'They'll be on their way back to somewhere,' Ruby said. 'I don't suppose they'll stay long. He may have a doo-dah, you never know. An appointment . . . He's probably a businessman.'

'Is that what Jenny said?'

'No, but if he's from Czechoslovakia, he's probably over here on business.'

'I wouldn't be so sure they have businessmen in Czechoslovakia. It's a Communist country, you know.'

There the conversation languished. After another sip of tea, Tebbutt allowed what was in his mind to surface. 'Ruby, I was thinking. About Mike Linwood. You know, he and Jean are no better off than we are. Just because we're poor, we don't have to be mean. I really hate being mean. I don't like to think of us as mean people, do you?'

'What are you getting at?' She was looking down at the table.

'What I'm getting at is that we don't have to be vindictive over this business. Perhaps we've got it out of proportion. They are our friends, after all, aren't they? For all we know, they need that three hundred more than we do. They have got those three kids to feed, poor little tykes. So I was wondering . . .'

She peered angrily at him over the top of her spectacles. 'Oh yes, and what were you wondering?'

'Look, Ruby, we can surely scrape by without that money, after all. Let's forget about trying to get it back.'

'What!' She gave a small scream. Bolivar, who had been sleeping on the windowsill, scudded from the room and into the garden without a backward look. 'Give away three hundred quid? Give it away? You must be off your rocker. Think how long it takes to earn that amount. I certainly wouldn't give it to the Linwoods, even if I had it to spare. They're miles better off than we are – and they always look down on us and try to be superior. Let him join the Church, let her go on the streets, let them all starve. That three hundred's ours by right, and we're getting it back.'

'But if Mike won't give it back—'

'Then we'll attack him. We'll get Yarker. We'll set fire to their bloody house, we'll kidnap the kids, we'll blow up the confounded doo-dah, the Chrysler. There's a thousand things we can do. We could even get a solicitor—'

'I thought you were against GBH,' he said mildly.

She had jumped up, the better to confront him. 'I'm just being realistic. You're being silly. You're too weak, Ray, that's your trouble, too eager to please. That's been you all along. If you'd been more prepared to fight, you could have stayed on at the press another eighteen months and got a golden doodah – a handshake – and then we wouldn't be stuck where we are today.'

This was opening old wounds with a vengeance. He went red in the face. 'Oh, and who was so keen to come here, to be a country lass, to keep a fucking goat, to have a view of bloody cornfields—'

'I never thought you'd have to work in the bloody cornfields, did I, you prick? I never thought I was going to be married to a bloody YOKEL, drunk out of his mind every Saturday night!'

To impress this sentiment more thoroughly on her husband's attention, she brought her right hand over with a gesture not unlike that of a fast Middlesex bowler and swept his half-full mug of tea off the table. The mug flew against the kitchen sink and shattered. Fragments scattered round the kitchen, tea dripped over the rug.

'Bloody hell!' he exclaimed, almost in a whisper.

'When you get that three hundred back, you'll be able to afford another mug,' she said, eyeing him contemptuously. 'Don't talk to me ever again about throwing your bloody money away, not while I'm in need of a new dress, not while we can't afford to take Mother for a day at the seaside. You can think that over while you clean up the bits.'

'I'm not clearing up your mess,' he said, but by then Ruby was marching off into the garden.

'What a shocking temper the woman has,' Tebbutt said aloud, standing helplessly looking down at the wreckage.

The doorbell rang.

Just inside the front door the gloom was so intense that Tebbutt, pulling the door open, could see only the silhouettes of his daughter and the tall man standing behind her. He ushered them into the living-room where Agnes – all spruced up for the occasion – sat in her wicker chair. He embraced his daughter, delighted to feel her arms round him.

Jennifer Tebbutt was a smart young woman of twenty-eight, dressed at present in a tailored dove-grey business suit cut on severe lines which emphasized the slimness she had inherited from her mother. She had always been rather plain; careful make-up now disguised some of those deficiencies. Her brown hair was cut fashionably short. Except for the slim gold watch on her wrist, she wore no ornament.

'Hasn't my little hippie girl become smart!' said Tebbutt, surveying his daughter admiringly.

'I never was a hippie, Dad.'

She appeared to bubble over with pleasure as she introduced her companion, Jaroslav Vacek, to her father. The latter noted that she slipped a hand possessively round the Czech's arm as she did so.

Vacek smiled broadly as he shook hands with Tebbutt. A gold tooth glinted in his upper jaw. He was very solid, and was wearing a shiny double-breasted suit which made him look wider than he was. His complexion was sandy, his hair sandy but made drab by the application of hair oil.

In his manner was something Tebbutt did not find reassuring. He stood stolidly before Tebbutt, hands in jacket pockets, thumbs protruding forwards, dominating the small room, which he surveyed with a calm stare, turning his head this way and that, even while addressing Tebbutt.

He answered a few questions noncommittally. Although his English was fluent, his accent took a while to become accustomed to. While they were exchanging remarks, Jennifer marched off to summon her mother. Tebbutt listened to her heels determinedly clicker-clack on the quarry tiles in the passage, passing the shattered remains of his mug on the way. 'Been having a row again?' she called.

Agnes, bolstered by Indian cushions, contrived a bob in her chair when introduced to Vacek. He bowed and enquired after her health.

'I can't get about, you see,' she said. 'My legs pain me all the time. My kidneys are leaking protein. And other problems. Well, I'm old. Fortunately, I have a very good daughter, very kind, yes. The doctor's worse than useless.'

'I'm sorry. Life is always hard for the old.'

'At least you're young, Mr Vacek. I'm on the scrapheap. Is Czechoslovakia a healthy place? At least you don't have these nuclear power stations, do you?'

'Oh yes, we certainly do. Mainly in Bohemia. Since our coal is of poor quality, we rely more and more on nuclear power, let's say.'

Tebbutt asked him if he was in Britain working with Jenny.

'No, I don't work with her exactly. I am in England merely on an economic advisory trip, that's how to describe it.' He turned his back as he spoke, to look at the bookcase with its imprisoned runs of Galsworthy and old boxes of jigsaws.

'Let's say I am escorted by your Jennifer.'

'I see.' Tebbutt was annoyed by the broad back. 'Are you in manu-facture, would you describe it?'

Turning towards him, Vacek sighed, as if answering questions only out of a sense of duty. 'I am a member of the Czech Scientific and Technical Council. Despite the nuclear power plants, our industry is in rather a backward condition in certain aspects, owing to unfavourable world trade. For instance, backward in shall we say infrastructure and computerization, let's say. And there are other difficulties. So I come to study Britain's economic miracle, about which we hear much.'

'Oh, our famous economic miracle!' Tebbutt gave a laugh. 'I've heard talk of our economic miracle on the television. You won't see many signs of it in Norfolk. A chap I know committed suicide only yesterday because he's been made redundant.'

With a slight dismissive gesture of his right hand, Vacek said, 'But Britain is very prosperous, Mr Tebbutt. We admire your achievements under firm, clear leadership. You have made great progress since the seventies.' He looked about, as if hoping that Jennifer would re-emerge and end this discussion. 'The revived British economy is the envy of Eastern Europe, let's say. We hope also to turn things around, as you have done, by study of your methods.'

'You mean laying people off work and increasing unemployment to bring down inflation? Millions off the workforce, thousands homeless, cutting children's allowances?'

'Mr Tebbutt, allow me to say that in every stride towards economic progress and revival of trade must be fall-out, you understand?' He was leaning forward, heavy, slightly patronizing. 'It's inevitable. It's an equation, a formula, let's say. Unemployment is necessary – even desirable, let's say – to combat inflation, to stabilize demand at home, to have a system responsive to market forces. Market forces is with us a new concept, you see. In our country, we have full employment, yet nobody works. Something must go on what your mother calls the scrapheap. More firmness must be demanded from the workforce.'

Tebbutt went red. 'How can sacking skilled men be admirable? Don't try to tell me unemployment is ever desirable. It ruins a man's life, and his family's. You're looking at one of the victims of unemployment, of deliberate government policy. You may see an economic miracle. I don't wish to be rude, but I see a country falling apart, able-bodied decent chaps kicked out of jobs they've done for years, misery, homelessness, families breaking up, the North disintegrating – not just the North, either – whole regions ruined, industries having to close, good old firms—'

The dismissive gesture cut him off. 'But this is all inevitable in a period of transition, isn't it? The sweeping away of the obsolete. These "good old firms", let's say, may not fit in the wider picture. I should not tell you when I am in your country to learn. Of course, there are casualties among the unqualified, but the general trend—'

'Unqualified? I wasn't unqualified. My print firm wasn't unqualified. We were quick to adopt new methods, to seize export orders. But when the industries in the Midlands were shut down, bang, our customers went down the drain just like that. We went bust. Do you imagine we got government compensation?'

Tebbutt could not make himself be quiet. 'I know of thousands of men like me. On the scrapheap. It's a bitter thing. You lose your self-respect, let me tell you. Over forty, you've no chance of finding another job. I'm a skilled printer and what do I do rather than go on assistance? I dig. This week, I've dug, I've sawn down trees. What for? For peanuts.' He snapped his fingers. 'For less than the statutory living wage. Don't talk to me about Britain's bloody economic miracle.'

At that juncture, Agnes heaved herself half out of her chair and said loudly, 'So you have been up to the seaside? How did you like it?'

Glad of the diversion, Vacek turned to her, summoned a smile, and said, 'It was beautiful. We went for long walks, and we stayed in a hotel which was clean and nice, with your splendid English breakfasts.'

Tebbutt stuck his hands in his pockets, and went to stare out of the window at the ruined cottage opposite.

'Oh, breakfast, yes . . .' Agnes pursued the subject. 'Very nice. But what about the sea? Your country's on the Mediterranean, I believe?'

He shook his head, half-turning away from her as he spoke. 'No, you are mistaken in your geography, let's say. Czechs have no sea coast. It was an error made also by your William Shakespeare in his play *The Winter's Tale*. We have no sea, so it's a fascination for us, naturally.'

'Have you known Jennifer for long?' Agnes asked.

He hesitated before replying. 'I met her last week. As the public relations officer for MTD, she was so kind to meet me at the airport.'

'I see,' said Agnes, 'but the two of you stayed in the hotel together,' and said no more.

Sounds came from the kitchen of cheerful voices, of smashed crockery being swept up and a kettle being filled. Eventually Ruby and Jennifer entered the room and they all settled down to a rather uncomfortable conversation. Tea followed, a little early, accompanied by one of Mrs Bligh's best sponge cakes.

'So you're doing well still, Jenny, love, are you?'

'It's not so hectic at this time of year, Mum,' she replied, casting an affectionate look at Vacek – a look not lost on her grandmother.

'I suppose you meet all and sundry in your job,' the latter remarked.

'All and sundry is who we try to sell our products to, Gran,' said Jennifer, equably.

She and Jaroslav stayed for two hours. After a walk round the garden they declared they must go; Jenny wanted to take Jaroslav to Yarmouth. Ruby and Ray stood at the gate to wave goodbye as the white car drove off. It was lost to sight as soon as it had climbed the low hill. Rather dejectedly, they returned indoors and Ruby began clearing away the tea things.

'What did you make of him?' Ruby asked. 'First Communist we've ever had in here . . .'

'I can't say I took to him. You've seen pictures of Prague. It's very grand. He probably lives in some damned great mansion. He had a contempt for this little hutch directly he saw it, that's my impression.'

'Oh, I don't think so.'

'He's a big-wig over there, isn't he? Member of some scientific council or other. Or so he said . . .'

'Well, you sorted out your guest, Ray,' said Agnes from her chair, addressing her comment more to the window than her son-in-law. 'Shame to lie to him, though.'

'How d'you mean, lie?' He was immediately defensive.

The old woman chuckled. 'Pretending things are so awful now and were so good before. You know you like the outdoor life. I remember how you used to complain in Birmingham about being cooped up in the office.'

He thought a bit. He had already had one quarrel since lunch, and was grateful that Ruby seemed to have forgotten it. Walking round to face the old lady in her chair, he said, 'Would you like another slice of Mrs Bligh's sponge cake before I put it away, Gran? It's hard not to lie to foreigners, really, isn't it?'

3

Despatched

The street was lined with birch trees whose leaves had already been touched by the drought. Some had withered and fallen as if anticipating autumn, to blow downhill towards the city. In the dying day, the little grey villas standing sentinel on either side of the street were anonymous, as if weighed down under piles of slaty cloud moving in from the west. Their dustbins were overflowing with rubbish.

As Petr Petrik walked slowly up the cobbled roadway, he kept a sharp look-out, pausing before he moved into the unkempt garden of the last house at the top of the street. As usual when returning from work, he walked round the outside of the villa, looking into every window. Starlings scuttled away from underfoot, taking low flight into nearby bushes.

Mrs Emerova, his landlady, was sitting in her kitchen, reading a newspaper under a dim light, clutching her neck below her bun of grey hair in characteristic attitude. She glanced up briefly as he ducked under her sill. His room was empty. The room of Mrs Emerova's other lodger, Martisek, was empty. Nothing was untoward.

Usually, Petrik did not return until after dark. In the summer, he often slept in friends' flats.

When he was sure all was quiet, he brought out his key and entered the house. The stale odours of the hall were reassuringly unaltered. He called a hello, and received an answer from Mrs Emerova. The blob of chewing gum in his door hinge had not been disturbed. He opened up and went in.

His room was small and already gathering dusk. As he crossed the floor to drag the flimsy curtains across the window, he checked the room.

A desk and chair were set under the window, the chair jammed against the foot of the bed with its high old-fashioned headboard. A wardrobe of similar vintage to the bed dominated the wall opposite the bed. On his improvised bookshelves, books in German and French mingled with Czech titles. What saved the room from anonymity was a line of photographs stuck to the distemper of the wall, stills from the two films Petrik had directed in his youth, the short feature *Faithless Creatures*, and his fantastic documentary *Sewers of Time*. The photographs had curled at the edges, as though growing wings to fly into the centre of the room and take a turn about the plastic lampshade.

Petrik switched on his radio, to listen briefly to a report concerning increased agricultural production in Slovakia before switching off again. He peered restlessly through the curtains, taking in the view of back gardens, and a waste space in which a goalpost stood, sinking into the fading light.

Taking a biscuit from a tin in the wardrobe, he munched slowly, staring at nothing, feeling at a letter in the hip pocket of his jeans without removing it from its place of concealment.

When the biscuit was gone, he unzipped his jeans and began to masturbate in front of a small mirror. To assist the process, he pulled a worn copy of *Playboy* from under the bed and opened it at the photograph of a naked American blonde.

Petr Petrik was a slender man in his mid-forties. His body was pale and bony, his face long and freckled. His hair was mousy, cut short. Only the fierce stare of his eyes gave him some distinction.

After his orgasm, he zipped up his jeans, put away the magazine, and lay on the bed, which creaked under his weight. He was no more relaxed than before. Taking the letter from his pocket, he began to read it once more, as if determined this time to resolve its mystery.

The letter was typewritten on flimsy paper without a water-mark. It bore no address. It read:

Petr Petrik –
    Greetings!
    Your motion picture based on Franz Kafka's life entitled *Sewers of Time* is considered of worthy artistic merit. An opportunity may arise in the near future to schedule it for some limited showings to selected audiences. This department trusts that the proposal will be of interest to you.
    If favourably received, *Sewers of Time* might qualify along with other works for wider viewability ratings. In such an eventuality, the Saradov Studios might provide a job opportunity in one of its departments.
    When you have had time and opportunity to consider this proposal, I shall forward a further communication.

        Comradely felicitations,
            Lubomir Cihak,
            Secretary, Prague Film Academy of Arts

12 April 1986

It was not only the bureaucratic jargon of the letter which was alarming: just being addressed by authority was ominous. Petrik read it over yet again before folding it and returning it to its envelope. Kafka's writing was still banned. How could his film be unbanned? The letter could only constitute a trap of some kind.

His cousin Jaroslav Vacek would know how exactly to deal with it.

That he should even consider going to see his bullying cousin was evidence of how seriously Petrik took the letter from Secretary Cihak.

While he considered the matter, a light tap came at his door and

84

a voice enquired if he was awake. Stuffing the letter into his bomber jacket, Petrik went to open the door.

Mrs Emerova was generous to her lodger and sometimes offered him a bite of supper. Petrik, knowing something of her history, understood she was lonely and welcomed his company. She smiled at him now and invited him into the kitchen. Mrs Emerova was a tall, thin woman, slightly bent with the years, her square shoulders caving in towards her chest. Her scrubbed face and scraped-back hair, topping her old black jumper, gave her a look of false severity. The old lady liked to laugh until her false teeth rattled; Petrik tried to amuse her in exchange for her soup. He knew her for a good honest woman. Most people were honest; it was the system which corrupted them; but Mrs Emerova was too old to be corrupted. She had survived the Nazis and all that had happened since.

Her kitchen was neat, clean, and rather cold. On the table two plates were already laid: he never refused to eat with her. She served the soup in plastic bowls, and there were helpings of Hungarian salami and potato to follow.

'How's the little hunchback?' she asked, when they were seated facing one another. It was one of her favourite conversational openings.

'Things haven't been going well for our unlucky friend.'

Mrs Emerova began to laugh immediately. She remembered the story, but like a child tempted him to tell her it again. Petrik spun it out over the soup; the hunchback's unfortunate life lasted little more than a minute so far.

'Well, as you know, he was pretty hungry. Starving, in fact. Couldn't enjoy a nice tasty soup like this . . .'

Her teeth began to rattle slightly in anticipation.

'. . . So he toddled down to the market square. He joined in with all the other hawkers. And he tried to sell his hump – to a butcher or to anyone who wanted a lump of meat.'

'Sell his hump!' The old lady dropped her spoon and rocked back and forth in time to her false teeth.

At that moment, one of Mrs Emerova's souvenirs of earlier days chimed the hour of six. Her black marble clock stood on the kitchen shelf next to her black saucepan; its face was embedded in a block carved with pillars, steps and pediments; evidently designed to represent an eighteenth-century bastille in which time itself was imprisoned. The tin notes of its strike always made Petrik uneasy, and he paused in his narrative.

'Go on,' the old lady ordered, impatiently. 'Are you really saying he went down to the market place and tried to – to sell his hump?' She started laughing again at the thought. 'It would be fatty, like sow's cheek, wouldn't it?'

'Well, there he stood, in the market square, temptingly offering everyone a carving fork, but no one would buy, not even one slice.

'No one would buy, and the poor little hunchie was very sad. He walked about the square like this . . .' Having gulped down his soup, Petrik pushed back his chair and slouched about the kitchen, left foot to the fore, left shoulder hunched, by way of demonstration. 'Until a little mountaineer from the High Tatras wearing a huge woolly hat came along and tried to use his hump for mountaineering practice . . .'

This was too much for Mrs Emerova. 'Oh, I must tell Lotti. I must tell Lotti,' she said, amid outbursts of laughter.

'You must tell no one,' said Petrik, all mock-stern. 'The life of our friend is a secret between us, Mrs Emerova.'

As they ate their salami, his landlady asked for more details, but he put her off, saying that the great feature of the hunchback's existence – apart from his hump – was that everyone took advantage of him.

'It's like life, you see,' he explained. 'Adverse circumstances.'

Mrs Emerova advised him to look on the bright side of things, serving him an extra spoonful of potato as she did so, to reinforce the advice. He smiled and thanked her. Just as he missed his mother, so she missed her son.

Back in his room and feeling happier for something in his stomach, he re-read the letter from Secretary Cihak, trying to understand its portents. They said things were beginning to change in Russia – but in Czechoslovakia? Never! He fell into a light doze, to be roused by the clump of boots in the corridor outside his room. He sat up tensely, swinging his feet to the floor. For some reason, the sound of those boots always alarmed him.

Mrs Emerova had rented out a part of her bungalow permanently to a man called Martisek. Martisek was a tall man in his forties. A moustache hung across his face like a bird with extended wings, giving him a sinister appearance. He walked with his head thrust forward, as if the moustache weighed heavily.

Petrik and Martisek had never spoken. They avoided each other. Petrik did not wish to know what work the other man occupied himself with during the day. Instead, he sat on the side of his bed with his hands on his knees, listening. It was just possible, he considered, that he hated this man, stranger though he was. 'Old Boots' – that was his name for Martisek.

The boots clumped over the worn linoleum. A door on the other side of the corridor was unlocked. Then came the sound of the lock turning on the inside. In a minute, bed-springs gave a creak. Then two separate bumps as the boots were removed and thrown to the floor. A radio was switched on.

'Old Boots' was a creature of habit.

It happened in the same way every evening Petrik listened. An intense loneliness filled his soul. He lay back on the bed, picked up a book of poems from beside the bed, and tried to read.

At last he bestirred himself. His girlfriend, Ondrej, would be coming from the university in half an hour. He needed to see her, as much for her own sake as to discuss the best approach to his cousin Jaroslav.

Now that dusk was enfolding the city, rendering it at once more mysterious and more tender, he walked down the street with greater confidence than he had climbed it. At the road junction at the foot of the hill he was in luck. A trolley car was trundling along, its arm sparking against its overhead cable, the very embodiment of normality. Whatever the regime in power, the trolleys kept going. A trolley was entirely apolitical. He jumped aboard and was carried towards the gaunt apartment blocks which ringed the ancient city.

On the third floor of one of these apartment blocks, a flat containing two other women, lived Ondrej Korinkova. Ondrej was married, but her husband had disappeared three months after the wedding, almost certainly arrested and imprisoned for treason to the state, in this case for printing a pamphlet in support of the Helsinki Agreement. The two women who shared the apartment with Ondrej were both divorced; they made their living by cleaning and occasional whoring, when possible with foreigners staying in the smart hotels in the centre of Prague. All three women considered themselves lucky: they had no kids to look after.

Ondrej's section of the apartment was partitioned off by an old yellow bedspread. It was behind this curtain that Petr Petrik found her, and embraced her. Though still a student, Ondrej Korinkova was in her late twenties, a full-bosomed girl with long lank hair which she had dyed a streaky ginger. Her eyes were as green if she were a true redhead; she outlined them with kohl for emphasis. When Ondrej looked at you, you knew you had been looked at.

Ondrej and Petr made love on her bed, ignoring one of the other women who was sewing sequins on to a dress in the far corner of the room, on the other side of the curtain. They did not undress fully.

About their love-making was a kind of spring-like familiarity, as yet not turning into dull summer of custom. He liked her slight movements; she was not one to throw herself about in a way he found annoying. And he listened with joy, his face to her face, as she neared her perfect pitch, sighing, 'Please, please . . . oh, yes, please . . .', quite unconscious of what she was saying, breathing that innocent word.

He savoured his own self-control, well able to let her spend herself, whispering, struggling, clasping her arms about him, before he allowed himself to climax in the sunsets of her emotion.

But after, as they sat on the side of the bed smoking cigarettes,

Ondrej said, in a light tone, delivering the sentence with a throwaway air, 'You like me only for the fucking . . .'

Immediately, Petrik turned on her a look of hatred. She had said such things to him before; he suspected she said it to many men, as if denying to herself secretly that she could be of value for anything else but fucking. 'Why do you talk sometimes as if we were enemies?'

She shrugged her shoulders and regarded the tip of her cigarette. 'There's enmity in every relationship.'

Afterwards, he took her out to a café he knew she liked on Jindrisska. It was already crowded. Ondrej enjoyed crowds, and passed whispered comments on other customers. He bought two glasses of red wine, and they smiled as they silently toasted each other.

He asked her what she had been doing with herself, rubbing his leg against hers under the table.

'I've been reading all day,' she said. 'I sat by the river and read. I was swallowed up by it.'

He smiled at her. 'Something in your words makes me sad.' Or perhaps it was the café. It had deteriorated since they were last here. The place was dim; some overhead bulbs had failed and not been replaced. The Russian vine on the terrace had ceased to flower. It might have been a railway canteen.

She chose not to respond to his remark. 'I have read an English poet all this afternoon,' she said, speaking stiltedly in English, not Czech.

'Shakespeare? Sturge Moore?'

She reverted to her native tongue to say, 'Samuel Coleridge. Early last century. It gives you an illusion of liberty, reading about that time. Coleridge walked all over England. Also, he was a drug addict, like me. He had an unhappy love-affair, like me. He was free to wander all over Europe, unlike me.'

'You're quite a free spirit, Ondrej,' he said lamely. He sipped his wine. She was so young. He did not want to think of his wasted student days.

'You know what?' She gave him one of her intense stares.

'Coleridge has written this remarkable book whose name I can't pronounce. He's talking about a play he dislikes. He gives it a real slating. I guess it was shit. And he talks about materialism, and do you know what he says? He says materialism may influence the characters of individuals and even of communities to a degree that almost does away with the distinction between men and devils. Isn't that great? And he goes on with a smashing bit of prophecy, "It will make the page of a future historian resemble the narration of a madman's dream." Don't you think he was thinking of *dialectical materialism*?'

'It's a good guess, anyway,' he said, looking round the café to see who was listening to them.

'I must try to get you interested in Samuel Coleridge some day,' she said, laughing lightly. 'Do you want to go and hear some jazz at Stompie's?'

As they walked down the boulevard, he apologized for being so abstracted, but was reluctant to say why. 'You know the Saradov Film Studios?' he said.

'Sure. They turn out shit.'

'That's what I thought.' Saradov turned out trivial films on safe subjects, many so pedestrian they were not even exported to the other countries of the Warsaw Pact, except Bulgaria. The Bulgarians watched anything. After the Soviet invasion of Czechoslovakia in 1968, many of the best script-writers and film-makers left the country. Others, like Petr Petrik himself, were forced to find other jobs. Yet the tradition of good film-making remained alive, sitting on a dusty back shelf.

Just supposing that this secretary, Lubomir Cihak, wanted to open the cultural door a little . . .

He had heard Cihak's name mentioned, generally with scorn. The man was always associated with hardline policies; the assumption was that he knew nothing at all about the movie business. Why should he be thinking about resurrecting Petr's old movie about Franz Kafka, with all its heavy overtones, politically slanted, of paternal repression? It was a mystery.

Perhaps his formidable cousin Jaroslav could solve the mystery.

When he and Ondrej were in the noisy jazz club, he tried to phone his cousin Jaroslav. Hardly surprisingly, he could not get through. The line seemed to be engaged.

The following afternoon it rained. Ondrej had arranged to meet Petr at six in the evening. The two friends who shared her apartment were going to see how business was doing at the Intercontinental. She joined them on impulse. She had gone to bed with foreigners before; it was nothing special, but she enjoyed seeing smart rooms, lying between fresh sheets, and maybe taking a luxurious bath too, if the man was agreeable – most of them wanted the women promptly out of their room once the trick was over. Westerners were worst in that respect, regarding 'Commie girls' as somehow inferior as human beings. Russians and Soviets generally – particularly the brutes on visiting Georgian delegations – regarded the girls as 'Western', and sometimes presented them with gifts of vodka, over and above the pay. Arabs paid most, gave grander presents, were cruel and haughty. All in all, Ondrej preferred Western men. In her limited experience, they used better soaps and were less inclined to haggle over the price.

She was in luck this afternoon. While Milada got a seedy chain smoker, she was immediately picked up by a tough-looking fellow, little older than she was. He had pleasant curly hair of an almost golden tint, and an open freckled face with a snub nose she found amusing. He could have been a boxer. He spoke a funny kind of English, and said his name was Frank. They often gave false names.

Ondrej paid him the usual compliments, and in fact he was quite a pleasure to be in bed with. Of course she knew the room would be bugged. So, presumably, did he. Foreigners were not so stupid as they used to be.

He allowed her to shower afterwards, climbing into the shower to feel her under the spray. When they were drying themselves, he became chatty and asked her if she had ever heard of Ireland.

'Of course. I'm not a fool.' She was annoyed by the question. 'It's where Bob Geldof and George Bernard Shaw come from.'

'Full marks. It's a great place, Ireland.'

'But not very important, I believe.'

'Sure, you're a bit of a cheeky little monkey!'

'Did you ever hear of Samuel Coleridge?'

'That's not an Irish name.'

She used his talc in a cloud, so that when Petr met her at six, he sniffed suspiciously.

They had chosen as rendezvous a small bookshop on Apolinarska run by a friend of Petr's. She saw immediately that he was anxious.

'We'll walk in the Botanic Gardens,' he said. She agreed, not wishing to upset him, although the trees were still dripping from recent rain showers. They strolled among other strollers deep in conversation; here, one could speak without much fear of being overheard.

'How's our friend the hunchback?' Ondrej asked. 'Any progress?'

'Not much. I showed you the latest sketches. Something could be trying to bite off his hump . . . A mail bin or something. That puts our friend in a dilemma. He wants the hump off his back. But will he survive if it is amputated?'

She laughed. 'Very subtle political thinking.'

'You have to do something.'

'Reminds me of that old riddle: "What stands on the corner of the square and doesn't kick people?" Answer: "A Russian-made people-kicker".'

'I wonder what it looks like?'

They paused by a pool where goldfish lazily circled. Petrik had a piece of stale bread roll in his pocket. When he threw the crumbs to the fish, they rose to the surface, seized a morsel, and darted away into the depths with a flick of their tails. Only momentarily did the small O of their mouths appear above the water.

'They're starving, you see.'

'Nonsense, everyone feeds them. You're too political, Petr! I'm going to treat you to a good feed tonight.'

Instead of asking where the money had come from he said, 'How was your Samuel Coleridge today?'

After a while, he took her arm and said quietly, 'Before we eat, I need you to come with me. I have made an appointment to see my cousin, Jaroslav Vacek. It would help if you accompany me.'

'Your big party boss cousin . . .'

'As boys we were very close. I looked after him when his parents disappeared. Now – well he's, quote, one of our leading industrialists, unquote, and was recently elected a council member of the Scientific and Technical Council, or some rubbish like that. Of course we don't have much to do with each other nowadays, but I'll make a better impression if you're with me. He won't think I'm such a failure.'

They both laughed. 'What's he going to do for you?'

'I've got a problem, a letter. Jaroslav is not a nice guy, but maybe he likes me enough to help me out. Though I'm sure to have to do something for him in return.'

'It's not dangerous? My profession is not hero but student and coward.' She turned her face up at him, pretending innocence.

'We'll be OK. It's not like the old days, really. In the old days, those goldfish would have been eaten long ago. Besides, Jaroslav'll like you. A bit of a womanizer. He speaks good English, I know, and makes lots of business trips abroad because he's trusted. Maybe you can talk to him about Samuel Coleridge.' He wrapped an arm around her.

They walked in the direction of the Jiraskuv Bridge. Vacek lived in what Petrik called 'Hollywood Prague'. Off one of the cobbled streets was an archway leading into an inner courtyard, defended by two great wooden doors, through which swagger coaches had once rattled. The entry phone on a side pillar was unostentatious. Petrik buzzed and a guard opened a small door in one of the large ones. They entered. In the courtyard, a big black Mercedes glittered under lamplight.

Ancient stone steps led to the upper floors of the building, but the guard escorted them to the first floor in an elevator.

Jaroslav Vacek opened the door to them, greeted them in a friendly way, and ushered them in. He shook Ondrej's hand and bowed politely. Vacek was in his late thirties, but looked younger, probably because of a healthy tan. His sandy hair was oiled and brushed back. His general athletic appearance was reinforced by the well-cut track suit he was wearing; a towel was tucked in at the neck. As he led Petr and Ondrej to the living-room, he gestured deprecatingly at the exercise bike they passed.

'I'm working out. Excuse me. I've just returned from an official visit to Semtin, where they are too hospitable.' He lapsed into English for a moment. '"Too utterly, utterly", as the English say.'

The room commanded a view of the Vltava. Ondrej went over to look out of the window while Petrik took in his cousin's furnishings. The room was more than comfortable; its elaborate display of objects made him immediately uncomfortable. On the walls were modern abstract paintings, set between ikons and framed pages from illuminated liturgical calendars.

'They're cheap ones,' Vacek said, with a smile and a dismissive wave of the hand, as his cousin stared at a golden ikon of the Virgin. 'That's to say, not from Russia but Macedonia in Jugoslavia. They're not only cheaper than the treasures of Zagorsk, they're a lot more cheerful as well. More to my taste. What may I do for you? I haven't much time.' He indicated that they should sit down.

'I'm sorry to bother you, cousin,' Petrik said, immediately regretting that he had opened the subject apologetically. 'I have received a letter . . . Well, it rather worries me. Do you know a man called Cihak, Lubomir Cihak?'

'Can I see the letter? Oh, excuse me – Ondrej, what would you like to drink? I admire your green eyes, by the way.'

'Cutty Sark whisky,' she said without hesitation, turning from the window so that he might enjoy her eyes again.

'I have some Glenfiddich. Will that do?'

'Oh, sure – I'm only a student, you know.'

'You must take a course in whisky some day.' While he was speaking, he moved rapidly to a drinks cabinet, pouring three healthy measures of whisky while Petrik brought the crumpled letter from his hip pocket.

When they were settled, Vacek read out the letter from the Secretary of the Film Academy concerning Petrik's film.

He dangled the letter in one hand. 'Sounds like good news.'

'On the surface.'

'God, you people are so miserable. You're so used to being trodden on, you want to go on being trodden on for ever. What's the matter with you, Petr? Afraid of ending up in Terejin, like some other pals we could mention? Here's someone with a bit of clout and he wants to show your film – just the sort of thing you've been rabbiting on about since you were a kid. You're in luck. Why hesitate? It isn't that *Sewers of Time* is such a fucking masterpiece, is it?'

Ondrej gave Vacek one of her piercing looks. 'My generation holds *Sewers* in great esteem, on a par with Forman and Menzel's work.'

'Yes – but have you ever seen it?' He laughed.

'She's not seen it,' Petrik said quickly.

Vacek regarded them both in turn, as if trying to decide which of them was lying to him, then folded his arms and turned his back on them.

Before he spoke again, he let silence thicken in the room. The sun broke through cloud, outlining the distant shoulder of Hradcany almost in silhouette, as it lit one of the ikons in the room with additional gold.

Vacek lowered his voice to make it flat and uncompromising. 'You're a bit of a bad lot, Petr. I told you a year ago to stay away from me. You do my reputation no good.'

Petrik stood up and spoke formally. 'You must understand my position, Jaroslav, please. I haven't been popular around here because I don't conform, and it's hard for me to see what's made these people change their minds.' He paused, confronted by the unsympathetic expanse of Vacek's back.

His cousin swung round abruptly. '"These people"? Who're you talking about?'

Remembering that tone of voice of old, Petrik spoke forcefully.

'Husak isn't dead or we'd have heard. This man Cihak is one of Husak's hardliners, isn't he? There's still a ban on Kafka. So why this letter to me? I just think the whole thing is fishy. I hoped you could advise me. It can't be they really want to show my film, can it?'

Vacek's face was unyielding. He drank his whisky. 'Why should they want to show your film? Ask yourself that first of all. It's long out of date in technique et cetera. No, I can tell you what's happening, though I wonder you can't see it for yourself. How some people survive in the rat race I'll never know. But first, you must promise to do me a favour in return.'

'What have I got to do? Come on, cousin Jaroslav, you needn't be like this. We were friends once. OK, I was in jail and got beaten up, but that's nothing in our socialist paradise, is it?'

Ignoring him, Jaroslav turned to the woman. 'Maybe you'd like to do a journey with Petr? I thought maybe a trip to West Germany Bundesrepublik for a few days?'

'You'll have to tell Petr about it, not me,' Ondrej said. She had folded her arms and sat on the sofa with her long legs crossed at the ankle, plainly disliking this whole conversation, refusing to do more than sip the malt whisky. Petrik thought as he glanced at her how thin and nervous she looked.

'As you wish, I don't care.' Vacek shrugged. 'Here's what you could do for me.'

He perched on the padded arm of a chair, clutching his glass. He explained that, on behalf of his company, he was in negotiation with a Western businessman whom he did not trust; the people behind him were a trifle shady. The line of business, too, was confidential. He wanted to see that this man, who was leaving Prague at the end of the week, got out of the country without making any other contacts. He wanted him watched. So Jaroslav needed to arrange that he had an escort all the way to the frontier. The businessman was travelling by train to West Germany. It would look entirely natural if another couple, a man and woman, just happened to be with him in the same compartment. 'And no one could be suspicious of a pair like you,' he said, smiling.

'What do we have to do?'

'See he doesn't get off the train. Simple enough.'

The question of money, visas, passports for them could be easily arranged. He would have them all ready by Friday. If they did this for him, they could part with the businessman once they were through the frontier, and spend three days in the West before catching an express back to Prague.

Petrik looked at Ondrej Korinkova. He could see immediately how she felt about the opportunity. She had shifted her position and was regarding Vacek attentively, looking at him more favourably.

'What's the catch? Who is this businessman we'll be with?'

'He's harmless, pretty well. He's a front man for a revolutionary force in his own lousy country. He likes money, he gets paid. The history of the world.'

'What's he buying from you?'

'Never mind that. Will you do it? There's nothing to it, no danger. You just have to speak English.' He pronounced the latter phrase in English, with mockery.

'Why us?'

Vacek sighed, as if his patience was running out. He glanced ostentatiously at his wristwatch. 'You've come along at a convenient moment. Your appearance will not make him suspicious; the sight of Ondrej and her green eyes will please him. In return, I'll do something for you. Now, don't bugger about with me – is it yes or no?'

'Yes,' said Ondrej. 'We'll go.'

Without waiting for Petrik's response, as if he took that for granted, Vacek said, 'Now, as to this apparatchik Lubomir Cihak. He is, as you rightly say, a hardliner. Also quite intelligent, in case that surprises you. Sensitive to the political atmosphere like a human barometer . . .

'Our friends and masters in the Kremlin are not what they were in the days of Josef Stalin, or even Leonid Brezhnev. Maybe because the Soviet economy is about to break down – so well-placed colleagues tell me. Of course, they've been saying that for years . . . at least.

Their new man, Comrade Gorbachev, is singing a different tune, The Dubček Blues. It makes people uneasy, particularly those who were happy with the old tune. They don't want destabilization, which appears to be what Gorbachev is about. You understand what I'm saying?

'Unsettling things are happening in Soviet society. The winds of this new creed of *glasnost* and *perestroika* are blowing round Russia and elsewhere, the Baltic states in particular. I was there last month. Gorbachev is rocking a pretty stable boat. There's not much reason to believe that the unrest will spread here, nevertheless ripples are already going out. So some clever men are anxious to secure their futures, to invest in life insurance by way of a little harmless liberalization.'

'You don't mean—' Petrik began, but his cousin silenced him.

'Shut up while I'm lecturing you. I've better things to do with my time, you know. Let's say that Cihak is such a man. Cihak's connected, however tenuously, with the arts, and the arts are always a weak point.

'So one day he decides while shaving to make some small gesture or gestures which could count greatly in his favour if the wind started to blow from a different direction. Like, say, digging up from the archives a banned film which he knows will cause few ripples, and letting it be shown on limited circuit – maybe in Bratislava or Brno . . .'

He burst into harsh laughter. 'Well, I need explain no more. Cihak's letter to you is no trap. His plans for his future create your golden opportunity.'

'There you are!' cried Ondrej, clapping her hands. In excitement, she swung her artificially coloured hair about so that it lashed her cheeks. 'It's your golden opportunity, Petr. Thank you so much, Jaroslav.'

Jaroslav gave her a calculating look. 'Of course, I could be lying.'

Petrik was irritated by her giving thanks to his cousin when there was nothing for which to thank him. Jaroslav had always wanted his pound of flesh, and something more if he could get it.

Nor did he like the smiles Ondrej was now giving his cousin, though the latter appeared to ignore the warmth coming from that quarter.

Gazing at the ceiling as if finding inspiration there – it was one of the most immaculate ceilings in Prague – Jaroslav continued to dispense advice to his cousin. 'Play into Cihak's hands. Of course let him show your lousy movie. You'll be rehabilitated . . . Of course, none of this will happen if you fail to return from Germany after the weekend.'

Again he folded his arms and turned his back on Petrik. The latter studied his cousin's neck. In its fashion, it gave away more of Vacek's character than his face did; this was a ruthless neck, evasive and worldly.

He rose to his feet, setting down his glass, and said to the neck, 'So it's settled then? It may surprise you, but I would like my movie shown, even in Brno. So we'll do what you ask. At what time do you want us to come back here on Friday?'

Vacek turned, arms still folded. 'I don't want you to come back here at all. There has to be no more association between us. On Friday at ten A.M., be at the Hlavni Nadrazi, the news-stand by No. 1 Platform. A man will meet you there and give you all the information – documents, money – you need. Is that clear? You'll be prepared to travel.

'Meanwhile, I will get a message to Cihak, expressing my support for the release of *Sewers of Time*. He'll know my name.'

Smiling, he made a dismissive gesture and rose to his feet. As Ondrej and Petr moved towards the door, the latter remarked that he hoped that they would be doing nothing illegal.

'The state itself operates on illegality. It could not continue otherwise. That illegality is a defence against the crimes of the West. Many of our dealings with the West are "illegal", according to the statutes, because we have a blocked currency. Therefore illegality is itself legal. You must have discovered that for yourself, cousin, when they threw you in the slammer.'

This he said absent-mindedly, as if it were something he had learned. Ondrej held out a thin hand to him. Taking it, he said, in an altered tone, looking intently at her, 'I see Petr wishes to leave. You stay behind, and I will advise you on some shopping that a lady might do in Nuremberg.'

'She's coming with me,' Petrik said, in sudden anger, grasping Ondrej's sleeve and dragging her from the room. She went without objection, not resisting him.

'As you please,' said Vacek, unruffled. 'However, since you are so unsure of yourself, Petr, I shall give you in advance a photograph of the Western businessman you will be travelling with. You can study his features at your leisure.'

He had opened the hall door, to reveal the guard standing alertly in the passageway. Retracing his steps into the living-room, Vacek pulled a half-plate photo out of a bureau drawer and returned to offer it to his cousin. Petrik was too angered and humiliated to accept; Ondrej took the photo instead.

Petrik marched off without a word of farewell. After a quick glance at Ondrej, at the pallid face, the unwashed hair, the painted eyes, he thought perhaps he really hated her: but what he really hated was the whole business of deception under which life was lived, hers as well as his, as well as everyone else's.

In truth, Petrik secretly did not believe that his Kafka film was a masterpiece; but he had made it in homage to a writer he greatly admired, one who seemed to have had a prophetic insight into Prague's troubles. He asked only that *Sewers of Time* – the title was a phrase taken from Kafka's diaries – be seen and judged. It was a record not only of Kafka but of Prague, and therefore of the whole ghastly world; a record, a witness. But what was judgement these days? Judgement was political.

Jaroslav had spoken contemptuously of Cihak's self-serving nature, yet Jaroslav was himself a self-server. He often represented himself as a good Communist, a loyal party member, yet the words meant nothing to anyone any more: all idealism had long since faded. And Petrik himself – he had agreed readily enough to go on this errand for which he had no heart. Everywhere was this betrayal of self, a cynicism backed by the armoured brigades waiting only a few kilo-metres outside the city.

He descended the winding stone stair, gazing grimly down at his feet. The steps had not recently been swept; crushed cork tips of cigarettes lay in corners. Ondrej followed, two steps behind him, staring at the face in the photograph Vacek had handed her. She recognized the blunt nose, the bushy eyebrows, the pugnacious expression. It was a photograph of the Irishman she had been in bed with in the Intercontinental that afternoon.

'It's like a journey up the Amazon,' Uncle Josef said. 'Strange terri-tory, much of it unmapped . . . All sorts of unknown dangers await you. The natives aren't always friendly, and even your friends can turn against you. So watch out.'

'Thanks for the warning, Uncle,' Petr Petrik said, smiling as he hung up the phone.

'He's such a pessimist, my uncle,' Petrik said, returning to the restaurant table. 'He says it's like a journey up the Amazon. He doesn't like the Germans.'

'Oh, the Germans are no worse than anyone else,' Ondrej Korinkova said. 'People are all the same, really, no better, no worse . . .'

The complacent views of a whore, he thought, but said nothing. He was nervous and smoked continually. They sat in the old restau-rant of the station, not in the snack bar in the modern underground hall. He liked the Art Nouveau of the old station, which he and his friends always referred to as the 'Wilsonjaak'; it was typical of his bullying cousin to refer to it as the Hlavni Nadrazi, or main station, a name imposed by the regime.

As Ondrej chattered in a cheerful way – trying to talk intellectu-ally, he thought – he let his mind wander to the one nook in the city that, apart from hers, gave him contentment. He had never taken Ondrej to it, not her or any other girlfriend; only his pleasant old uncle Josef had been there, in that cubbyhole which was a substitute for the freedom of the Bohemian countryside he had known in the optimistic years of boyhood, when all adults around him had believed that the institution of a Socialist state boded well for the spirit; and for self-denial.

The nook was underground, in a repository of old bones and lost aspirations. He barely had room to move in it. There on the narrow bench was his secret project, his little hunchback who moved only by stop-motion photography, the little man who plunged through a world defined by Petrik's pen and his ability to mould modelling clay. And round about, close as branches of trees to a hunter hiding in a copse, were the pieces of apparatus he had saved from his more prosperous Kafka years or bought on the black market: his camera, his lights, his developer, the monitor and the radio-cassette, most of them imports from West Germany.

It was when his cousin Jaroslav had mentioned the possibility of a visit to West Germany, put as a sly suggestion, in that indirect way in which power was expressed nowadays, that Petrik saw his chance. He could acquire brand new equipment, above all new lenses, in Germany, and dispense with some of the outdated tools with which he was forced to work at present. With the new equipment, he could make his work more brilliant than ever. His little hunchback would rise up and enact all the injustices of society, helping to sweep them away, as swept away they must surely be one day – sooner or later. The hunchback would be his voice, stifled for too long. Everyone should hear it.

Or so he had reckoned, coming away down Jaroslav's stairs, scuffing the already squashed cork tips, nursing a secret little thought of victory to himself.

Now, sitting in the metal restaurant chair contemplating Ondrej as she enthused about a play she had seen in private performance, he found himself considering how much he was motivated by gain. He was really no better than his avaricious cousin. His goal was, after all, to gain advantage, so that he could shine before his fellow country-men. No self-denial there, only self-deception. Superstitiously, he touched the burdensome packet of money and documents in his pocket as he accused himself.

Adventure was not for him. Ever since boyhood, witnessing the shooting of his father, cowardice had invaded him, undermined him. He should not be going on a shabby secret errand, waiting for a westbound train. He wished himself back in his underground cubbyhole, with its damp floor, and him sweating under the lights as he moved the shaped clay, frame by frame, safely towards a shaped conclusion.

He thought, I may not exactly be able to love Ondrej, as perhaps a better man would, but I do see she has more courage in her beautiful body than I in my parsimonious one . . .

Yet he viewed her with some disfavour. Ondrej wore a green travelling cloak over a too-short dress. As she sat smoking at the table, the skirt had ridden up to reveal her shapely legs encased in patterned tights with love birds embroidered low on either calf. Such garments had surely not been acquired legitimately. Students did not wear such things.

For this occasion, she had dyed her hair black and, most remarkably, was not wearing make-up. Without their kohl, her eyes were small and tired-looking. That too made him uncomfortable. It was almost as if she were in disguise.

Ondrej stubbed out her cigarette in the remains of the meal on her plate, shooting Petrik quick glances as she did so. She was annoyed that he had insisted on coming to the station so early. It was only nine thirty in the evening, an hour before their train left. It was due to pull into Nuremberg station before six the next morning. He did not know why she was so tense and smoking so heavily.

He had come to the station that morning, as his cousin had demanded, and met the contact. The contact informed Petrik that he was to travel with Tom Driscoll; that was the name of the man whose photograph he held. He handed over to Petrik the documents necessary for their journey, together with a little spending money in both koruna and Deutschmarks, which Petrik checked over carefully under the eye of the contact.

Something unexpected had also been passed over: a tightly packed and sealed manila envelope. This, the contact instructed Petrik, was to be delivered to an address in Nuremberg, which address he made Petrik memorize; it was not written down.

As they sat in the restaurant, Petrik fingered the envelope in his inner pocket every few minutes.

'Leave that thing alone,' Ondrej whispered to him across the table. 'You're getting on my nerves. Every idiot in here must know by now you have something worth stealing in your damned pocket.'

He withdrew his hand, laid it on the table, fiddled with a knife. 'It's bound to be a bundle of money. What else could it be?'

'Dope?'

'You would think of that. It's currency, I can feel. It's obviously illegal. Trust Jaroslav to stick this on me, the bastard. It wasn't part of the deal at all.'

'You were a bit of a fool to accept it then, weren't you?'

They smoked, not speaking to each other. After a while, he called the waitress over and ordered another hot chocolate for Ondrej and another espresso for himself.

They waited, keeping a watchful eye on the passers-by beyond the restaurant window. It was a few minutes past ten when Ondrej rose hurriedly from her seat, saying that she had just spotted Tom Driscoll.

As Petrik started to rise, she pressed his shoulder down:

'No, you stay here, Petr dear. I'll tackle Driscoll to begin with. It'll look more natural for a woman to bump into him and start a conversation.'

'But we don't have to bump into him. That won't look right. You know the arrangements. We already have reservations next to him in the sleeping car. That's all it needs.'

'Leave it to me,' she said, and left the restaurant. Nonplussed, Petrik stayed where he was, peering from the window, gnawing his lower lip.

Ondrej marched straight up to Tom Driscoll as he paused by the news-stand. 'You look like a foreigner, and a little lost,' she said, in her fluent English. 'Can I help you? Stations are often confusing.'

Driscoll was well-built, as she remembered, and little taller than she was. His heavy features and snub nose were as she recalled them from their encounter in the hotel. He was wearing a rather unseasonal gingerish top-coat and carrying a small metal case. The impression he gave was of a hard, capable man. She could not resist a flicker of approval.

He looked the girl over, not smiling. 'I know the station well. I'm not lost at all, miss.' There was no recognition of her in his grey eyes.

'Sorry. I thought you were hesitating. Excuse me.' So saying, she turned round and walked back to the restaurant, swinging her hips and sighing with relief to think that her ploy had worked. He did not recognize her, this man who had called himself Frank. She had been afraid of trouble on that score.

Petrik was paying the bill at the counter inside the door. 'What did he say?'

'It's Driscoll all right. He looks just like his photo. I asked him in Czech where the ladies' toilets were. When he said he didn't understand, I apologized and walked away. I wanted to be sure we had the right man. Have you settled up? Shall we go?'

Dozens of people were besieging the express, which stood dignified and immobile, its interior lights gleaming, being readied for its journey westwards. The boards were up on the camel-coloured sides of the carriages: PRAHA-PLZEN-CHEB-NURNBERG-STUTTGART. At the far end of the platform, a minotaur-shouldered diesel was in place, simmering to be off. Ondrej climbed aboard the train, Petrik following close behind. They struggled to gain their second-class sleeper, pushing past men and women moving this way and that along the narrow corridor. Many passengers were weighed down with luggage, and many were in military uniform.

Ondrej was excited by the bustle. She thoroughly inspected the compartment and the six bunks folded back into the walls. An old man joined them, pulling a heavy suitcase behind him. His pallid leathery face supported a two-day growth of white stubble, although he was smartly dressed. They watched him covertly as he wrenched down one of the lower bunks, kicked off his shoes, and climbed into the bunk. When his eyes closed, he appeared to fall asleep immediately.

A few minutes before the train was due to leave, Driscoll came aboard. He stowed his case away and sat down next to them without removing his coat. When they gave him a greeting, he nodded, saying nothing.

The conductor walked through the train, calling to everyone without a ticket to leave. The bustle increased. Ondrej went to the corridor window to watch their departure, calling to Petrik to see what a long train it was. Prompt to time, the express began to move with gradually increasing strength, to roll past the waving groups of people on the platform into the darkness beyond the station.

For a while Ondrej was content to stand in the corridor, peering out of the window at the lights and signs of industry in the night. At last, she came back into the compartment yawning, to say to Petr, 'Well, I'm going to turn in. I'll leave it to you.' She avoided looking directly at Driscoll.

The bunk reserved for her was above the sleeping man. Without disturbing him, she pulled the bed down and climbed into it, turning her cloak-clad back on Driscoll and Petrik. The latter thought to himself, 'She's shooting some shit into her veins up there, sure enough.' He did not know what she was hooked on, and never enquired.

It was impossible for Petrik to retire to his bunk as long as Driscoll remained where he was, since Petrik's was the other middle bunk; Driscoll had reserved the lower bunk on which they were sitting. The two upper bunks had not been taken. Driscoll showed no sign of moving. He continued to sit immobile, staring into space, his lower lip protruding as if in deep thought.

Petrik too fell into a daze, his thoughts turning as always to the question of his film-making. He had taken a job in a back-street garage, repairing Western makes of cars, which always fetched good prices in the capital. His boss operated out of a disused chapel. The boss was a scholarly and decent man who understood Petrik's love of film-making, and had been heard to say proudly to customers, gesturing to his assistant, 'Yes, he used to be a film director in Dubček days.'

The boss lived with his current mistress in the crypt under the converted chapel. In a fit of goodwill, he gave Petrik a space at one end of the crypt little bigger than a large cupboard to use as a studio. This was his nook.

Here Petrik had installed some equipment and was putting together the black-and-white animated feature starring his small hunchbacked figure. He had one minute eight seconds on film so far. In moments of idleness, his thoughts went to the next scene, for which he had partly drawn the set. A postbox was getting ready to open its mouth and swallow the little hunchback. The working title of the feature was *Legacy*.

It was just after midnight, when the express was drawing out of a dark Plzen, that Driscoll produced from one of his capacious ginger pockets a silver flask. He unscrewed the cup and poured an amber liquid into it. Then, catching Petrik's eye upon him, he proffered the cup.

'Would you be liking a drink?'

Petrik was surprised, and could not immediately think of the limited English he possessed.

The great bulk of the man edged slightly nearer, still offering the cup. 'It's Irish whiskey. *Verstehen*? It'll do you good. Make your hair curl.'

'No. No, thanks.'

'Go on. We've hours to kill on this bloody train.'

Petrik accepted the cup, and sipped. It was strong and good, waking new sensations in his throat as it went down.

'There's no sense in being miserable. I always say it. My mother always used to tell us, if you walk around under a black cloud you're going to get many a wetting.'

Petrik looked out of the window. 'It's good to be cheerful, even in rain,' he said. He fingered the plump packet in his coat.

'My sentiments precisely. People have to create their own lives.' Driscoll accepted the silver cup back, steadying his elbow against the rear of the bunk in order to pour himself a generous dose before continuing. 'Yes, people have to create their own lives. It's a must. The more miserable the outlook, the brighter should be your hopes.

You have to fight for what you think is right and to hell with the rest of them. Isn't that so? On either side of the Iron Curtain, that's so, eh? I take it you're Polish – sorry, I mean Czechoslovak. I'm forgetting which bloody country I'm in.'

'It is not always possible to "create your own life", as you say it. There are limitations and circumstances. Our own life is set for us, in many ways.' He found English difficult.

Driscoll preferred to ignore this last remark. Gesturing with the cup towards Ondrej's back, he said, 'Do you think your little missus would like to join us for a sip?'

'She's in sleep.'

'We could wake her up. She's a nice-looking lady, your little missus. There are quite a few birds I've seen in Prague look a lot like her.'

'I have not seen them,' Petrik said. He was displeased by these personal comments.

Silence fell. The train rattled through the night. Driscoll unbuttoned his coat and, leaning forward, rested his elbows on his knees, the better to enjoy his drink. After a while, he turned again to Petrik. 'You Czechs are good businessmen, you know that? You make a tough deal. You ought to be capitalists.'

'Many of us think it.'

The dark countryside through which they were passing became punctuated by a few scattered lights. Soon they were entering Marienska Lazne. To avoid further discussion, Petrik went to stand and look out of the door of the compartment. Driscoll rose and joined him. He started up another conversation, passing the cup again.

Petrik found his English returning, though he did not speak it well. They talked of general things, in the cautious way of travellers; but the subject of what was to be made of life seemed never far from Driscoll's thoughts. Conscious always of being on his cousin's mission, Petrik was careful not to annoy the man, who he suspected could be of uncertain temper. He found it best to agree with most of his sentiments, although a mild demurrer awoke the other's wrath.

'You got to make your own life, that's what I say. If someone oppresses you, you fight back against the bastards.' Saying this, Driscoll thumped the window bar for emphasis.

'Well . . . that isn't possible sometimes,' Petrik said. 'Then you have to make the best of the things. I suppose it is a different case for you English.'

Driscoll flared up immediately. 'I'm no bloody Englishman and I'd cut me own throat if I was. Don't you call me English. I'm Irish to the blood and bone.'

Petrik apologized hastily. 'I should have said Westerner.' He gave the man a cigarette by way of apology. They smoked together in silence.

The little whiskey cup went round.

'I shouldn't have spoken as I did,' Driscoll said, reflectively. 'What do you know of how I was brought up, how my family has suffered? You aren't the only lot who suffer oppression, you know, you Poles.'

'Czechs.'

The repetitive noises of the train, its slow but steady movement forward, had lulled most of its passengers to sleep. The roar it made travelling through the Bohemian countryside acted as a lullaby. In the second-class sleeper, Ondrej remained asleep, while Petrik and the Irishman stood in the corridor, talking and sipping whiskey. Petrik was scarcely aware that the alcohol was going to his head. His English improved.

It was after two in the morning when the train began to swerve as it negotiated points, so that they wedged themselves into the threshold of the compartment with their shoulders. Peering out of the window, they saw by a single melancholy light that they were passing through Cheb station.

'We come to the national frontier,' Petrik said.

'I'll be glad to get back to the West, I will that. I like Prague well enough, it's a fine old city, and you can have a good time in the Intercontinental, but there's something about the whole country which depresses the hell out of me.'

'Yet you come here.'

'I've business here, haven't I? Like I say, it's a grand old city, that I'll give you, but soon as you cross the frontier into the West you can feel the difference in the air – yes, even at two in the morning. It's a fine place, Germany. What I'd call a real nation. I admire the Germans. They've got themselves a good thing going, and they don't oppress nobody either. It's the best place in Europe, and the most democratic, to my reckoning, bar none.'

'You have also business in Nuremberg?'

Driscoll passed the cup again. 'It may surprise you to know, but there's a whole lot of Irish living in Nuremberg. I'll tell you, there's a lot of Irish living everywhere in the world. Because of what the English done, there's more Irish living in New York than there are in the whole of Ireland, and that's a fact. It's amazing, isn't it? More of us in New York City than in all Ireland.'

He went on talking. Petrik half-listened. The train had slowed and finally stopped. All was dark outside, and there was not a sound to be heard. Driscoll ceased his chatter and peered long and hard through the window.

They started to move again, so gradually that the movement was scarcely perceptible. Without actually going to the window to peer out, Petrik thought he could see, outlined against a distant bar of neon light, dark figures moving along the track. For no clear reason, he became nervous and wanted to wake Ondrej Korinkova. Like Driscoll, he fell silent. Driscoll pocketed his whiskey bottle, looking to left and right.

The train travelled on with a stealthy movement. When they passed a lighted hut, Petrik saw how slowly they were going. In his excited state, he felt something dreamlike was happening. They were passing from the country he loved and despaired of, into that other world: the journey up the Amazon, Uncle Josef had called it – so big and loud and sexy and successful. Where movie-makers shot real films starring forceful men pursuing women in fine clothes, instead of making pinched little cartoons about hunch-backed plasticine figures being chased by huge grey office blocks on legs.

The door at the end of the coach was thrown open and four uniformed men entered the corridor. They wore caps and large overcoats and a look of serious blankness which Petrik knew well. One of them turned into a small reserved compartment by the door they had entered while the others moved straight into action, waking passengers and checking their documents. Petrik did not need Driscoll to tell him the Czech customs police were aboard.

As they drew nearer, stirring up the sleepers, issuing commands, bringing men out into the corridor to be searched, apprehension seized Petrik. The package Jaroslav's contact had thrust on him burned in his pocket. He was convinced it contained illegal foreign currency. Perhaps he might hide it under Ondrej's blanket. Then she would be in trouble if it was found . . . And she might be in trouble anyway if they found drugs on her . . .

He turned back into the compartment and shook the girl. 'Wake up, Ondrej. Customs officers are here. We're at the frontier.'

'Buzz off! I just want to sleep,' she mumbled.

'If they discover drugs on you, you're in trouble.'

She sat up slowly and turned a pale face to him. 'God, I was having such an awful dream. I need a coffee.' She began to light a cigarette. He left her to it, stepping back to the doorway to look at what was happening. The officers were about to emerge from the neighbouring compartment.

It was a time for haste. Petrik acted.

'Hold on to this for me till we're through,' he said to Driscoll. As he spoke, he pulled the package from his pocket and rammed it into the Irishman's breast pocket under his raincoat. 'They won't search you. You're Western. You're safe.'

Driscoll had no time to argue, had he wanted to. The three police appeared and confronted them, both flashing torches.

'Passports!'

When they had examined Driscoll's passport and given him a hard look, they handed it back without comment and took no further interest in him. Petrik's Czech passport was the signal for a brief interrogation and then a body search. He knew they would be looking for illegal currency. They found nothing. He hated the search and stood scowling at them as two of them went in to Ondrej.

The officers made a crude joke as they got Ondrej out of the bunk and searched her. Looking in her case, they laughed at what they found and threw it back at her. She blew smoke in their faces.

The old white-haired man in the lower bunk had got up and stood in one corner, hands clasped together, shuddering. The police took a long look at his passport. They flashed a torch in his face and asked a few brief questions, to which the man replied in heavily accented Czech.

'Come on,' they said. The old man was marched down to the other cop at the end of the corridor. Petrik and Driscoll stood motionless while this happened.

'What a lot of fascists,' Driscoll commented. 'What a country!'

The searchers moved on down the train and into the next coach. Ondrej stubbed out her cigarette and went back to sleep.

After twenty minutes of near silence, the train began its serpentine movement, to clatter over further sets of points. Distantly ahead line after line of glittering lights appeared. The other world, the world of the West, the fabulous Amazon basin itself, was approaching.

'They've gone now,' Petrik said. 'You can give me my money back.'

'What money would that be?' Driscoll demanded, looking him in the face.

'The package. I knew you to be OK, I knew they do not search you, with your English passport. Thanks for you to keep it safe.' He held out a hand.

'Supposing I hold on to what you gave me?'

Driscoll put his right hand up to the region of his pocket, but made no further move, regarding Petrik steadily.

'I shall have it back now,' Petrik said, laughing nervously. 'The police have departed. We're in West Germany now. The West. Your West.'

The man travelling as Driscoll made his move. Putting the power of his shoulder behind the blow, he brought his right fist smashing against Petrik's jaw. The latter fell to the floor without a sound.

'Teach you to call me a fucking Englishman,' Driscoll said.

Vacek was entertaining friends when his phone rang. He took the call standing in his bedroom, making no comment until his cousin had finished breaking the news.

'Mm . . . Driscoll, or whatever his name is, is the opportunist I took him for . . . What a sheep you are, Petr . . . Is that green-eyed person still sticking with you? So you have some luck . . . Goodbye.'

He set the receiver down, unperturbed. The loss of his Deutschmarks meant little. And the IRA was pretty small beer. The Syrians were much more important to him: he would be meeting one of their representatives soon. In fact, when he visited London in just two weeks.

He turned to rejoin his party.

4

Adopted

As a general rule, the great house seemed to sleep at night, in a natural conclusion to its heavy, drowsy aspect during the day. The only lights to be seen after dark would be the bright lights, burning late, from the rooms on the first floor which Dominic claimed as exclusively his, and the dimmer light from the room on the top floor at the rear, in which his wife, Fenella, increasingly spent her time.

The house presented to uncritical eyes a certain grandeur. Certainly it was big. Its front elevation was saddled with a number of bays and gables, the work of romantic Victorian restoration. An overhanging upper storey made the building appear to suffer from an everlasting headache. This forgery, inspired by the medieval fictions of Sir Walter Scott, was topped by mock-Tudor chimneys, twisting above the hunched roofs like old-fashioned sticks of barley sugar. A variety of aerials sprouted there, evidence of Dominic's way of keeping in touch with the world.

The previous owner of the property – a complete thug in Dominic's estimation – had turned the garden into a carpark and a crazy-golf course. That had gone. So had an inappropriate conservatory. An area inside the front walls provided a proper parking space, shielded from the house by a colonnade on which roses trailed. The rest of the space was down to lawn, set off by clumps of pampas grass and

114

a goldfish pool. The odd job man kept the area in order. Dominic's wife sometimes walked there.

To the rear of the house was an old stable-yard, inhabited by two active young mastiffs and surrounded by various torpid outbuildings. Here Dominic kept his cars. Here too stood a stable-block converted into living accommodation for the Bettses, the husband and wife who worked for Dominic and helped with the running of Shreding Green Manor.

If strangers ventured into the grounds of the manor after dark, its silence and its darkness terminated immediately. Powerful intruder lights came on. A warning siren sounded. The mastiffs began to rush along their wire runs in search of malefactors. At the touch of a switch, Dominic from his upper rooms could cause his amplified voice to sound alarmingly all over the area.

These precautions were considered necessary because Shreding Green was no longer the convenient distance from London its first Georgian owners had intended. London's outskirts now lapped about its protective walls. The congested airport of Heathrow was no more than five miles distant. London was full of opportunists, thieves and villains, as Dominic knew. He made most of his money there, and from them.

On a Saturday evening in October, early in the eighties, the intruder precautions were lifted. The dogs were kennelled. The entire alarm system was switched off. The electronically operated gates were unlocked. The estate was awakened from its slumber. By six in the afternoon, music filled the house and spilled over into the grounds. Fountains played. Caterers' vans appeared. A large marquee of blue and white stripes was erected in the paddock behind the stables. A live rock group arrived and began to set up its amplifiers. Dominic Mayor had decided to throw a party.

He stood in the paved hall of Shreding Green Manor, instructing four security guards hired for the evening. He showed them the signal he would give to indicate any gate-crasher at the party. They in turn explained how they generally worked. He then walked out with them to their van to inspect the two dogs, built like Kodiak bears, which they had brought along.

'I wouldn't muck about with 'em if I was you, sir,' one of the guards said.

'I had no intention to do so,' Dominic replied stiffly. 'Keep them on a tight leash until they are necessary.'

He stood unmoving, watching to see them disperse about the property. Dominic Mayor was a small young man, neatly built, as if designed for a tailor's window. He had a small brown beard, possibly intended to lend a pale, wistful face strength. He stood with feet close together, frail hands clutched behind his back, watching, quick to follow every movement.

He was already dressed for the evening, in a lightweight white suit, double-breasted and buttoned up. Beneath it, a crimson frilled shirt showed, open at the neck. White and crimson were his favourite colours.

He stood there, dainty hands behind him, surveying the mansion he had won for himself. This evening it would not be dark. All the lights would be on. Flags were out, large expensive flags, for Dominic would have nothing resembling the little plastic flags he had seen at village fêtes; these were flags which lapped the grey masonry with rectangles of blue, yellow, and a rather sombre ox-blood. From the high fake tower flew the Union Jack.

As Dominic regarded this display with his usual expression, in which there was less satisfaction than a look of waiting alertly for a satisfactory verdict, a middle-aged man wearing an old dinner-jacket came smartly from the main portal, advanced towards Dominic at a half-run, and saluted as he halted before him.

'All present and creck, sah,' he said, giving a shadowy imitation of an imaginary sergeant-major.

Ignoring the play-acting, Dominic said, 'Look, Arold, one little thing you could do. Mrs Mayor's mother, Mrs Cameron, will arrive soon.'

'Don't worry, suh, I well recall the lady. She drives a Rover 2000 if I'm not mistaken. I'll see to her, park the car, everything.'

'What I want you to do, Arold, is to see – well, that everything is made sufficiently easy for Mrs Cameron, yah? In particular, you tell me the moment she arrives. No irritation for her, understand?'

Arold Betts bent his left arm and raised his left hand in a gesture

116

of denial, at the same time canting his head so sharply to the left that his protruding teeth grazed his fingertips. 'Rely on me, Mr Mayor. Situation understood perfeck. A touchy lady, Mrs Cameron, Doris and I know it, having experienced the back of her hand, so to speak, more than once. That car has but to appear and you shall know.'

'Perhaps you might park her car for her, Arold. The lady has a difficulty with reverse.'

'Understood perfeck.' He gave a conspiratorial wink and a nod, before turning smartly on his heel and marching off, head thrust forward, teeth leading.

Arold found his wife Doris in the kitchens, smoking a cigarette and looking on as the caterers unloaded food from their vans.

'Ooh, it's like olden times here, Arold,' Doris Betts said. 'A Tudor feast day, no less. Take a shufty at all this grub, and marvel.'

He was hastily pouring himself a glass of wine.

'These are great days for us, Doris, and great days for England. If our lad could see us now, I imagine he'd be proud.' He raised the glass in a silent toast to the great days, or possibly England, or possibly their lad, and drank appreciatively. 'All the same, gel, with that woman Cameron coming it spells trouble. 'E 'ates 'er. The dogs 'ates 'er. And I reckon 'er daughter do too.'

'Well, I certainly do,' said Doris indignantly, annoyed to be left off her husband's list. 'Rudest woman I ever come across. I know I'm an orphan and all that, but I don't care to be treated like a lump of dog-dirt, thanks. Arold, dear, don't get too tight tonight, for God's sake.'

He shook his head at her, grinning. 'A mere vassal, me, Doris, but not incapable of enjoying myself when the occasion arises.'

And he sipped more deeply at the wine. 'Mayor wouldn't grudge me a drop. That's not like him. He may be a foreigner but he's a gent, a lord . . .'

'Don't be daft. He's no foreigner. He's got a British passport.'

'You know what I mean. Born foreign.' As he spoke, his wife was turning away to polish up some glasses, which one of the hired staff was unloading. This man, who was dressed in a light blue uniform, asked if there was a 'do' on.

'I'll say there is,' Arold replied, proudly. 'Three 'undred and fifty guests expected on parade 'ere this evening. It's like an entertainment of old, with lords and ladies. And the boss is only twenty-six and a bit. A youngster. That's what I call success, on the grand scale, modern-style. Come from nowhere, now worth a million. See his car out in the garridge? That's a Porsche Carrera Targa, with special interior fittings. Not another like it in the whole country. And he lets me drive it on occasions. That's your new aristocracy for you, mate.'

He lifted his glass, negotiated it past his teeth, and drank again.

'Ere's to 'im, says I.'

The subject of Arold Betts's admiration had gone indoors. Before confronting his wife, he went into the library and took down from the shelves a leather-bound volume with a title on the spine, *Great Expectations*. The volume was in reality a box disguised as a book. Inside was his supply of cocaine. Dominic crooked his left hand and poured himself a generous shot on the stretched skin between thumb and forefinger; this he snorted up both nostrils. He returned the book to its shelf. Then he went briskly to see Fenella Mayor.

Fenella had moved out of the Mayors' communal bedroom a month earlier, following a quarrel. She now slept in one of the guest bedrooms, on the door of which Dominic knocked. After a pause, he heard her ask who it was.

'It is me, Fenella. Who else?'

She unlocked the door, opened it a crack, and looked out at him. Her long anxious face lacked colour. She studied her husband without comment.

'Well – may I come in, dear?'

'What do you want?'

'Oh, come on, dear, we are married, if you remember it.'

She opened the door further and stepped aside to let him into the room, still clutching the doorknob. She was a tall woman, an inch or two taller than Dominic, and eleven years older. A yellow chenille dressing-gown loosely draped her figure. Clothes were spread out on the double bed.

Dominic went to stand by the window. Rubbing his hands together, he put on a genial tone of voice. 'Nearly ready, are you? Our guests will arrive soon. I want you to be down to greet them with me. Host and hostess. Will you wear that pretty dress you bought in Richmond yesterday?'

She continued to look at him without expression before speaking. 'I don't like you in my bedroom, that's the trouble. I told you that all that sex thing is over between us until the quarrel is settled and you apologize.'

'OK, fine, Fenella. No sex. I understand. I have apologized. I do again. This is different. It's party time. I have come to see you are OK and have on a nice dress to meet people. It's getting late.'

He glanced nervously at his watch before clasping his hands behind his back. He was aware that he spoke to her as if she were a child to be humoured. About that, Fenella rarely complained.

The room in which she had taken refuge suffocated him. His mother-in-law, Morna Cameron, had provided most of its furnishings from her estate in Scotland. The brass bedstead rattled as he paced back and forth at its foot. The dressing-table which stood to one side in the bay window was a relic of Victorian days, its frontage of little drawers bearing complex wood inlays. It was laden with lace mats, cut-glass pots with silver lids, and cut-glass trays.

Like sentinels on opposite sides of the room stood two matching wardrobes, one for a lady, one for a gentleman. Their austere mahogany fronts imposed silence on the room. The lady's wardrobe stood open, to reveal a line of dresses, hanging imprisoned and limp.

These relics from a British yesterday he did not share were not to Dominic's taste. Nor was the tartan carpet underfoot.

'Bloody hell,' he said. 'Look at the time.'

Seeming to ignore him by not following his movements, Fenella merely stared ahead, in the direction of the window. 'I don't know all these people. Why are they coming? I didn't ask them.'

'We both sent out the invitations, if you remember. The pink invitations you selected in Harrods. The occasion is to celebrate the making of my first million. It's a cause for celebration, Fenella, and the chairman of Schatzman's Bank will be here. Josh Rund.

You remember him. Put on your dress like a dear and let me see you in it.'

'How are we to get three hundred people in here? I don't want them coming upstairs. Besides, the reception rooms are filthy. I'm sure Arold never cleaned them as I instructed. He drinks too much, that's Arold's trouble.' She gave a brief laugh. 'I'd sack him but I know how you like him. What will the chairman think? You ask the chairman of a bank to a filthy house and you think that's good for business? You don't understand British ways, that's half your trouble.'

He smiled, saying in a mollifying tone, 'I don't suppose anyone will notice a bit of dust. I guarantee the rooms were thoroughly cleaned. The important thing is to make everyone feel welcome, yah? Now, tell me you're almost ready.' Even to himself, his words sounded artificial; he could not force himself to be natural in her presence.

'How can I do anything with you standing there talking? If only you'd leave me alone and stop bullying me, I could get on. The guests will soon be arriving. They don't want to see me anyway. It's you they're interested in. It's not my million.'

'Correct. But it is our house. Our home.' With a malicious smile, he added, 'And of course you must be ready to receive your dear mother.'

She moved. She came closer to him and said, 'Is my hair suitable? I didn't like the way the man did it, and I told him so.'

'It looks just lovely, dear. Put on those pearl earrings your mother gave you – don't forget – and she's certain to be pleased.'

'Are you sure she'll come?'

'You invited her.' He could not help giving her a look of loathing.

'What are you accusing me of? I had to invite her.'

'Good, good.' He started shaking his head. 'It will be nice to see her again.' He had a quick glance at his watch.

'Do you think so, Dominic?'

'I said it, didn't I? Now, be a dear and hurry to put on the dress.'

He looked back at her as he reached the door. There his wife stood in the middle of the room, one hand to her sallow cheek, giving him one of her lonely stares.

On impulse, he went back, put an arm round her waist, and kissed her. 'Don't worry. All will be fine, yah.'

She sighed. 'Oh, you can twist me round your little finger, that's the trouble. The things I do for you, you'd never believe.'

Dominic giggled. 'Never.'

He went slowly downstairs. After some hesitation, he took a turn into his library and consulted *Great Expectations* again. As he did so, he heard an early guest arriving, and footsteps on the stone paving outside.

Once they turned off the M4 or M40, Dominic Mayor's guests found themselves in an uncomfortable landscape reflecting many of the get-rich-quick tendencies they themselves exhibited. The country round about Shreding Green was low-lying and dispirited and afflicted by something greater than itself: progress.

The upper windows of the manor, from which Fenella Mayor was gazing despondently, looked over an unkept wasteland of twenty acres which Dominic had bought up to save them from developers. Beyond the wasteland could be seen two filling stations, the towers of an 'urban development', pylons, and a new industrial estate, to which Federal Express lorries shuttled along on the narrow roads, brushing past Iver's quota of Range Rovers.

The area was pocked by building sites. The fashion was for so-called 'greens': arrangements of small brick houses, their mock-Georgian doorways guarded by carriage lamps, huddling in a geometrical pattern. Where planted, infant trees stood like policemen beside garages with up-and-over Regency doors. A new pub, the Avengers, stood only two miles from the manor's front gates. For the occupants of these 'greens', newly-weds, gays, and other combinations, a massively utilitarian shopping centre was in the course of construction in Langley.

This newness was peppered with 'For Sale' signs. Nothing was consolidated. Marlborough Green, Royal Thames Green, Princes Park Green, all manifested empty houses, uncut lawns, tokens of distress. Some of the intended boutiques in the shopping centre had never opened.

Sainsbury's had stayed away. Many of the town houses had an abandoned air. Many of the people who had moved to Shreding last year wished to move away this year: they did not like the neighbours, they had lost their jobs, or they were moving up or down the social scale; Shreding for them was either too posh or too naff. This was the dawn of the 1980s and the hour of the estate agent. Stagflation ruled.

Tokens of an earlier time remained. Among reservoirs and driblets of river, leafier enclaves prevailed, expressed in golf courses, studs, and riding-schools. Winding lanes, up which container transports now lumbered, led past thirties bungalows which the retired owners, besieged, had surrounded by the blight of the seventies garden, *cupressus leylandii*.

One or two of this retired class came to the party, happy to have as a neighbour someone as rich as Dominic Mayor. But the guests on the whole were enjoying the flood-tide of their youth. A bald head or a greying one among their number was an anomaly, genially tolerated much as the occasional black was tolerated. After the hired man helped them park their cars, they teemed into the manor, cheerful and confident, to be greeted by blasts from a live group, Mortal Wounds, and waitresses with trays of drink.

The most eminent bald head belonged to Josh Rund, chairman of Schatzman's Bank. Josh, at forty-five, was considerably older than most of the other guests. He and Dominic greeted each other in the hall with a measure of real affection. Josh had backed Dominic when he was an unknown nineteen-year-old, and Dominic had then proceeded to funnel money into Josh's recently founded merchant bank. They had triumphed over uncertain times together. After Dominic switched from computer whizz-kiddery to short-term trading on the financial markets of the world, he had grown mushroom-rich. The Iraq-Iran War was proving equally good for Josh Rund.

The two men had something else in common. Both had married older women. Elegant Suzy Rund, dressed in a glittering black gown for the occasion, was still blonde in her mid-fifties, and greyhound thin.

'Where's Fenella?' she asked Dominic as she clutched his hand. He could hardly believe the rosiness of her cheeks was rouge.

'She has somewhat headache. She'll be down soon.' The pupils of her eyes were large, commanding attention. It occurred to Dominic that she was on drugs.

That also they had in common. Also, like Dominic, Suzy and Josh were not born in England. England had made them. England was their home, their refuge. But it was not in their blood. Deep in their minds were other languages, other landscapes.

When a waitress came up with a tray of champagne, Suzy, Josh and Dominic each took a glass, raising them solemnly to each other.

'Here's to many more years of Tory misrule,' Josh said, and drank deep. Dominic took a sip and then set his glass aside. They fell into discussion of the latest political scandal.

The young men at the party were of what journalists had christened the yuppie class. They dressed elegantly and with some discretion, to be outshone by the frolicsome ladies who accompanied them. Many of these ladies were independently rich. The stock exchange was still predominantly a male preserve. Professions in photography, design, couture, publishing, and the art world had opened up to women. Their lives were more interesting and, on the whole, more precarious than those of the market-slaves they accompanied – who, like Dominic, often worked an eighteen-hour day.

Many of them, of both sexes, had broken away from provincial homes they despised. They now lived in expensive London apartments, rich while still in their mid-twenties, a relatively exclusive body of gate-crashers in society. They drank and laughed this evening: tomorrow at nine many would be back scanning the green figures ghostly in their VDUs.

Dominic moved among them, carrying his wine glass, not drinking, chatting to all and sundry, exchanging gossip.

He noticed immediately when Fenella started down the stairs, and went over to escort her down the last few steps.

'What a mêlée. I don't know anyone,' she said, looking about rather short-sightedly. 'Aren't they noisy? What are they talking about?'

'Come and meet some of them, dear. There are the Hartridges. You remember them? Do you want some wine? Champagne?'

'You know it gives me a headache. Is everyone here? I've let you down again, Dommy, haven't I? I should have stood by you like a good wife. No wonder you hate me.'

'Don't start that again, there's a dear person. Just enjoy yourself.'

He took her over to meet Pete and Dru Hartridge. The Hartridges had formed a very successful leisure consultancy in the City, and could send overworked executives at a moment's notice to an unknown beach in Martinique, a grouse moor in the Scottish Highlands, or a health farm in Esher, with escorts if needed. As Fenella began talking with sudden animation to Dru, Dominic studied his wife's dress. Suzy Rund looked so marvellously right in her black number; Fenella looked ridiculous in her gauzy mauve – or was that word violet? – outfit. The hemline was the wrong length and unfashionable. The spray of artificial flowers at the shoulder was absurd. He felt bad.

She caught his eye. 'Do you like the dress, Dommy darling?'

'Correct. You look really marvellous in it, dear.'

'Yes, it's brilliant, darling,' Dru said. 'I was noticing it. A most unusual colour. Just your colour, soft, totally mysterious.'

He turned away, and there was Suzy Rund. She saw the look on his face and grabbed his arm, laughing as she did so.

'I've been watching you, Dominic, you scoundrel. It's your party and you're not drinking.'

'Suzy, do all the people lie? How do you understand which is praise or which is "taking the piss"?'

She laughed, with a real note of gaiety. 'Isn't praise always insincere? I hate it, personally, myself. But the English with their downbeat humour – you can't tell it one way or the other. Don't worry.'

'Maybe I do need a drink!' He snatched a glass of champagne from a passing tray. 'Let's get outside a minute.'

'I'm happy to do it. Josh is talking shop to the Patels. You realize I am about the only woman here who does no work at all. Instead I live on my husband's immoral earnings.'

'Oh my God,' he said in sudden good humour. 'Come outside, Suzy, and let me kiss you. How I love to hear that laugh of yours. And your pale lips. I never laugh, you know that?'

Night had fallen. The outside of the house was floodlit. Guests were still arriving. Dominic waved to them, while steering Suzy Rund behind a sheltering clump of pampas, where he flung his glass into a flowerbed.

He stood on tiptoe to kiss her.

'Put your hand in here,' she said, leaning towards him. 'Not much tit, I'm afraid.'

'I love it. How hot your tits are.' He pressed his mouth to her left nipple. 'Oh, Suzy, you're such a life-giver.'

'Lifesaver, you mean. I'll be fifty-five next January. I feel so desperate. Josh isn't interested.' She pushed him off and adjusted her dress.

'Has he a mistress?'

'No. I've checked. He's just lost interest. It's money, of course – money kills everything. Christ, Dominic, what do people *do*? No, sorry, no feeling my cunt. Just kiss me. It's the human warmth I want. Then we must get back.' They nuzzled each other, till she turned to sneeze, cursing the cold.

'I adore you, Suzy. You're human.'

'Keep saying it. I know you're in a fix with Fenella, Dominic. I just want to say I'm sorry. She has an unfortunate personality.'

They stood against each other, sighing, unwilling to break away.

He was suddenly aware of someone coming round the pampas bush, and stood back from Suzy.

It was Arold Betts. He flung one of his salutes, at the same time giving a quick glance at Suzy. 'Evening, Mrs Rund, I thought as it was you. Bit nippy for the time of year. Mr Dominic, suh, you told me to inform you. Mrs Cameron is just arriving this minute, suh.'

A strong smell of drink surrounded him.

'Get inside, please, Arold. I'll deal with Mrs Cameron.'

'Very good, suh. Orders is orders.'

As he disappeared, Dominic stared at Suzy. The semi-darkness softened the lines of her face, making her look younger.

'Take good care of your dear self,' he said, and went to confront his mother-in-law.

Morna Cameron was a tall bony woman, given to wearing thick tweed suits which made her look even more sizeable. She loomed over Dominic. Although she was now in her eighties, age had not impaired her activities or her temper. She moved constantly between an estate in Scotland and a flat in Kensington. The latter proved a useful base from which to descend on daughter Fenella.

Fenella had become Morna Cameron's chief interest since the death of her husband five years previously. There was also a son, James, Fenella's brother, but he had long since escaped from the family's spell and was living in California, growing mushrooms with great success and never writing home.

'I have a strong suspicion your man was drunk,' were her words of greeting to Dominic as he came up and attempted an embrace.

'It's good to see you, Mother,' he said. 'Do come in. It's nice of you to come. Fenella's longing to see you.'

'I'm surprised she didn't bother to come out and greet me.' Her Scottish accent was slight.

'She's waiting inside. The party's going well.'

'It's very noisy. The Beatles, I suppose.'

'It's Mortal Wounds.' He showed her into the house.

'They're all the same to me.'

'Mortal Wounds are very popular this year.'

The old lady adjusted her hearing aid. 'Everything's a terrible noise. Just noise. It's no good speaking to me in here, Dominic. I can't hear a thing.'

This last remark was thrown out as they entered the main reception room, now full of groups of people, all laughing and talking. Clicking his fingers, Dominic summoned a waitress to his side. The girl stood there, waiting for Mrs Cameron to take a glass. Instead, the old lady embarked on a long story about some trouble she had had in a shoeshop in Kensington. Dominic clasped his hands behind his back, nodding, muttering sympathetically. He gazed dully at the scene. Time went by.

'But there – what do you expect today?' It was Mrs Cameron's punch-line, good for any number of downbeat stories.

Some couples were dancing at the far end of the room, enjoying tapes while Mortal Wounds took a break and a puff.

Dominic could feel his tension rising as Mrs Cameron finally refused a glass. She was looking about her with the air of disapproval which rarely left her. Her face with its guardian wattles on either side of pursed lips was covered with a light sandy fluff, as though perched on the margins of a desert. Behind her spectacles with their desert-coloured frames, her old flinty eyes were alert for targets for her displeasure.

She settled first for the décor. 'All this white, Dominic, it's so depressing.'

He knew her weak points. 'It's very expensive. And fashionable.'

'You should have restored the manor to its former glory. White walls go with poverty. I know an excellent man in Edinburgh, a specialist in all things Jacobean. You and Fenella should have asked me for advice.'

'We brought over an Italian from Milan.'

'Milan,' she echoed contemptuously. 'Malcolm took me there once. Didn't care for the place.'

Malcolm was her dead husband.

Dominic had, he would concede to friends, overdone the white. White was everywhere, set off by crimson upholstery and the occasional crimson carpet. But white was what he had wanted. White was neutral. He couldn't stand the old British stuff which Morna and his wife liked.

'Umberto Fascetti. I'm sure you know his name, Mother.'

Morna Cameron made no answer. She had sighted her daughter. The hairs of the desert trembled.

Fenella was still talking to Dru and Pete Hartridge, being very animated about it. Pete was nodding and smiling rather automatically, saying, 'Quite, quite,' at intervals. When Fenella found someone to talk to, she always latched on to them, for fear of being left to face new people.

She turned as her mother came up, fell silent, and then went to kiss her. The embrace was followed with anxious enquiries as to health, the running of the Fuarblarghour estate, and other matters. Dominic stood alertly by, accepting a glass of champagne from a passing tray. Dru and Pete faded away rapidly.

'It's lovely of you to come, Mother,' said Fenella, wringing her hands. 'Dominic will get you a drink. Dominic. Isn't this fun, the party?'

'Och, you're enjoying it, are you, Fenella? If so, I'm surprised.'

A moment's suspense, while Dominic signalled a waitress frantically for a drink.

'Why – why surprised, Mother?'

'Wearing that ridiculous dress. No one gives parties in a dress like that, even a party like this one.'

The drink arrived, Dominic moved between mother and daughter as the latter fell back, and thrust the champagne at Mrs Cameron, laughing and begging her to drink. When she refused, he pointed out some of the other guests, naming them rapidly as if calling a roll.

Fenella came forward again. 'Mother, this is a new dress. I bought it to try and please you. Don't you remember you once had a dress this colour?'

'I would never wear that colour. It suits me no more than it does you, with your washed-out complexion. Don't insult me.'

'When I was a little girl, Mother. I came with you to buy it in Edinburgh.'

'Oh, why, here is Colin Cohen, Mother,' Dominic said. 'Please don't upset Fenella. She's not feeling well. Colin's in telemarketing and doing fabulously.'

'Going broke, you mean,' Colin said amiably, clasping Morna's hand. 'What can I sell you, Mrs Cameron? It's my proud boast I can sell anything, even if I lose on the deal.'

She stared at him in amazement. 'You're a salesman, Mr Cohen, do I understand? Perhaps you know something about hearing aids . . .'

Taking advantage of the respite, Dominic turned to Fenella. He had witnessed that look of agony before. Gripping her arm, he said, 'Don't let the old bag get you down, darling. She loves to stick the knife in, and you're her favourite target. The more you try to please, the further goes the knife in ... The dress looks just smashing, *wunderbar*.'

'What have I done? What have I done? Oh, Dominic ...' Words failed her. Then she said, 'I must go upstairs and take this horrible thing off. I knew it didn't suit me, that's the trouble. I'm sorry to ruin your party, dear. Stay and enjoy yourself.'

'No,' he said, pleadingly. 'Don't let her win.' But Fenella had turned away.

He stood, glass in hand, watching her push through the crowds, watching her climb the stairs, watching her run along the upper landing until she disappeared in the direction of her room. Then he proceeded to drink.

Friends came along to congratulate him, to pat him on the back, and to be cheerful into the small hours. Many of them had held First Million parties.

As he moved with friends towards the bar, Dominic was surprised to see a woman he recognized standing alone against a wall holding a glass of fruit juice. It was the physiotherapist who came every day to give Fenella her exercises, by name Lucy Traill. Fenella must have invited her to the party. Leaving his companions, he went over and spoke to her.

Lucy Traill seemed bored. After a moment's talk, he said, 'I know you're here only as a guest, yah? But make me a favour. Go up and attend to my wife, will you?'

Lucy smiled pleasantly. 'Sure, I don't know anyone here. I'll be glad to see her.'

'Comfort her.'

'Your wife's an unhappy woman, Mr Mayor, if I may say so.'

His anger showed. 'Mind your own business, Miss Traill. Everyone's unhappy.'

As she went upstairs, he rejoined his companions. He had no close friends. These were business acquaintances, mostly of his own age, mostly too busy to establish friendship. They communicated by phone or computer network. But they had much in common, and respected Dominic's flair for playing the market, based on his understanding of commodities.

He took two or three people into the library to share some coke. They found a couple making love behind the sofa. No one interfered with them.

'Nice place you have here,' Colin Cohen said, stretching out on the white rug in front of the fire. 'I hope it was a bargain, Dom. What did you have to pay?'

Dominic said he had bought it reasonably off a man who was going broke. 'He had several other big houses round the country. A private yacht and so on. He had debts totalling £24 million.' He laughed. 'Of course he was soon in business again. People respect big debts. His name was Cracknell Summerfield, and his taste in interior decoration was real bad.'

'That's old Charlie Summerfield,' Colin said. 'He still owes money, believe me. But he's into double-glazing and décor now, and mixes with Kuwaitis. I heard he was thinking of standing as Tory MP for somewhere up North. Carlisle, could be.'

'Carlisle deserves him,' Colin Cohen's girlfriend said, and they laughed.

Later, Dominic was summoned by one of the guests to look after his mother-in-law, who wished to leave. She stood in the entrance hall, her coat about her shoulders, with her look of unpreparedness to be pleased.

'Sorry you're going, Mother,' Dominic said. 'Allow me to escort you to your car.'

'I appreciate it, Dominic. You are always polite, that I must say. I should not have hoped that Fenella would come to see her mother off. She's never behaved like a daughter of mine. I don't know why I bother.'

'That's what mother-love is all about, Mother, yah?'

As they walked over to where the Rover was parked, rather jammed in by other cars, Dominic looked about for Arold, but the man was nowhere to be seen. He said in a low urgent voice, 'Mother, dear, if you don't mind my saying this, Fenella loves you very much. You'd get on so much better if you made allowance for her shortcomings. It would make her happy.'

She gave him a look that perhaps attempted humour. 'That's aye rich! It's your job now to make her happy, not mine, thank God. I could never please her. She never loved me, whatever you say.'

They had reached the car. He took the keys from her and began to ease into the driver's seat. 'She does love you in her way, as I suppose you love her in yours. If you could let it show it should be a great help.'

She was on him immediately for that impertinence. 'That from you! I never heard such a thing. Haven't you had a row with Fenella too? Haven't you threatened to desert her? I suppose it's all about this sex business. Well, you've had a bairn between you, poor wee boy, and you should be satisfied. It never appealed to me, but I suppose sex is all people think about today. I didn't bring Fenella up to be like that. I think it's disgraceful.'

She pulled at her hearing aid, as if it too offended her, saying 'You're to blame it's come to this, Dominic, though I know she's difficult. You're making too much money, that's the trouble . . . A rotten situation. It makes me feel ill.' She put a hand to her chest. 'Not that you'd care about that.'

He squinted up at her from the driver's seat. 'You find life very bitter, don't you, Mother?'

The headlights glinted in her spectacles. She hesitated momentarily, before saying, 'I manage my life better than some people I could mention.' As he started the engine, she stood back out of the way.

Once the car was outside the gates, he let her take his place at the wheel.

'Go carefully, Mother,' he said. 'I'm sorry you feel as you do.'

She looked up at him, gave him a smile from the desert, and drove off without another word.

Dominic walked slowly back to his party.

*   *   *

The great crush of people began to thin rapidly after two in the morning. Although it was a Sunday, many of these yuppies would put in several hours of work today, or perhaps pay some attention to any children they might have acquired. An intense shunting of automobiles took place.

The security men came to Dominic, leading in their patrol dogs. He paid them off from a roll of banknotes in his back pocket, tipping them generously.

By two forty-five he was alone. A little green Morris stood solitarily in the carpark. He assumed someone had been too drunk to drive and had accepted a lift.

He went back into the house, where Doris Betts was endeavouring to clear up some of the mess. 'Terrible, in't it, Mr Dominic?' she said. 'Some people don't half make a muck.'

'Leave all that, Doris, and tell your husband to get the Porsche out.'

Straightening up, she said indignantly, 'Why, it's near three in the morning. Time we was all in our beds.'

'I can't help that, woman. I want to go for a drive. Get Arold, if he's not blind drunk.'

'Drunk?' she muttered, hurrying towards the servants' quarters. 'Never touched a drop. What do you take us for?'

He walked about in his white suit, glancing at his watch as if the time would not register on his consciousness. Going over to the drinks cabinet, he poured himself a liberal tot of Armagnac and rolled it about in the glass. After taking a sip, he set the glass down. Staring at himself in a mirror proved no more satisfactory. He smoothed his little beard and tried to adjust his expression so that it looked less hang-dog.

'What am I to do?' he asked himself aloud.

He had resumed his pacing up and down among the debris of the party when there came the roar of a car engine outside, a terrible grinding sound, and then a protracted noise of disaster, followed by the barking of the mastiffs at the rear of the house.

Dominic went outside, not exactly at a run.

Beyond the clump of pampas, his Porsche lay nose down in the ornamental goldfish pond. Its side was scarred and buckled. As he approached, the rear lights glowed and died.

'Shit,' Dominic said.

Arold Betts was climbing from the driver's seat. He fell into the pond, cursed, and crawled out on hands and knees to sprawl at Dominic's feet, groaning.

'Oh my gawd – I swear as I never saw that particular bit of wall before. The car lights couldna bin working. Then I had to swerve to miss that pampas . . . Oh, whatever have I done?'

'What you have done is you're drunk, man, and you have completely buggered up my car.'

'Creck. Creck in every point, my gawd. Oh, bloody hell . . .' He drew himself up on to his knees, covering his face with his hands, so that his words were barely distinguishable. 'And ain't that just what happened to our lad Haubrey when he come back from the war where he covered himself with onner, and lost a finger, and the night he come back I says to him, "Aubrey, if onner 'as a name it's Haubrey" – right proud of 'im, we was, and the 'ole street turned out, and then he goes and runs his car right into the canal.'

'Never mind that. Get up, Arold.'

But Arold stayed kneeling, feeling safer in his puddle. Clutching his face, he looked pitifully up at Dominic. 'You was the best boss I ever 'ad, Mr Dominic. I know how you values this car, and what an expense it was, and I'm right sorry for what I done, honest. I'm a bastard, a real bastard, don't know my own best interests. Now I've gone and very like broke your heart and proba'ly got me and Doris sacked into the bargain.'

'Get up, Arold,' Dominic said again, taking the man's damp elbow to encourage him. 'It's OK, yah, really OK. Worse things happen.'

'I'm ever so sorry, Mr Dominic,' Arold said, standing and sober now. 'I wouldn't have 'ad this 'appen for the world. It was just that wall come at me . . .'

'I understand,' Dominic said gently. 'I don't mind. Now we should better all get to bed. Worse things happen.'

He walked off. But Arold stood where he was, still voicing his regrets by the ruined car. 'You bloody well should mind,' he said, squeezing water from his trousers.

A cup of tea stood by the bedside. He looked at it for a minute, seeking a meaning to it, before bringing a hand from under the duvet and reaching out to feel it. The cup was cold.

The bedside clock told him it was almost nine.

Dominic groaned. His head throbbed, his nose was blocked. He felt generally second-rate. At this time most days, he would be along in his work suite, the ten IBM monitors switched on, and he would be taking the pulse of stock exchanges all round the world: not only New York, London and Japan, but the Paris Bourse, Hong Kong, Singapore, and other centres.

Doris Betts had come in and left the tea without waking him. As a general rule he slept lightly. Now he lay on his back, breathing through his mouth, sniffing, his thoughts dull.

The fool party. Sheer ostentation. He wished he had not done it. Heavy-eyed, he looked at a watercolour, mounted and framed, hanging on a wall where sun could not reach it. Marshes and a broken fence stood in the foreground; behind was an old barn, outside which stood a tractor, and the remains of a windmill, with blue distance beyond. Dominic had painted it when fourteen or fifteen, picnicking with his adopted mother, Daphne; Daphne! who treated him to a holiday in Great Yarmouth on the Norfolk coast. Happy bygone days. Perhaps he should have been an artist. But it was years since he had held a brush. Despite the regret (regret was the permanent backcloth of his mind) he always gained pleasure from looking at the picture; amateurish though it was, it represented a real act, a true event, to set against the world of deception in which he had become an actor.

As his thoughts wandered, they lighted on Suzy Rund, his one consolation in the disaster of the previous night, remembering her flushed cheeks, her hot breasts, her sneeze. Had he caught a cold from Suzy? Even for that moment of pleasure, there had to be punishment.

Oh, Jesus, I suppose I deserve all the blows you rain on me, yah? he said to himself, and staggered out of bed to find a box of tissues, treading as he did so on the white Italian suit which had been cast on the floor.

A tap on his door. At his command, in came a woman with another cup of tea. Not Doris, as he expected.

'What are you doing here?' he asked, surprised, standing at bay by his chest-of-drawers, checking instinctively to see his pyjama trousers did not gape.

'I've brought you another cup of tea, sir,' said Lucy Traill, moving confidently, and setting the new cup by the cold one. 'I wanted to see if you were all right before I left. Mrs Betts is collecting your son from next door.'

He liked the aura of calm surrounding her. He had seen her only rarely on her regular visits to give Fenella the physiotherapy a doctor had recommended. Lucy Traill made a neat figure in her stone-washed jeans. Her sharp features, clear-cut lips, and inquisitive blue eyes were sheltered under a mop of interestingly disarrayed golden hair. Something in her smile told him she enjoyed seeing him at a disadvantage, and he climbed back into bed.

'You've been here all night?'

She nodded.

'Did my wife ask you to stay?'

She put her hands on her hips and showed white teeth as she bit her lower lip. 'Your wife was in rather a bad way, Mr Mayor. I must tell you. She threatened to commit suicide. Since there was no one else, I thought I should stay with her. Entirely my own decision.'

'How long have you been coming here, Miss Traill?'

'I'm Lucy. Eighteen months. No, more. I drive over from Acton.'

'My wife infrequently speaks of suicide. It's not too serious.'

'Do you take no notice? Perhaps it is serious.'

He was annoyed that she challenged him in this way. 'Look . . .' He paused, uncertain that what he was about to say was for the best. 'I regard her threats as part of her emotional blackmail of me.' He blew his nose on a tissue.

135

She sat down on the end of his bed, tucking her jean-clad left leg under her.

'I have to go. I've got to get back to my kid. But I should perhaps say to you, Mr Mayor, that your wife is in a very bad way emotionally in my estimation. Perhaps you know, or perhaps you don't, that Mrs Mayor has been prescribed a lot of drugs – far too many, to my way of thinking. I'm attached to a hospital and I see a lot of what goes on. Doctors love ladling out pills indiscriminately. Saves them having to get to know their patients. Your wife – Fenella – has accumulated a cupboard full of pills.'

Dominic felt uneasy. He picked up the cup from the bedside and then set it down again without drinking. 'I do find – the situation is difficult. I can say that much.'

With a flash of humour, she said, 'You can say that little . . . She is upset because you said you wanted to leave her. Is that right?' Then, reading the expression of pain on his face, she added, 'Sorry, I know this is none of my business, but she talked to me for a long time last night, wouldn't let me go . . . Huh, well, she spoke continu-ously for two hours before falling asleep.'

He leaned forward in sudden interest. 'She did? What did she talk about in that two hours?'

Lucy looked confused. She cast her gaze downwards, for the first time less than certain in her manner. 'Um . . . well . . . it was a sort of – I can't really remember. A sort of general complaint against life.'

'I understand. Miss Traill, I also have had to listen to those mono-logues. Two hours. Once three. Very terrible. You can only listen, but once launched, she needs no listener, yah? The monologue is followed by sleep. Very terrifying. The sick monologue. Is there such a thing in medical science? And, even worse, the listener cannot remember. Not a word. Somehow, the memory rejects it, throws it out. Like a dream.'

He shook his head, clutched the cup of tea again, looking pained. The physiotherapist was about to reply when he cut into her words.

'Let me tell you – I've confided this to no one else – that sick monologue, even Fenella does not remember it after. It's like another person who speaks with her mouth. I was so frightened. It's true I did say her "I want no more of it, I want to leave", but it was only in a moment of anger. I was frightened. You cannot always keep the temper with Fenella. You know how it is to talk with her, do you? Like a maze . . . You think I'm trying to – how do you say? – win you over, get round you? No. Not that.'

'Go on,' Lucy said, regarding him steadily from the end of the bed.

'That's all. I said it once, I wanted to leave her. She hung on to it. I can't understand. Grasped it, like a rope. Then she forced me, really kind of forced me to say I did not love her. I swear it was what she wanted to hear. And of course – of course I love her—'

She spoke softly. 'But you do want to leave her . . .'

He found he was crying convulsively. Her arms were round his shoulders. His tears and saliva poured into the crimson peony pattern of the duvet. She rocked him gently, saying nothing.

Such was their situation when the door of the bedroom opened and Malcolm Mayor walked in.

'Hello, Dad, hello, Lucy.' Life was so full of astonishment for a five-year-old that Malcolm saw nothing unusual in the scene before his eyes. He climbed on the bed, hugging his father, saying, 'Don't cry any more. I was only with the Barnabys. I'm back now.'

Reg Barnaby, a motorway consultant, lived just down the road with his wife and three boys, one of whom was Malcolm's great friend. Fenella had sent Malcolm there to be out of the way of the party.

After drying his face and beard, Dominic essayed a laugh and cuddled his son, telling him he was happy to have him back.

'I won't go away any more, Daddy. Not if it makes you sad.'

Lucy stood up and said in a formal voice, 'A little help is needed, that's clear. A close friend of mine, Joe Winter, has a brother in practice in Oxford who would be helpful. I shall ring you and give you his address, Mr Mayor. It would be a good idea to get in touch with him.'

'We've been through all that,' Dominic said, wearily. 'But thanks all the same, Miss Traill.'

She offered him her hand. It was small and tough.

'Can I have a ride round in your car?' Malcolm asked her, following her from the room. 'Daddy's Porsche is in the fish pond. Did you see? It looks ever so funny. Its nose is right in drinking with the fishes.'

Three days later, Dominic Mayor drove to Oxford in his second-best car, parked it in the multi-storey carpark, and entered a small waiting-room at 13 King Edward Street. After a few minutes, he was shown into the presence of Clement Winter, the psychotherapist whom Lucy Traill had recommended.

After some preliminaries, Dominic confessed he did not know where to begin.

'You can begin where you like. Everything will lead very shortly to the heart of the problem.'

'I sometimes think I'm going mad.' He was surprised to hear himself make such a definite statement. It silenced him for a moment, while Winter sat at ease on the other side of a small electric fire, apparently in no hurry for anything more to happen in the history of the world.

'I don't know what's what any longer.' After another pause. 'I blame myself . . . My wife's very – but I blame myself.' Pause. 'You see. Well, there were my parents . . .'

'Perhaps they would make a good starting point.'

Not without surprise and delight, he found himself relating the confused story of his early years, and how Daphne Mayer had come to adopt him. The words began to flow easily. Everything unrolled, so that he had a sense of sitting back and listening to himself. The longer he talked of earlier times, the longer he kept the problem of Fenella at a distance.

Dominic had little sense of history, only a series of pictures. He always pictured his grandparents – who had never been *his* grand-parents – fishing by a lake in south-east Russia. Grandfather, the story went, was a great fisherman as well as a brave soldier. These grandparents bore five sons and a daughter. The eldest boy, Vasili, married Dominic's mother Lena, his real mother.

Lena was born in 1919, a time of great hardship in the newly established Soviet Union. After she married Vasili, she and her new husband moved to Moscow to find work. Life was tough. They had two sons, one of whom died of diseases related to malnutrition. When the Great Patriotic War was declared against Nazi Germany, Vasili joined the army. His courage became renowned. He was soon promoted, and given command of a supply train.

This story Dominic learned only through his mother. Details were obscured by hate, even many years after the events. It appeared that Vasili had led a raid somewhere and captured a German field hospital. A blonde nurse was spared from the general carnage. Vasili held this woman himself, and raped her.

It seemed that he had kept this German woman on his supply train during its long journeys, and was fascinated by her. He had never travelled beyond the boundaries of his own country before. All that was new he found wonderful. He developed the wish to learn the nurse's language. Along with German, she taught him something of the West. She showed him a photograph of her home in Hamburg, and he conceived a wish to go there.

Once, he managed to get back to Moscow to see his wife and child. He must have been in two minds about the women, or perhaps he was deficient in his sense of danger. He found Lena and the surviving boy starving. He disguised his wife as a soldier, and smuggled her and the boy aboard the supply train, where food rations were comparatively plentiful. They were travelling through Poland when Lena discovered he was keeping a foreign woman in another carriage.

Her fury was boundless as she told the tale. Lena was a strong woman, and she had attacked her husband. He hit her right in the face, breaking her nose. She bore the token of his violence ever after.

Vasili had stopped the train. Throwing down a sack of rations, he kicked Lena and the boy off. The train then moved on again, leaving them there, standing in a Polish field a foot deep in snow.

Lena never saw Vasili again. But by roundabout means she eventually learned what happened to her husband. The German nurse must have come to love him. She stayed with him when he joined a Cossack force fighting against Russia on the German side. When the end of the war came in 1945, both he and the woman fell into British hands, and were confined in a prisoner-of-war camp, where they were kindly treated. The British then handed them, together with hundreds of others – men, women and children – over to the Russians. They were shot, and their bodies buried in a mass grave in the Ukraine.

It was only by good fortune that Lena had survived in a hostile country. In war it was a matter of luck who lived, who died.

Clement Winter listened to Dominic's account with only two interruptions, to clarify something Dominic had not made clear. Now he said, 'I'm afraid that our time is up.'

Dominic stood. 'I'll buy another hour. I wish to go on. I have hardly started, don't you see that? I'm not even born yet.'

'Perhaps you'd care to make another appointment with my receptionist?'

'Look, here's money.' He brought a roll of twenty-pound notes from his rear trouser pocket. 'Let me please buy the next hour.'

Winter consulted his watch, and also rose.

'Forgive me. I have another client in ten minutes' time.'

'You see, my name isn't Dominic at all. It's Dimitri. I'm not real, I'm a pretend person. Dimitri. Dimitri.'

He felt himself at the heart of some terrible drama. The day had turned cold and wet. He walked in the Oxford streets. There was an injustice, a cruelty, pervading human lives, something inherited. He could not go back to Winter until ten past four on Friday afternoon, in two days' time; it was the first available appointment. His story was suspended. Yet it was not even his story. He had, as he said, not yet been born. He could not think ahead, but was encased in what had transpired, in what he had revealed, blurted out – a secondhand story, after all. He took shelter in a college doorway, feeling his cold still on him. When the rain faded away in inconclusive fashion, he walked on.

He bought a suitcase. He bought toilet things, pyjamas. He booked into a hotel and lay on the bed staring at the ceiling. He could not go back to Shreding Green, not until he had talked to Winter again. When he tried just once to phone Fenella, there was no reply.

He thought briefly of his work, then dismissed it. He could, of course, go to London to stay with his adoptive mother, Daphne. But he was caught in the heart of the terrible drama beside which even work was irrelevant.

Why had he said he had blamed himself? He was a victim of circumstance. A millionaire victim.

He ordered dinner in the hotel, but left it almost untasted. Upstairs, he unlocked his room door and entered, switching on the lobby light as he did so. The bedroom, its curtains not being drawn, was faintly illuminated by beams from a street-lamp. On the far side of the room, by the bathroom door, Fenella was standing. She wore a dress which swept to the floor.

A shock ran through him. He found himself unable to move. Yet it was confusing – he was going towards her, against his will.

She put up a warning hand. In the metallic light from outside, her face was bleached ghastly white. The other hand went up to clutch her throat, as so often it did.

'How did you get here?' he asked.

She spoke. 'I have seen you. The real trouble is—'

But what was the real trouble? What did she say then? He could not hear or understand. Desperately, he asked her to repeat what she had said. 'Was it all my fault, Fenella?'

Giving him a sad smile, or at least a rictus he interpreted as a smile, she turned, went into the bathroom, and closed the door firmly behind her.

'Oh Jesus,' he whispered.

He stood in the dark, looking about. The wallpaper was mottled. No comfort there. The room felt cold.

Going forward, he tried the bathroom door. 'Fenella, please let me in. Don't always lock me out. Let me come in to you. Please.'

He dragged the door open and pulled on the light cord. The room with its sky-blue suite leapt from darkness into light. It was empty. He rushed in, peering into the shower. She was not there. Of course.

Sitting on the bed, sprawling, sitting up again, peering about, Dominic struggled for rationality. She had definitely been here. 'I have seen you.' That baffling sentence. 'I have seen you.' Oh, he had heard it in a voice outside his head. And what was the rest of that vital message?

Half afraid to enter the bathroom again, he went and rinsed his face.

She had been here. He was convinced of that. He had no truck with the paranormal. The episode was more chillingly truthful than ordinary deceptive reality.

He fell into a swoon, sprawling face down on the bed.

That night, in his overheated room, he could not sleep. Scenes of violence haunted him: the attack on the German field hospital, with deaths he could only imagine, the repeated rapes of the woman on the train as it forged from one scene of carnage to another, the abandoning of his mother in the snow, by the side of the track, the mass shootings and the mass grave that ended it all. That Second World War, the Great Patriotic War as the Russians called it, was to him some terrible distorted Homeric tale, ended long years before he was conceived, yet somehow living within him, corrupting him.

When he roused himself enough to look at his watch, it was almost two in the morning.

He dressed and went down to the lobby. An old porter sitting there reading a newspaper seemed glad of his company. He related an anecdote concerning a pair of real leather shoes an American tourist had left him, with all the details of how the gift had come about. 'And do you know, sir, the right shoe fitted me a treat, but the left one – why it was far too big, so I had to stuff it with newspaper.' He gave a creaking laugh. 'Now what do you make of that?'

In the morning, by daylight, Dominic phoned Fenella, saying he had been called away on business, and would return as soon as he could: though in his mind the idea formed that he might never be able to return.

He steeled himself to ask her the vital question. 'Where were you at about nine o'clock yesterday evening?'

Her answer was cold and disinterested. She was at home. Where else?

'Do you want to tell me something, Fenella?'

'You have put yourself in the wrong. You have left me, as you said you would.'

'That's not true. I'll be back soon.' Again, he could not tell whether or not he was lying.

It was ten past four on the Friday afternoon. Greying, distinguished, Dr Clement Winter sat on one side of his electric fire; Dominic Mayor sat on the other. Winter's expression was open, receptive, though he seemed mainly to study a point on the ceiling of his room.

'The evening before last, I had a vision. I haven't been home since our meeting. I stay locally. My wife came into my hotel bedroom. Then she was not there. I'm sure she was physically present. Or perhaps it's just strain. Do such things happen?'

'Did your wife stay for long?' So he did not show disbelief . . .

'No. She told me something. I feel it was extremely important. Unfortunately, I could not understand quite what she said. Perhaps it's all to do with trying to make sense from my life. I'm only twenty-six, yet I feel ages old . . . I suppose I'm . . . well, I try to make sense from my life, speaking with you. Yet I thought I came to seek assistance for my wife.' He clutched himself as if against external cold.

'You probably see that the two questions are related.'

'Ah . . . yes. Perhaps that is why she was with me.' And he found himself plunging again into the terrible drama of the past.

Lena, his real mother, always remembered the desolate field, the snow, and the train pulling away into the distance. She was well aware that, as a Russian, she was liable to be killed by the first Pole she encountered. When she saw that someone was coming, leading a horse, she made her son hide in a hedge, so that he at least would stand a chance of surviving.

The someone was a woman, and some spark of female sympathy must have crossed between them. She took Lena and the boy to a ruined farm, where she lived in a barn with three men. The

143

relationship was never clear. All the farm animals had been killed, either by Russians or Germans. Without a word of the language, Lena existed in a kind of mist. They lived on turnips. She slept on the floor, on sacking, cuddling the boy against the winter cold. It was a brutal form of existence.

Although they never molested her, the three men were like animals. They seemed to have no blood bonds between them. Only the youngest one, whose name was Wiktor, showed a semblance of kindness towards her. He was often absent.

In order to increase her chances of survival, Lena tried to pick up some Polish from the old woman. The woman was a poor teacher, very impatient, and away most of the daylight hours, gathering wood for the fire. Many a day they were without warmth.

The spring came late. One day, Wiktor returned in haste. He had a revolver, which he exhibited as a preliminary to making a long and passionate speech to the other men, with frequent reference to Lena. She became very agitated.

A bottle of vodka was passed round. Finally, the other men came to an agreement with Wiktor, despite lamentations from the old woman.

At dusk, Wiktor indicated that Lena should go with him. She gathered that they had far to travel. Her son was to stay behind in the barn. Then came a scene which Dominic's mother had acted out for his benefit or her own many times when drinking brandy at night. The lad had run to her and clung about her neck. She had fought to keep him, but the two older men pulled them apart, and Wiktor had dragged her outside.

Lena re-enacted this scene with great earnestness, without showing compassion for the boy. Either she was glad to be rid of him and looking forward to going off with Wiktor, or she had invented the scene, perhaps as an assuagement for some other sorrow she preferred to keep within herself. Dominic did not know.

Lena and Wiktor covered almost two hundred miles on foot, so she said, taking many weeks, hiding from Germans. Wiktor was a sniper and joined other partisans. She was never clear about, or else

Dominic had not listened to, this part of her saga. What was clear was that Wiktor was shot, and she passed into the hands of the Wehrmacht.

It was a time of terrible degradation for Lena. Somehow she survived until the end of the war, when she was caught up with the remnants of the German army fleeing westward before the Russians. When the great swirl of conquest, destruction, and defeat settled somewhat, she found herself in ruined Dresden, penniless and homeless and alone.

'She was then the age I am now,' Dominic said, 'ragged, dirty, with no country. It was the state of many people in that dreadful time. All Europe in ruins.'

He found himself compelled to go over the story again, like a hound running back and forth to pick up a scent, searching for clues. But there were links in the story, contradictions even, not to be brought to mind, even in the calm Oxford room. Part of his history, his prehistory, was lost for ever, and he felt its loss keenly.

Winter was accommodating (so Dominic guessed). He agreed to see Dominic at the same time every day of the following week.

Dominic bought a track suit and spent the weekend walking by the Isis. He could not eat. He moved to a better hotel and liked it no better.

On Monday he looked round an art gallery and saw nothing that moved him. He hated art. He looked round a bookshop and found a book called *Phantasms of the Living*, but could not find strength to remove it from its shelf. He hated reading.

Although he also hated music, he went to a music shop and bought a Walkman. For this he obtained a tape of the one piece of music he did like, Shostakovich's *Sonata for Viola and Piano*, with its dialogue between the two instruments. It was meditative in character. A Russian critic had once said of it that it would make the world a better place. For that reason, Dominic had grown to love it. And because Shostakovich's first name was Dmitri. He lay on his double bed and listened to the noise between his ears.

*   *   *

During the week, he continued to unfold the patchwork of his narrative in the room in King Edward Street, while Winter listened. In the
narrative was something cleansing. Dominic began to feel that it
would release a new phase in his being. Possibly Fenella's apparition
in the hotel bedroom had been a farewell to the previous phase.

His mother had become involved with a German in Dresden, an
ardent Communist, who was helping to rebuild the Dresden ballet
after the end of the hostilities. This man set great store by Lena
because she was a Russian woman, and therefore presumably
Communist born and bred. Although she had had to imbibe many
of the slogans of the regime, she cared not a fig for politics.

The ballet company began to acquire a reputation. The new
authorities of the new country, the German Democratic Republic,
funded it generously. The company began to travel, performing in
such places as Weimar and East Berlin. Lena and her Communist
friend, Wolfgang, went with it. Dominic believed that his mother,
perhaps out of fear, never revealed that she had been previously
married. Wolfgang married her in 1955, when she found she was
pregnant.

A son, her third, was born to her on 1 May. The date delighted
the Stalinist-minded Wolfgang. They christened the baby Dimitri.
When Dimitri was seven years old, the Dresden ballet made its first
tour of non-Warsaw Pact countries. It visited Helsinki, then
Stockholm. When it was performing in London, Lena claimed political asylum.

'It was in the English papers. She showed me the cutting. She just
walked into a police station in Kensington. With me.' Dominic paused
for Winter's response.

'Why did your mother wish to leave the DDR?'

'I think she hated Wolfgang. She was a good hater. He would beat
her often when drinking, and sometimes without drink, yah? He
beat me too. Also, she was afraid of the occupying forces, the Russians,
in the DDR, in case Vasili caught up with her again. She never wished
to be dragged back to the Soviet Union. At that time, she had not
learned that Vasili was already dead and buried in the Ukraine.'

There followed the English years.

'Lena had the constitution of a horse, but I was always ill.'

When she was granted permission to stay in Britain, she got a job in a London supermarket and lodged with the Mayer family, Eric and Daphne and their three children. The Mayers were a cheerful tribe, and treated Lena and her son with great kindness. Both adults worked, Eric being the manager of a small building-supply firm, Daphne teaching German and other subjects at a secondary school in Islington.

Lena's life took a turn for the better. She was forty-five, and began to look and dress better. She learned English rapidly, and obtained a better job. She was good with her hands, and helped in the house, to Eric's admiration. Unfortunately, her son, little Dimitri – whom she now took to calling Dominic – remained withdrawn, and kept to himself, unable to mix with the Mayer children, despite Daphne's encouragement.

For a year or two, life sailed on an even keel. London was a pleasant place to be.

One fine summer Sunday morning, there were notes for Daphne and little Dominic. Lena had run off with Eric. They had gone to Spain, to start up a hotel on the Costa Brava. She sent love. Love and apologies.

Dominic got to his feet and wandered restlessly round the room. He could not speak. The old memory choked him.

'Was there someone you could turn to in your shock?'

'I was glad she had gone. At first I was glad. I was nine. She was an awful mother. It was not her métier. Lena beat me – she who was so accustomed to being beaten. What she would do was smack me sharply in the face.' Rage overtook him. He stood over Winter, demonstrating in the air. 'She would do *that*, flick of hand, right in my face. Always when I was unprepared. I feared her, I feared Lena. Her tales when she was drunk tormented me also. It's only this last year that I've come to miss her, and to feel sorry for her. What a life she had! And two sons lost . . . Three? She must regret it . . . Maybe the smack also, yah?'

'And are you in touch with her?'

'A card from Portugal, soon after my twenty-first birthday. No address. I suppose she's still alive. Lena.'

After a long silence, during which he went back to his chair, he said, 'I sometimes wish I could speak to her, maybe forgive her. At least she got me out of the DDR . . .'

Winter asked, 'Do you feel it is important to forgive your mother?'

'Excuse me, she is no more my mother. When she left, I acquired a better one.'

When he spoke of Daphne Mayer, he thought of light. Daphne herself was a light-coloured woman with short-cropped fair hair. Although substantially built, she wore mini-skirts for a while, for this was the mid-sixties, and he loved looking at those solid pale legs. She sang when she went to work; she sang when she came home. If she was tired, she never showed it. She looked after her own children uncomplainingly. She gave a special show of affection to little Dominic. There was never a question of her turning him away although Lena had run off with her husband. For the first few weeks after Lena had left, Dominic reverted to wetting his bed, much to the disgust of the Mayer children, but Daphne never scolded him. She sang as she rinsed his sheets.

Daphne's younger sister Rosemary, who worked nights at a bakery, came to live for a while. She was some support during the day, and stopped the other children bullying Dominic.

Dominic had been terrified of Wolfgang, his father. Now that both parents had faded away, he began to develop. He liked the house with the two singing sisters. It was light and bright, unlike the grim block in which they had lived in Dresden, and had a back garden with a swing and visiting cats. The music on Daphne's transistor was light and cheerful, not heavy and patriotic. He quickly learned the names of the four Beatles.

Overcoming bureaucratic obstacles, Daphne eventually adopted Dominic as a Mayer. Unfortunately, owing to a malfunctioning type-writer somewhere in the ranks of officialdom, he emerged as Dominic Mayor instead of Mayer.

He laughed as he told Winter of this error.

'Isn't that symbolism for you?' he said to Winter. 'Some mindless thing decided that I should never become quite a Mayer. Only a Mayor.' He paused. 'No, perhaps mindless things decide nothing. Maybe it was God. I remember Daphne laughed and said it was God – "he must be illiterate," she said. So there I was, a little English boy, learning to speak good English from the German teacher.'

Daphne coped well with reduced circumstances. The sixties were an easy time in which to live. She worked on translations in the evening, sitting at the table while the TV blazed and four children noisily played round about her. Novels she translated, and even some poetry. On Sundays, she often managed an excursion out of London, taking them all by Green Line bus to Beaconsfield or Chesham. Did she miss Eric? She never said.

By his mid-week session with Winter, Dominic was prepared to talk about Fenella.

For all Daphne Mayer's kindness, to which he happily responded, his experiences had left him isolated. Daphne had a good understanding of children, and never gave up, even ignoring her own children on occasion in order to help Dominic. Seeing his dexterity with crayons, she bought him some watercolours. Rosemary looked after the Mayer children when Daphne took him on a special weekend holiday to Great Yarmouth, arranged through the kindness of another teacher. It was his first sight of the seaside. Then it was he had painted his picture of the barn and old mill. But nothing had changed his withdrawn nature.

'When I struggled to reject my father, he came back in dreams,' Dominic told Winter. Winter merely nodded encouragingly. 'I hated Wolfgang, yet one thing he gave me. I was street-wise from an earliest age. You had to be in the DDR. I ran messages for him. You know what, he had a "secret hobby" – as he said. Messing with telephones, bugging. Wolf could bug anything. Electronics I learned from him, and didn't forget when I was with Daphne. It became my secret hobby. Something told me it was a dirty little DDR secret, even when used in London.

'You see . . . I realized much later Wolfgang was with the ballet but also worked for the Stasi. Only secret police had such modern equipment as was in his room. As a kid I found a way to key into computer systems – mainframes of banks. Early in the seventies, I was ordering goods on forged accounts. You understand? A little crook, thinking it a game.'

His repertoire was greatly extended when home computers arrived. Dominic was the first boy to own a Sinclair ZX, the youngest member of the computer generation. Size did not matter in this unexplored world.

'Imagine! That poor child could obtain things like any adult. And he soon learned to play the stock exchange game . . .'

In no time, he was able to lavish small presents on his adoptive mother. His room began to fill with fraudulently acquired equipment.

Fenella Cameron was working for one of the mushrooming computer trading firms in London. She had been deputed to check on frauds and failures. At that time, she lived with her mother in a flat in Kensington, only a short distance away. She took it upon herself to visit Dominic personally.

He was shocked when she called. He had scarcely visualized human beings at the other end of the line. Fenella had threatened him with the police, but he had promised to return the equipment, and all was smoothed over. He was impressed by her calm demeanour. Daphne gave her a coffee. While they were talking round the kitchen table, the lights went out. There was a power cut in Islington. The nation's miners were on strike.

'I walked some way back with her before she caught a taxi to Kensington. Of course, Fenella seemed immensely grown-up to me. I don't know what she saw in me, spotty, just reaching puberty. Perhaps she saw my excitement. I liked escorting a woman in dark streets. It made me feel big. And I knew she was scared. Poor Fenella. Always scared. She told me how lonely she was, how she lived with her mother, how she thought she'd never marry . . .' He fell silent.

'Did she talk about her mother?' Winter asked.

'Her father was still alive. She talked about him. He lived up in Scotland. Malcolm Cameron. Malcolm James Cameron. She loved him, but her parents lived separately. She never said anything against her mother . . . Come to think of it, she never has done so. More's the pity, Dr Winter. I believe she needs to throw the old witch out of her system . . .'

He was sitting forward, hands clasped. Looking up, he saw his fifty-minute hour was nearly over.

He went on hurriedly, 'The upshot was, I saw her again. It was a new, strange experience for us both. I soon persuaded her to have sex. She was lonely and thought she would never marry. Daphne also said she would never marry after Eric had run off, though there was a chap interested. Of course, the Cameron Scottish estate sounded romantic. Anyone born in the depths of Europe has a curiosity about Scotland . . .

'I was slightly ashamed of this new relationship, and hid it from all my new friends.'

He caught Winter's eye. 'Tomorrow, yah?' he said.

On the Thursday afternoon, Winter came into the reception room to greet Dominic as usual in his slow polite manner.

'I notice you always leave me with what is called a cliff-hanger as you depart, like a true storyteller,' he said, showing Dominic into the consulting room.

Dominic looked guarded. 'I've forgotten what I said.'

'Really? Yesterday, you paused at the door and said, "I'll tell you tomorrow how she invited me up to Scotland."'

'I have to keep your interest.' He smiled. He clasped his hands behind him.

'You have my interest.' Smiling in return, he indicated the armchair by the fire. Dominic sat down.

'Look, Dr Winter, I realize we have only today and tomorrow. Fenella thinks I've deserted her. I must go home for the weekend. Really, my first intention was to bring her to see you. Not me. Her. I think she's really in trouble in a way I'm not. That's what Lucy Traill believes.'

'Did you think that when you married Fenella?'

'Mmmm . . . I imagine not. I had had little experience of women, did not know how they would behave.'

'You had experience of two deeply troubled women, Lena and Daphne.'

'They were older . . .' His sentence died away. 'You're saying I'm fatally attracted to older women?'

'You're saying it.'

'Shit. I'm not saying it. I don't think it. But I suppose I saw Fenella as an escape from all my past, even including Daphne. At that time, being young and thoughtless, I wasn't half as grateful to Daphne as I've lately become. She deserves – well, everything. Everything I could give her.'

'And Fenella, nothing?'

'I married her, didn't I? Look, somehow I find it hard to go on. I'm at the end of the narrative, which I hope you enjoyed, by the way, yah? Now there's just entanglements. The marriage, I mean.'

'The narrative was interesting, I agree. But it was somewhat impersonal, not being so much about you as your parents. Now that you reach more personal matters, you naturally find it more difficult. So you tell me you must finish tomorrow.'

'I'm not trying to avoid . . . OK, perhaps I am. It's so painful. Listen, there are two salient points as I see it. First, Fenella's wish not to be loved. Second, these terrifying sick monologues she gets into, which no one can understand.'

Suddenly, he came up against her apparition in the hotel bedroom, when he had not been able to grasp what she said. It had been a projection of his brain; it summed up the situation: she always spoke and he never could hear, never grasp her meaning.

He felt truth swim like a fish just below the surface of his comprehension.

He became agitated. 'It's no good . . . Jesus, she is trying to communicate with me and I just refuse to hear. It's my fault, and I'm to blame for the failure of the marriage, and I am coming to you just to try to shift the guilt from my own shoulders. I'm really a bastard, just as Lena always said. Doctor, I can't go on with this. It'll always be a farce. I'm lying even when I think it's truth. I'm too messed up for anyone to mend.' He stifled a sob, glancing swiftly at his watch.

'Forgive me, I'll pay but I must leave. It just gets worse. You can't believe – I can't believe – a word of it. It's all too twisted up in my head, yah. I never loved Fenella, never loved her properly. All she needed was to have someone to listen clearly to the pain she got from her fucking mother – and I wasn't listening. That's all she needed. Now – too late! I wasn't listening. Too busy making money. Money! As if it's worth anything . . . Why do I blame her at all for my faults? I act as if I hate her. So I do. When I told her I would leave her, that was what I really meant. I didn't know . . . What do I know?' He spoke fast. 'Yes, what I really meant . . .'

'In the heat of the moment, possibly. Yet you entered here telling me you wished to go back to Fenella at the weekend. I see you need fortitude to return. But words are not set in concrete.'

Dominic brushed his hair back from his forehead. 'When you tell something to Fenella, then those words are set in concrete. In stone. Marble. There for ever. One day after a row, she looked so sad. She has a good expression of sadness. So I put my arms round her, just to comfort her.

'"What do you do that for?" she asked. Such a silly question. "What do you do that for?" Isn't it the common language of compassion, understood even in a war? "Lust, madam, pure lust," I replied in annoyance.'

'And what did she reply to that? "Very well then, no more sex till this quarrel is over." That's what she said. In great horror, I said to her that perhaps if we had no sex we could never cure the quarrel. But what she said had already become marble. She has no way to make . . . um, concessions. No way. I bend before her, take back my own words, eat humble pie, lose all my pride, and hate myself for it, all for the sake of peace and happiness. She? No such thing. She's so unbending, like her mother – and I admire it. The slab of marble moves forward towards me like a glacier, blocking off my options, till my back is against the wall. You understand that?'

Staring wide-eyed at Winter, he added, 'Do you grasp a word? There's a sword in my heart! – do you grasp what I say?'

Winter was sitting upright, all attention, his hands resting peacefully on his lap. The landscape of his face was humane – benign but slightly weary. After a pause, as though he had deeply considered Dominic's question, he gave a slight nod, encouraging his client to continue.

'I understand. You put it well.'

'Put it? It's what I live with six years now. I don't understand, I really don't understand whether she wants me or not . . . No, that's a lie, another lie – under it all, I understand – well, I think I understand – that she does want me, needs me even. Desperately. But on her terms. Terms which would kill me.'

A stony silence fell. Finally, resignedly, Dominic said, 'But I'm trying in some perverse way to impress you. You see why I work so happily with computers? I don't lie to them, they don't lie to me. I have done here a whole lot of self-blame. Perhaps it is so that you in your mind will think I am not to blame. This I will say. If you had Fenella here, she would not blame herself. She would blame only me. Her old mother likewise. They are quite unable to see any fault – any little fault in themselves, yah?

'Lucy Traill worries that Fenella may commit suicide. I feel like it myself at times. It's an escape from the living trap.'

Again the silence, in which the minute hand of the clock on the mantelpiece moved perceptibly.

'I suppose I'm saying that only to impress you? I would not really do it. Suicide.'

'And you think Fenella might?'

'I think I had better return home. I don't know what she will do. Not suicide. But you see my problem. She speaks in two voices. Does that mean she is mad? If she is mad, then the more important that I stay with her. At the same time, the less I wish to be there. I must drown my wishes for the sake of little Malcolm. And for Fenella's sake. She has no other friends, only that all-devouring mother.'

He rocked back and forth in his chair. 'I wish the old hag was dead. That's the truth.'

He took a long walk after his session, heading westwards without thought, without heed of traffic. He was furious with Winter, who offered him no comfort. He was furious with himself. He had given too much of himself away, for no return. Shostakovich played in his ear, but he tore the headphones off impatiently.

He walked uphill, turned off the main road, became lost. He found a long unending road almost free of cars and wandered along it. Thoughts blew through his head like leaves before an autumn storm. The idea of being lost had its appeal. Glimpsing a building in a field, he climbed over a locked gate and went to sit in it, thinking to pass the night there. The building, like the gate, was locked, and surrounded by mud. He conceived a sudden hatred for the miserable spoilt countryside, hostile to humans and animals alike.

He came to a small village with a pub. The pub was closed. On the edge of the village, by a council estate, he found a telephone box, where he rang for a taxi to collect him. It took a half-hour for the taxi to arrive, the driver complaining about rush-hour traffic. He ordered the man grumpily to take him to his hotel.

After 'the phantasm of the living', he was still wary of entering his room. Fenella was not there. He packed up his few belongings, went downstairs with the new suitcase, paid his bill, and walked through into the hotel garage for his car. He climbed into it and drove back to Shreding Green down the M40.

He could live without his Friday session with Winter. His duty was with young Malcolm. He could not desert the boy as his mother had deserted him. Not that Fenella had ever been other than kind to her son; that he had to admit. And he would live with the situation as it was; there was always the money game to play; it kept his kind occupied.

Just no more silly lavish parties.

He thought too of Mrs Cameron, realizing how he feared her. He had no doubt that her life-long disparagement of her daughter was at the root of all Fenella's problems; something vital in her had been killed. And yet – the mother too had an incurable misery, she too was to be pitied. Maybe her problems went back to her treatment as a child. And back and back through generations, a scroll of human misery extending all the way to the Ice Age. Adam and Eve had been unfit parents. Hadn't one of their sons killed his brother?

Dominic laughed. Maybe he had a half-brother still alive somewhere in the wastes of Poland. Those wastes were nothing to the wastes of the heart.

The great frown of the manor was caught in his headlights. The electronic gates swung open for him. At his coded infra-red signal, the intruder alarm system switched off before it could begin to howl.

The front of the house was in darkness, with not a light showing, though that could signify nothing. The mastiffs barked in their run, and Dominic gave them a word to calm them.

He unlocked the front door and entered the house. Switching on a light, he looked about him. All was silent and orderly; the reception rooms presented a rather ghostly appearance. He thought to himself: The old hag was right, white is a depressing colour. Why have I liked it for so long? It symbolizes ice and isolation. His hours with Winter had given him an uncomfortable awareness of symbolism.

Kicking off his shoes, he prowled through the rooms without switching on more lights. Everything was in order; the catering firm had, as usual, cleared up efficiently after the party, and Arold and Doris had followed to see all was well. An empty magnum champagne bottle stood unobtrusively on the mantelpiece in the rear room, next to a Dresden china pair of shepherd and shepherdess.

He paused before the half-length portrait of Fenella which he had commissioned from Oscar Mellor as a wedding present for his bride. The portrait showed her in a white blouse with a dove-grey jacket over it, looking warily in semi-profile over her left shoulder. Of course, the name Fenella meant 'white shoulder'. Mellor had painted a background featuring only a misty castle, tall and impregnable. Dominic had never understood its meaning; the Cameron house in Scotland was not at all like that, although he had provided the artist with photographs of it.

Looking up at the canvas, he thought, nodding to himself, Perhaps I'm mad. Could be that's the reason why I married so young in the first place? Nineteen. Still a child. All that rubbish I spouted to Winter – why did that have to come out? That business of Lena standing in the snow with the kid by the railway line as the train pulled away. It wasn't my life. I was unborn.

Yet it stands for something in my life . . .

The ice, the isolation . . .

He looked about at the white rooms, shrouded in shadow.

Maybe I was traumatized by all that stuff in my early years. Change of country, change of language, change of mother. Traumatized. Still traumatized. The snow represents some kind of freeze on my mentality.

He sat down on the arm of an Italian sofa, the better to think.

That's why I have this silly preference for white. It's a miserable non-colour. That old bitch Morna was right. White's the snow. The snow of coke. The snow of insanity. Oh Jesus . . . I'm really stuck in some awful infant age. That's why I can't help Fenella. Fenny. Not man enough. Still child-sized.

All I've learned in life is this money game, played out like a video game, the BCT, as Colin Cohen once called it. The Big Computer Trick. Trade swiftly, never let your money leave the bank. I've nothing of myself to invest, only money, common currency.

He sank into the sofa.

Let's face it, I'm really fucked up and done. To hell with shrinks. I'd better go and see Fenella, tell her I'm back. She must have gone to bed early. Drugged, as Lucy Traill said. Who knows what goes on?

Rising, he slipped off his coat and let it fall to the floor before going into the library for a fortifying snort of *Great Expectations*. With the warmth coursing through him, he went to the door and called softly: not to Fenella. To Arold.

No answer. Jesus, they're all dead, he thought. Murdered. But in that case, he might have seen Fenella lurking in the shadows, by the long white curtains covering the front windows.

He stood listening, wondering what was wrong.

In his stockinged feet, he padded through to the back hall, to call again, and met Arold coming through from the servants' passage.

'Bit dark in 'ere. 'Ow about shedding some light on thinks?' His mouth looked monstrous, his lips glistening round the protruding teeth. His head rolled to one side. He stood swaying slightly, clutching the door frame for support. 'You're back, Mr Dominic, I see. Wasn't expecting you this late. Doris 'as gone to see a friend, if you wanted summink.'

'It's only ten thirty, Arold. I didn't mean to disturb you.'

'Like a drink or a cup of tea? I was just ringing Aubrey or I'd 'a come earlier. I mean to say, I did hear the car arrive and guessed as it was you. Couple of days ago, I was telling Aubrey, I got the garridge to come and tow the Porsche away. Bloke said it could all be fixed, shouldn't set you back more nor one K.'

He put his elbow to the door frame, the better to support his head. 'I still feel very bad about all that, Mr Dominic, like I was saying to Aubrey. Very bad indeed. You took it like a good 'un. Tomorrow morning I'll get busy sorting out the goldfish pond. Lucky it seems none of them carp was killed.' He burst into laughter, which turned to coughing. 'Funny to think of running over a blooming carp, ain't it?'

Dominic smiled. 'Very funny. Something not in the Highway Code. Arold, is my wife upstairs?'

Arold looked startled, cleared his throat, and managed to stop coughing and laughing. 'My Christ, don't you know yet, suh? I thought you had the info and that was why you was back here. I'm sorry to have to tell you, but truth is the old girl's dead.'

He lurched forward and patted Dominic clumsily on the shoulder. Immediately the thought flew to him, Now I understand that phantasm – it appeared at the moment of Fenella's death . . .

'Dead, Arold? *Dead?* When?'

'Oh, let's see now, today's Friday, is it not? No, hang on, Thursday

. . . Yes. Monday, it would be. No, I tell a lie. Tuesday. 'Course, we couldn't get in touch with you because we didn't know where you was. I said to Doris, "How the 'ell are we to find the master?" and she said—'

'Arold! Sober up, will you? Are you trying to tell me that my wife died on Tuesday and no attempt was made to trace me?'

Arold spluttered in his distress, rolling his huge head wildly. 'You are in a state, suh. I better get you a tot of grog. It weren't Mrs Mayor what died, 'course not. Like I said, it was the old girl, the old girl, suh, Mrs Cameron.'

Dominic grabbed his servant by the shirt. 'Who's dead? Tell me properly.'

'I just told you, suh – old Mrs Cameron.'

'What's that noise, Arold?'

Arold looked startled and peered back along the passage behind him. 'Vietnam War, Mr Dominic. I got a video running about the Vietnam War. *Rambo*. Want a look?'

'Come and sit down and speak properly. Mrs Cameron is dead? How? Where? Where's Fenella? Where's Malcolm?' He locked his hands together to control his trembling.

As Arold followed Dominic meekly to a pair of chairs, he said, 'To answer your questions in proper military order, suh, Mrs Mayor's gone up to Bonnie Scotland, taking the boy with 'er. That's where the old girl died. Up in Scotland. She was in her eighties, when all's said and done – had a good run for her money.'

Dominic raised his hands helplessly above his head.

'She died at Fuarblarghour – on Tuesday?'

'Creck. According to my intelligence, she decided to drive back up to the estate after the party last Saturday night – rashly, in my opinion. Stopped somewhere on the way. Reached Fuarblarghour afternoon of Sunday, feeling a bit dickey. The bailiff called the doctor Monday, but she had two heart attacks Monday night, the house being that cold, lapsed into unconsciousness. Mrs Mayor was called then, flew up by plane with the kid early Tuesday – I drove 'em to Heathrow Terminal One to get the shuttle flight. Very upset I was, and Doris, though I never liked the old girl, suh, to tell truth. In fact, I did offer to fly up with 'em, but offer was rejected out of hand.

'Anyhow, to cut a long story short, apparently when your missus got to the bedside, Mrs Cameron was in a coma and sinking fast, and never a word more she spoke – except one.'

He paused for dramatic effect, and then said, "'Shame it is . . .'" He repeated the phrase, adopting a Macbeth-like voice. "'Shame it is." That's what she said, as I learned from your wife's lips over the phone. Though exactly what was a shame we shall never know. A tragic end, suh. Doris and me, we offers our condolences.'

'So my wife is still at Fuarblarghour?'

'Creck. Where I assume you'll be joining her?'

'I'll catch that same early Glasgow flight tomorrow, Arold.'

'I'll be delighted to drive you over to the airport, suh. My pleasure. Now perhaps a cup of tea, or maybe summink a bit stronger? You're looking very pale, natural in the circumstances.'

'Tea, thanks, Arold. Would you mind bringing it up to my room?'

'Pleasure, Mr Dominic.'

At Glasgow airport he hired a car and drove north rapidly on the A82 along the western shore of Loch Lomond. The rain, falling in curtains, rendered the loch all but invisible. Cloud lifted slightly as he rolled down towards the long narrow gash of Loch Awe. He slowed, turning left along the southern shore.

At Heathrow, Arold Betts had begged to escort him on the trip. 'Sort of a back-up unit, Mr Dominic, you might say.' With some regret, Dominic had ordered the man to stay behind and look after the manor. He put out one of his small neat hands and clasped Arold's large puffy paw. Arold and Doris were irreplaceable.

On reaching the village of Blarghour, Dominic turned up a gravel track which bore a sign saying 'Fuarblarghour House only'. Climbing above the loch, the way led at first through wooded land, followed by stretches of moorland with wide views. A whitewashed cottage stood sentinel as he entered the Fuarblarghour estate. Lines of cloud were sweeping away over the distant Firth of Lorn, admitting patches of blue sky overhead.

Fuarblarghour House perched on a granite shoulder, looking towards Loch Awe and the opening to Loch Avich. The heights of heather-covered Beinn Breac loomed in the distance behind it. The inhospitable Cameron manse was a tall grey building, constructed of local granite; through one of the windows of its tower could be seen the distant ruins of a castle which had once guarded or failed to guard the loch against the depredations of the Campbell clan.

Malcolm was playing in the wide hall, running a fire engine up and down the parquet flooring. He took his father out to a back scullery to see a cat which had given birth to four kittens. While they were admiring the little blind animals, Fenella appeared.

Dominic was on his knees. He jumped up to embrace his wife and kiss her pale cheek. This she took in good part, saying that she was glad to see him because there was much to be done. No reference to his earlier absence; no reference, for that matter, to her dead mother lying upstairs.

'Trixie will get you something to eat,' she said. 'I expect you're hungry.'

'Mummy, poor Tibbs is starving. Can we give her some milk?' Malcolm asked.

Dominic felt sorry for the cat, and for the small lives she had brought into the world. Above her bed – a grocery box – loomed an enormous weight of masonry and ponderously empty rooms, all loaded with Rob Roy furniture. Following the death of the elder Malcolm, Fenella's father, Morna had hired the manse out for holiday lets. British, American, and even Japanese visitors had come. But the building had never been adapted for such purposes; the kitchens were inconveniently old-fashioned, and overseas guests demanded heated swimming pools. The enterprise had died a natural death, under the stern eyes of Denis MacManus and his sister Trixie, Mrs Cameron's northern substitute for Arold Betts and his wife. Morna Cameron had become the sole and intermittent denizen of her property.

It occurred to Dominic, not for the first time, that someone had to inherit the estate, and it was not difficult to guess who that might be, if not the local cats' home. Unless Morna had had one last attack of spite, it was more than likely Fenella would be her heiress; which, he foresaw, would bring a new series of problems.

Trixie MacManus was a small, gaunt woman plainly without tricks. An immense jaw gave her an aspect of immutable seriousness. To distract attention from this feature, she confined her brown hair in two large buns, which hung on either side of her face like earphones. She entered the chilly dining-room, greeted Dominic politely, and set a large cold ham before him. While he carved, she brought in reinforcements of vegetables in two tureens. 'The cabbage is local-grown,' she told Dominic.

'All is arranged,' Fenella said, not without complacency, as they ate. 'The doctor has been and provided a certificate. The wee woman has been and laid out Mother's body. The undertaker from Inverary has been.' She ticked these items off on her fingers. 'The funeral will take place on Monday, conducted by the Rev. Nickerman, who was a friend of Mother's. We can stay up here over the weekend. And the Will has been read.'

'Oh? Who read the Will?'

'Our solicitor, of course. Bruce Dower, of Stirrup and Dower, London Wall. You have met him.'

'Dower flew up here to read the Will?'

'Certainly. Stirrup and Dower have a branch in Edinburgh, but Bruce flew up here as an old friend of my mother's. His father was my grandfather's solicitor.'

He would not ask the question on his mind. He took more mustard and ate his ham. After a silence, Fenella answered the unspoken question, 'I am not my mother's sole beneficiary. She left you a cut-glass decanter, together with small bequests to the servants. Everything else, the entire estate, devolves on me.'

'A cut-glass decanter? Why a cut-glass decanter?'

'I suppose she thought you would like it, Dominic. What a

162

funny question. She left you nothing else – if that is what you are thinking – because she assumed you were rich enough already, I suppose.'

'You mean no sentiment was involved.'

'Mother merely did what she thought was right. She was not sentimental. I see you think she was not generous enough.'

He asked in lowered voice, 'What provision did Morna make for her grandson?'

There was a pause. Before Fenella replied, Malcolm asked if his grannie had left him the toys in the house.

'You're a bit too young to be mentioned in a Will, dear,' Fenella said.

'Of course he's not. Even the unborn are mentioned in Wills by those who care about them,' Dominic said.

'Not in Mother's Will.'

Nothing more was said until Trixie brought on bowls of prunes and custard.

'And your brother, Fenny,' Dominic said, striving for a relaxed tone of voice. 'Jamie. Did Morna leave anything to James?'

She smiled at the idea. 'Mother disowned James long ago.'

'And how do you feel about James?'

'As I say, the trouble is Mother disowned him long ago.'

He put his spoon down. 'Fenny, I don't understand. James is or was your brother, your only brother. You must have played together when you were small, perhaps you were bathed together, slept in the same room, cuddled each other, loved each other. Don't you feel anything for him?'

'James went off to the United States long ago. It was his decision, and that's the end of it.'

'No, it's not. Maybe you'd like to see your brother again. Maybe Malcolm would like an Uncle James. The United States isn't the end of the world, you know.'

She looked down into her prune bowl. 'Can we leave the subject, thanks. James is nothing to do with you. Or with me.'

Dominic leaned across the table towards her. 'Then I want to ask you another question. What did your mother say just before she died?'

'Oh, these questions! She began a sentence but was unable to finish it. In any case, the words were indistinct . . . I think she said, "The shame it is . . ."'

'Or maybe just "Shame it is . . ."'

'Possibly, yes. It means nothing. Her mind was wandering.'

'Suppose that what she said was "Jamie is . . .", yah? but was unable to complete the sentence. Didn't you tell me she called him Jamie in the Scottish way? Couldn't it have been that at the last moment before she died that grim old lady repented of her treatment of her son, the way she never repented of the treatment of her daughter, and wished – who can say? – to make some amends, perhaps even to summon him home, perhaps even to permit you to be a sister, a loving sister, as you could be, to this exiled brother, Jamie Cameron?'

'As you yourself remark, Dommy, who can say? It's immaterial, Mother's dead, and besides, you are frightening Malcolm.'

Malcolm, in fact, was sitting with a dessert spoon in his mouth, looking pop-eyed from one parent to the other, more full of curiosity than fright.

'Have I an Uncle Jamie in America, Mummy? Can we go and see him?'

'Certainly not, Malcolm. He may be a criminal for all we know. Your father is just guessing. Get down and go and play – and take that spoon out of your mouth.'

When the boy had gone, they sat and looked coolly at each other.

'Have you really no curiosity about that brother of yours?'

'Things will be very different now,' Fenella said. She looked out of the long window.

'But not different enough,' Dominic said, rushing on to have his say, conscious of plunging into dangerous waters. 'Despite this house and the estate, Fenny, despite years of knowing your mother as well as you, despite all that, I feel I have no – no contact, yah, with you. You realize you have never said a word to me about your childhood—'

She put her hands on the table; the fingers were long and blunt, without polish. 'If this is to be another of your criticisms of me, I don't want to hear it. I shall ring for Trixie to clear away, and go upstairs to sort out my mother's possessions. There's much to be done.'

She stood. Dominic stood as well. He spoke in an urgent voice. 'Fenella, dear, my dear wife, let me get through to you while your mother lies dead upstairs and you are presumably conscious of the frailty of life. I still love you and have no wish to criticize, only to heal. You know all about me. I have told you – I told you when we first were lovers – if you remember such a time – all there was about me, all my tragic past, and the whole business as far as I knew it – as I believe lovers should do. Perfectly frank and open, *able* to be open.'

'Oh yes, I had all that Russian business by heart, believe me.' She folded her arms across her chest, giving him a supercilious smile.

'Fenella, *able* to be open. And what did I get back from you? Nothing. Only this defensive silence, as now. Silence. A brick wall. Now your mother is dead, now Morna is dead at last, please renounce her, yah? Throw her out of your mind and be open, happy. Forget! I know she has injured you. Now's the time to throw her out, now.'

She moved towards the door, looking over her shoulder. 'The trouble is, you hated Mother, just as you hate me. How you twist things! It was you who were going to throw me out, remember? I don't want to hear you speaking ill of the dead any more.'

She was about to leave the room. He fell on his knees. 'Fenella, I beg you, please. Break down now, show emotion, cry, tear your clothes. Now's your chance. You're still young and the old hag has gone . . . You're free—'

She slammed the door behind her. Slowly, Dominic rose to his feet. Despite the electric fire, the room was as cold as a grouse moor.

Fenella was busy all that weekend, walking about upstairs among the furniture and possessions. She would occasionally summon Trixie MacManus and her surly brother to her side. Some rooms upstairs were empty and uncarpeted, their floors echoing as she prowled them to peer from their deep-set windows or investigate the contents of a fusty cupboard. Other rooms were overfurnished. And there were attics, draughty and dim, full of relics belonging to past Camerons piled up like memories, draped in dustsheets like catafalques, a great family treasure trove with no one to treasure it but Fenella Mayor. Dominic wondered if she was sad or pleased as she found her way among these responsibilities.

Trixie was occasionally despatched downstairs, carrying hat boxes or piles of old picture frames or broken-stringed tennis rackets of Edwardian vintage. These ancestral trophies were stacked outside the back door in the light of day. Dominic and Malcolm, feeling themselves in the way, walked down to the edge of the loch, where they climbed about, in the ruined castle. Not another person did they see there, only an ancient horse which kept its distance.

By night, silence prevailed over Fuarblarghour House. Everything imitated the stillness of the body in the shrouded main bedroom, as if its halitus exuded paralysis. Dominic marvelled that his son was unafraid. When he kissed the boy goodnight on the Saturday, he asked him if he would like a light in his room.

'I can see to go to sleep in the dark, Daddy,' Malcolm replied.

Dominic himself was installed in a long narrow room to the rear of the house, the walls of which were hung with photographs for whose frames a whole oak forest had gone down. Between two long narrow windows stood a grandfather clock. From above the face of the clock protruded the carved head of a Highland stag. He stood looking at it, touched it, for a moment almost believing he had seen it before. The clock was unwound. When he tapped its case, the chime struck one with a parliamentarian voice, as if declaring that the Noes had it.

He quizzed in the drawers of a high chiffonier. They were choked by carefully folded sheets with lace edges, shawls, blankets, all smelling of mothballs. The drawers were lined with issues of the *Scotsman* dating from early in the century. In one drawer he discovered a photograph, mounted on brown card and tucked under a stack of lace napkins. It showed a pair of children, elaborately dressed, sitting on a rug. Behind them was a painted Japanese screen. The children were boy and girl. The boy, with as many curly locks as the girl, was the older of the two. Both had the long Cameron face. It could be Fenella and Jamie. He did not know. He sighed and closed the drawer. It was no business of his. Had Morna hidden it there? Poor comfortless Morna.

The past lay suffocating as camphor in the room. Other people's pasts . . . as if one's own was not bad enough. A large study of Malcolm Cameron, Fenella's father, all drooping moustaches, wearing a deerstalker hat, dominated the wall above the brass bedstead, entombed in another oak. Dominic had discovered of this man only that he had died of drink, although cancer was generally given out as the cause of death.

'The Laird of Blarghour!' exclaimed Dominic, addressing the portrait in a sportive way. 'What sort of a life, yah? Maybe you caused all the grief. Bet you were made to sleep alone . . . In this very room. Why was that? Were you bully or victim? What did you do to your wife? Your children?' The portrait remained silent. 'Pity research can't be done into such matters, everything computerized and analysed. Sorted out. Filed. Happiness programmed. Break up the solid blocks of misery, the chains of circumstance.'

He lay uncomfortably between cold sheets, staring out into the room, his thoughts turning to Lucy Traill. She could warm his bed, make it a paradise. The endearingly cheeky way she had come in and perched on the end of his bed at home. Must have been after something . . .

No future in thinking like that! He pressed the switch dangling over the head of the bed and put out the light. Lying flat on his back, he tried to calm himself with thoughts of work, the refuge in figures he so often sought. Before leaving Shreding Green, he had inspected his offices on the first floor of the manor. His assistants were keeping everything under control while he was absent. At present, Dominic was particularly interested in the price of copper on the commodities market. Copper had been expensive and in short supply a few years back, when he entered the game; with new glass fibres coming into use in place of copper, demand had slackened. He bought and sold profitably on a falling market. Dominic was a master of price movements. His assistants were trained to commit huge sums of money in one market and sell within minutes in another; no Mayor money ever left Schatzman's or his other banks. It was Colin Cohen's BCT.

He was dozing. A noise somewhere in the house roused him. He sat up, thinking of his son. Silence. Then the noise again, a brisk noise, very small, muffled by thick walls, and the massive furniture of the house. Silence again.

He lay back, still tense. As for his investments, this refrigerator of a house represented another sort of investment, an investment in bricks and mortar and land of which the British were traditionally so fond. No ten-minute switches here from market to market. Inheritance, with its unseen powers, took years, decades, generations. It was a stone-age way of getting rich. Though no one here knew it, the microchip had rendered Fuarblarghour House obsolete. Fenella didn't know it; certainly her family solicitors, Stirrup & Dower, were not going to break the news to her.

The noise roused him again. Without switching on the light, he climbed out of the high bed, slipping on his jacket against the chill. On the corridor walls beyond his room hung threatening things, huge oils of Highland scenes, framed documents, the odd shield and sword. He went quietly round the right-angle of the corridor.

Turning the corner, he saw that a door on the landing above was open. Light fanned from it on to the patterned carpet. Fenella was moving about in the room. He could now identify the noise as the snapping closed of trunks.

Dominic went forward silently, barefoot on the carpet, until he could see what she was doing.

Fenella was in stockinged feet, wearing only a vest and a slip. She was bending over a large black cabin trunk, lifting from it items of clothing. Tissue paper rustled. She spread out a woman's two-piece suit of heavy tweed. After feeling in the pockets of the jacket, she started to try the garments on, watching herself in a cheval glass.

Soon she was fully dressed in her mother's clothes.

The mortal remains of Morna Agatha Cameron were laid to rest in the Blarghour graveyard, the service being conducted by the Rev. Anstruther Nickerman, black of habit, white of whisker and face, red of nose, and dark brown as regards voice.

It appeared from all the Rev. Nickerman said that he had every hope that the recently departed would even now be on her way to, or had actually arrived at, a state of eternal bliss. To Dominic, holding Malcolm's hand, this statement seemed countered by the ugliness of the narrow slot freshly dug in the soil. Nor did the Chapel of Remembrance allow bliss great priority. It was of the meanest possible dimension inside; outside it sprouted numerous pinnacles and minispires in advanced stages of nigrescence, like a mass of stalactites turned upside-down. Of all the buildings he had ever encountered, it was the one least to be associated with a state of eternal, or even fleeting, bliss.

After the ceremony, hastened by a light, pleasant rain, Fenella grasped Dominic's arm and turned away from the grave with the same abruptness with which the Rev. Nickerman closed his *Book of Common Prayer* and made off towards his small black vehicle.

Dominic remembered, was encouraged, by that firm grip on his arm when they were back home again in Shreding Green. He regarded himself as a vacillator. She showed no weakness: he admired most the characteristic he feared most.

With settled determination, Fenella drove over to Kensington every day, to clear up in her mother's flat. Dominic drove over there too one evening, and offered to take her to dine in a restaurant he knew before going home.

'Splendid,' she said. 'In that case, I shall try out a coat of Mother's, which has hardly been worn.'

October had turned to November. There was the excuse to wear a coat. Even Dominic could see that this heavy mannish coat was out of date and ill-suited his wife; having no wish to upset her, he said nothing. Perhaps it was an endearing feature that she was blind to the trivialities of fashion.

They went together in the newly repaired Porsche. The restaurant was already bustling when they arrived. Dominic had reserved a corner table.

Fenella swallowed pills with her wine.

'I shall put Mother's flat on the market in a few weeks,' she said, as they drank coffee at the end of the meal. 'The possessions I wish to keep can be temporarily stored at the manor.'

'We might get a better price for the flat in the spring. Why not hang on till then? Perhaps you could let the apartment for the next quarter, yah?'

'The trouble is I've decided to sell at once.'

'That's it, is it?' He smiled. 'Why not wait a bit? You know there's a recession at present. House prices may improve next year.'

She returned his smile. 'I want to get it off my mind. The flat was only Mother's pied-à-terre. It wasn't the family home.'

He felt she was holding something back. She would say what she wished to say in her own time. He changed the subject.

'How's the physiotherapy? Do you feel it does your back good?'

She lifted the coffee cup to her mouth – 'I sacked Miss Traill on Tuesday' – and drank.

Dominic took a deep breath, and smoothed his beard. 'Really? You sacked her? I thought Lucy was rather a friend of yours. You asked her to the party. She was always very concerned about you. Why on earth have you sacked her?'

Fenella gave him the frosted look, her eyes blank as she looked through him. She set down her cup precisely in its saucer before replying, 'I believe you know why.'

'I most certainly don't.' Yet he felt within himself that familiar uncoiling of guilt, like a snake awakening.

'How stupidly innocent you look, Dom. You most certainly do. Didn't Miss Traill, Lucy as you call her, enter your bedroom after the party?'

He threw back his head and gasped. 'Jesus, Fenella, what new thing have you thought up against me? This is too much. I can't take it. I can't take any more. It's impossible. Let's pay the bill and go, get out of here. Whatever's in your mind, forget it – it didn't happen.'

He stood up, signalling angrily to their waiter. Fenella sat where she was, looking up fixedly at him. 'The trouble is, she did enter your room, didn't she?'

'No, she bloody didn't. Not in the way you think.'

'She waited till Doris was out of the way and Arold was in the garden and then she came into your bedroom. Do you dare deny that?'

'Wait till we're outside.' As the waiter came over with the bill in leather folder, Dominic produced his American Express gold card, saying to the man, 'We're in rather a hurry, if you don't mind. Thanks.'

She stood up. 'Very well, you refuse to admit it. But Malcolm came in and saw you and Miss Traill cuddling – if that's all it was – on your bed. Of course I sacked her. What else could I do?'

This was said in a loud conversational tone, rather as if she were addressing a slightly deaf mother. Conversation died at tables nearby, heads turned a polite few degrees.

'Shit,' Dominic said, standing there, feeling embarrassed. It did not help matters that she was taller than he was. He glanced quickly at his watch, anxious to escape.

Holding his head downwards and towards her, he said in low tones, 'You could have asked her what really happened, that's what you could have done. Or you could have asked me. Come to that you could have trusted me. If you think we were screwing, then you are mistaken. Unfortunately.'

'Oh, what were you doing then? Talking about me, I suppose.'

He hurried away across the restaurant, waiting impatiently at the cashier's desk, drumming his fingers on it, until he had his card back. The waiter, returning it, gave him an oily smile, half-way between conspiratorial and gleeful, as male chauvinism vied with the pleasure of seeing a customer discomfited. Dominic left the restaurant without looking back, leaving his wife to retrieve her hideous coat.

'What a weakling I am,' he said, pacing on the pavement outside. 'Why didn't I hit her? Why don't I drive off now? Because I'm scared to. I'm forever putting myself in her hands. Of course she has a contempt for me.'

When Fenella appeared, she was in her usual state of calm; a calm that had intensified since her mother's death.

'That was a fine performance you gave in front of everyone,' she said.

'Let's get in the car and get home.'

At the wheel of the Porsche, he was able to control himself. He chose to take the Old Bath Road home, driving slowly, mollified to see other people about, squeezing a little pleasure from the evening. After all, there had been a time when he and Fenella had delighted in each other's company. Before he made a million. And, after all, he would have liked to have screwed Lucy Traill when she had sat down so freely on his bed; the impulse had not been absent from his mind. Or from hers? Since he had not told his wife of that incident, or of his visits to Winter when he was away – she had asked nothing about his absence – she could not be blamed for her suspicion. It was silly of him to lose his temper in the restaurant.

He pulled the car into the forecourt of a silencer centre which was closed, and cut off the engine.

'Are you going to make me get out and walk from here?' she asked, with a small attempt at humour.

'Fenny, Lucy and I did nothing sexual. OK? Please believe me. I'm sorry I lost my rags.'

'Rag.'

'Rag, yah. There was a time between you and me when everything was so happy. I still remember the evening of the blackout when I walked you a little way back to Kensington, and felt immense joy. You were so cool, so gracious.' He was looking at her, turned as far as the seating would allow, while drumming with his right hand on the steering wheel. Fenella stared ahead into the shadowy recesses of the station, as though listening intently.

'You too perhaps remember the promise of those days. I can say only that for me it was then like spring. Spring and a new life. But now after only a few years, where has the summer sunshine gone? I feel we live together, but without – oh, my dear Fenny, without the warmth that grows between a man and woman, without the summer sunshine, the natural confidences, the . . . the flowers of . . .' He hesitated over the dangerous word. '. . . Of love.' And went on hastily, 'I do not speak in reproach at all. It's just that between us – really ever since the birth of little Malcolm, yah? – there is a terrible . . . you know what I'm saying? . . . a cold state of something like – well, not at all like the gentle summer sun we could enjoy together. The sun, the music. You see what I mean.'

She was silent for a long while before turning to look at him. She spoke gently. 'Those days are gone. We've got Malcolm, haven't we? I don't understand what you mean, all this business about summer and flowers. It's too continental for me. I'm not used to that. We get on as best we can. You'd better save the flowers and sunshine and stuff for Lucy Traill and whatever girlfriends you went off to see the other week. All I want is peace.'

'So do I.'

'You have come under the influence of that drunkard Betts. I'd have sacked him long ago if I didn't know you liked him so much – I can't think why. Anyhow, he and his disgusting wife will have to find other employment when we go to live in Scotland.'

This was said in such a level voice that he was almost robbed of words; he had never accustomed himself to her way of delivering small death sentences.

'We're not – You never said anything about this. We've not discussed this. What the hell are you talking about? You're going to sell that dump up there in Blarghour, yah? – same as the flat in Kensington.' He banged his fists in fury against the wheel.

Fenella sat perfectly immobile. 'So much for your fine talk of sunshine and roses. Have you found another reason to quarrel? You always think you can wind me round your little finger. We aren't going to live in that damned manor of yours for ever, are we, with planes roaring overhead all day and all the filth about. We've inherited a family home now. Isn't that what you've always wanted, Dimitri, you with all your relations vanished behind you?'

He let in the clutch with a jerk. The car bounced forward. It burst through a plastic chain guarding the entrance to the station and shot on to the road, narrowly missing three men walking by. They yelled their abuse, but he was off down the road, gathering speed. The acceleration had thrown Fenella back against the seat.

'You're insane,' she said. He was savagely glad to hear her shriek. 'If you're trying to get us killed, go ahead!'

'*You're* insane! You know what, you're mad and don't know it. Look, there's no way I will live up in Blarghour in that bloody house of your mother's. Even if there was, you've gone the wrong way about – Jesus!' He had burst through a red light, and missed hitting a turning lorry only because its driver swerved on to the pavement at the last instant.

The near collision calmed him little. Perhaps they were both frightened, for neither said a word more until they arrived at Shreding Green and were inside the house. Arold came lolloping out to see if they needed anything, but was immediately ordered back to his own quarters.

'Say le vie,' he exclaimed, disappearing without so much as a salute.

'Come into the library and let's have this thing out once and for all,' Dominic said. He switched on the lights and paced up and down, not daring to look in the direction of *Great Expectations*. She stood inside the library door in one of her watchful poses, a hand crossed over her chest.

'Now, Fenella, tell me I didn't hear correctly. You cannot think of keeping that mock-castle your mother has left you?'

She said, with a half-smile, 'Perhaps I should preserve it for Brother Jamie. You're keen to meet him, aren't you?'

He rushed at her and barely prevented himself from hitting her. 'None of that snide talk. Try for once to be honest and straight, because we have to have this clear. That bloody Fuarblarghour is no good for you. It's full with shadows. Even your mother couldn't bear to live there in the wilds all year. We certainly will not go live there. Malcolm would hate it, I'd hate it.'

'It's only an hour's drive from Glasgow.'

He stood back, furious. 'Do you even listen? Can you listen? Can you even hear in there, woman? I don't care how far it is from Glasgow. I have to make our living, I have to work in London, I have to work right here, where my business is set up, where communications are, where all my colleagues are, where everything is – not up in some vague psychotic dream in the wilds of somewhere in some place whose name I can't even pronounce. How many times do I have to tell you this, how do I make you understand, you lunatic, that there's no way it would be other than destruction for us to pack up and go to such an isolated dump when we've already got a really first-class difficulty of communication between us? You won't speak to me properly, you won't let me screw you any more, how the hell do we to get out of that one issue alone without complicating the whole miserable scene by we go to some rain-soaked ruin in Scotland?'

With a sneer, she said, 'Oh, you're planning to leave me again, is that it?'

'You bet I'll leave you. Tomorrow. This evening. Now.' He tapped his watch for emphasis.

She moved towards the door. 'You are violent. The trouble is you had too much to drink in the restaurant. You've been at those drugs of yours, I can tell. I'm going, and I'll speak to you at some other time.'

He jumped up and grabbed her, pushing himself at her, yet at the same time holding her away. 'No, you're not going yet, Fenny. This is how you wind me up, get me mad with a dreadful proposition, then creep away, leaving me sunk and dead. Come and sit down and let's for once talk this out.'

He swung her violently around. She was laughing, encouraging him to be violent.

He slapped her across the face. 'Laugh at that, you bitch,' growling like an animal.

She remained laughing in a kind of way, mouth half-open, eyes half-closed.

In an altered voice, she said, 'I know I deserved that. Of course, of course, I see . . . Go on, hit me again. Do it.'

He hit her again, so that her head rocked back and crimson spread across her cheek. She put on a little girl's voice. 'Yes, I deserve it, I know, I see. I'll go and throw myself in the loch, if you like. Would you like that? I'm not worth anything. Tell me again.'

Anger overrode all his other feelings. He pushed her into one of the uncomfortable Italian chairs by the fireplace.

'You'll stay there. Now, speak. Why couldn't you discuss it with me properly, if you wanted to keep this fucking Fuarblarghour House? Why couldn't we sit down in a friendly way and talk it over? What's wrong with you? How could you dare to think—? We can't live there. Why should you want to? It's because of your mother, isn't it? She still has power over you. Beyond the grave. More power than I'll ever have. If that isn't the problem, what is?' He stood over her as she drooped against the hard white upholstery. 'Come on, let's have it finally. Confess. What's wrong with you?'

She was not looking at him. 'You don't love me, do you?' Again the tiny voice. 'The trouble is, I'm not very lovable. I realize I'm not the person for you. All you've made me say is true and I believe you. It isn't just that I'm cold, although when the wind blows I hear it saying all kinds of things. Nothing about me, nothing about me, best to ignore me. Some things are just an interruption, to be trampled underfoot . . .' The voice as it continued seemed to change colour, to a sickly yellow tone, deeply disturbing to him, no less disturbing, because he had heard it before.

He dropped down on his knees by her and held her hands.

'Fenny, dearest, you're frightening me. Do stop it. I'm sorry, really I am. I never meant to hit you, yah? Understand? Fenny?'

She withdrew her hands gently, with the tenderest gesture like a child's, tucking them for safety into her armpits, all the while looking away from him, head to one side, staring with a shy air into a corner of the room. Talking in the same strange way, lips barely moving, ghostly in appearance. There was no way of interrupting her, and he sat huddled by her, silenced, trying not to listen, trying to listen.

On and on it went, abject, rejecting. It was the sick monologue.

Fenella talked on without pause in the same unvarying monotone. Once he tried to break the flow. 'Who are you?' he asked. 'Tell me who you are and I will try to help. Don't be frightened.'

But he was frightened. Whoever was speaking was beyond his aid.

At last there was an end . . . The voice died, uttering something that might have been construed as a feeble threat or an entreaty.

Fenella looked up and said in a more normal voice, 'Well, I don't know about you, Dom, but I'm going to bed. I'm tired.'

He also was exhausted. 'Are you all right? We'll talk about this in the morning. Discuss what just happened.'

'Good night, Dominic.'

He remained sitting on the hearthrug long after she had gone upstairs. It was two twenty in the morning. The frightening voice had prevailed in this room for over two hours. It was the sick monologue he had mentioned to Lucy Traill . . . Once again, he found himself unable to recall anything it had said.

Singing quietly to herself, Doris Betts was stuffing some of Malcolm's clothes into the washing machine in the utility room. Arold came in through the outer door from the yard, stomping in his boots. 'Arold, you nearly made me jump, coming in like that.'

Her husband put a cautionary finger up to his nose. 'Be like dad, keep mum. Doris, love, come over to the kennels, will you?'

She was wary of his conspiratorial air. 'What's up? Are the dogs OK?'

'Yes, love, fighting fit. Just step across the yard, there's a pet.'

She rammed the washer door shut. 'Can't be long. I've the upstairs rooms to do this morning. Don't try any monkey business, that's all.'

'Trust an old soldier,' he said, standing back gallantly to let her pass.

He led the way across the yard to a building that housed the generator, looking round to see the coast was clear as he did so. Once inside, he pulled the wide door to and pointed up the wooden steps to the loft above.

'Doris, love, I was up there sorting out 'is reference boxes, and what do you think I saw? Rape. Rape, that's what!' Nodding with grim satisfaction at his wife's look of astonishment, he went on. 'From the window in the loft you gets a good view of 'er bedroom 'cross the way. As I 'appened to be looking, who should pull apart 'er curtains but our Mr Dominic.'

''E never goes in there these days,' she said indignantly.

'I'm telling you, gel, he was in there this morning, not half an hour past. Next thing is, 'e throws open the window. Then 'e appears again – with 'er. 'E's clutching 'er, and shouting something fierce. 'Course, I can't make out a word. She's fighting 'im and struggling in 'is arms. Then 'e carts 'er orf and I can't see a blind thing. No doubt 'e 'as 'er on the bed. 'E's a strong little devil, for all 'is small stature.'

'Yes, Arold, but 'e wouldn't rape 'is own wife, surely? There's not much fun in that. Rape's somethink gentlemen do with strangers.'

Arold lifted his best finger, speaking as one who had served in the forces of the Crown. '"Brutal unlicensed soldiery", my dear. A man's capable of anythink when aroused.'

'Oh dear.' She put a hand up to her mouth as if kissing a favourable view of mankind goodbye. 'Perhaps you should phone the police, Arold . . . No, don't do that. We don't want them round 'ere. They might arrest me as an orphan and vagabond.'

'Remember you're a female orphan, my dear, and as such incap'le of rape. No, what worries me – in my opinion a bit of rape would do our high-class Fenella no harm – is that this means us two have got the skids under us. Their marriage is breakin' up. If it's breakin' up, then this place'll be sold up. If this place is sold up, then we'll be chucked up. If we're chucked up, then we're fucked up. Aubrey can't 'elp us in 'is situation, poor old lad, and we aren't likely to find another billet good as this, not at our age. Not with three million unemployed.'

'Oh dear. What can we do? She is a hoity-toity piece and no

mistake. Perhaps a good rape will bring 'er to 'er senses. 'E's not still at it, is 'e? Shall I go up there and 'ave a look?'

Arold patted his wife's arm. 'No, no, a rape ain't like an ordinary bunk-up. It's over in a flash. A bunk-up's about sexuality, as you well know. Rape, now, that's about power.' He raised a clenched fist under her nose to demonstrate his meaning. 'Point is, 'ow can we save the situation?'

'Just let me think a minute, Arold. You talk so much.'

He shook his head at her, opening his mouth to show off his teeth to better advantage. 'It may be too late for thinkin', ducks. Last night when you was out, I 'appened to be passing the library and couldn't 'elp 'earin' our Fenella goin' on at 'im. I dunno what it was all about, I'm sure, but she kept on and on summink terrible. What I did gather was she had developed a strong dislike for the sexual act.'

Doris snapped her fingers. 'As we always suspected. Now, I've an idea. We've got to get that young Lucy Traill back, what she gave the sack to. Dominic was 'aving it off with 'er, wasn't he? That's why she got the push. So what does our lady do? Why she tries to wipe young Lucy out her mind as if she never existed, just like her little pekinese, if you remember that incident. Wipe her right out. So she chucks out every possible bit of paper with Lucy's name on. Including a rotten vicious letter she wrote to the hospital where Lucy works, demanding the sacking of an immoral woman destroying a happy marriage. That was her words.'

He looked at his wife suspiciously. 'How do you know all this, old love?'

'Ah. Because she wrote out the letter first to see how it went. Practice, like. Then she tore it up into four and screwed up the bits. But I found 'em in her waste-paper basket. "Immoral woman destroying a happy marriage". That's what she wrote.'

'Cow!'

'So I kept Lucy's address, you see, Arold. You could give it to Mr Dominic, he could get her back – or if not back, he could always meet her in secret, 'ave her as a mistress, if she was willing, of course.

Then he'd be happy and have reason not to fret about the deflects of his wife. So we'd stay on here and live happy ever after.'

He scuffed his boots on the ironstone bricks underfoot. 'You're a clever old dear. It might work. We could give it a try. Give us Lucy's address and I'll pass it on.'

He clasped Doris to him and gave her a kiss. 'Back you go now, ducks, before he catches us off duty. Chaps can be of funny temperament following rape.'

Dominic never knew what impulse prompted him to go to Fenella's bedroom that morning. Her door was not locked. Directly he saw her, he knew things were not as they should be. An open bottle of pills stood on her bedside table by other bottles, perhaps a dozen of them. Fenella was lying, mouth open, across the bed in her nightdress, head and arms dangling. Pills of various colours lay spilled on the sheets.

He called her name and ran to her. Her head fell forward as he lifted her, pulling her into a sitting position. Despite the central heating in the room, she was cold; for a fearful minute he thought she was dead. She groaned.

'Fenella!' Pronouncing her name, he found himself calling endearments, shaking her. Gasping, she put her hand limply to her throat, as if bringing to his attention how beautiful her neck and breasts were.

Not knowing what to do, he ran and threw open one of the windows. As he carried her to it, to give her fresh air, she began to struggle, to cry, and feebly to hit him.

'Leave me! Leave me!'

Even then, in his panic, he wondered why she was not saying, 'Leave me alone.'

They fought at the open window. He tried to make her walk about, but she slumped as if her legs were boneless, and struck out wildly. Dumping her on the bed, he phoned her doctor, Fay Mee.

By noon, Fenella was sitting up, drinking hot chocolate and looking more herself: or possibly less, for a kind of mirthless cheerfulness possessed her. Her colour had returned. She gesticulated more than usual, now and then throwing her hands to left and right, saying, 'What a shock for everyone! How the servants must have feared I was dead. Or perhaps they hoped I was. And you, Dom, poor dear, you must have run down at once to tell your friend Arold that I had gone for good.'

'No, Fen, I was too busy reviving you.' He had just been allowed back into the sick room.

She gave a strained laugh, appealing to Dr Mee with an artful turn of her head. 'And I expect Dom was just a little bit hopeful too, don't you, doctor?'

Fay Mee was an intense chunky person, short-haired and efficient. She belted herself into a business-like raincoat in preparation for leaving. Taking a pace nearer the bed, she tugged briskly at the duvet. 'Mr Mayor was intensely upset, Fenella, so don't let's have any silliness of that kind.'

'Ah ha!' The patient fiddled with her bed jacket. 'We can see whose side you are on! I suppose you secretly imagine I deliberately took too many Temazepam and –' she gestured coquettishly to her piled bedside table '– other little treats you have brought me.'

'There, there. You're still over-reacting, dear. Perhaps we'll cut down on some of the prescriptions.'

Fenella pretended to fall in with the suggestion. 'Quite right, doctor. It would serve me right, punish me. Forget all about my being in constant pain.'

When Dr Mee was ready to go, Dominic saw her out of the house and to her car, where she paused and asked him if he wanted a sedative.

'I'm fine. She didn't do it on purpose, did she? She was pretty strung up last night.' When Mee reassured him, he said hurriedly, in a low voice, 'I would like to ask your professional advice. Can it be that my wife is – well, two people, who talk in different voices? One perhaps a small girl? Isn't there a medical term for that, multiple personality or some such?'

She looked at him rather hard. 'Such things exist mainly in the world of fiction. I see many unhappy women, Mr Mayor, and frequently their bouts of depression spring from their husband's not caring for them. As for instance – being unfaithful, threatening to leave them, saying they love them no more. All such psychological acts have physiological consequences.'

Dominic clasped his hands behind him. 'Do you ever see any unhappy men?'

She got into her car. The gates opened for her and she drove away. Dominic walked about the lawn, trying to breathe deeply, while jumbo jets climbed steeply overhead.

Returning to the house, he found Arold lingering in the porch. He proffered a piece of paper on which was a name and address.

'I just found this blowing about the place, suh, and thought as it might belong to you, suh.'

At three thirty that afternoon, after shedding his car in the carpark, Dominic was sitting in the small office in the West London Hospital which Lucy Traill shared with other physiotherapists. He had been waiting twenty minutes when she arrived, pulling off a wet raincoat and dumping a Samsonite case on the desk on top of a pile of papers.

She looked at Dominic in no particularly friendly way.

He began with apologies. 'I can see you're busy but I didn't know how else to contact you.'

'Mr Mayor, I don't think we need have anything else to do with each other. I am, as you say, busy. The administrator showed me the extremely unfair and offensive letter your wife wrote, accusing me of immorality and destroying her marriage. Fortunately, we're used to neurotic letters. It was ignored, but that doesn't soothe my feelings.'

She regarded him stonily as he sighed. 'I looked after your wife for two years and I deserve better treatment than that. I don't want anything further to do with you or your wife.'

As she stood there, confronting him angrily, her face red, he dropped his gaze. 'I didn't do this. I didn't know this. I knew only she had unfairly sacked you. She told me yesterday. Any rude letter was nothing to do with me. I am innocent of this. It's terrible, terrible!' He felt impotently on the verge of tears.

'It's not terrible. It's just disgraceful. What are you doing here? I don't need your lousy apologies.'

He held out a hand to her, from which she moved away. 'Lucy – Miss Traill. I didn't want this to happen, I didn't know about it. I was away, I talked with your friend Clement Winter. I'm not involved.'

She gave a snort. 'God, you're a bit of a worm, aren't you? And to think I rather fancied you, seeing you in bed in your fancy pyjamas. Please get out of here and let me get on with my work. I have to see another patient in five minutes.'

'No. Wait. You may insult me, I understand your feelings. I mean to put this right, to show I'm deeply regretful at what has happened. He felt in his inner jacket pocket and produced a cheque book and pen. 'I'm sure we owe you payment.'

'Forget it. I don't want your money.' The blue eyes were bright with anger. 'You'll only add insult to injury.'

He stood with the pen at the ready, as if it were a sword. 'Perhaps you remember how this all started, Lucy – with you marching uninvited into my bedroom.' He spoke steadily, looking at her directly. She clutched her case and stared back. 'You got yourself into this trouble, and you know best what was in your mind at that time. Now, I shall write you a cheque for one thousand pounds in – what's the word, damn it? – in return for what you have suffered. Then that's the end.'

'A thousand pounds! You must be mad.'

As he stooped to the table to write the cheque, he said, 'No, I am not mad, Miss Traill, just sad. Very sad about this whole misfortune, because I came here hoping we might be friends. You have been unjust in your judgement.' In a moment of pride and pique, he made out the amount as two thousand pounds.

Accepting the cheque from him, she read it carefully. She blushed furiously. 'I don't know what this is all about. I'm ashamed to accept. But I do desperately need the bloody money.'

Hoping the gesture might in some way soften Lucy, he paused; but there was only shame to be read on her face.

'You might as well have it then. Money means not a thing to me.'

'Very well. What do I say?'

He pushed past her and closed the office door behind him. Leaving the bustle of the hospital, he walked out to where the car was parked. The rain had stopped, leaving the pavements of Hammersmith Road to glisten with an oily residue.

'Still for ever protesting your innocence, Dimitri,' he said.

Only a week earlier, one of the Squire family had been in the same West London Hospital. Jane Squire worked in a small business in a mews off Thurloe Place. The property had been a carriage-house in Edwardian days. Together with three men and another woman, she was part of a company called Astro Nought One, which devised software for CD-ROMs. The company had begun by devising shoot-'em-ups for arcade games. Now, with Jane's inspired input, they were moving up-market.

While wondering how to devise a sequence whereby a wizard turned into a dragon and then a butterfly, Jane was walking to work one morning from her two-room flat. As she crossed from the South Kensington tube station, a car hit her.

After several spells of drug-induced sleep, she woke to find her parents at her bedside in a one-bed ward. Her face was bandaged; she peered at her mother through one blackened eye.

'Nothing more serious than a broken leg, my sweetie,' Teresa assured her. 'That will heal and you'll be fine.'

'All your bruises will be gone in a few days,' Squire said.

She turned her face from him, sinking further down the bed. 'Let me alone.'

'We've brought you some flowers and grapes, darling,' said her mother.

'Go away. I know you're only pretending to care.'

She would not speak again. Outside the ward, a young Portuguese-American consultant, Don Barrieros, took Squire and his wife to one side, assuring them that their daughter was mildly in shock, nothing more. He patted Teresa's arm. 'She is my best patient, Lady Teresa.'

Teresa was shopping next morning. Her husband went to the hospital to sit for the best part of an hour by his daughter's bed. The flowers Teresa had brought the previous day stood in a vase on the window ledge. On his entry, Jane had turned her back, huddling up in the bed. While he made no attempt to disturb her, he hoped that his silent presence might provide some solace; faint was that hope, for the relationship with his younger daughter had never been an easy one.

She had left home early, dropping out of university, rarely returning to Pippet Hall, rarely communicating, except with her mother. Anxious for her well-being, Squire had made periodic checks through friends, and knew that Jane was making a name for herself in the shifting world of computer animation.

Thomas Squire had reason to feel melancholy, that cool London morning. A friend in the Foreign Office had phoned to say that an old friend, Vasili Rugorsky, had died in Moscow. Only three years earlier, Squire and Rugorsky had been together in Sicily. The Russian, Squire recalled, had looked unwell even then.

His thoughts were drifting when suddenly Jane turned in the bed, wide awake, wide of eye, angry, and said, with her distinct elocution, 'Why bother to sit there? You've never shown the slightest interest in me before.'

'I'm showing some now, Jane. The bruises on your face are healing, I see.'

'You see nothing.' She slammed her head down on the pillow again, while continuing to glare at him.

'What can we bring you? Books? Magazines?'

'My friends bring me all I need.'

After a short while, she said, almost as if communing with something inside herself, that he was sitting there enjoying acting the role of a fond father.

'I really am a fond father.'

'Baaa.' She made an angry sheep noise. He remembered her angry sheep noise. He sighed and sat tight, knowing more was to come. It would do her no harm to let it emerge.

'Oh, you doted on my sister but not on me. You were only interested in your career.' As she spoke, she gripped her sheet tightly, perhaps in some fear of his response to this challenge. 'I've had to lie here for hours and think it over, think it all over.' Then she came out with it, raising herself to say that he showed no interest in anything but his career, as if she had not uttered almost identical words the moment before.

Squire considered before replying. 'I enjoyed fame when it came my way, yes. For a while I felt that I was needed, was necessary. That I could somehow make the world just a trifle happier, make individuals happier. Maybe change the way people thought. Folly, I suppose. Hubris. But retribution came. Retribution is a dependable quality, with a reliable timetable.'

There was a silence.

'We girls were not such fools as you might think. We were only kids then, but we knew all about your bloody Laura. That surprises you, doesn't it, Daddy?'

He was rubbing his hands together. 'Of course I knew you knew about her. It was a tragic episode and I really cannot discuss it with you.'

'You had the affair but she really meant nothing to you.' Her tone was suddenly supplicatory, as if she was near tears.

'You're wrong there.' He shook his head, baffled by the way in which communication – of which an influential critic had called him a master – was so poor a medium for conveying any depth of meaning, particularly when that meaning involved gentleness, love, concern.

'My dear daughter, never think that anything that happens means nothing. If you have not yet experienced it, the time may come when you will love someone dearly yet find that love to be impossible. We are granted only so much.'

Jane's voice was gruff. 'You trying to make me sorry for you?'

He rose, took a pace or two, reconsidered, and sat down again.

At that moment, Barrieros put his head round the door and asked if everything was all right. Squire waved him away. The head disappeared.

'We both must feel this is a ghastly conversation, Jane. Under emotional stress, we might say things we could regret later. Or we might say things the other would misinterpret. Be sure I do love you greatly. You're my dear daughter – it cannot be otherwise . . . I may have been lousy at showing it. You have a good creative job, and that makes for happiness. Let me tell you that being a public figure, that holding forth on every possible subject, does not create happiness, only self-delusion.'

She levered herself up in bed as if coming more alive. 'Ann always said you had another occupation, a secret one.'

'Well, if it was secret, that is because it cannot be discussed.'

After she thought about that and decided not to pursue her accusation, she said, 'So what's so wrong with self-delusion? What I really hate is self-knowledge. It makes you see what a little worm you are.'

'Nonsense. That's just self-pity, which you must not encourage in yourself. It's bindweed in the garden of the psyche – as any gardener would tell you.'

His metaphor had made her smile, at least with one side of her face. 'Talking of bindweed . . . Why isn't Mummy here?'

He did not say what he suspected Teresa meant when she said she was 'going shopping'. He only knew she was quieter than usual after such expeditions.

'She's gone shopping. She'll be along soon. Then she and I will lunch at the Travellers' Club with some old friends. And we shall raise a glass to an old friend who just died in Moscow.'

'Did I know him?'

'No. Listen, Jane, if you can live without delusions, you'll be doing well. I popularize modern art, I promote all kinds of art, because I believe people secretly thirst for it, especially in a secular age. It took me some while to realize that I have no art in myself, none. Pontificating is a lesser thing, a substitute for art. Your mother's grotesque winged insects she makes are a better thing than anything I can do. I cannot paint, compose music, write.'

'Come off it, Dad. You've written several books.'

He shook his head. 'Nothing creative. Merely digestive.'

She gave him a sideways glance. The scorn had gone from her face. Only the bruises remained.

They held hands in silence.

Although Dominic had switched on the engine of the car, he did nothing more than sit in the driver's seat, letting half-thoughts and semi-feelings whirl like snow in his brain. The puddles in the carpark were filled with dead-fish colours of oil, blurring before his unfocused sight. The colours changed as rain fell again and turned to snow. Dominic closed his eyes against an immense roar filling the space, as of aero engines passing overhead or a train hurtling onward.

Frightened at last, he roused and stuck his head out of the window, ignoring the wind and speed. As he had anticipated, the woman stood rigid in the field, dwindling fast, her small boy beside her. Grief at a terrible lost chance took Dominic, distorting his vision. He waved frantically. 'Mother!' he called, but the small figure, black against the snow, made no response. 'Mother!' – again – but no sound uttered by human lungs could compete with the defeating definite onward machine progress.

The train ran on a curve, and the woman in the snow was lost from view behind the clattering carriages.

Rubbing his eyes, Dominic brought his head in and closed the train window.

Various stenches surrounding him reminded him of that cattle boat, Noah's Ark. Where had it been? Notions of space and time were hazy. When Lena and her Communist husband had taken him away from Dresden, they had made him leave behind all his toys, everything – including that precious little carved wooden Noah's Ark. He could have clung on to the Ark, or at least to the painting he was in the middle of – his little box of paints! – to leave that behind! – but this was the terrible lesson of life, that everything had to be left behind, paints, mothers, father, money – his Ark, with its little red roof and the giraffe looking perkily out of the top window, and that delightful curve of the bow rising from the spume, to curl back on itself in an ornamental yet practical way, like the unfolding of a fern leaf. Gone. Gone. The leaf would never properly unfurl.

He could smell the giraffe now, he thought, as he stood there in his little-boy breeches, disconsolate. The corridor of the express was choked with livestock: cockerel, pullets, an angular goat chewing a haversack, little black pigs of hirsute disposition, all guarded or not, as the case might be, by Vasili's cohorts, lounging, smoking, laughing, caring little for the ordure underfoot. Evidently a successful raid behind enemy lines had recently taken place. These boys knew that war was fun – better a soldier than a peasant. In the near compartment, so crammed was it with inebriated infantry that they had been forced to nurse an old tan cow across their corporate knees, and to swig their home-made vodka over the cordillera of her backbone; fun was in escalation mode.

The master of the revels stood nearby, conducting a long monologue through a fog of cigarette smoke. His cigarette blazed at the tip like a damp firework. Still struggling with grief and loss, Dominic, from the position of the man's knees, fur-booted, filth-caked, made bold to interrupt the disquisition.

'Why did you do that to her?' he asked Vasili. 'She'll die in the snow.'

His mother's first husband, unshaven rogue, it could be discerned through the smoke screen, was a tall gaunt man with a dark moustache and eyebrows curling sadly towards his dark, deep-set eyes. His square jaw bore a ragged scar. He wore a dirty white sweater under his Soviet greys. A hard man, but not a brutal one: indeed, he looked, at this moment, merely sorrowful, and slightly bizarre with a black-faced lamb draped over his right shoulder.

'Why did you turn her away?'

'An ancient Kirghiz saying puts it far better than I could, boy. "Good riddance to bad rubbish" – a piece of folk wisdom you might well bear in mind in your present circumstances. I did what I did because I love Ursula more than Lena. Ursula is more to me than all the stars in the heavens.' He delivered this inarguable statement in a deep voice, lending emphasis to each word in the sentence.

189

Ursula, the German woman he had made captive, sat beside him, a magnificent example of Prussian femininity, if slightly beady-eyed, arms folded in her fur coat, contemplating little unborn Dominic with detached interest. Beside her, propped up with a lot of other baggage, was a Nazi flag with a swastika at its centre, evidently one of the spoils of war, like Ursula herself. Although she wore a thick cloth skirt – perhaps part of a nursing uniform, he imagined – it had ridden up to reveal her plump, appetizing calves and thighs. To be taken into Ursula's orbit of ministration would be, he felt acutely, no small thing.

'You may understand some day,' said Vasili – not unkindly but implacably, as if reading from some sacred script – setting the lamb down gently on the floor of the compartment, as if for emphasis.

'You're a victim of circumstance. I'm not. There are certain key times in life when God Above gives a man a rare chance to decide his own fate. There are seven such times, one for each decade of your life. In all other whiles, we are in the hands of God Above, and he has charge over us, as I have charge of this lamb whose throat we shall be slitting tonight, and also this venerable clock here, worth millions, and appropriated from a certain Scottish manse of which you know, or will know after you are born.'

Vasili smote the clock to which he referred, which gave out a hollow bleat of protest. A carved stag's head protruded above its enamel face. The compartment was so loaded with loot, with oil paintings, carpets, water-closet pedestals, fire tongs, vacuum cleaners, chests-of-drawers, armchairs, and other prerequisites of civilization, including the grandfather clock the commander of the supply train had just struck, such as simple clean-living Cossacks had never encountered in their born days, that there was barely room to move. This congestion confused Dominic almost as much as the temporal convolutions contained in Vasili's statement. He shook himself, for a moment almost crediting himself with sitting in a white car in a carpark in Hammersmith; although this improbability was washed away in a flood of lamb urine over his right foot, as he attempted once more to grapple with Vasili in conversation.

'Excuse me, but I was told you were a Communist and believed in Lenin. I mention this because I am surprised at your reference to God.'

Unruffled, stroking Ursula's thigh, Vasili said, 'Oh, God Above you mean? I do believe in Comrade Lenin, and Lenin has charge of God Above.'

'Wait,' squeaked Dominic, terrified at his own courage in disagreeing with this eloquent giant. 'That can't be right. Surely Comrade God – I mean—'

Vasili swept away the objection with a dismissive hand. 'It has recently been scientifically proved in laboratories in Sverdlovsk-Petrovsk that Comrade Lenin thought about considerably more things than God Above; for instance, the rise of the proletariat. Whereas God Above in the main concerns himself throughout eternity with moral problems which by now are obsolete anyway. As the Kirghiz admirably put it, "Eternity is a hell of a long time." Why else are we waging this war? Say if my lamb's annoying you . . . But to continue with the main thread of my discourse, how many of those seven special times, those key times, have you already wasted in your short life?'

When no answer came from the boy, Vasili continued in his same calm, remorseless way, raising his voice only to counteract the terrible roar of the train, so closely resembling the sound of planes taking off from Heathrow. 'Your silence tells me that you have no awareness and no feeling for destiny. Our great Comrade Lenin had charge of destiny. He went aboard a train much like this one in order to deliver the Russian nation from its decadent capitalist Tsarist fetters. You will observe how easily victory fell into his hands. That was because Lenin had seized one of those seven vital times, those key times – recognized it and seized it, as I in a lesser way seized upon this tremendous Ursula here when I came upon her –'

'And raped her . . .'

'– And raped her repeatedly. Women on the whole dislike the act of rape, it being a violation of their bodies, particularly if it happens regularly. Ursula, however, has a very special attitude towards her body and, I must add, towards the bodies of men, regarding any embrace as a mystic union fore-ordained which, if accepted in the right spirit – and by that I don't mean with old-fashioned prayer, such as neither she nor I believe in, nor even in the spirit of any ideology, not even Marxist-Leninist dialectical materialism – but rather in the sort of mystical purgative spirit such as was understood in the Ancient World, long long ago – You understand my meaning, boy?'

'Not entirely, no. You mean she liked what you did to her?' Dominic glanced anxiously at Ursula as he made reference to her, but she remained immobile as ever inside her furs, not speaking, not moving, regarding him much as she might have regarded, say, her next meal.

'Ah, now there you touch on an entirely different matter. Suppose I take up this rifle –' Dominic had long been uncomfortably aware of the weapon Vasili now hefted in his leathery hands – 'and proceed to blow your brains out with it, with a single bullet – no, let's for vividness of argument say with a whole stream of bullets – then we would not say you enjoyed the experience, or could enjoy it, but you might nevertheless, if imbued with the spirit – thank you, meine liebchen . . .'

Ursula had suddenly roused, selected two black cigarettes from a silver cigarette case, lit them, and passed one to Vasili, which he stuffed into his mouth with the hand not balancing the rifle, while scarcely interrupting his discourse.

'. . . accept the metal into your person, which is to say your cranium, with a calm and positive spirit, embracing, so to say, the experience, turning negative force to positive.'

'As in the Ancient World?'

'Long long ago, boy, before men and women were ever thought of . . . Now how could I demonstrate the truth – the revealed truth – the positive force – of all this to such an ignorant unborn lad as yourself? Possibly the best way would be for Ursula to exhibit to you her sexual quarters, which are of a formation and beauty unrivalled, capturing entirely the great spirit of which I speak. No queen, not even Queen Cleopatra, who ruled over the lands of the Nile in ancient times, could boast such exquisite sexual quarters. Ursula, meine liebchen, show this young boy here your sexual quarters.'

The woman rose languidly from the bench, blinking her violet eyes against the smoke from the cigarette gripped between her lips. Balancing herself against the jolting of the train, she hitched her skirt still higher to reveal an absence of knickers. Dominic stared at her sexual quarters as if hypnotized; though bereft of speech, he felt inclined to agree that here was something monumental.

'There's amplitude,' said Vasili, admiringly, and indeed Ursula appeared to the boy's untutored eye to be generously endowed, not least with a curly mat of brunette hair, entangled like honeysuckle between the pale portals of her upper thighs.

'Aryan,' said Vasili, winking and giving one of the curls a tug. 'Pure Aryan. It gives you a new respect for Adolf Hitler.'

In order to demonstrate her delights more fully, Ursula, wreathing her head and shoulders in a fresh puff of smoke, opened her legs slightly. An index finger went down into the brunette curls. She hooked the finger into her nether mouth. Dominic was privileged to glimpse the pink satin lining thereof, though he could not avoid a notion that the lip involved was wrinkled in a sneer at his lack of manliness.

He gasped and leaned back in his seat. 'It is a beauty, miss,' he said, addressing Ursula for the first time while colouring slightly. 'It reminds me a bit of Mum's old tom cat.' She continued to regard him, skirts still hitched, smoke pouring from her nostrils as if she was afire with sexuality. 'I hope I can find one like that somewhere when I grow up. It is a real beauty.'

'But who are you to judge, young man?' asked Vasili, his voice growing slower and deeper. 'Judgement is evidently beyond you. You have asked me enough questions. It's my turn to ask you a few.'

Ursula smoothed down her skirts and resumed her seat, staring out of the train window as if she had lost all interest in the proceedings now that her part in them was over.

Leaning forward, Vasili grasped Dominic's shoulder to steady him for the questions. 'Do you see yourself, in your relationship with

Fenella, as a man walking alone down a street or as a splendid horseman, a Kirghiz, let's say, amongst whom I spent many memorable years, galloping over the steppe?'

'Well, put in those terms . . . It's hard to say . . .'

'Come, boy, no shilly-shallying. You'll grow up one day and have to face Fenella, realize that. It's fated in the cards, as Kirghiz women say. Which is it, street or steppe?'

'I'm no horseman.' He felt oppressed by the authority of this huge man, feeling instinctively that he would never grow up to be as formidable, or to recognize when they turned up those key times of which Vasili spoke. He would be the sort of fellow even lambs piss on. Looking miserably out of the window, he was not surprised to see that the little black figure of his mother was still there in the Polish field, disappearing, disappearing, for ever disappearing.

'I'd probably buy myself out of trouble.'

Vasili laughed and made rasping noises down his cheek. 'As I thought. Just as I thought. You're your mother's boy, or will be. You've no fight in you. Now, mark well what I'm going to say.' He grasped Dimitri by the throat, the better to secure his attention.

'Follow my example. Be ruthless. Never mind if you get shot in the end, like me. Defy circumstance. Seven times, seven key times.' He shook the unborn boy seven times.

'This is one of those key times. You have to kick Fenella off the train, Dimitri, that's what you have to do . . . Are you OK?'

A terrible knocking sounded in Dominic's right ear. At first he imagined that the monstrous clock was falling on him. He struggled to get free. When he looked out of the window, there was only a small anxious face staring in at him, rapping on the glass. 'Are you OK?' it asked again. 'Are you OK?'

The advice came once more, chilly now with distance: 'You have to kick Fenella off the train, Dimitri.'

'Jesus,' he said. His mouth was dry. He pressed a button and the car window slid down, allowing a gust of cool damp air to his cheeks.

'Are you OK, mate?' A small man in a porter's uniform stood against the car, looking in with an expression of concern: a normal

English careworn face with no additional extras in the way of features. He jerked his head in the direction of the bulk of the hospital behind them. 'I was coming off duty like. I saw you slumped over the wheel like . . . A lot of people get took bad after they've been visiting.'

'Thanks, I'm fine,' Dominic said. 'Thanks very much. Just a nap like. It's time I got home.'

He had always lived on the brink of terror, in fear of the things he was forced to remember and those he was unable to remember. The imagery of the speeding train, of Vasili with his gross desires, and of his mother-to-be lost in the snows of a foreign field – these were in part no more than embodiments of a submerged something greater than all of them, of which his translation across Europe had been an enactment. The great predatory train sped along a line of betrayal operative before his birth.

Sitting alone in his offices in Shreding Green, Dominic understood why he had been afraid to confide in Clement Winter. That submerged thing could not be allowed to see the light of day: it was a hatred of life itself, with all its inevitable betrayals.

This was why he had buffered his abridged week of consultation with a narrative which involved – no, not his own toils – the toils of his mother's drama before he had been born or conceived in a Dresden garret. His motives? Yes, self-protection certainly, to guard against some ultimate dissolution of self of which that submerged thing was a vital component. But also because his emotional life seemed to begin and end with a simple and terrible story of a defence-less woman being cast out into a foreign field.

That incident held a living meaning for Dominic. It foreshadowed what, years later, Lena had done to him. He had been left by her as callously as she by Vasili. Dumped on the wife of the man she was running away with.

He turned over these old coins of his existence, still not defaced by constant circulation.

The wonder was that he – well, not unlike Lena – had been spared. For the woman his mother had betrayed, Daphne Mayer, had proved a good woman: even in a Biblical sense a Good Woman. In her dwelt a legendary disinterested goodness. She had not acted out on that small deserted boy the anger and misery she must have felt.

It had been a kind of miracle. He owed everything to Daphne Mayer.

Now here he sat, contemplating leaving Fenella and his son. That was the next instalment of the narrative. He was about to act out the very essence of the drama of which he had fallen a victim: the compulsion to do so was strong enough to override any ethical scruple. And no less strong because it had as much to do with the past as with Fenella's difficult nature. The past never died, even the past he had not lived.

To his labouring thoughts came a memory of what he had read concerning child abusers. No crime was more despicable than a sexual crime against a child. Yet who were these profane people? Why, those who had been themselves abused in childhood. People under compulsion.

The undertow of his reflections brought him back to the psycho-drama he had endured in the hospital carpark. It was a mistake to humiliate Lucy Traill by throwing money at her. Or had his real motive been to pay her off, so that the temptation to break free of his sterile marriage would be lessened? To leave Fenella would be to humiliate her further. He could wrestle with the submerged thing in himself: it was familiar, his familiar. But Fenella – she had locked her incubus away inside her, had no communication with it. One day that fury would erupt. As cancer?

Shying away from the thought, he said to himself: But what ails her is a mental cancer. I hoped to assuage it. Perhaps I can yet. Or perhaps I can't. Either way, what do I matter? What if the future's as bleak as that Polish field . . . I can throw myself away without regret, yah.

Someone had to be by Fenella's side to help her. If not for her sake, for Malcolm's. He was that one, self-chosen. He had married her.

This was one of those key times of which the phantom Vasili

spoke. He had to struggle against his natural compulsion to escape. He must not throw her from the train of marriage.

Oh, he believed in divorce. But not for those filled with self-hatred. He could forgive himself only if he stayed with her.

This decision was reached slowly. By agonized catechism. Throughout a sleepless night.

Next morning, he phoned Daphne. At the weekend he drove to see her.

The Islington house was still the same. The front door was still the same. He recognized some of the scuffs on its paintwork, where children had kicked the door impatiently to get home to warmth and tea.

But the street had changed. A comfortable little corner shop had gone, making way for an office block. The large houses on the other side of the street, facing the terrace where the Mayers lived, had been turned into some sort of council flats. As Dominic parked, he saw a nurse come out of one of the flats and walk briskly down the street in the direction of the Angel Underground station.

Soon he was in No. 11, and his arms were round his adoptive mother. He always kept in touch with Daphne, had written to her occasionally, phoned her occasionally, given her and the children lunch in a restaurant occasionally, but it was almost three years since he had seen her. He had become too fascinated by the game of making money.

'I look an awful mess, Dom. Come and see what I'm doing.'

She was redecorating the bedroom where her two sons, Bill and Reggie, had slept. They were gone now. She explained that she hoped to rent out the room to a lodger.

'Do you need to take in a lodger, Ma?' he asked.

'Oh, you know how I like looking after people . . .' She laughed. 'I'll get someone nice. They'll be company.'

It gave him pleasure to recognize a Daphne Mayer response when he heard one. The real answer to his question was everywhere about him. Since he was last here, the house had grown smaller, dingier, and darker. At least there was objective reason for the increased dark. Daphne had to have an electric light burning in the kitchen; the new office block cast its shadow over the whole terrace.

Daphne was a plump, comfortable woman. Like her body, her face seemed based on the curve; she had round cheeks, a plum for a mouth, and a button nose. Perhaps she had never been beautiful, but it was a face he delighted to look upon again. She was now in her fifties, but – as he told her – still strong and as active as ever. Although she laughed at the remark without contradicting, he saw when they sat down together on the kitchen sofa with mugs of tea that she was tired. She still taught German at the local school. She also worked part-time in the local doctors' clinic.

Forgetting his own troubles, he gradually uncovered hers. She placed no blame on the authorities, but the fact remained that teachers' pay had not kept pace with rising inflation. She was a good deal worse off than she had been. Eric had ceased to send her money. She had no idea where he was, or if he was still with Lena.

Both Bill and Reggie had had problems finding work. Bill went from job to job, indifferently taking whatever came; he was hoping to get married – if he got a better job, 'if things improved'.

'He told me it would be better under this new government, but it's worse.'

Reggie had soon given up the struggle to work. He was now living – well, she was not sure where. Last she had heard of him, he was living in a squat in St Albans with some sort of pop group. Relating this, Daphne kept her gaze fixed on the carpet on which Dominic had once played on his hands and knees.

He could read her mind: she believed that Reggie had needed a man in the house to steer him through his early years.

'How's Crystal?'

Oh, Crystal was fine. She had the same job as before and the company was doing well. She earned quite good wages. No, she had no boyfriend at the moment – the last one had been a bit of a flop. Crystal worried about her firm's legality, fearing she might end up in court. The company sold armaments on the international market.

Its relationship with the Foreign Office was rather dodgy. But the Department of Trade and Industry continued to give out licences. Crystal suspected the directors of handing out bribes. What Crystal and Daphne, loyal citizens both, found it hard to believe was that apparently the government was quietly breaking its own arms embargo and permitting firms like Crystal's to sell to countries in the Middle East.

Daphne was a scrupulous person, going into this complex matter of her daughter's firm in some detail until Dominic grew bored. He made a fair percentage of his money from Israel and the Arab states, and believed in selling them anything they were foolish enough to purchase.

She perceived his restlessness and talked of other things. 'Do you remember when we took a trip to Yarmouth, just you and me?'

'Of course, Ma.' They beamed at each other. 'I painted a picture. I've still got it.'

She laughed. 'You ought to have kept up your painting. You could have been an artist. Crystal is quite artistic. Oh, I love Yarmouth – all those miles of lovely sand. And the Pleasure Beach. I suppose that's still there.'

'I had a ride on a donkey.'

'Best fish and chips in England. I'm sick of London, tell you the truth, Dom. Wouldn't it be nice to live in Yarmouth? Retire there? See the sea every day.'

'You'd never look at it if you lived there.'

'You were such a good kid. Have a little boarding house on the front. All painted white. Easier to keep things clean there . . .' She roared with laughter at the thought.

'No more German.'

'No more marking grubby exercise books. A dog perhaps. I always liked those little – what are they called?'

'Rottweilers?'

'No, you chump. Jack Russells. Cheeky little dogs. You know.'

Crystal came home. She was the child among the Mayer offspring who most resembled her mother, with her pretty round face and sparkling eyes. Once, she had teased the life out of Dominic. Nowadays they were on a different footing. She was twenty-three and attractive to him. On impulse, he invited her and her mother out for a curry at a nearby Indian restaurant.

He forbore to mention his own painful decision. Just being with Daphne again was comfort enough. And the meal was relaxed and enjoyable.

As the two women accompanied him back to where the car was parked, Daphne signalled to Crystal. Making a moue to show dislike of her mother's hint, Crystal kissed Dominic's cheek and walked off briskly in the direction of No. 11. He saw her go with regret.

Daphne took Dominic's arm, making him walk more slowly. 'I know you've got trouble with Fenella, Dom. You've never mentioned her once. Can I give you a bit of advice? You'll think me mad.'

He did not try to pretend. 'I'll be glad of any advice, Ma. I know you never took to Fen. I certainly need some help just now.'

She stopped a few yards short of the car. 'Pray.'

When he looked at her in astonishment, she smiled and repeated the word. 'Pray, Dom. I don't believe in God any more than ever I did. But I do believe in prayer.'

'One without the other? You must pray to God, yah? You can't just pray to . . . no one.'

'Dom, I'm telling you this most feelingly.' Looking at him with a worried expression, she clutched one of his hands. 'I know it's not the sort of thing people usually go on about. But we two are different, aren't we? I couldn't – wouldn't dare say this to my other sons. I don't believe in God, still can't make myself believe. But I pray to him.

'It's not God that's important. It's the prayer. There's my discovery. My secret. We live in a hard materialistic age with little place for God. But prayer sweetens up life and strengthens us. It has sweetened and strengthened me.'

He was embarrassed. 'Ma, I know life's difficult for you—'

'Nothing that can't be borne,' she said firmly. 'What prayer does – praying aloud – is concentrate the mind. You have to formulate in words what you desire, what you must do next. "Oh Lord, make me as kind to the naughty boys in the class as to the good, to the stupid as to the clever." That sort of thing. Then you know. Then you're clear in your own mind. You're really addressing your higher self. Provided you have one. Maybe prayer encourages a higher self to develop. Anyhow, it works. Next time you're about to be angry with a lout of a boy, you remember your prayer. 'Cos that prayer contained what you really wanted. So you aren't angry.'

Dominic looked away from her. 'Yes, but – what you say, Ma – well, we know prayers don't work.'

She gave a strained laugh. 'You think I'm turning into a religious freak in my old age? Not a bit of it. I'm just telling you prayer works. If all the people in the world got down on their knees today and prayed for a better world, on Monday we'd have a better world. Go back to Fenella. Do as I say. Be brave. Dear Dom.'

They embraced in the street. He kissed her cheeks. As he had done so often in the past. Then they parted.

But if Dominic had come to a decision, so had Fenella.

She was returning to Scotland as soon as possible.

He responded to the announcement in his usual conciliatory fashion.

'Fen, I know I have offended you. I'm sorry. I sometimes don't know my own mind. Just let's forget some of our little problems, shall we, and try to start again? I do love you – you know that really.'

She was standing in the north reception room holding a glass vase. She gave Dominic one of her searching stares, almost as if she had not heard, before setting the vase down.

'What's all this leading up to?' Folding her arms across her chest, defensive, looking beleaguered.

Dominic gave a nervous laugh. 'Well . . . it's leading up to . . . whatever you like. Depends on you. Can you hear the – Fen, the implications of my words, is that what you call it, not just the words?'

'Why does this have to depend on me so much? It wasn't my idea we should part. I've always been faithful to you.'

He sighed. 'Let's sit down and talk, shall we?' When she picked up the vase again, he took it from her hand and placed it on a side table.

She sat down meekly as instructed, crossing her legs and leaning forward with an arm raised defensively across her chest. 'I'm tired of seeing that expression on your face, Dom. Why don't you cheer up and realize how lucky we are? We shall be able to get Fuarblarghour estate into working order again. Stirrup and Dower say there were fishing rights in Loch Awe which have been allowed to lapse, but can be revived. And the old farm, Fuarblarghour Farm—'

He raised a cautionary finger. 'It is exciting that you have come into this inheritance. But there is something we must put right first of all. You know what I mean. A terrible coldness between us – a quarrel. We must try to ease that situation before we even discuss to go to Scotland to live. Isn't that so? Obvious, yah?'

It was as if she was a long distance away in the big white room.

'If you refuse to come up to Fuarblarghour, the quarrel, as you call it, will never be settled. You just want to get rid of me. You want me to go up there where I belong, alone with Malcolm. Don't deny it.' She gave him a sly look, a mixture of tease and hatred. 'When I'm gone, you can see as much of Lucy Traill as you want. The truth is, you have ceased to be interested in me.'

Letting out a wild, bitter laugh, Dominic said, 'Don't start that again. I'm still interested in you, Fenella! Jesus, yes! I'm interested, yah – as I am in life and death – I just can't get through to you.' In a fit of desperation, he rushed over to her so that she flinched back in the chair. He merely flung himself at her feet and clutched her dress.

'Fen! Please! Stop this internal game you play. You are caught in a web of your own making. I see it, I see it clear. Confess.' He buried his face in his hands, saying to himself, How can prayer stand against all this? I travel through this stony wilderness. Rejection. Death of the soul. I don't stand a chance. Can I take much more? She is – she lost something, something in her was poisoned by that mother . . . Better if her mother had left her, jumped into Loch Awe.

He broke into whatever she was saying. The truth was, he hated to hear her talk. A conversation with her was pretence. The custom of loving her had been eroded, a knife-blade worn thin on a grindstone. 'I shall not hurt you. I just wish you to see that you make your own difficulties. This is such pain. All pain. Please, Fenella . . . I'm afraid of you, because whatever I say to you is twisted in a way to hurt us both. Stop it, break free, why can't you, when I'm here to support you? I know of a quite famous psychotherapist in Oxford. Let's go together to him and let him help us.'

Something in her face closed, and he saw it. The line of her jaw altered.

Later, he thought that among all the waste of moments, the desert of their life together, this point was a decisive one. His offer to bring in an outsider convinced her of a conspiracy against her. For that was what she now proclaimed, mouth narrow and bitter in a hard face. When she asked him if he had spoken of her to this person in Oxford, it seemed to Dominic wiser to answer Yes, not to lie yet again. That for her was the needed confirmation. He had been talking about her behind her back; all that she had feared was now out in the open.

He had betrayed her. It could never be explained, but he had betrayed her.

Just for a moment, staring at her face to face, he seemed almost to catch her thought, to penetrate through to the conceptual world of Fenella Cameron, the bleak land through which she was destined to travel. A prevailing wind would always be blowing against her. There could be no joy here. Equally, with feelings deadened by cold, there was no pain.

Anyone who appeared over her horizon was axiomatically an enemy. Despite the passions they had enjoyed before they were married – those passions soon to wilt so inexplicably – hers was a strangely asexual world: and, because without sex, without colour. Those she loved most, being phantom-like without colour or character, could never be allowed in close. They carried a general contamination. This was a frigid land: all there was to stand against it was will. And the will could not be trusted; it too might fail. But as yet it kept her moving towards magnetic north.

'You have prepared this Oxford person,' she was saying. 'You talked to him secretly. This silly plan you speak of. Of course he will be on your side.'

His attempt at a placatory smile was a mockery. She saw that.

'It isn't a question of sides. The man's a psychotherapist.' He sighed, wondering whether it was worth the effort of going on. His will too would fail. 'If it was a question of sides – look, I come over to you, to your chair. I'm at your feet. I'm begging you. I'm at your feet, look, Fen, damn you. When would you ever come across to me? I'm on your side. Why don't you see this?'

'You have been talking about me secretly behind my back. You admit it. This person will know all about me. He will be against me, like all the others. I saw the way your friend Colin Cohen looked at me. Don't think I don't see the way those servants of yours look at me – the horrible Betts you like so much. How he looks at me. He treats me with contempt, just like everyone else. It's quite clear to me why you employed him and his wife in the first place – I've seen through that.' She gave a queer little laugh. 'I've seen through a good many things this last year.'

'Do you wish us to be together or not? Tell me that.'

The train roared on down the track.

'Oh, I've seen through your plan. Betts is here to watch me, to keep me imprisoned in this horrible place with the planes hovering overhead. Lock me up, chain me, beat me! You don't care anything for me, you just want me prisoner. Yesterday there was an IRA bomb outrage in the centre of London. I saw it on TV. Oxford Street was closed. Some poor woman carried off on a stretcher. It could be Shreding Green next time. Do you care? Do you want to see me dead, carried off? We'll all be blown up. We'd be safe in Fuarblarghour, but that doesn't suit you—'

'Hush, Fen. The Irish aren't after us. Don't be silly.'

'Betts is probably Irish. Hired secretly, like this man in Oxford. I've read of such things. You've seen them marching. It's peaceful in Blarghour. But of course you have your plan, you will do as you like—'

He jumped up. She was already launched on a sick monologue. 'Stop it, Fen. Stop it at once. You know what you're doing, you're killing our marriage.'

She leaned back in the chair, laughing at him without humour, mouth open, eyes stony. 'Marriage, what marriage? I've never meant a thing to you. You don't even like me.'

He spoke very quietly, his face white. 'Fenella, I can't go on pretending for ever. You are mad. Destruction is somehow in your brain.'

'Oh yes, you always blame me . . . I know it's my fault. I'm always in the wrong. You think I'm drugging myself. You'd like me to kill myself, wouldn't you, just because I'm worthless? Just because I failed once . . . Shall I do that, Dom, shall I? Would you like me to be dead and gone? A small thing carried away in the river?' Her lips were dry, flecked like a beach with a dry white foam.

As he rushed from the room, he found Arold polishing a bronze in the hall. The man gave him a sympathetic wink. 'Don't take no notice, Mr Dominic. They're all the same, yak yak yak. Don't mean nothink.'

Fenella was not deflected by her husband's behaviour. She dismissed him from her mind and went about her preparations for the move to Scotland and Fuarblarghour. Much packing was needed. Everything had to be washed. She was scrupulous about the washing. Many things had to be washed more than once.

At this time of crisis she was extra kind to young Malcolm, greeting him when he came back from infant school; hugging and kissing him. She told him how exciting it would be in Scotland, with a whole eighty acres of their own to roam in. And in one of the outhouses was an ancient tricycle which she had ridden when she was a small girl; it would be his. She would buy him a pony. There used to be ponies. She meant to hire a ghillie and go shooting.

'Will Daddy come and see us?' Malcolm asked. 'He doesn't like shooting.'

She fondled him again. 'Oh, I'm sure he'll come and visit now and again. The air is so good up there. You could climb Beinn Breac. You may see an occasional stag. One day when I was small, my father took me fishing on Loch Awe, Malcolm. It was so lovely. Just the two of us. I've lost my scissors. The cook had packed a splendid picnic basket for us with hot coffee in a silver thermos, and I remember we had salmon and cucumber sandwiches. That was the first time I ever tasted wine. Daddy let me have a sip. Ugh, I hated it. I've never touched the stuff since. He did laugh at the face I pulled.'

'Was Grannie there?'

'I told you, just Daddy and I. He recited a Robbie Burns poem. I sat on his knee and he recited to me. We didn't get home till it was dusk and everyone was in such a panic in case we had drowned. I mustn't use that word. It was so silly. I knew I was safe with Daddy.'

'Did you catch a lot of fish? Did you visit the castle, the old ruined castle? Is it haunted?'

'Of course not. There's no such thing as a ghost. Though a lot of men were killed there in a siege.'

'How many? Was there a lot of fighting and blood? What were they fighting about, Mummy?'

'We shall have to look up the history when we get there. Oh, we'll have such fun. You'll see.'

Malcolm peered into the case she was filling with towels. 'We better be sure to pack all my toys. We don't want them left behind.'

'Yes, dear,' she said vaguely, stooping to sort through the bottles in the drawer of her bedside table. Taking up a small brown bottle, she shook two red and white bombs into the palm of her hand, transferring them into her mouth. 'We'll leave nothing behind worth having.'

Standing in his offices at the top of the house, Dominic watched his assistants down in the garden, as they climbed into their cars and drove off one after the other. It was late afternoon. His mood was sunken. There was a sullen pleasure in neglecting his work, as he had done recently. The assistants, both bright and younger than Dominic, had commented neutrally on his lost enthusiasm. He knew they would leave soon, equipped with the knowledge they derived from him, perhaps to establish their own businesses. Well, let them go. To hell with them.

A stand of trees showed over to his left, their fine bare branches reaching up into the sky. Lights began to spangle the unestablished landscape visible from where he stood. Darkness was setting in. The sky was everywhere grey with mottled cloud, except behind the entanglements of the copse, where the setting sun showed through.

He tried to think of the English word for that colour, not quite yellow, not quite orange, not quite gold. And how you would paint it, suppose you were the painting kind.

While he stood there, the car he was awaiting arrived. The gates stood open for it. He identified it as a Bentley before turning from the window and making his way downstairs to greet the visitor.

Bruce Dower of Stirrup and Dower, the prominent solicitors of George Street, Edinburgh, and London Wall, was a son of the founder of the firm. His father had acted as solicitor for the Cameron family, as he now acted for Fenella Mayor. However, it was Dominic who had summoned him on this occasion.

Arold had shown Dower into the hall by the time Dominic got there. Taking Dower over, Dominic led him to the library, and explained the situation to him before Fenella arrived.

While listening, Bruce Dower folded his arms and allowed his head to turn in a complete survey of the room, rather like a falcon surveying a barren field. Dominic became conscious of the poverty of his library. The built-in shelves he had inherited were filled on one wall by calf-bound eighteenth-century theology bought by the yard, never read, never opened. Cheap ornaments decked the other sets of shelves. He pulled nervously at his beard while addressing the solicitor.

Dower was a man of late middle age; he kept his precise years to himself, as he kept many other confidences. The suit, the striped shirt with button-down collar, the discreet tie, the general air of a man being encased rather than merely clothed, all proclaimed someone accustomed to keeping confidences. Dower's manner was always guarded, almost cold, despite the hectic colour bannered across his cheeks and the bridge of his nose. This bridge was high, and gave him a hawk-like appearance, not entirely undeserved. It was apparent nothing would ever shake his equanimity.

Dower looked down at Dominic, observing but making no observations.

'Would you like something to drink, Mr Dower?'

'Thank you. A dry sherry would be appreciated.'

Dominic poured two sherries. He found his hands were trembling. The moment had come to stage this crucial meeting. Fenella's and his future would be decided. He began to wonder whether he was equal to the task. Prayer or no prayer, he could not convince himself that he had the will any longer to continue with Fenella. Yet he loved her. Whatever kind of love it was – and that desertion in the snow before he was born lent its overpowering colour – it operated on him still. He loved her because of what once had been. But he could no longer breathe her atmosphere: it was too chill even for him.

As he and Dower raised their glasses, the lawyer said, 'I am here as you requested, Dominic. But I should remind you that I am engaged as solicitor by your wife.'

Dominic was diminished by the way in which Dower pronounced his first name, as if reading a sermon from a pulpit. It hinted at condescension rather than intimacy.

'We – Fenella and I – we have a marital problem, Mr Dower, yah.' He was not certain he had pronounced the word 'marital' correctly, confusing it with 'martial'.

After a pause, Dower said, 'Fenella has informed me that you intend leaving her.'

'That was said, yes, in the heat of the moment. Unfortunately.'

'In effect terminating the marriage. And do I understand that, now Fenella has inherited considerable wealth, you wish to retract that statement?'

Dominic flushed with anger. 'That is not to be understood. Not at all. If you think that, you make a mistake. Her inheritance makes only a difference to her, not to me. In any case, I have no interest in the Fuarblarghour estate. Plus the fact that—'

He was about to say that he was richer than his wife. A kind of pride prevented him. He was overwhelmed with confusion. Taking a pace back, he said, 'Well, you will see, you will understand, when Fenella appears. She's upstairs. Perhaps I shall enquire what keeps her.'

Rushing from the room, he encountered Fenella in the hall. She was wearing one of her mother's tweed suits, and had draped a plaid shawl about her shoulders. The mothbally smell of these garments had been damped down with a dose of perfume.

'I've come since you asked me, Dom,' she said with her usual neutral air. 'But I'm really unwell. Is Bruce here? Perhaps Doris will bring me some coffee, if she's about.'

She entered the library and talked for a while with Bruce Dower, the subject under discussion being mainly a disputed right of way through the Fuarblarghour estate. She spoke with some animation and every appearance of being friendly with the solicitor. Watching, Dominic thought that any onlooker would take her for normal – but then, perhaps the poor girl is normal and I'm mad. He read her every gesture, and knew she was dosed with drugs. But he too had had a snort beforehand, to help him through this occasion.

Fenella, while talking, went over to seat herself in the most uncomfortable chair in the room, a large wooden construction vaguely resembling a coffin. Morna had presented this piece to her daughter when the latter married. It had belonged originally to an earlier Morna, a member of the Wilson family, who drowned during an Italian holiday. As Fenella seated herself, she became framed in a wooden hood. It narrowed over her towards a small shield on which, set in a scroll, was carved the word 'Beloved'. It was a translation of the Gaelic name Morna.

The discussion of the Fuarblarghour right of way was concluded.

Dower nodded his head in a way that emphasized the immobility of the rest of him. He would tackle the local legislation immediately.

Dominic took this opportunity to invite Bruce Dower to sit down. Dower, however, preferred to stand. He commanded the field, his hands clasped behind his back in a manner perhaps intended to remind Dominic that handcuffs existed in British society. He lowered his gaze to the white carpet as Dominic went and sat in a scarlet armchair opposite Fenella's coffin.

Dominic rubbed his hands together, demonstrating unconsciously that the gyves were not clapped on yet.

'It's good of you to come here, Mr Dower,' he said. 'I appreciate what you say, that you are Fenella's solicitor and not mine. I regard that as an advantage. You see what I mean? An advantage. I need a witness and I wish to have got a few things correct. Things, I mean, between Fenella – matrimonial things—'

'Take your time,' said Dower, his gaze penetrating.

This piece of condescension steeled Dominic's nerve. 'My problem is not with time. It's with English grammar. You will have patience with me as a foreigner, yah? The important thing is her and me.' He pointed at Fenella as he spoke. 'She is making life impossible for me – driving me crazy, I can say it. So, you have to listen. That's what I request from you. I wish to tell her in your presence –' here he swerved to look full at his wife – 'that I love her, that I do not wish to break apart our marriage, whatever was said in past times.'

Fenella said coldly, 'Bruce, you see, he's trying to trap me. He's so cunning.'

'No, no, I'm not cunning. I'm a simpleton, Fenella. Only clever at the computer. You know it. At all else a simpleton. At human relations a simpleton. That's why I cling to you. I found you, you found me, remember, when we were young, innocent, when I was still living at Daphne's house. You know it. Those dark streets. And I – so lost, left by my mother. Don't you remember how we loved, how I admired your – what is it? – poise, your face when it was gentle and soft? That can't be left behind, I won't let it.'

'But you refuse to come up to Fuarblarghour with Malcolm and me.' She shrank back into the chair, so that her face was obscured, so that the upper part of her body was in shadow, as if she would fade altogether from life. 'You're trying to trap me with your words. I don't understand why you lie to me all the time. I know you don't love me.'

Abandoning the sanctuary of the scarlet armchair, Dominic went across to her and sat at her feet. 'No, no, Fenella, the more you say these things the more it chokes me. You push me away when you say them. See, will you, please see I am in two minds. Yes, I admit it, I am tortured in two minds. I wish to be close and I wish to escape away when you are cold like this.'

He had forgotten Fenella's solicitor, who all this time stood cool and solid by the bookcase, occasionally raising or lowering his head, presumably to score a point with himself in some internal register; but otherwise refusing to be part of any scene where emotions broke loose. Nor did he do more than steer his head a few degrees to one side to observe what followed when a knock came at the library door.

What followed was Doris, bearing a silver tray. On the tray were coffee pot and cups. She came half-way into the room, proceeding with her usual series of bounces, then stopped. Her mouth fell open at the sight of Dominic, who had made no attempt to rise, kneeling by Fenella.

Still holding the tray, she made a half-turn towards Dower, addressing her remarks to him, instinctively recognizing the senior authority in the room.

'Ooh, Mr Dominic there on his knees! What a bit of luck I hoovered this carpet last week, or whenever it was. Anyhow, ever so sorry to interrupt. Do go on with what you was doing and I'll just set this coffee down for you. All nice and fresh brewed.'

Making a great performance of it, like a maid in a stage farce who grabs her one opportunity to shine, Doris dragged tables about and made various attempts to dispose of the tray until Dominic told her to leave everything. Still talking, she backed towards the door, dropping one final remark at the solicitor's feet as she went.

'I was brought up an orphan, sir, you understand, so many apologies for int'ruption and do give us a ring if there's anything else.'

Dominic had risen and went back to his previous post. He hung his head so as to study his watch.

The procedure of pouring coffee gave Fenella a little authority. She spoke directly to her solicitor. 'As you will be aware, we have another orphan in the room, Bruce. Dominic was brought up in the back streets of Islington. Fuarblarghour is an historic seat – a gentleman's seat. I am offering him the chance to leave the squalid environs of London – Shreding Green is almost as bad as Islington – and become a gentleman, engaging in gentlemanly pursuits. He refuses, as you see.'

The solicitor's head went up so that the broad blunt chin pointed at Dominic. Fenella's stricture had registered.

'As I see.'

'But this is not the – it's not . . . the point at issue. That's right? This whole business of Fenella's inheritance comes late to the argument. First is the estrangement.' Dominic paused. If only he could provoke Fenella into one of her sick monologues, the solicitor would see he was trying to stand by his wife, despite the odds against him. 'I don't know this excuse of being a gentleman. How can I ever be a Scottish gentleman as she would like? It's impossible, all would agree.'

'You have no wish even to try,' she said.

He leaned forward. 'Very well, Fen, then let's try something over shorter distances than Scotland. I gladly came across the few metres between us to your chair, to kneel at your feet, to tell you I love you still. Now, you come across to me, will you?'

She regarded him, as if waiting for something.

'Come on, Fen. Come across to me. I don't ask you to kneel as I did. I don't ask you to say you love me, as I did. I don't try to tax your pride, yah? All I ask is for you to make an approach.'

Looking puzzled, Fenella shook her head dismissively. 'Don't be silly. Why should I? I have nothing to say to you in your present mood.'

'OK. OK. But still just come. For the proof. To show you can. Just these few short metres. Please, Fen. For me. To show you still care, you sleepwalker.'

She sighed impatiently and addressed her solicitor. 'This is the kind of thing I have to endure. Names. All the time he challenges me, says he'll leave me, says he doesn't love me . . .'

Dower said, in a level voice, as if not asking a question, 'Do you find what he is asking of you now so particularly challenging?'

A flush of anger showed on her sallow cheek. 'You don't expect me to fall in with what he wants, do you? When he refuses to join me in Fuarblarghour?'

'Fen, it is easier to cross the carpet as an act of love than to throw up my business and go to Scotland. Have some sense.'

'You have no wish to try,' Fenella said coldly. 'You hate Fuarblarghour. I know it. Don't deny it. You are not worthy of the trust I placed in you when we married. You're like everyone else. I know your plan. Doris had no business in here. You're trying to make Bruce hate me, make me the laughing stock of Stirrup and Dower. You would humiliate me by making me come to you like some puppy dog. Well, I'm not your puppy dog. The Camerons don't behave like that. People keep up pretences of loving you. Cruel! Cruel! It was just the same at school – fair words, foul pretences. Believe me, I wasn't fooled once.'

She was gazing into the distance now.

'I met someone – I have held her in my arms, I so trusted her, yes, gave myself to her – oh, when I think how she fooled me! – and I could have drowned, yes, drowned with her, right down to the bottom of the loch, and when they pulled us out I'd still be holding her, my arms tight about her, pressed to her body. Then I found out how worthless she was. Mother showed me. Immediately—'

Bruce Dower set himself in motion and crossed to a position between the husband and the wife, from whence he could look down on both of them, as one come to judge the living and the dead.

'Getting down to the present case, Mrs Mayor,' he said. 'Getting to the present case, it is my duty to remind you that your husband has stated a) that he loves you, and b) that he has no wish to break up the marriage. He retracts whatever he may have said on that subject in the past.'

Fenella had raised her hands to her face. She continued to talk in low, rapid tones, ignoring the solicitor.

'It's always the same. The little hypocrite, she cared so little for me – whatever she said, she really cared for Jamie more. Oh, their lies, their tricks.'

'Excuse me, Mrs Mayor, but what we have here is something of a different case. Mrs Mayor!'

He spoke in peremptory tones. Fenella had shrunk back into the Beloved chair, her hands folding over her chest, so that, if canted backwards through ninety degrees, she would have appeared ready for the sexton. In anticipation of that dignitary's arrival, she relapsed into silence, lips and eyes closed.

Dominic came over to regard her with concern. Both men, looking down on her, heard her faint whisper, 'Go away, I'm ill . . .'

There was no doubting that Dower had interrupted the beginning of a sick monologue. When Dominic lifted her hand, she made no response.

'Jesus,' he said, 'what am I to do? Sometimes she will talk for one hour, two hours, all I suppose in . . . I don't know what. A different person speaks. What am I to do?'

'It's not within my brief to offer you advice, Mr Mayor,' said Dower, making himself an extra inch taller, and his voice a shade quieter, to show respect to the corpse, 'but I would suggest ex officio that a) you call a doctor, and b) though you must understand from this moment on that I have never said what I am about to say, I would consider your best course of action is to permit Mrs Mayor to retire to her estate in Fuarblarghour. Alone.'

'With Malcolm?'

'Accompanied by the child. Bearing in mind I have not said whatever you believe you have heard me say.'

These chill official words went like a dagger to Dominic's heart, producing not blood but tears. To his shame, he found himself weeping in front of the solicitor. Dower ran his tongue round between his teeth and his lips, continuing to study Dominic.

Fenella came to life with a terrible scream. She jumped up from her coffin-like chair.

'Liars! Traitors! Have you no pity? I heard you whispering together. I can't trust any of you. Pretend to love me, serve me! You're all against me. Well, I'll stand no more. The worm has turned at last. Get out! Get out!'

Waving her skinny arms above her head, she gave every appearance of being demented. She rushed at Dower, succeeding in knocking over the coffee tray, which fell to the floor with a crash. A dark stain spread across the carpet. The accident brought Fenella's activities to a halt. She stood there looking blank, as though totally unaware of what the three of them were doing in this room.

'Well, I will take my leave of you, Mrs Mayor, thank you,' said Bruce Dower. 'Perhaps we should talk again tomorrow. If you care to give me a ring. Or I shall be going up to Edinburgh on Thursday. Thank you for the coffee. Good evening, Mr Mayor, thank you.'

With these courtesies, he bowed slightly and moved towards the library door. Dominic hurried after him.

They emerged into the hall in time to see Arold and Doris scuttling for cover. Perceiving he was spotted, Arold called out, 'Sorry, Mr Dominic – thought I heard a scream. Must of bin the wind. Sorry!' He scudded out of sight.

Dominic, feeling a compulsion to leave the house, followed Dower out towards his car. As if touched however remotely by Dominic's unmanly display, Dower made a tut-tutting noise and wiped his forehead with a folded handkerchief.

Then he offered an unexpected remark. 'Suppose you think we English hard-hearted?'

Swallowing back a last sob, Dominic replied, 'I am English.'

They reached Dower's car. Dower unlocked it and climbed in. Sudden fear and anger took Dominic, to think the man was going away without further comment. He stuck one of his small feet in the way of the car door.

'Look here, I know you think it is not your bloody professional business to comment like a human being, but I want to know what you think of Fenella. You saw a bit of what she's like – really like. I can bet you never met anyone like that before, yah?'

The legal face, with its flush of colour across the high bridge of the nose, craned itself up at Dominic, with a fresh touch of the hawk.

'I am empowered to act only for your wife, as you are aware. It may be that when and if legal proceedings are instituted, Stirrup and Dower will be instructed to act against you. Pending that eventuality, there can be no further communication between us. I must advise you, moreover, that anything I have witnessed here this evening – irrespective of the fact that my firm will be submitting their account for my services – I cannot have witnessed, and have not witnessed. However, I wish to assure you there is and will be no personal animus in the matter. You understand my meaning?'

Dominic nodded. 'I see it. Jesus. That answers my question.'

'Not so. It answers only the first part of your question. To answer your second part: I take it you are no reader, from the impoverished state of your library shelves. When I am not involved professionally, which is rarely, I read the English classical novelists – Fielding, Austen, Reade, and so on; to use an old-fashioned phrase, they improve the mind. Should you ever have occasion to take up Charles Dickens's novel *Little Dorrit*, you will discover there a minor character, Miss Wade. Miss Wade is characterized by Dickens as "a self-tormentor". It may well be that you will be struck by the resemblances between Miss Wade and certain living persons with whom we are both acquainted . . . Good evening, Mr Mayor. Good luck.'

The Bentley pulled slowly through the manor's electronic gates and drove away in the direction of the M4. Dominic stood watching it go before turning back to the house.

The dogs in their caged runways were barking furiously. In the blackest mood, Dominic slammed the front door shut behind him. That bastard Dower, full of middle-class snobbery, barely concealing his contempt, telling him to read Dickens at a time like this. Why, he

216

could probably buy up that rotten firm of solicitors and close it down and put Bruce Dower out on the street – together with all those old books which so improved his mind.

Dower was ideal for Fenella. The blinkers were torn from Dominic's eyes by what had transpired. OK, the meeting had not gone as he hoped. What had he hoped? But he saw there was no possible future for him and Fenella together. Whatever he'd previously decided, it was better to let her go off with the boy. She'd be happier. She'd be free. It was undeniable that he was now reduced merely to nagging and accusing. He felt too bitter. She'd worn him down. She'd eaten his fucking heart out.

He had never said, had never had the courage to say outright, 'You must learn to hate your mother.' He should have said it. He owed it to her. But over and above that disease of the mind conveyed through the proud family line was that more prevalent British disease, the scourge of class. He had not realized that she hoped for him to become a gentleman. She had always regarded him as . . . well, he did not understand this nebulous thing: you had to be born to it. Was it how he spoke, how he held his knife and fork? Was there something wrong with his secondary school? Was being an orphan in itself a crime in her eyes?

It was something he would never understand. Something that made Fenella feel even worse, even more like a worm.

She had been taken up by some preposterous dream. Morna's Will was her last strike against her daughter. Her final act of domination. She had wished that Scottish morgue on her.

Fenella would rush to tumble into the cobwebbed yesterday that Fuarblarghour represented. The coffin of inheritance, of something to be kept up, a Name. Its ancient furnishings, its decay, its mouldering oils of Highland scenes . . . Oh, Jesus . . .

Of course he had always been unsuitable for her. For whom was he suitable? He had no place. That was the truth. Only in the illusory world of high finance, of the stock exchange, of the IBM VDU, of the BCT did he have any sort of function. How could he possibly live in that remote, stony place, submitting to her rules and the rules of those already dead? Could she not have some sort of empathy for his feelings in the matter? Or in any matter?

How attracted he had been at first by talk of the Scottish background: by that sense of continuity in her family he so lacked in his own life.

It was impossible even to consider going to Scotland with Fenella. She wanted him. But more strongly she did not.

It was the same with him. He wanted her. More strongly, he did not. He wanted to kill her. She was killing him.

This was how a marriage ended. Misery. Disillusion. Confusion.

Entering the library, that hollow-shelved place, he stood surveying it. Fenella sat shadowy in the coffin-chair, art nouveau strands of ivy ascending from the floor to climb over her arms, to claim her in the name of all Camerons. It was a trick of his vision. All the structure contained under its wooden wings was shadow. Fenella had fled upstairs.

A smart double knock like a rat-tat on a drum sounded on the door behind him. He stepped aside as it opened.

Arold stuck his turnip-shaped head round the door, exhibiting his teeth in an apologetic grin. "Scuse me, Mr Dominic, suh, but I know as things is a bit much for you. Can I bring you summat to eat? Like there's some nice sirloin of beef, cold, and some smoke salmon, whichever.'

'No. I don't want a thing. Wait. Arold, have you ever eaten smoked salmon?'

'Well, suh . . . In my position, you unnerstand . . . I mean, the likes of Doris and me, we don't . . .' He straightened up. 'To be frank, Mr Dominic, I'd say that smoke salmon is a rich bloke's dish.'

Dominic confronted his servant. 'But you must have tasted it here, in the kitchen, when there was some left over from a meal?' Seeing Arold's silent assent, he said, 'And you like it?'

'Quite creck. Hambrosia, suh. Even better than the tin stuff.'

'You squeeze lemon on it, Arold. You eat it with brown bread and butter. As you say, it's a rich bloke's dish. Only I now realize I hate the taste of the salmon. It's the lemon I like, and I like the brown bread and butter. The rest's just snobbery.'

Vigorous shake of the head. 'No, no that ain't so, suh, excuse me. Smoke salmon, blimey! Why, royalty likes it, royalty eats it, gets it down by the ton.'

'Thanks, Arold. I'll give a call to you if I need you.'

When the manservant had gone, closing the door behind him, Dominic lapsed back into his anger. What he needed was coke and Shostakovich. The coffee tray lay on the carpet where it had been spilt. He trod over the broken cups, to discover his Walkman smashed in the fireplace.

The childish spite of it cleared his mind. He hastened from the library and ran upstairs to Fenella's room, bursting in without knocking.

Her cluttered chamber was lit only by a standard lamp in one corner. She stood by the mantelpiece, having shed her shawl over the bed, where it sprawled like a lost wing. On the mantelpiece stood an open brown glass bottle of pills and an uncorked bottle of Kir. As Dominic entered, Fenella was in the act of washing pills down her throat, standing nose in air, swallowing. She set the glass down, and leaned against the shelf, elbow supporting head, looking down rather than at her husband.

'I don't wish to speak to you, Dom,' she said.

'Still guzzling down those pills? We've come to the end of the trail, Fen, haven't we? You won't move an inch towards me, will you? Suppose I told you there was another woman, that I was screwing someone else? You'd seize on that, wouldn't you? That would be the excuse you needed to throw me out of your life. You can't think how to get rid of me, to take hold of little Malcolm and be off somewhere to live out your sleepwalking fantasy of Scottish baronial life, or whatever it is . . . But another woman – oh, you'd love that!'

Still she chose not to look up. Instead, she concentrated on standing as before, trying to dislodge the slipper on her left foot with her right. She spoke without colour or emphasis.

'I suppose you have some prostitute or other. Sex is all you think about, isn't it?'

'Why don't you look at me? You're about to change into that other person, are you, that phantom kid, whoever she is?' From his inner breast pocket he pulled a micro-cassette recorder and waved it. 'I recorded every batty word you said when Dower was here. Would you like to hear yourself, eh? Would you like to hear what I've had to put up with for so long?'

Fenella flung herself on him. The cassette recorder went flying and smashed against a wall.

'I'll give you sex! You want sex? I'll show you what a prostitute can do!'

Afterwards, he never understood their frenzy. He was cursing her, tearing his clothes off. Just as savagely, she was tearing hers from her. They snarled at each other, face to face, lips drawn back in similar snarls. He ripped himself out of his trousers and fell on her. Amid screams and shrieks, they collapsed on the floor, rolling on her white reindeer rug.

Fenella was slapping him wildly on the side of his head. Biting at her neck, he prodded at her stomach with his erection until she grasped it as if it were a dagger and thrust it up into her body. She writhed on it as he drove it in with the force of his lower body behind it. Still they cursed and damned each other, legs entangled, one flesh.

Her fingernails were tearing into his back, ploughing the skin. Roaring with something beyond pain, he managed to get his arms about her, to pin down her flailing arms, to lock her against him. As he forced one of her breasts into his mouth, she bit his ear. So they stayed locked, fucking and kicking, until the cataclysm of sensation rocked them.

They fell apart, gasping and angry. She crawled on hands and knees over to the bed to grasp one corner of her shawl and drag it down to cover her nakedness. 'That'll show you I can be a prostitute too,' she said in a low voice, burying her face in the duvet.

'You want me to pay you?'

He pulled his trousers about his buttocks and slunk from the room. His ripped shirt and blood he left behind on her rug.

That night, he went to Malcolm's bedroom and kissed the boy goodbye before packing a suitcase and driving away from the manor.

He never went back. His adopted mother, Daphne Mayer, put him up that night and for many nights to come.

He received notification from Stirrup and Dower that his wife had taken up her inheritance and was now living in Scotland at Fuarblarghour House with her son. She was suing for divorce on grounds of desertion. /

Dominic lost touch with all his old friends. He gave up his work. After a blank spell which Daphne's doctor pronounced to be a nervous breakdown, he set about improving the quality of Daphne's life. They decided to escape from London, which was becoming dirtier and more sinister.

Something of both their wishes was fulfilled when he bought a small hotel, the Dianoya, in Great Yarmouth. The Dianoya stood on the front at Yarmouth, overlooking promenade and beach.

Dominic took a large attic room for himself. From its east-facing windows he swore he could see across the North Sea to the Continent.

The hotel was under Daphne's management. She was assisted by her new boyfriend. Dominic's task was to keep the accounts, to be civil to guests, and to do odd jobs. The first members of staff they engaged were Arold and Doris Betts. Under the previous management, the hotel had become run down. Dominic had it redecorated from top to bottom, and a conservatory added at the back, where guests breakfasted and dined. For a few years, the hotel was a modest success.

Dominic took up oil painting, and soon married a second time, a local artist by the name of Caroline Lambert. They produced two children, a boy and a girl.

While these children were still infants, the Dianoya took in an Irish guest calling himself Jim Donnell.

5

Accepted

Midsummer 1986

The castle was built of yellowing bone. A solemn parade of guards moved along its ramparts. Prompt on the first stroke of twelve, the main gates opened wide, to reveal a grim scene in the courtyard beyond. There the condemned prisoner stood, a thread of rope about his neck. The executioner, albeit a trifle creakily, pulled a lever. Down went the trap door, down went the prisoner with it, to hang limply by his neck. The main gates closed.

A white card propped against the castle walls read: 'Constructed by prisoners in Norman Cross during the Napoleonic Wars. Repaired, with new mechanism.' And a price was quoted, far above Ruby Tebbutt's purse.

Even after the mechanism had stopped, Ruby stood gazing in the window of the antique shop, one hand delicately up against the glass by her face, to shield the reflection of Fakenham market place. The macabre souvenir of past miseries fascinated her. She would have liked to buy it for her mother. Ray would be amused too. Still, it was something just to see it, all built from bones, and she could tell Agnes about it in the evening. How clever those French prisoners must have been.

Ruby's shift in the cake shop was finished. After a visit to the supermarket, she went with her purchases to the weekly lunch with her sister. Thank goodness, this week it was Joyce's turn to pay.

She was first in the Crown as usual. She entered the building, saying a word to one or two of the occupants of the public bar she recognized as she headed for the lounge, with its prints of long-dead racehorses. Dumping her carrier bag at her regular table, she bustled into the toilet and applied some lipstick, staring into the misty mirror at what she called her pasty old face. 'You never were pretty, you bitch,' she said to her reflection. She thought about having a wee and decided not to bother.

As she returned to the table, Joyce Lowe appeared, chirping her greetings. The two women trotted towards each other, uttering friendly squeals of recognition.

Although Ruby had put on a dress for this occasion, it was an old one her sister had seen many times. Even as she moved towards Joyce, she took in her sister's floral-patterned dress with white collar and its cry, 'New, new!'

'His hygienist gave me a perfect bill of health, was terribly compli-mentary, in fact,' Joyce said, without preliminary, in continuation of a phone conversation held two days earlier, hugging her sister and exploding a kiss two inches from her right ear without interrupting herself. 'But no, still I've got to go back to Denys this afternoon, so I mustn't linger too long. I know he's good but he is really being officious this time. Anyhow, how are you, Ruby? OK? Come back to Norwich with me and do some shopping.'

The saga of Joyce's wisdom teeth, and her love-hate relationship with Denys, her Norwich dentist, had been a long one, and no less long in the telling. Ruby was not at all discomposed by the flurry of information, while reflecting on how much of life was spent listening to the troubles of others. She knew her younger sister well. Before the wisdom tooth an ingrowing toenail had dominated conversation for some weeks. Both tooth and toenail had been exhibited to her more than once, though not in the Crown.

In the present impoverished state of the Tebbutt household, she was not about to go shopping in Norwich; the thought of shopping anywhere alarmed her.

'I've got something I want to do this afternoon,' she said, aware the answer sounded feeble.

Joyce got out a compact and proceeded to apply lipstick. 'A change would do you good. What are you doing? Where's the waitress? I need a G & T.'

Ruby was never sure whether to be pleased or annoyed her sister refused to acknowledge the fact that the Tebbutts were markedly less wealthy than the Lowes. 'Tess has got mange. On her left flank.' She indicated her own left flank in order to make matters clear.

Her sister laughed with affection. 'That bloody goat of yours!'

'Just a touch of mange. We aren't sure if it will affect the milk. I'm giving her vitamin pills.'

'Get the vet in if you're worried,' Joyce said.

'It's not that bad.' She did not say that a visit from the vet would set them back fifty pounds they could not afford.

As Ruby was about to impress her sister with the news of Jennifer's new Czech boyfriend, the waitress brought the menu and exchanged a few pleasantries with them. She told them about her son, who was doing so well at Creative Modelling. They ordered drinks, which arrived promptly, Joyce's G & T and Ruby's half-pint of bitter. Although the pub had been serving lunches for some years, it retained its traditional drive to get drink into its customers in preference to lasagne.

They talked about an old British film they had both seen recently on TV. It starred Stewart Granger, an actor both women had fancied in their youth. From there they moved on to other themes of childhood days, talking comfortably together while eating steak pie, chips and peas. They smiled at each other as they conversed, forgetting their small rivalries.

But Ruby found it hard to forget completely her sister's husband, Norm. She had never confided in anyone, not her sister, not her closest friend, about her intense early sex life with Ray; it was too precious, too private; to have spoken of it to a third party would have been to rob it of something of its magic. But soon after her sister had married the Norwich builder, Norman Lowe, she had become the unwilling recipient of Joyce's confidences.

And Joyce, in a first flush of matrimonial concupiscence, had told Ruby – they had been sitting together in Jarrold's cafeteria in Norwich – Ruby remembered it well – that Norman enjoyed rimming her.

'What's rimming?' Ruby had asked and, even while asking, had regretted her question. She knew the answer would be something awful. She felt herself blushing before Joyce replied, 'Surely you know what rimming is. Don't you and Ray do it? Norm likes to lick my bum, my arsehole. After a shower, of course.'

On the bus back home afterwards, Ruby could hardly stop laughing; but, out of the same instinct for privacy with which she kept quiet about her own activities, she never mentioned Norman's predilection to her husband. All she said to herself was, 'Lowe by name, low by nature.'

Joyce had never again offered such confidences, perhaps seeing that her sister was offended. After fifteen years of marriage, Joyce, like her husband, had grown somewhat on the portly side. Try as she might, Ruby could not banish from her mind a prurient curiosity: was Norm still able or inclined to indulge in that bedroom sport? And exactly what positions did they take up for its accomplishment?

She felt a similar sense of shame now, as she leaned over the little round table in the Crown and broke one of her own rules by blurting out, 'We've got trouble at present, Joyce.' And she found herself telling her sister how Ray had lent Mike Linwood three hundred pounds for the repair of his car. She became flushed as she spoke. Joyce lit a cigarette.

Her fear was, as she spilled out details of the scene at Stanton's garage, and the week which had passed since then, the money still not repaid, that Joyce would merely laugh and tell her not to be so silly. She thought the dress with the flower pattern and the white collar probably cost more than half the sum which so distressed her. But when she shed a tear or two, Joyce put down her cigarette and took her hand, uttering comforting nothings, much as their mother had once soothed them in their infant sorrows.

'I know the amount doesn't mean a thing to you, Joyce,' Ruby said, dabbing her eyes with a tissue. 'But it means a lot to us, and there will be interest to pay on the credit card, and poor Ray blames himself, and it has buggered up our friendship with the Linwoods . . . Oh, I shouldn't say anything to you about it . . .'

'You were always the one who bottled up your feelings,' Joyce said, sympathetically. 'Cheer up and I'll get the waitress to bring you a brandy. You do drag out that half of beer, I must say. Gloria!' This last cry was to the waitress. 'It was generous of Ray to do what he did. Serve Linwood right if he'd had to leave his car with Stanton and walk home.'

'Oh, Ray wouldn't let him do that.'

She accepted the brandy and sipped it noisily. She hated balloon glasses, which made it difficult to get at the liquid.

After the meal, she retired to the toilet to touch up her face. Joyce came with her, all motherly. 'Look, darling, don't be upset. I must head for Norwich in a mo', but I'm sure everything will be fine. The blighter is bound to pay up – especially if he's got religion.'

'That doesn't follow,' Ruby said, regretfully.

After her sister had left, she had a wee and went home to see how Tess was.

When the Fakenham bus had deposited her, Ruby retrieved her old bicycle from the hedge and pedalled slowly along, down Clamp Lane to No. 2. She went in the back door, calling to her mother, dumping her shopping bag on the draining board.

Agnes was sitting in the wicker chair in the front room, sleeping, propped erect by cushions, with the radio talking by her side.

'Are you all right, Ma? I'll get you some dinner.' She switched off the radio to save the battery.

The old lady raised her head and looked round woozily. Having been dozing with her mouth open, she began to munch, as if dinner had already been delivered, in order to induce a little moisture back into her mouth.

'Is that you, Doris? The brown paper's in the cupboard. Don't forget the dustcart comes today. If it wasn't for this wind . . .' Her mumblings became more obscure.

Her daughter knelt by her, smoothing her brow, thinking compassionately of the ageing mind lost somewhere in the mazes of the past. With a paper tissue from the box by the radio she mopped a trickle of saliva from Agnes's chin.

The action roused Agnes. Her eyes opened, and she said with perfect clarity, 'What was that they were saying about the Germans on the wireless? Did I hear someone's voice? What's his name?'

'I've only just come in, Ma. Would you like some parsnip soup? Bread, cheese, OK?'

'I used to love it when we went to Clacton as kids,' Agnes replied. 'I had a donkey ride once. Lovely beaches when the tide was out. We could go back there, Ruby, couldn't we? Have a paddle, just the two of us?'

'Clacton's a long way off, Ma.'

The old girl sighed heavily. 'What a nuisance. When was that? They've probably sold the donkeys, too. I can almost smell the sea air. It would do me good, a day by the sea . . .'

'I've got the saucepan on. You're not too hot, are you? Can I take this rug off?'

'Why do you and Ray never take me to the seaside?'

'I had lunch with Joyce, Ma,' Ruby said, moving back to the kitchen and turning up the decibels as she did so. Thank heaven the old dear wasn't deaf. 'She's still having her tooth problems. She'll be at the dentist right now, poor thing.'

She didn't add that Joyce had not asked once about her mother. It was rather a sore point that the old lady lived with her poorer daughter. The temporary arrangement had become permanent, and not solely because the Tebbutts found they derived some benefit from

Agnes Silcock's old-age pension; there was also Ruby's secret pleasure that she was her mother's favourite or, conversely, that Joyce was not greatly in favour.

'We could go over to the seaside. What's-her-name might be there,' Agnes said in a low shriek. 'Who turned this wireless off? People are always interfering.'

Her bad days were becoming more frequent. Soon it would no longer be possible for Ruby to work part-time at the cake shop, and one of their slender sources of income would disappear. The old lady would need someone all day. As it was, Ruby was not happy about leaving her mother alone in the mornings. Perhaps Joyce and Norm would have her in Norwich – though they would be more likely to send the old lady to a home.

She made herself a cup of tea before taking her mother in a tray with home-made parsnip soup, bread, margarine, and a pat of Tess's cheese.

Agnes was not the only problem looming. With dull foreboding, she thought of that three hundred pounds. Although she would not willingly criticize her husband, Ruby could not help feeling it was pusillanimous to have lent Mike Linwood their credit card; he had surrendered too easily to emotional blackmail. He should have thought up a good lie. The surrender opened up a wider question: how much of their present situation was owed to Ray's general mismanagement of their life together? Although he blamed their misfortunes on a rotten government, there was a point at which everyone had to stand up and admit responsibility for their own lives. He had never been ambitious. He was too easily deceived by Cracknell Summerfield. Did he perhaps enjoy hard rural life too much?

These cloudy questions had crossed Ruby's mental skies before. Then she turned on herself, asking, OK, girl, who would you rather be married to? Who do you know'd be cosier in bed? More equable generally? Be thankful he's not a money-grubber. A faint echo came back, saying: Still, it's a pity you can't take the old lady to Clacton for the day; that's not asking much, is it?

'Do you still believe in God, Ma?' she asked Agnes as she fed her bread and cheese in small chunks.

'Oh, times are different,' Agnes said, nodding in agreement with herself. 'I can remember the time when—'

'But you used to go to church a lot. You used to take Joyce and me, remember?'

The old lady stopped her munching and wiped her mouth on a tissue. 'Times are different. No one goes to church now, do they? I never see anyone going to church.'

'God might still be about, for all that.' She laughed as she formed a mental picture of an old man with a white beard sitting waiting hopefully in a dark empty church for a congregation that never came. Ever.

'Well, God once valued humans. It's different now. After two World Wars . . . After that battle . . . What was it called?'

'Stalingrad?'

'No, no, not Stalingrad . . . Lord Hay, was that his name? Doesn't matter . . . Waste of human life . . .'

When she had fed her mother, Ruby went out into the garden. She had changed her dress for a sweater and jeans, and had put on some old gardening shoes. This was a time of day she much enjoyed, spent in the company of Tess.

Tess lived in an enclosure at the bottom of the garden. Her twelve-foot chain was attached to a wire firmly staked at both ends, so that the white nanny goat had plenty of room to graze, and could retreat into her hut if it rained. Ray had built the hut from old timber, and thatched it with some Norfolk reed stripped off the ruinous outbuilding to the rear of No. 1 Clamp Lane.

'Here we are, darling,' Ruby called, in her sweetest tones – the tones she had used to Jenny when Jenny was a baby. The goat came slowly towards her mistress, giving a single deep 'mheeeer' as she approached. She was milked at the same time every day and regularly yielded about two pints; Ray would milk her when he came home.

Having fondled the animal, Ruby fetched a steel comb from the shelf inside the hut and sat down by the goat to comb her. Tess stood still for this procedure, occasionally shaking her head, as if not in entire accord with the endearments Ruby was whispering.

God took up some of Ruby's thought. Before going to work that morning, she had provided a galvanized bucket full of water for the goat; the bucket was wedged between three stones brought from the beach so that Tess would not accidentally kick it over. Ruby looked at the water, at the face of the goat, she inhaled its sweet breath and its pleasant scent. She regarded the grass, clipped short by grazing, with its maze of detail, the moss, the tiny twigs, the worm casts, the filaments of buttercup, daisy, clover, and thought to herself, 'I don't know about the grand effects God's supposed to bring off, though I know they exist. I've seen them on television. But someone is awfully good on minute detail.'

She was conscious of the smallness of her own life. She liked it that way. If only they had a bit more fucking cash.

The mange on the goat's flank was no better. She rubbed Intensive Care into the patch while the goat tried to eat the plastic bottle.

Unhitching Tess from the run-wire, she led her round the house and out by the front gate, taking care to avert her eyes from No. 1 Clamp Lane on the other side of the road. Its derelict state constituted a threat to orderly existence. Broken, dismal, its garden overgrown, it stood as a reminder of how the rural poor of an earlier generation had fared. The previous summer, vagrants, two men and a woman, had arrived one night and taken over the vacant premises. They moved on after a few days, to the relief of the Tebbutts. Ruby and Ray had gone over to inspect, and found that the vagrants had painted swastikas and crude cruel drawings over the faded wallpaper, as well as using the small front parlour as their toilet. Ray had brought in disinfectant and soil to cover the mess; the feeling that the cottage was defiled was more difficult to bury.

Turning right, Ruby took Tess for an amble down Clamp Lane in the direction of Binham. The sun shone warm upon them, woman and goat, as they sauntered. Birds sang, the goat's chain rattled as she foraged contentedly in the hedgerow, nibbling at this and that.

Later, Ruby would work along here with a pair of shears and a sack, cutting grass to dry for winter fodder.

Pulling Tess out of the hedge, she made her walk a short way on the paved road; the hard surface was good for her hooves. No traffic passed that way. The afternoon dreamed. She and the animal moved amid the deserted farmland. To her right, over the shoulder of the field, she could see a distant line of trees and the rooftops of Field Dalling Manor farmhouse.

Where the road reached its lowest point, thistles grew thickly by a ditch on one side. Tess enjoyed thistles, ignoring the clumps of poppies flowering nearby. Vetch with its modest purple flower entangled itself among the grass and dock, ground ivy and dead nettle, which sheltered under a hawthorn hedge. The attention to detail was pretty good here, Ruby thought. Beneath the leaf cover, the soil was crumbled and dry.

She dragged Tess away from a laurel bush which would have poisoned her. Would God do as much for her? She recalled her mother's words, 'Once God valued humans . . .' What had He thought about the vagrants? Had He valued them? Had they done something to deserve their horrible way of life, shitting on all they came across? What was He planning for her and Ray? To her mind came a dreadful picture of being turned out of No. 2, to wander the countryside, pushing Agnes in a wheelchair; her deepest fears painted such a scenario.

'You'd come with us, Tess,' she said aloud. 'You could help pull the wheelchair.' She climbed up on the bank at the roadside in order to let the goat forage more deeply into the hedge.

Her anxieties were not allayed next morning, when she went in to Agnes first thing and found her in a lethargic and confused state. Ray was sympathetic, but drove off to work as usual. After dithering a while, Ruby rang the doctor, who told her to give Agnes an extra pill. Ruby went upstairs and drank a strong mug of tea by the bedside, before hurrying downstairs again to ring Bridget Bligh at the cake shop, to announce that she would be late.

So it happened that she was at home when the post van roared along the lane and the postlady flipped a letter through their front door. Letters arrived rarely at the Tebbutt household. Ruby picked this one up from the mat, perched her glasses on her nose, and studied the blue envelope cautiously. The postmark was one which covered the whole county, 'Norwich, Norfolk', and so gave her few clues. The typewritten envelope was addressed to her. It felt too fat to be a tradesman's bill.

Taking the letter through into the kitchen, she got a knife and opened it. Inside was a brief handwritten note on the same hard blue paper as the envelope; it enclosed three hundred pounds in six fifty-pound notes. The note was signed Joyce, with love and kisses.

Ruby took the note to the wooden milking stool by the back door, removed her glasses and cried quietly.

When she had regained her composure, she folded the money and Joyce's note back into their envelope and hid it in a Toby jug on the dresser. She went outside. She walked about slowly on the paved way which led up the garden, gaze lowered.

The money changed everything. A grave joy filled her to feel how hard it made her, how it fortified her. Unexpected though the gift was, she felt small gratitude towards her sister; Joyce owed her this at least for the way she alone cared for their mother; it was Joyce's conscience money – though Ruby acknowledged to herself that it was something to have a conscience nowadays.

The same pleasure in being hard made her secretive. She would not allow this unexpected gift to become an easy way to let either Mike or Ray off the hook. Ray had particularly annoyed her when he had suggested allowing the Linwoods to keep the money; she had interpreted his suggestion as weakness, not generosity. Once she showed the fifty-pound notes to Ray, he might give up the pursuit of what she saw as justice. She wanted him to force the Linwoods to honour their debt. Accordingly, she resolved to hide this morning's unexpected windfall. It would be her secret, and the Toby jug her secret bank.

How thrilling! It was like plotting an adultery. The power of money . . . ! Even in this modest sum.

Like a vision – was this God taking care of detail again? – she saw that now she could afford to take her mother to the seaside.

She smiled as she thought of trying to heave Agnes up on the back of a donkey. In any case, they'd better avoid Clacton. She had heard that Clacton was completely spoilt. There was always Yarmouth. Yarmouth was nearer, and probably cheaper than Clacton.

A spasm of anger against Ray overcame her. He would be furious if he discovered she had told their troubles to Joyce. It wasn't that he did not get on well with Joyce and Norm, but he had his pride. Of course he had his pride. But the silly ass would probably order her to send the money back, and that she certainly was not going to do. Considering that Joyce never contributed anything in support of her mother, she could bloody well afford to let go of three hundred pounds. Why hadn't she sent more? If she knew they were in diffi-culties, she could easily have sent five hundred pounds. Five hundred pounds was nothing to that little bum-licker Norman Lowe.

What a lousy unjust world it was. Scowling, she marched back into the house to see how Agnes was. It was high time she went to work.

The cake shop was not the smartest place in town. It had been a greengrocer's until a nearby supermarket, selling more expensive vegetables, had put it out of business. Bridget Bligh had bought the premises at an advantageous price. She lived with a cat in the two cramped rooms upstairs.

When Ruby entered the shop, red in the face and out of breath, Bridget gave her a smile which lacked her usual warmth.

'Look what the cat's dragged in,' she called to her son.

Teddy Bligh, aged twenty, had occasionally been known to do odd jobs about town. As far as Ruby knew, Bridget had never married. It was hard to imagine that Teddy had been conceived in anything other than a fit of generosity between two other engagements.

Teddy was helping out in the shop this morning, wearing a blue baseball cap which said 'Kansas' on it.

'Sorry I'm late,' Ruby said. 'Have you been busy? It's quite extraor-dinary, I had a – well, a vision, I suppose it was, on my way here.'

Bridget gave a toss of her head. 'The meringues have had a vision and all. Summat must account for them collapsing. They're about as crisp as a baby's wet nappy. Get that batch of filled rolls in the window, will you? We can natter later on.'

'I had a vision, Bridget, a real vision, cycling to get the bus. I must tell you.'

Bridget made a sort of 'tsk', half-scowling, half-laughing, as she bustled about. 'It's a weird bloody place, is Norfolk. People seeing visions cycling to work . . . Woman told me the other day she'd seen a ghost in her bathroom, of all places.'

'This was no ghost, Bridget. I was coming through Field Dalling and suddenly I was in Germany. Somehow I knew it was Germany. Well, it was on the Continent. There was an ornate stone bridge over a wide river. People were walking on the bridge – no traffic. It was definitely foreign. I wasn't frightened a bit, not at that moment. I just stood looking at the river.'

'Did you see any meringues floating by?' She was disinclined to take in what Ruby was saying, although Teddy lounged across the counter, mouth open.

'Listen, a woman approached me, taking a long time about it. She was old, bent double, dressed in black. I saw her as clear as I see you. She had a scarf over her head. And she was leading some kind of animal, I don't know what.'

'That would be Swaffham market, not Germany, love.'

'Shut up, Ma,' Teddy said.

'For some reason, I was frightened of her. I couldn't see her face. And she pointed at the water. She took hold of me by the arm and she pointed at the water and she said – I'm scared to tell you, Bridget! I'd better not tell you, in case it comes true.'

'Tell me. Whisper it.'

'Well, you see . . .' Ruby paused anxiously. Two customers had entered the shop. Teddy turned reluctantly to serve them. 'I can't quite explain how, Bridget, but you see we were standing under the bridge. There was this massive stone arch over us, as if we were in a cellar. It was very dark. I felt – well, as if I was already dead. And

234

this voice came from a long way distant, saying . . . Well, it said, "People saw you die by the seaside."'

Bridget stared hard at her. 'You've gone as pale as a sheet, Ruby. You'd better come in the back and sit down. I've got a nip of brandy. "People saw you die by the seaside"? What does it mean?'

'I don't know.'

'Oh, it probably doesn't mean a thing. Load of rubbish. First sign of madness. Have you been sleeping all right? What happened after that?'

Ruby revealed her muddy shoes. 'When I came to, I found I'd got off my bike and was standing in a ditch, by the old Grendon place. I've never had anything like that happen to me before.'

'Didn't something dreadful happen on the Grendon farm once, so I was told? A murder or something? Get some more carrier bags out, will you, love?'

'What do you think it all means, Bridget?'

As she asked this, she was moving into the little crowded rear room to sit down as advised. Bridget, however, was emerging from her brief sympathetic mode and thinking of her meringues.

'Means you're going daft, if you ask me. Germany, my foot! In Field Dalling! Now let's get busy.'

Although Ruby had her nip of brandy and got busy as instructed, she remained preoccupied. Normally she did not worry; she had cultivated forgetfulness. Behind the ominous vision which had visited her, unpleasant enough in itself, lay an anxiety that in some peculiar way she might have invented it all herself: that it had been a product of will rather than accident, just as, she had once seen on TV, there was a debate going on among people to whom such things mattered as to whether the universe itself was a product of will or accident.

Nor had it escaped her troubled mind that the old crone in her vision might well have been her mother. Perhaps at this moment her mother was lying on the floor of No. 2 Clamp Lane dying of a heart attack. The vision had been a psychic projection, whatever that was. The strange message, 'People saw you die by the seaside', must connect with her mother's desire to revisit Clacton.

Yet, Clacton . . . With its bright banal sands, its coarse amuse-ments, its stinking food shops . . . How different it was from the melancholy cellar-encased atmosphere in which the voice in the vision had pronounced, as if it were a note of doom, the picture-postcard word 'seaside' . . .

She could not wait to get home and see that all was well. Yet she feared to go. The vision undermined her simple courage in existence.

That day, Ray Tebbutt was far from his wife's thoughts. It was also true that she was far from his. As he worked in the garden centre, he worried about his three hundred pounds. The morrow would be the last day of the month when – so he believed – the credit company would start to charge him interest on the unsettled account.

He had to get the money back from Mike Linwood; yet he would humiliate himself in so doing. Mike's dreadful decision to enter the Church . . . well, it put Jean and the boys at risk. Perhaps the Linwood family could afford that piddling sum even less than the Tebbutts. He was furious with himself for the way in which the loan had come to dominate his thinking. It was untrue, as he had once supposed, that only the rich were obsessed with money; the poor thought about it all the time.

The BBC news was currently full of admiration for the new man in Russia, who promised sweeping changes.

While Ray had never had any affection for the regime in the Soviet Union, he had always – even at the height of the Cold War – admired the way in which the Russians had lived simply, in poor housing, without many material goods, and without complaint. Now, if what he heard was true, he had been mistaken. All the while, ever since the Russian Revolution, the people had been oppressed and unable to protest.

Now they could speak. And what did they say? Why, that they longed for material possessions. They longed for what the West had to offer.

You bastards, Ray said to them all under his breath, as he went to the shed to refill the chainsaw with petrol; you bastards, do you dare envy me, working for this sod Yarker? Just think of Yarker in Russia! Comrade Yarkovich, paid-up member of the KGB, responsible for little massacres here and there on the Kola Peninsula, given the order of the Red Star and Bar by Comrade Leonid Brezhnev himself. Now promoted to Governor of the Lubiyanka. Is that what you bastards want?

You don't work your guts out in Russia, do you? OK, you have no justice, but the system looks after you in some fashion from cradle to grave, doesn't it? Over here, we have justice, Great British Justice, and they charge you for the shagging grave, so much per foot per decaying body. Do you know – have you any idea, Comrades? – what it costs to bring up a child in this capitalist country – what was the figure? Well, we must have spent close on thirty thousand pounds bringing up Jenny, wouldn't you say?, so that she could grow up and run away from home and become a feminist, despising her father, rightly, you might claim – while at the same time trying to destroy the defences of this country. Yes, defences against you bastards, who were perfectly ready to blow us up yesterday and today are whining for Western aid and hoping to join the Common Market. I never wanted to join the bloody Common Market – well, European Community it is now – Christ, the change in name . . . Europe's still for businessmen only, isn't it? For the rich? Why should you want to join it? Oh dear, what a bloody world . . .

The chainsaw roared and bucked in his grasp as it bit into another tree trunk. Still his thoughts flowed on.

Let me just ask you this, though it's a question for us, whoever *us* may be – the West, the Brits, the Yanks, the Germans, the French, the whole lot of us, as well as you Ruskies: how much do you reckon the Cold War has cost? A straight fucking question. *How much has it all cost?* The bill's got to be paid. I mean, not just the price of all the useless armaments, the missiles, the soldiers standing to, the rations, the whole loony espionage superstructure, the space race, the military bureaucracy – you know what I mean, all that crap . . . And not only all that, but the miserable pollution of the planet, the hole blown in the ozone layer, the overheating stuff, the ruination of your industries and everyone's countryside, all in the name of military preparedness. The Cold War. And not just that, Comrades, fuck you, but the poisoning of all our lives on most of the planet. You follow what I'm getting at? The last forty years, millions of us petrified with terror in case either one of your mad scientists or one of ours launched a nuclear bomb, or a general more eager for promotion – no, let's just say some poor common squaddie who had been pissed off just one inch too much by his sergeants, his officers – let's just say the annihilation had started . . . fire, smoke, radiation, destruction, death . . . That was the scenario we all had boiling in our cranial pressure-cookers for that long time – a whole generation plus, right? It doesn't bear thinking of. There you are . . . That bill will never be paid, will it? You can collect on three hundred pounds, but on billions of hag-ridden lives – never. Talk about collective guilt . . .

But that's how life is. Never better, never worse. Always shit. Filtering down from the top of the system to the bottom. And the bottom of course flinging it back again. Believe me, whenever I get my hands on a bit of it, I'm certainly going to fling it back again.

Even his boss, the porcine Yarker, was giving him shit. Tebbutt was currently engaged in sawing down the poplars as ordered. His thoughts found harmony in the growl of the chainsaw. He operated it without protection, without helmet or eyeshield or gloves, wrenching at the heavy machine, which fought and leapt in his hands.

Yarker revealed his ignorance by insisting on having the trees down at this time of year, when they were still in leaf. It simply added to the difficulties of felling. Tebbutt was now working on the fourth tree along; three raw stumps stood behind him. Bent double, he guided the revolving chain to bite at an angle into the trunk. Deeper it went, screaming, sending up a spume of sawdust. As the tree gave a warning groan, Tebbutt stepped smartly back. A woman and a child from nearby bungalows watched over the fence in delighted terror as the poplar crashed down, bounced once, and settled like a defeated gladiator in the dust.

Tebbutt straightened, eased his back, then began sawing the fallen tree into logs, which he bagged on the spot in yellow polythene sacks. After some while, setting down the chainsaw, he took out a hand-kerchief and wiped his brow.

A lanky figure was entering the garden centre, looking about in a short-sighted way. It came on a few paces, saw Tebbutt, halted, made a salutation. It was Noel Roderick Linwood, Mike's father, his white hair afloat.

'Hello there,' he called.

'Perhaps he's brought the bloody money,' Tebbutt said to himself.

Noel stood his ground, waiting for Tebbutt to come to him. The salutation had been a summons. Tebbutt pocketed his handkerchief and trudged over to where the old man stood.

Noel Linwood clasped a walking stick in his right hand. His left was in his blazer pocket. He held his head back, squinting down his strawberry nose as Tebbutt approached.

'You look a trifle hot.'

'I am hot. Fucking hot. Are you after some plants?'

'Shouldn't you be kneeling towards Mecca, or some such nonsense?'

Tebbutt laughed. 'You didn't come here to ask me that. I'm sorry if I was rude to you at dinner that time. It was the wine. Plus a naturally bumptious disposition.'

Without changing his expression, Noel Linwood said, 'I was amused. There's a paucity of humour in our house. I was particularly amused afterwards, to watch from the dining-room window as your wife beat you up by the car. She's what they call a bit of a joker too, isn't she?'

Tebbutt did not reply. He simply stood there, letting sweat trickle down his face. He spoke again only when it seemed as if the other would never break the silence.

'Mr Linwood, your son Mike owes me a considerable sum of money – considerable to me. Have you come to pay it back? Why exactly are you here?'

Lifting his stick, Linwood half-pointed it at Tebbutt. 'I can see you're not in a good mood. Physical labour always took me the same way. Made me truculent too. I am not responsible for my son's activities. I've been paying off his debts for God knows how long, and now I've stopped. I've sworn off it. You may know the old Iraqi saying, "A donkey must be fed, but a son finds his own grazing."'

'You sound just like Mike. Now I know where he got it from. Sorry, I must get back to work.' From the corner of his eye, he saw Pauline Yarker watching him from the window of her mobile home. She had switched off her radio, the better to overhear the conversation.

'You enjoy what you're doing, eh?'

'I'm a peasant.'

'No, no, Tebbutt. "Not so fast", as they say in the cinema. I came by because I wanted to ask you – and that amusing wife of yours, of course – what's her name? – to dinner again on Saturday night. And really I don't care a bit what you say at table – within limits. Lie as much as you wish. A counterbalance to Michael's preachments . . . Eight o'clock, Saturday. You look as if you could do with a good free meal.'

'I don't need a free meal. I just want my money back, and I certainly don't wish to meet your son socially until I get it.'

The old man showed his rows of too-white teeth in something that could be construed as a grin. 'If you turned up, you might get the money, mightn't you? My friend Tom Squire will be there, by the way, with his missus. So try and look smart.'

With that, he gave a genial nod and turned away.

Back from work that evening, Ray entered the kitchen at No. 2 Clamp Lane, kicked off his boots, and told Ruby of Noel Linwood's invitation.

She pretended to be more astonished than she was, and sat down heavily on a chair. 'I can't believe it. I feel quite faint.'

'Put your head between your legs.'

'I can't.'

'I'll put mine there.'

'Tonight, darling. I take it we're not really going round to their bloody place on Saturday, are we?'

'We're less likely to get our money back if we don't go. Besides, remember what a good cook Jean is.'

'Oh yes, you'll get a look at Jean too, won't you? Does she let you have the odd feel now and again?'

'Nothing odd about it.'

After Ray had milked the goat, they settled down to discuss the unexpected invitation. They rarely went out, except to some people they knew in Bale, for whom Ray had once worked. They could not understand Noel, never once considering that he might simply be bored. And they had a certain wariness of Sir Thomas Squire, as one of the landowners of the district, and a man who was famous to boot.

But Ruby was prepared to go along with whatever her husband wished. She was preoccupied with her disturbing vision on the way to work. With her usual reticence, she was not ready to tell Ray about it. It remained safe in her head, like the cash in the Toby jug. For the more she thought it over, the less certain she was that the old woman by the dark river had said, 'People saw you die by the seaside.' Had the figure been her mother, saying, 'People saw *me* die by the seaside'? Or had the figure in some way been Jennifer? Was it a warning from her daughter?

The more the vision frayed round the edges, the more Ruby directed her fears towards her daughter.

Ever since Jenny had called with the Czech whose name Ruby had already forgotten, she had worried about her. It was understandable that mother and daughter were no longer as close as formerly. Jenny had transformed herself into a real city lady – 'yuppie' was the word – after her silly period in CND; Ruby herself – well, what was she now but an old country cabbage?

It was worth something nowadays to look back to the happy days of Jenny's childhood, when they had had no money problems. How nicely the little girl had played in their walled garden in Birmingham, 35 Long Eaton Road. As a tot, she had enjoyed her sandpit, making sand-pies and pretending to have a shop. Later, she had tended her own little patch of garden, sowing blue cornflowers and love-in-a-mist. Before Joyce married that builder, she and Ruby used to take Jenny to the seaside, to Skegness or Hunstanton. They liked Hunstanton best. She could picture the small figure now, running delightedly along a margin of tiny waves, waving her plastic spade in excitement or chasing a seagull.

She had been afraid even then, even as she and Joyce sat on the sand behind a hired wind-break. Afraid that the dread day would come when nuclear war broke out and they were all destroyed; war had so often seemed inevitable. And afraid, more immediately, that something awful would happen to Jenny and she would drown. Fire or flood, it would surely come. She dreamed of it.

As far as she knew, Jenny was even now at a coastal resort like Hunstanton, showing off bits of England to her foreign boyfriend. Happy. Let's hope you're happy, Jenny love. You'll never know how much your old mum loves you. I'm sure that daft vision thing was just a projection of my inner worries for you. Be all right, there's a dear.

What a bugger that we can't live rational lives. There's always that other layer going on, behind the eyes. Another dimension, so vivid. I'm not sure I haven't had visions ever since I was a girl. You tend to put them out of mind and forget them quickly, like dreams.

Perhaps I should worry more. Perhaps I worry too much.

Remember how things used to be, before Ray lost his job and Jenny was just a little tacker . . .

Hartisham was an ancient village. Many Saturdays had passed it by. In the fifteenth century, Margaret Paston of Norfolk had written to her husband in London of the great increase of lawlessness in Hartisham. 'Sir John Partrich passed to God on Tuesday last past, whose soul God assoil! His sickness took him on Tuesday at eight of the clock when he was out riding, and by three afternoon he was dead. Now who will controul the mischief?'

By the mid-1980s, things were quieter. Sir Thomas and his wife, Lady Teresa, presided over what remained of the small community. A lad's suicide was the one current token of unrest.

The Squires rolled up to St Giles House in their black Jaguar only a minute before the Tebbutts' orange Hillman arrived.

Noel Roderick Linwood had evidently been watching for his distinguished guest. He rushed into the garden, waving his arms above his head in effusive greeting, with barely a glance at the Tebbutts.

Not quite knowing what to do, Ray and Ruby stood by the open doors of their car, looking on. Ruby gazed with awe at the knight whom she had seen on television, thinking to herself with self-deprecatory amusement that she might as well have a good look since, so obscure was her life, she would probably never again meet in the flesh anyone who had been sanctified by the TV cameras.

Squire was tall and upright, with a slightly theatrical air of authority about him. The hair that remained to him appeared crisp and well-groomed, in contrast with Noel's wild mop. His smile as he shook hands seemed to Ruby to be excellent and unforced. She took in his profile, with adequate forehead and nose and a strong jawline, eyes deep-set and grey – searching but not judgemental.

Ignoring not only the Tebbutts but Lady Teresa as well, Noel plunged into conversation with his guest.

Teresa Squire seemed to expect this. She did not step forward, but remained at the car. Having gazed sufficiently at Squire, Ruby turned her attention to his wife. Teresa, aware of this scrutiny, looked at her and then away without changing her expression in the least.

She leaned against the side of the Jaguar, clutching her elbows in her hands. She contemplated, or appeared to contemplate, the rickety chimney of the Linwood establishment. She wore gold bracelets on the upright arm.

Ray stuck his hands in his pockets, to stand in a rather sullen attitude, angered at being ignored.

Meanwhile, Noel Linwood was commiserating with Tom Squire on a threat to his life, as reported on television and elsewhere. 'So the KGB are after you, Sir Thomas, ha ha!'

Squire was explaining that he had been involved in a symposium held in Luxembourg on relationships between art and economics. Soviet delegates had been present, as well as a West German kremlinologist, Klaus Leberecht. At one point, the argument had become heated, when the Russians made derogatory claims about Western art being degenerate. Squire had contradicted, stating that art in the West was free – within certain financial limits – and in no way subject to state dictates.

After angry exchanges, the Soviet delegation had marched out, uttering, it was true, vague threats about seeing that 'international discourtesy' would be punished.

This situation Squire explained dismissively in a few sentences, evidently tired of the whole subject.

Mike Linwood had meanwhile emerged from the front door with a child at his heels. He made no attempt to approach, standing mute with eyebrows drawn together. Squire gave him a cordial wave of the hand.

Laughing at what Squire had told him, Noel Linwood clapped him familiarly on the back.

'They'll kill us all one day. Bomb us, invade us, who knows what. If you ask me, our days are numbered. We're in decline, that's the truth.' He laughed again.

Ruby saw the shadow of a smile cross Teresa's face, although she continued to gaze towards the rooftops.

'My information somewhat contradicts that view,' Squire told Noel, giving every indication of being about to make a hasty move towards the house without actually stirring a foot. 'According to Klaus Leberecht, who is generally to be relied upon, and other authorities I have spoken to – well, it's pretty common knowledge – the Russian economy is in an extremely bad, if not terminally decrepit, way.

'In fact, Klaus goes so far as to predict the collapse of the entire rotten Soviet system by 1990.'

Noel looked incredulous. 'That's all rubbish, dear boy,' he said with a dismissive gesture. 'You'll see. Once they've mopped up Afghanistan, the Ruskies'll invade India. India will fall like a slice of rotten cheese. Gorgonzola. Then they'll turn on the West.'

'Are you going to introduce us to your other guests?' Squire enquired.

'He's drunk,' Ray told his wife quietly. 'Old Linwood's drunk!' He began to feel interested in the evening.

Ruby, flustered by the introductions, informed Squire she had seen him on TV. As they moved into the hall, Mike Linwood managed to avoid speaking to Ray Tebbutt. Nor did Tebbutt get much of a smile from Jean, which angered him again. An ancient unspeaking lady, who sat in a corner as if a hallowed part of the furniture, ignored them all.

Over everything boomed the voice of the self-constituted host, offering, threatening, making jokes about this and that, demanding drinks.

His voice, thick as treacle, made the house seem more crowded than it was. It calmed a little only when everyone held a glass in their hand. In the silence that followed, Teresa complimented Jean on the lack of ornament cluttering the room.

'They've been sold, Lady Teresa. What we had.'

It was not a promising start to the evening.

Squire talked easily to Noel Roderick Linwood about safe parish matters, such as the imminent closure of the local post office, as they sat in the Linwoods' drawing-room in St Giles House, from which the Linwood boys had been ushered, Alf resisting every inch of the way. A white square of Lego on the hearthrug marked his passing.

Having forcibly ejected her sons in deference to her father-in-law's bidding, Jean Linwood moved in and out between drawing-room and kitchen, putting the final touches to dinner, in the scents of which the Tebbutts tried not to seem interested. Teresa Squire sat sideways in her armchair, resting her naked right elbow in her left hand, the better to support her chin as she gazed at the ceiling above her husband. Her body language clearly stated that she was not available at present for conversation. Mike Linwood stood by a window, subdued in the presence of an employer who was also his father's honoured guest. What he needs, Tebbutt thought, is a set of worry beads.

Tebbutt himself was not in the best of tempers. He answered tersely the low-spoken comments of Ruby, who sat next to him. His mood had not improved when he parked their Hillman next to Squire's Jaguar. Nor was the sight of Mike – who made no attempt to speak to him – calculated to improve matters.

He turned to the woman on his other side, who sat remote on a stiff-backed chair, occasionally brushing an imaginary hair from her cheek. This scraggy old person was in her eighties, her face as lined as a moorland track. She wore a straggly dark wig, crisp and untidy as bracken after a heath fire, which gave her a wild look; yet she sat on her hands, impaling them under bony buttocks, like a child told to behave. This was Noel's sister, introduced as Auntie April, over from Blakeney for the evening.

'This is an interesting house,' Tebbutt said to her by way of opening a conversation he might later regret.

'Priests once lived here,' Auntie April said. 'I can smell their garments.'

'I think that's supper cooking. Rabbit, possibly.'

'Long ago, young man. Their vestcements. Hidden by centuries. Still visible to those of us who are gifted with second sight.'

Noel Linwood overheard at least a part of this exchange. He broke off his conversation with Squire, to point a finger at his sister and shout a warning to Tebbutt. 'Barking mad . . . That's her. Beware! Barking mad.' Raising the finger, he attempted to bore a hole into his temple while rolling his eyes, to give some indication of how mad barking mad really was.

Auntie April turned the upper part of her plank-like body towards Tebbutt. 'My brother spent much of his life in Iraq. Speaking a foreign tongue. Under a curse. Babylonian.' Her large violet eyes, the pupils of which were ringed by pale moons, looked intensely through Tebbutt without holding any anticipation of a response.

Teresa Squire, overhearing this exchange, broke from her boredom to tender, in a low voice, a sentence across the room. 'I've often

246

speculated about the motivations of people who spend long periods of their lives voluntarily outside their native country: whether it could be an indicator of some specific struggle in their inner make-up. An Oedipal conflict of some kind. It would be interesting to know.'

'Yes,' said Ruby. 'My mother longs to go to the seaside again.'

There that morsel of conversation died. Teresa returned to her impenetrable distance, chin locked in pale be-ringed hand.

Tortured by the aroma from the kitchen, Tebbutt tried to decide whether by refusing to eat he might make Mike Linwood feel guilty. He wondered if such a course of action would retrieve his three hundred pounds. Then he remembered an old Norfolk saying, perhaps first heard in the Bluebell, from whence all wisdom flowed: that when invited out to dine, one should always eat as much as possible. If the host was a friend, he would be flattered to think his wife's cooking was appreciated; if an enemy, his larder would be the more depleted.

Squire and his wife were in their late fifties. A certain beauty and grandeur hovered about Teresa's expensively coiffured head. She appeared ready at any moment to have her portrait painted. Ruby was studying her with interest, as the first prosperous woman she had met in a long while.

As for Squire, he still retained the presence that had made him in the seventies a successful presenter of a long series of TV documentaries on contemporary culture. He was now president of a distinguished art gallery in London. This evening, he wore a comfortable pepper-and-salt tweed suit; a heavy digital watch on his left wrist was his only adornment. Tebbutt experienced a surge of envy, regarding him, as they all rose at Jean's request to move to the dining-room. He saw as they followed Squire and Noel how Noel shadowed his guest, his hand cupped under, but not quite touching, Squire's elbow.

'I'm ravenous,' Teresa said companionably to Ruby. 'It smells gorgeous.'

'Animals had to be made dead by shotgun and chopper,' said Auntie April. 'God's will, mighty inventor of shotgun and chopper.'

Noel's head whipped round angrily. 'Barking mad,' he said.

'Arab boys,' Auntie April replied. 'Roderick Randy.'

As Jean indicated their places, Tebbutt observed that the portrait of Noel Roderick Linwood which had previously hung in the kitchen was now installed over the mantelpiece; his heavy painted countenance peered down at the table. The narrow room faced north over a stretch of lawn on which light was rapidly fading, to sheds beyond and the Hartisham almshouses in the distance. It was cold and stuffy in the room, as if it had not been used for a while. A dim electric fire, with two orange bars stretched under a curved hood, glowed in the grate. Tall white candles created a sparkle on the table. The dog, Thelonius, was shooed out of his hiding-place.

'No mercy to those of lesser breed,' commented Auntie April. 'Dogs. Wogs.'

As soon as they were settled at table, Mike circulated, pouring wine.

This is going to be hell, Ray told himself, nudging Ruby not to drink too much. She turned pointedly to Noel and asked him if he liked goats.

'There are enough difficulties and annoyances, inextricably part of normal life, without encumbering oneself with *goats*,' Noel said, lifting his hands to sketch two horns on his forehead, while making a moue of dislike.

'Particularly,' Mike said, pausing by his father's side, 'if those difficulties and annoyances are self-created, eh, Father?'

'Goats are great destroyers of the Middle East environment, dear boy.'

Without replying, Mike made his round of the table, pouring no wine into his own glass. When Jean entered with a samphire appetizer – '*spécialité de la région*,' intoned Noel – Mike said grace.

'May the Lord make us truly grateful,' repeated Auntie April in a stage whisper. She gave a cackle. 'What's truly? We'd die first.'

'She's woofing mad,' Noel told Squire, confidentially.

After the samphire, Jean brought in a grand tureen, apologizing as she ladled out the soup. 'It's an old Norfolk recipe I got from Mrs

Price down at the cottages. Terribly simple, but I hope you'll like it, Lady Teresa.'

'Mm, and simples in it,' said Teresa, sampling.

'What's it called?' Noel asked. He was generally on bad terms with his daughter-in-law, but the hatchet had been buried for the occasion.

'"Cottage Soup".' Jean's dark hair, swept up in horns on either side of a central parting, curled down over her cheeks, almost concealing both eyes as she glanced swiftly at Noel.

Noel roared with laughter at her answer. For a moment Jean caught Ray's eye through her ambush of hair. It was her first acknowledgement of his presence since the Tebbutts' arrival.

'These wholesome old country traditions cling on despite what we call progress,' Noel said, sipping at the herby mixture. 'There's a treasury of wisdom stored up in cottages round here.'

He addressed this remark, like most of his remarks, to Squire, who asked, 'What sort of things are you thinking of, Noel, apart from recipes for excellent soup? Fennel in here somewhere, I believe.'

'Oh, I don't know . . . Well, even in quite humble homes you'll see as you pass by little racks of books standing on the window-ledge. While the rest of the country's turning more and more to videos of sex and violence, in cottages up and down the land people are still enjoying a good read.' He dropped his spoon to gesture grandly with his right hand, perhaps in unconscious imitation of Shakespeare or Milton holding forth.

'Harms the books,' said silent Auntie April. 'Sunlight. Bad for them. Yellow. Deterioration. Decay.'

'Mad as a hatter . . .'

'Those books you praise are often nothing but trash, Father,' Mike said. 'Nothing at all worth reading. Perhaps an old *San Michele* here or there, mainly trash. Agatha Christie.'

'I'm not sure I agree with what I take to be your basic thesis,' Squire said, addressing Noel. 'That is, that the cottages of England – rather a miscellaneous lot, when you think about it – are *not* repositories of anything but a trivializing culture. Visit car-boot sales hereabouts and see if you can find anything but old LPs of sixties pops, or Edmundo Ross on shellac, or paperbacks of the frothiest of romantic novelists. It's a sad feature of lower culture that it does not develop and reject, clinging only to what it first came to enjoy.'

'Well, you wouldn't exactly expect Henry James in your average council house, would you now?' Noel said, giving a bark of laughter. 'Nor would I buy James if I saw him. Can't stand his stuff. Personally, I don't frequent car-boot sales. Sorry. You know what Rebecca West said about James. "With sentences as immense as the granite blocks of the pyramids, he sets about telling a story the size of a henhouse . . ." Words to that effect.'

'Reading M. R. James,' Auntie April said, half-turning her corpse-like torso in Tebbutt's direction. 'Creepy stories. Makes your flesh creep. Runes. Ruins. As things are.'

'Madwoman at the table,' Noel said. 'Apologies. Barking mad.'

'Circumcision,' Auntie April said. 'The back entrance.'

'The great intellectual movements of the last two centuries were hardly generated in cottages,' Squire said. 'Hardly even filtered down there.'

Mike said, in a timorous voice, 'But who causes it "to rain on the earth where no man is, on the wilderness wherein there is no man"? That's how God sees the poor . . .'

His bid to enter the conversation was unsuccessful, although his wife smiled down the table at him, nodding in a kindly way.

Having finished his soup, Ray felt bold enough to say, 'People in cottages are too hard-pressed to earn a crust to bother about anything else.'

He was surprised at how warmly Squire agreed. 'Exactly so. The poor people of England have always existed on the breadline, often in acute distress. Moreover, my belief is that the poor in this country were never worse off than when the great ideas that have formed our times were being enunciated – over their lice-infested heads, as it were.'

Ray was unsure what ideas Squire was talking about. Perhaps this showed in his face. Perhaps Squire was glad to speak to someone other than Noel, currently crumbling his bread over a wide area of table.

'You need idleness in order to formulate new ideas. Of course, idleness is a naughty word today; we associate it with the even naughtier word, unemployment. Nor am I sure that new ideas are exactly what are required at present. We need time to recover from a bombardment of ideas.' He spoke lightly and amusedly, looking from face to face as Jean collected up their soup bowls.

'It was only in the eighteenth century that men and women ceased to hark back to previous civilizations for models for their own. Such men as Gibbon, and Montesquieu, in whom Gibbon found inspiration, came to regard their world as not being in decline – a new idea in itself. Far from being in decline, the Enlightenment was seen as at least the equal of the past. Indeed, wealth and knowledge were on the increase, according to Gibbon.'

'Monk Gibbon. Very creepy. The Nun,' said Auntie April, shivering. 'Something grindling in the woodwork.'

'Crackers!'

'This is another Gibbon, Auntie April. *Edward* Gibbon,' Squire said. 'The old prevailing notion of a past Golden Age was banished at last, though it's true the French court had its cult of simpering shepherds and shepherdesses. The myth that the past is always better – "There were giants in the Earth in those days" – still lingers among the uneducated. A fallacy, particularly where the rural poor are concerned.

'Progress, to the élite of the eighteenth and early nineteenth century, meant simply that such increased benefits as wealth and knowledge should be controlled by rational minds. You see the idea cropping up in Shelley's *Defence of Poetry*, for instance. That was the belief, the vision, powering the Enlightenment and such manifestations of it as Diderot's great *Encyclopédie*.'

Lady Teresa, who wore a short-sleeved dress in a twenties style, leaned a bare elbow on the table and said, 'Of course, Diderot also wrote novels once regarded as naughty. *He* wrote a book called *The Nun*, Auntie April, *La Religieuse*.'

'Terribly creepy,' Auntie April said, brushing the imaginary hair from her cheek. 'Terrified of nuns. Dormitories, the vestibule of life. Chastity departs from there.'

'Dumb and daft. Have to excuse her.'

'Paediatry and puggaree,' his sister muttered, looking down at her lap. 'Foreign bodies. Ishtar and dusky bewitching hags . . .'

Jean entered bearing a large rabbit pie, sweltering under a bronzed pastry crust with a fluted edge, and set it before her husband to serve. Everyone admired it.

'You'll like this, Sir Thomas,' Noel said genially. 'Jean's rabbit pie takes a lot of beating. Michael, let's have more wine. Wake up.' Noticing Ray taking a deep gulp at his glass, he observed, 'I see you Muslims have adapted to alcohol. Well done.'

'Is this another cottage recipe?' Teresa asked Jean.

'Rabbit pie is traditional in these parts,' Jean said. 'But this recipe owes more to Mrs Beeton. As well as rabbit, it contains chunks of pork, bacon, and forcemeat.'

'We have an old receipt at Pippet Hall. A delicious pie. It includes onion, some chopped steak, and I don't know what else. Very fattening.'

'You've had trouble at Pippet Hall,' Noel said. 'Several sackings and a suicide, I hear, yes?'

Mike Linwood spoke up. 'Yes, poor Billy Lamb killed himself, rest his soul. I knew him quite well – worked with him in fact. I phoned Jean directly I heard the dreadful news.'

Helpings of the rabbit pie were passed down the table. Auntie April took hers and stared at it as if transfixed before prodding it with a finger.

Squire proceeded to explain that the vegetable- and fruit-packing business he had established in his grounds on the Wells road had been losing money for some while. Early profit had turned to loss following the import of cheap fruit from the European Community. He had had to give five men a golden handshake. For two more he had found other work about the estate. Billy Lamb was one of those receiving a golden handshake.

'He had another job in prospect,' Squire said. 'Unfortunately, he also had problems with his lady friend.'

'That was Margy Sulston, who once worked at the Ostrich,' Tebbutt said knowingly, remembering what he had been told.

'What was the problem?' Ruby asked, looking at her husband with raised eyebrows, suspicious of where this information had come from. She signalled to him to drink less. He passed her the potatoes.

It was Teresa Squire who answered Ruby. 'After Billy's death, I drove over to see the girl's mother. Well, Margy is scarcely a girl any more. Twenty-nine, I believe. According to the mother, Margy was desperately in love with Billy. She found love poems in her room. However, poor Margy faced Billy with a psychological dilemma. She had no taste for the mechanics of love-making.'

'What are *they*, for heaven's sake?' Ruby said, over a forkful of rabbit. 'You mean vibrators?'

'I mean the sort of condition from which Frederic Chopin suffered. Cold when it came to the actual physical transactions of sex. The ups and downs of the business.'

Her quick eyes caught – as did Ray's – the glance Jean gave Mike. As if aware her look had been intercepted, Jean asked how the pie was. All agreed on its excellence, and of the succulence of the meat.

After a moment, Teresa continued, evidently fascinated by the case. 'Some took Billy's side, some Margy's. I believe he was rough with her on occasions, calling her frigid. The engagement was twice broken off.'

'How did she take the news?'

'Very badly. Margy's run away to a relation in Coventry. Her mother cried a lot. She said that Margy had had treatment from an old gypsy woman in Swaffham market. I dread to think *what*.' She paused. 'The mother was hiding something. My belief is Margy was possibly the victim of incest as a small girl. Her father's a known bad lot.'

'Common as crosswords,' said Auntie April, croakingly sotto voce. 'Iceni insects. I could tell you . . .'

'Perhaps it's as well that people like that don't breed, tragic though

253

the death may be,' Noel Linwood said grandly, with another of his gestures.

'Presumably Margy will abstain from "breeding", as you call it, on a voluntary basis,' Teresa said. 'I would prefer to see the poor woman receive proper psychiatric assistance. Tom and I are trying to get in touch with her.'

A communication of agreements flowed between the Squires, both of whom had now given a polite snub to Noel Linwood's opinions.

Watching them opposite him, tackling their full plates with relish, Tebbutt was torn between wishing to attack Squire and wishing to fawn on him, this embodiment of wealth and knowledge, the qualities on which he had been eloquent. Possibly people had always felt so divided when confronted by the lord of the manor.

He hoped in some way to challenge Squire so that he betrayed himself. Squire had expressed little sorrow over the death of Billy Lamb; on the other hand, to his credit, he had made no display of false remorse. And Lady Teresa, the gilded hussy with her bare elbows, she had at least driven over to see Billy's girlfriend and was trying to help her. Do-gooders. They could bloody afford to do good. He wanted to hear Squire speak again, though he felt himself too ignorant to argue with the man.

'Sir Thomas,' he found himself saying, 'you show some sympathy for poor people. Why do you think it is that the poor never seem to have any power? Why are they always trampled all over by the powerful?'

Squire gazed thoughtfully at him until Tebbutt lowered his gaze. 'If you are asking me why Lamb committed suicide, I should have to say because of a weakness in his character. A lack of sensitivity. Couldn't he have cultivated some insight into Margy's problems?

'If you are asking why I sacked him – well, I'd say it was because of a weakness in the economy. As a farmer, I'm not subsidized to the same extent as French farmers. My enterprise was closed down by much bigger ones, beneficiaries of the CAP. I'm sorry about Lamb.

I'm also sorry – damned sorry – to have to shut down an enterprise into which both Teresa and I put our hearts.'

Fiddling with his bread roll, Tebbutt said, 'I mean more generally, why are the poor always downtrodden?'

'Because they ask for it, that's why,' Noel said from his end of the table. 'Because they won't work unless they're made to.'

'We're certainly better motivated if we are working for ourselves,' Squire said cheerfully. 'But a better answer is – well, if it won't vex you, I'll take that question back to the Enlightenment. It's my pet subject at the moment – we are preparing an exhibition of paintings of the Enlightenment. Only a short while ago, common people were nothing. Nothing. Chattels. They were owned by the king, along with the land they tilled. The kings of France before the Revolution called themselves "France". "*L'État, c'est moi.*" They embodied the nation, swallowed it whole. In Shakespeare we have "time-honoured Lancaster", and the rest of it. The nobles owned the serfs, had the power of life and death – and labour – over them. The notion that the common herd owned the land too, might have a vote, a say in the running of the country, is a novel one, historically speaking.'

'In Communist countries, the ordinary people own everything – in theory at least.'

'Only in theory, Mr Tebbutt. Be assured of that.'

'What about the peasants in China?'

Ruby kicked him under the table for his boldness.

'I fear I know too little about Chinese peasants to answer you. But I'd guess that Chairman Mao, himself a peasant, was too clever not to see to it that they worked harder than ever.'

'But he did attempt to share out the land – so I heard.'

Squire looked thoughtfully at his plate. 'The question of how power should be deployed, not abused, has never been satisfactorily answered. Chiefly because the powerful themselves determine such matters. Occasionally, power does devolve into the hands of what you'd call a poor person, the underprivileged. Mao's a case in point. We can all think of examples to show that underdogs wield power no more wisely than the rogues they supersede.'

Auntie April sat upright in her chair and sang to them – in surprisingly girlish tones, to the tune of 'The Red Flag':

> 'The working class can kiss my arse –
> I've got the foreman's job at last . . .'

Squire laughed heartily. 'Precisely, April. Joe Stalin also got the foreman's job. If you visit his birthplace in Gori, you find a one-room hut, preserved like the stable in Bethlehem. Stalin was born a peasant, dirt poor. Expected when a boy to become a priest. When he gained power, he was directly responsible for the deaths of millions of his fellow countrymen. Another nasty example is the shoemaker's son, Nicolae Ceaușescu, present dictator of Romania, who unfortunately visited Buckingham Palace a few years ago. One of Her Majesty's few mistakes in a long reign. According to what I hear, this son of the people is a monster, corrupted by power, starving his wretched fellow countrymen.'

'So anyone who gets hold of power becomes a monster?' Tebbutt said.

'Not at all. There are examples on the other side. Horses for courses. The poor are no better and no worse than the rich. It's just that there are elements in human nature on which power operates like a devouring cancer. Elements of compassion, tolerance . . .

'What one requires, therefore, is a sturdy constitution to protect the state from circumstances where the ruthless – whether rich or poor – are able to seize unlimited power. We have that protection so far in this country.'

'You can read about abuses of power every day in the papers.'

'Our good fortune is that we *can* read of such things in the papers. We have a free press – one of the few countries in the world to do so. What example would you give as an abuse of power?'

Tebbutt knew he was trapped. He had no skill in argument. Whatever he said would be contradicted by this easy smiling man sitting opposite, now wiping his lips on his table napkin. Then he thought of his dear daughter, and the months she had spent with the CND, opposing the deployment of American nuclear weapons on a Norfolk airbase.

'This country squanders far too much money on defence,' he said. 'Isn't that an abuse of power?'

Squire shook his head. 'Power would be abused by any government who decided not to invest in defence – in effect, to disarm itself unilaterally. Since earliest days, nations have had to defend themselves. Otherwise, sooner or later, they disappear. I know such arguments are pallid set beside the strong emotional drive we all have for peace. But, as we learned in the school playground, you have to defend yourself. Peace requires muscle. Otherwise, you must bend to the mercy of bullies, the Stalins and Ceauşescus and Hitlers.'

He seemed intent on letting Tebbutt down gently. In softer tones, he said, 'Personally, I grieve most about the defence spending poured into Northern Ireland. There's where we need wise statesmen on both sides, to get us out of that sad entanglement. The Irish and English should be kissing cousins. Northern Ireland has us caught in a moral maze and I think every one of us, English as well as Irish, has to pay for that ancient wrong.'

'Are you talking about the IRA?' Jean asked.

'Yes. Also about the situation of which the IRA is a part. The IRA is a striking symptom of power mania – the power of the bullet. The IRA may be fighting a lost cause and fighting it in a cruelly wrong way, but they serve to remind us that a cruel wrong was done the Irish people. There indeed the poor were abused, just as the English poor were.'

'You think they should have been better armed?' Jean asked.

Squire roared with laughter. 'Frankly, yes!'

The talk became general.

Ruby was attempting to persuade Auntie April to try some food, but the old lady spat out a piece of potato and would have nothing more. Teresa had already pushed away her half-emptied plate and was looking bored again. Mike ate heartily, occasionally shaking his head as if denying what was being said.

Startled, Ray realized that Jean was making covert signals, wiggling fingers and frowning. Following her gaze, he saw that Alaric, Aldred and Alfric were pressing their noses against the window pane and making funny faces. Jean rose and drew the curtains, shutting her sons from view. It was now dark outside.

The powerless always get locked out, Ray thought. Talk doesn't alter the fact.

The men were eating and drinking more heartily than the women. Noel Linwood, who was holding forth about Iraq, began to recite poetry – perhaps a sure way of annoying his sister.

> '"We are they who come faster than Fate:
> We are they who ride early or late:
> We storm at your ivory gate: Pale Kings of the Sunset, beware!"

Marvellous stuff!'

'Coming faster than fate,' repeated Auntie April, and cackled. 'My lips are sealed! All some people think about . . .'

'Barking mad . . . Wonderful place, Iraq. Chap that runs it is a bit of a blighter. Can't be helped. Too many people there, that's the trouble. Bad neighbours . . . You're right, Sir Tom, have to arm yourself to the teeth. A lot of those people should be done away with, quite frankly. It's as I said earlier, though you didn't agree – some people shouldn't be allowed to breed. Over-population . . .'

'Eugenics was another Enlightenment idea,' Squire said. 'Francis Galton had a theory that there were indisputably superior people in the world, as well as multitudes of inferiors. People who hold to such theories invariably rank themselves with the superior minority. They don't see that many of the despised cottagers who read Catherine Cookson may be in many ways "superior" – you have to put the word in quotes – to themselves. In kindness, for example. In conscience and forbearance. Just as Hitler, in whose regime the eugenics theory comes really unstuck, could not perceive that many Jews were "superior" to many of his SS troopers. Moral qualities versus muscle . . .'

Noel was determinedly not disconcerted. 'All the same, Sir Tom, I think you'd like this chap Saddam running Iraq. He's burdened with a war against Iran, but he's got his head screwed on the right way. There's another example of a man with a humble background . . . Different kettle of fish from Adolf Hitler, of course . . .'

He ordered his son to fetch another bottle of wine. Everyone attended to their plates in silence for a moment, until Teresa spoke, drumming her fingers on the table.

'Perhaps it was Hitler's singular lack of rationality which finally put the kibosh on the Enlightenment, with its brave confidence in the idea of Progress. As you say, Tom, rational minds had to be part of the equation. The appearance of railway timetables must have served as an affirmation of rationality. The steam locomotive as ethical proof . . . By the beginning of this century, trust in reason was on the wane. The moths, and Sigmund Freud, had got at it. Then there was the calamity of the Great War – or World War One, if you accept that countdown – which opened the gates for Adolf Hitler to strut in. Thus did rationality create from Progress its own Frankenstein's monster.'

'*Frankenstein*. Love it,' Auntie April said. 'Genesis, Hubris, Nemesis. Terribly creepy . . .' She pushed her plate away and brushed the imaginary hair from her cheek.

Noel sighed. 'Barking again. Right up the creek, poor lady . . .'

Most of the diners accepted second helpings, and more wine.

'I don't think I'm rational,' Ruby said suddenly, putting down her fork. 'Perhaps it's because I live in a cottage. I see things. Just the other day I had a – well, I call it a vision. Something spoke to me about death. Gosh, I shouldn't mention death at the table, should I?'

'Certainly not,' said Noel, looking offended. 'None of us is going to die, are we? Let's take a vote on it.'

'Oh, death can be very funny,' Squire said, accepting more braised parsnip. 'Provided it's kept at arm's length.'

Auntie April stretched out a stringy arm. 'That's the length of an arm. Perfect. It's never been married and it's never died – yet. Maybe next April . . .'

She gave a grotesque laugh. Her brother hid his face in his hands. Silence fell, until Squire interposed with some haste. 'Marriage has many hazards, as we all know. You're fortunate if, like Teresa and me, you have survived a few crises and gone on to make a solid marriage.'

'I ran away from him once,' Ruby inserted mischievously, pointing at Ray.

'Well, that's more or less what happened with the Lawrences of Stanhoe.'

'Oh, yes, tell them that story, Tom,' said Teresa, beginning to smile. Ruby looked sulky and lodged a small rabbit bone on the side of her plate; she had wanted to tell her tale, but the Squires outgunned her.

'The Lawrences, Silas and – what was her name? – Hermione, yes. They lived in the big house in Stanhoe. It's divided into flats now. It was his house originally, the old Lawrence family home. Silas was thin and bald and a rather miserable-looking old chap, whereas Hermione was quite a fatty, and came from a long line of fatties. Silas's portrait hangs in the National Portrait Gallery. He was famed in horticultural circles for identifying three sub-species of goosegrass, or something of the sort.

'Anyhow, Silas and his wife fell out. I believe it was over a house-maid he was caught in bed with. Or perhaps Hermione simply was not amused by goosegrass. The marriage broke up. She kept the house and all her fat sisters moved in with her.'

'A fat brother too, I believe,' Teresa added.

'You're right. Also a fat brother. Silas moved out, minus housemaid, to live in a flat in Lymington and muck about with his yacht on the Solent. I sailed with him once, and we crossed to the Scilly Isles. He was not what you'd call a mariner.

'Silas was old enough to be my father. When he became pretty decrepit, he wrote to Hermione, rather throwing himself on her mercy and asking if he might return to the family house in Stanhoe to die. This was in the sixties.'

'And could he bring the dog?' supplemented Teresa.

'Hermione wrote back to say no to him and no to the dog. She told him in no uncertain terms to go and die somewhere else. I don't know what happened exactly, but a year later poor Silas ran his yacht into a dinghy, which sank. A woman on board was nearly drowned. For Silas, this was the end – a terrible disgrace. He got in his old car and drove all the way back up here. Some time long after midnight, there he was in Stanhoe, banging on Hermione's door. His old door.'

'Can you imagine the scene?' Teresa said. 'It was pouring with rain. Winter. Big Hermione bounces downstairs in her nightie, peers out into the darkness, and sees her ex standing there. It's three in the morning. She refuses to let him in. He pleads with her. He says he only wants to collect some possessions from the cellars. He left a tin trunk of family documents down there. Eventually – when she sees he hasn't brought the dog – Hermione lets Silas in, all dripping, and forces the poor man to go down to the cellars immediately. I imagine she rather lacked a flair for hospitality.

'The house stands on a slight eminence. Perhaps you know it. With extensive cellarage. Silas staggers down there. She goes back to bed, grumbling.

'Easterbrook. That was her family name before marriage. She and all the Easterbrooks get up next morning. Hermione, her three sisters, and of course the brother. They go down to breakfast. While they're tucking into their eggs and bacon and all the rest, they hear groans in the cellar.'

Jean was clearing away the dishes and making Mike rise to assist her in bringing in the pudding, a fine summer pudding with cream and custard to accompany it. Sir Thomas smiled appreciatively at her.

Teresa continued with the story. 'So of course they all troop down into the cellar.' She began to laugh. 'They leave breakfast and troop down into the cellar still munching . . . You'll have to tell them the rest, Tom.'

Tom smiled widely. 'Ruby, you say you see things. That's something else the Enlightenment sought to suppress. Visions didn't fit the world picture. Save them for the Romantics. Only the material world had a right to exist. One result is all those soap operas followed avidly by – *pace* Noel – people in cottages and palaces: dramas set in houses without spiritual dimension. Nourish your spiritual life, don't feel ashamed of it. Work on it positively and it may reward you with positive visions.

'Anyhow, there was nothing spiritual about the Easterbrooks. The flesh had taken over. And what did they find down in their cellar when they got there? Poor old Silas Lawrence! There lay the discoverer of goosegrass, helpless on the floor, calling "Help me!" He had prised open a wooden chest and then suffered a heart attack.'

Tebbutt observed that both Mike and his father were horrified by this tale.

'It was many a year since Silas had set eyes on his ex-wife. Hermione had blossomed into a real fatty. And her sisters and brother were all just as enormous. Silas was in the Land of the Fat, they had been living on the fat of the land. They were all so round that they could not bend to pick Silas up off the floor. Circumference rendered them powerless, and he died before their eyes.'

The whole table roared with laughter and passed round the bottle of wine – all except Noel, who shook his head, and Mike, who crossed himself.

'It's a horrible story,' he said.

'Oh, horrible,' agreed Teresa, and they all laughed afresh. Jean helped them to more summer pudding. As the blackcurrants, redcurrants and raspberries tumbled on to their plates, she assured them she had another pudding in reserve.

'I'm certain his ghost lives. Haunts Stanhoe House still,' Auntie April said, with sudden animation. 'Only this morning, I was sitting in my room. Alone. Doors closed. Windows closed. No flowers. Just a fly flying round the room. Round and round. It made no noise. Just went slowly round in circles. As if I wasn't there. Awful.'

The company fell into an uncomfortable silence.

Auntie April found it necessary to explain. 'Think of that fly. My brother. Absolutely alone. Round and round. Not another fly anywhere. Just silence. No escape. Closed universe. Hope we aren't like that.'

After another silence, Mike Linwood said, 'Yes, that would be terrible, Auntie. What did you do?'

She looked up at the ceiling for a moment. 'Round and round. I wasn't going to have such nonsense. Not in my room, of all rooms. I rolled up my newspaper. Yesterday's. Charge of the Light Brigade. Squashed it flat. Against the window. Very little blood. I was surprised.'

'Well,' said Jean, rising. 'I'll fetch the coffee if you'll get the liqueur, Mike.'

'I bought the liqueur,' Noel said. 'I'll get it.' He rose unsteadily to his feet. 'I paid for this meal, I'll have you know. What an affront . . . Anyone else got any funny stories about death? Dear, dear – we'll be talking about money next.'

'Money's a sore point, Mr Linwood,' Ray said, standing up. 'Some of us are owed money by members of this very household. Ugh!' He grunted as Ruby kicked him, and sat down again.

Auntie April began slowly to clap her hands together. She fixed her faded old eyes on Teresa. 'You will understand, dear – money owed, blood owed. Always the history of families. Family involves history, just like a nation. You remember the Norman Conquest, don't you?'

'Not quite,' Teresa said, with a brittle laugh.

April ignored her. 'All this talk and talk – Noel's speciality. The Irish refuse to forget their history. So do I. So do I, you hear?' Her voice rattled. 'It's what you're made of, history, and blood owing.' She sank back in her chair, covering her eyes.

Mike went over to her, patting her thin shoulders, saying, 'It's the wine. She always gets like this.'

'Perhaps something should be done about it, then,' Teresa suggested.

Noel gave her a wink, saying with forced geniality, 'Like that as a girl, Lady Teresa, all brine and britches. Don't worry yourself. All's fair in love and war, ha ha.'

With a nod at his wife, Squire rose. 'We must be going. We have to attend Billy Lamb's funeral tomorrow. Hence, I suppose, all our talk of death.' As the Squires made their farewells, he said to Noel, 'I'm sorry we can't help you with your plans.'

Noel tossed his white hair and stared down at his plate. The

Tebbutts stood uneasily to one side. Only Auntie April remained in her place, now gazing up at the ceiling as if searching for flies. When Squire approached to say goodbye, she clutched his tweed-clad arms.

'Take me, take me from here. The assassin's billet. I don't want to stay here all night.'

Pulling herself up, she clutched at Teresa too.

Noel blundered round the table, gabbling away, waving his napkin. 'Sorry, sorry. I told you about her. Ape, you will sleep tonight in one of Jean's hard little unaired beds upstairs and tomorrow I will drive you back to Blakeney, muzzled, OK?'

He pulled her away from the Squires, tugging at her brittle mottled arms.

'Gently, gently, please!' Teresa exclaimed. 'You'll hurt her.'

'That never stopped him,' Auntie April said.

'Leave this to me,' Noel said, wrenching his sister away. 'She's no idea what's going on.'

'Oooh, abyss!' the old woman shrieked. 'You sadomite, you. Babylonian! Help!'

But there was no help in family quarrels, and he dragged her away, holding her body like a plank before him. The Squires looked at each other and beat a hasty retreat with Jean following to open the front door for them.

The Tebbutts remained rooted to the spot, watching as Auntie April tottered out of the room towards the kitchen.

Victorious Noel raised a fist above his head. 'I'll have the old bitch put away, see if I don't. Barking mad. And I'd like to have that bastard Squire put away . . .' Catching Ray's eye, he said, more soberly, wiping flecks of foam from his mouth, 'What do you Muslims reckon? All I wanted from him was to hire out his confounded packing sheds as a gun club. He's not using them now. Might have made a bit of money. Not he – landed gentry, no sporting instincts these days. Bastard.'

Mike, keeping his distance, said in a low voice, 'They put you down, Father, both of them. Couldn't you see that? Curse if you like.

Sir Thomas will never do business with the likes of you. You can forget about that.'

'We'd better be going,' Ruby said, tugging at her husband.

But Noel, in real anger, had turned on his son. 'Keep your mouth shut! You love to see me in difficulties, don't you? I shall move out of this dump tomorrow – then we'll see how you and that slut of a wife of yours manage without me. I've had all I can take of you and your pious ways.'

As they began to shout at each other, Thelonius ran in, barking with delight to be back in the house.

The stone-flagged hall was in gloom, its outer door open to the night. Jean Linwood stood in the shadows, leaning against the hall-stand, listening to the rumpus taking place over her dinner table.

Ray took her hand. 'Lovely meal, Jean. Thanks so much. And I'll be round to speak to Mike tomorrow morning, if you'd tell him that.'

'Tell him your bloody self,' she said. As she turned her shoulder to him, she began to cry, dragging her hair over her eyes.

'Lovely evening, Jean,' Ruby said, and bundled her husband into the night.

Three boys, crouching behind a clump of pampas, anxiously watched them go.

As Ray reached their car, Jean screamed after them, 'It wasn't always like this!'

The Tebbutts had an argument over their Sunday morning breakfast – quietly, because Agnes was still asleep.

Ray insisted he could not go back to Hartisham and try to collect the money from Michael Linwood; they had trouble enough without him pestering them.

Ruby insisted he must go. The money was theirs and had been promised. It was not scruples but cowardice which made him hesitate.

In the end, he gave in, driving off while his wife went out the back to look at Tess's mange.

At St Giles House, he left the orange Hillman in the road and walked round to the back door. Mike's Chrysler was not in the carport. Only the broken-down Toyota truck stood among nettles, a permanent fixture. The house was silent. After waiting a moment, he knocked. Thelonius barked and whined on the other side of the door.

Eventually, one of the boys opened up. It was either Alaric or Aldred; their pale faces, like their names, were much alike. The lad's expression became even gloomier on recognizing Tebbutt. Without a word, he let him into the kitchen and then disappeared up the back stairs, the dog following.

Tebbutt stood in the worn room, with its stale odours, listening to the tick of a wind-up clock. I'm getting old, he thought – and weird. Some things give you the pip. It was a phrase inherited from his mother, long ago. Well, Norfolk was a repository of forlorn things. He remembered Auntie April's remark about priests in their 'vestcements', still to be smelt. To his mind, religion was yet another of the claims the past had on the present, insidious as tick of wind-up clock.

When no sounds of human movement came to him, he crept into the passage and peered into the dining-room. Nothing had changed since he had left it twelve hours before. The dirty dishes were still piled on the table. A slice of surviving summer pudding was beached on a serving plate, staining it red. Discarded napkins lay here and there. The painted face of Noel Roderick Linwood regarded the debris.

When Jean entered the room, she came noiselessly on bare feet, in a mustard-coloured gown, startling Tebbutt. She stood, arms akimbo over her breasts, defiantly. He shuffled. He made a facetious remark about the previous evening. Dismissing it as worthless, she told him Michael was at church. Her manner was chill and lifeless.

'I'm really sorry if things are bad, Jean.'

'Look, I've got this stuff to wash up.'

When he said he would wait, smiling in an attempt to appease her, she said he could not: she had too much work to do. He would get his money in good time, if he stopped pestering them. Her face was drawn, forbidding argument.

As she followed him to the back door, he asked where Noel was. She replied that if it was any of his business the old man was driving his sister back to Blakeney. At this point – as he had his hand on the latch, the door half-open, cheerful morning sun spilling over the threshold, lighting the drab interior of the house – she appeared to weaken, to soften.

They stood close, not moving, not looking at each other.

'Oh, hell,' she said.

He put an arm round her waist.

He knew she had wished it. Yet the arm was in its place only a moment, curling round the slender trunk of her body just above her hips, when she threw it off, showed fury, told him to clear off or she would set the dog on him.

He went to sit in the car and wait.

Perhaps we should go and live somewhere else. I'll never make any money here. Perhaps after Agnes is gone . . . Perhaps Ruby might welcome a change. Of course she'd be sorry to sell off Tess. And we've got the cottage more or less fixed up . . . It wouldn't fetch a lot of money. People who come up here want somewhere near the sea. Besides . . .

Shortly before one o'clock, the Chrysler appeared, rolled across the grass, and stopped a few yards from where Tebbutt waited.

Mike Linwood sat at the wheel, staring across at Tebbutt, evidently having trouble deciding whether or not to get out of the car. When he did so finally, he was clutching a Bible in one hand.

He came straight over to the other car, his face drawn into lines of disapproval, his furry eyebrows twitching, and began speaking before Tebbutt could leave his seat.

'This is unjust. You're persecuting me, Tebbutt. You are trying to make a victim of me. I once thought there was trust between us – I see now I was deceived. You think that I do not intend to repay your miserable loan. Your miserable grudging loan! That's what's in your mind. I know. Nothing could be further from the truth.'

Tebbutt pushed open the car door, climbing out to confront Linwood face to face. When he spoke, he repressed his rage at the other's tone of voice, so weary, so righteous.

'You broke your promise, Mike. You have not returned the loan.

You promised it at the beginning of last week. You broke your promise. So I've come to collect now.'

'You're persecuting me. I haven't enough money to get the boys to the optician.'

Turning to stare into the distance, Linwood began to speak of his embracing spirituality. He supposed Tebbutt would find such a grave matter funny; yet it was a decision based on months of anxious thought and prayer. He repeated the words in case they were unfamiliar to his listener: thought and prayer. It had been his vision on the way to Damascus. Didn't, he asked, even Ruby claim she had visions? He hoped to do his mite to turn the tide against all the greed and despair with which the world was threatened.

'You should be telling this to Joe Stanton, not me,' Tebbutt said. 'Come on, I got you out of a hole. Don't give me this shit – pay up. That's all I ask. I don't care if you're going to turn Buddhist.'

At which Linwood gave a snort of contempt, spun on his heel and marched towards the house. After a moment's hesitation, Tebbutt sprang into action, following him as he entered at the back door. Thelonius jumped delightedly up at his master. Jean entered with a tray from the passage, giving her husband a wan questioning look without a smile.

'As you can see, I'm being pursued.'

'Oh, for God's sake, give him the money and be done with it,' she said. She set down the tray of dirty dishes by the sink, turning her back on the men as she started to run the hot water.

Taking no notice of Jean's remark, Linwood perched himself on the edge of the table.

'Since you've barged in here, Ray, we'd better have a talk, you and I. I want to tell you something. You know my father, Noel. You had the doubtful pleasure of meeting him again last evening. He's a materialist of the old school. He grew up in an age of materialism, when to make money was the main aim in life, no matter at whose expense. Father is—'

'What did he invite me round here for?'

'To embarrass me, of course. Didn't you gather that? You lied to him and he enjoys lies. That nonsense about being Muslim. Father is utterly destitute of spiritual values.'

'Oh, shut up about spiritual values,' Jean called from the sink, clattering dishes, and was ignored.

'Noel's a money-grubber, a miser. His occupation in life was to sell arms to the troubled nations of the Middle East, to any little dictator with the finance. It was under his creed I was brought up and, as a good and dutiful son, I laboured long under his spell. My eyes were blind and I saw not.

'I'm throwing it away now, that dreadful creed. I'm going to be free at last.'

'Then come and help me clear up these dishes,' said Jean in the background.

'Patience, dear, I'm trying to help Ray. You see, Ray – a change of heart! A little late in life, you might say, but the Lord rejoices in a sinner come to repentance, whatever his age. Even a failure like me. You may laugh inwardly to hear me use the time-honoured language of the Bible. So be it. But—'

'Mike, look, all this stuff is between you and your family. I don't care what you do. Don't tell me. Just pay up and I'll be off.'

A plate came sailing in their direction, missing both of them, to crash on the floor.

'Pay up! Get out of here, the pair of you!' Jean screamed.

When neither of them moved – were, indeed, transfixed by surprise – she gave a muffled cry and ran for the back door, shedding another plate as she went, to disappear into the garden.

'She's very upset,' Tebbutt said. 'Shouldn't you go to her?'

'She'll be back. Don't worry. I know Jean. Emotional. The sort of person prayer would greatly help.'

'"The sort of person . . ." Christ, Mike, is that how you think of your wife? I'd say she's out of her mind with worry.'

'No, listen, Ray, calm down. I don't wish to quarrel with you or any man. You and I are of the same generation, almost. You must surely be sympathetic to what I have said about my materialist upbringing. The odds were loaded against us. There are millions like us. The unhappy post-war generation, deceived from birth. As Proverbs truly says, Where there is no vision, the people perish. We've lived out an awful dilemma, captives of economic necessity. Have you ever considered that the Cold War is a macrocosmic projection of inner death? All that stuff we were getting from Sir Tom last night the – Enlightenment and all that – utter guff.

'Millions of us have served as units of state, without spiritual dimension. Isn't that so? Our brief existences should be full of faith, hope, love. Instead, if we live as the state requires, we throw our lives away. You're nothing more than a work unit, a statistic, an "X" on a vote paper – a consumer.

'Don't you know that's so? I'm certain you do, really. Think of young Lamb. Job gone – he had no other identity. So he perished. Isn't that so?'

Tebbutt felt bound to agree with this proposition, at least in part. 'I've never had doubts about my identity, but I see what you mean.'

Setting his head quizzically on one side, Linwood said, 'I'm not sure that you do see. Otherwise you would not let this paltry sum of money upset our relationship, my dear Ray. I would like to bring you to God one day.'

Rushing forward, Tebbutt caught Linwood by the collar and wrenched him from the table. There he paused. Another car had roared up behind the house, hooting as it stopped. Mayhem was averted.

Noel Roderick Linwood had returned. He breezed into the house, white hair trailing like a horse's mane, grunting, as he urged Jean back into the house. She fled before him, rushing into the dark interior, in a mustard-coloured flurry. Thelonius began a furious barking.

Tebbutt released Linwood and dropped his hands.

Halting in the middle of the kitchen, Noel did a slow turn, cartoon-fashion, his shoulders drooping, arms trailing, mouth agape, to stare at Ray.

'You back again? Come to finish off the summer pudding? Or did you never leave? Is he converting you to God or you him to Allah?' He allowed his son no glance. 'Opium of which people?'

'I'm here for the shagging three hundred pounds he owes me. Nothing more, nothing less.'

Noel smote his forehead. 'Blood from a stone . . . And now you're intending to strangle him. Why? As usual he's preaching, eh? Out of the mouths of boobs and suckers shall come forth prose, as the Bible says, in its amusing way . . .'

Still maintaining his slumped carriage, Noel wove his way from the kitchen and disappeared into the house. A door slammed. Upstairs, the boys turned up their rock music extra loud, celebrating their grandfather's return.

Mike was pale. 'You see how terrifying it is to live here. They're all in spiritual crisis.' He spoke almost in a whisper. 'Money's their god, as I fear it is yours. You were about to resort to force. Everywhere one looks it's the same story nowadays. Art, literature, music – the cash nexus rules. That's why I wish to take Holy Orders. Perhaps you might understand from my example. What do the majority of townspeople do on Sundays, instead of going to church? Why, they go shopping. Shopping! It's degradation.'

'Maybe. But at least it's something the whole family can do together.'

'And so is praying.' Linwood looked pleased, having scored a point. More confident now – though still darting glances in the direction his wife and father had taken – he crossed to the sink, poured himself a glass of water from the tap, and sipped it.

'I suppose you see no difference between shopping and praying. That's precisely what being an economic unit means.'

'Don't be such a prig. People do what they can. We work for a living – the trouble is, the living isn't good enough.'

'You might as well be in Bulgaria, or some atheist state – Albania, China . . . You must perceive that the world is being overtaken by a creeping form of spiritual death. All then becomes clear. That's the reason I'm joining the Church. Why be so adversarial, Ray? It's for the good of my soul. Don't grudge me that.'

'And what about the good of Jean's soul?'

Linwood smiled. He set down his glass on the draining board where the dirty dishes were piled. 'It's not quite the same for women, is it? Basically, I mean. Read your Bible. Despite all the feminist nonsense being talked . . . I mean, that's a different kettle of fish, somehow, isn't it?'

A door slammed in the house. Noel Linwood returned to the fray, showing his unnaturally white teeth in something between a grin and a growl. He waved a piece of paper at Tebbutt.

It was a cheque for three hundred pounds, written in Noel's spidery hand. Thrusting it at Tebbutt, he told him to take it and get out; as he spoke his grimace was switched on to his son, who had drawn himself up as if before a firing squad.

Tebbutt grabbed the cheque.

Without forethought, he launched a lie to save his dignity. 'I shall donate your generous cheque, Mr Linwood, to the Anglo-Muslim Society of Great Britain.' He almost ran to his car.

At No. 2 Clamp Lane, a warm welcome awaited Tebbutt. Ruby, who had become anxious at Ray's prolonged absence, embraced him, kissed him, kissed the cheque, declared she should never have forced him to confront the crazed denizens of St Giles House, praised his courage to her mother. Mother joined in the admiration society, protesting she did not know where all the money came from, and she personally was grateful to the government for her many blessings.

They celebrated with a glass of wine, home-brewed elderberry.

Ray and Ruby walked out into the garden, leaving Agnes to nurse the cat. There, leaning over the gate into Tess's enclosure, Ruby told her husband that Jenny had phoned an hour earlier. She was with the Czech fellow, Jaroslav, and they had found a comfortable little hotel on the sea front at thing-me – Yarmouth. She had invited her mother over for the day.

'She sounded quite keen to have me.'

Ray agreed immediately that she should go, fingering the cheque in his pocket as he spoke. Whereupon Ruby announced that she had secretly saved a little money – by coincidence, it amounted to three hundred pounds – and with that she was determined to take her poor old mother to Yarmouth. It would fulfil Agnes's dream of seeing the sea once more.

Surely Ray could come along too, just take a couple of days off? The break and the sea air would do him good.

Ray thought that Yarker might agree, since he had put in overtime recently, cutting down those bloody poplars.

They hugged each other again, sharing their pleasure.

Ruby had even remembered to write down the name of the little Yarmouth hotel.

The Dianoya. Very quiet, Jenny said.

6

Salvation

Professor Hengist Morton Embry walked from the university carpark at his usual brisk pace. Raincoat open, hands clasped behind his back, he was enjoying the crisp November air.

He found English weather pleasant. This pleasure was enhanced today by the news that the east coast of Florida was being assailed by winds of hurricane force. In the precincts of the Anglia University all was calm. The deciduous trees, planted in the sixties to offset the cheapjack architecture, shed their leaves without fuss, dropping them tidily round their roots.

Tucked under Embry's right arm was a summary of his report on the bomb outrage at the Dianoya Hotel. He was about to present it – or rather, his case – informally to the principal of the university, Sir Alastair Stern. Embry had worked hard during his British year. He wanted this project to go through.

He wanted it to go through for academic reasons. *Amour propre* was also involved. And at the back of his superficial but fertile mind lay the possibility of turning the story of those involved in the IRA bombing into a screenplay for the movies. Maybe transpose the setting from England to America . . .

The principal's rooms were in a renovated manor house. The house had become derelict during World War II, when the RAF had taken it over and ruined it. House and extensive grounds had sold cheaply to the university foundation during one of the periodic recessions which afflicted England.

As Embry ascended the stairs to the second floor – there was of course no elevator and the second floor was the third over here – he reflected that the theoretical basis of his thesis was not entirely sound. He recognized as much privately, while not acknowledging it publicly. However, he liked Stern and believed Stern liked him. Stern might come up with further funding. Much depended on whether Gordon Levine would also be present at the meeting. Embry was aware that the younger man had both influence on Stern and no affection for him (Embry); they had failed to hit it off in Florida the previous year.

Sir Alastair Stern greeted Embry and helped him out of his coat. Stern was a tall man with a stoop, in his sixties, silver-haired. His drooping lower lip gave him a good-humoured air which his nature did not belie. Standing discreetly by the drinks cabinet was his son-in-law, Gordon Levine. Levine moved forward to shake Embry's hand, after which he moved back against the linenfold panelling that lined the room.

When greetings and conversation regarding mutual friends were over, Stern sank into his chair and opened the copy of Embry's report which lay ready on his desk. Thus prompted, Embry opened his own copy, tapping it importantly.

'It's good of you to spare me an hour on a day like this, and I promise to take up no more than sixty minutes of your and Gordon's time.'

'If you could just run over your report for us . . .' Stern said in his dry voice.

'Sure thing,' said Embry. 'This paper is merely my preliminary summary regarding the Dianoya Hotel Explosion.'

He cleared his throat, set half-frame glasses on his nose, and commenced to speak rapidly, following the printed page with a substantial forefinger.

'The Dianoya Hotel is No. 1 Dunes Drive, on the sea front at Great Yarmouth. It is a small private hotel, with front windows overlooking promenade, public gardens, the sandy beach, and the North Sea. It was converted from a private house into a hotel in 1922 and has since been much modernized. At the time of the explosion, July 1986, it was owned by a Mr Dominic Mayor and his second wife, Caroline Mayor.

'Great Yarmouth is mentioned in the Domesday Book, 1086. It was an important fishing port for many centuries and is now a popular seaside resort. Its industries—'

At a slight interjection from Stern, Embry smiled, nodded, skipped that passage, and continued.

'The Dianoya itself was a pleasant small hotel, well-recommended, and giving personal service. Its public rooms comprised a hall, a dining-room with bar extending into a conservatory, and a lounge with access to a smaller bar. On the first floor were three double bedrooms, one single, one bathroom, and a toilet. On the second floor were two double bedrooms, one single, and a toilet. The five double bedrooms were all fitted with cubicles containing showers and toilets.

'From this it can be seen that the Dianoya could house a complement of only twelve guests at any time, although children could be accommodated in addition.

'The third floor is given over to private accommodation, the Mayors' apartments.'

'Er . . . the explosion. The victims . . .' Stern prompted.

Embry smiled broadly. 'That's what the report is all about, Sir Alastair. Just let me run through these ancillary points first.'

Using his finger as cursor, he read rapidly from his summary.

'Broadly speaking, that was Section One.

'Two, the Hotel Staff. The hotel is owned by Mr Dominic Mayor and his wife, Caroline Mayor, as stated. It is Mr Mayor's second marriage. The Mayors have two small children and live on the premises. They take no part in the running of the hotel.

'The hotel is managed by Dominic Mayor's adoptive mother, Daphne Mayer – slight difference in spelling there – and her friend "Andy" – Andrew Rawlings. They also live on the premises.

'Daphne Mayer has some assistance of a daily nature, mainly a waitress, Betty, plus a cook, and Arold and Doris Betts, two servants who live in a small converted store plus caravan to the rear of the hotel.

'Three, the Bomb. The bomb consisted of eight pounds of the plastic explosive Semtex, manufactured in Czechoslovakia. The Semtex was probably paid for in Prague by an IRA agent calling himself Driscoll, and the delivery made via Libya. A ship, the *Eksund*, was loaded in a military dockyard in Tripoli. As well as the explosive, the *Eksund* probably contained Kalashnikov rifles, ground-to-air missiles, mortar bombs, etc., all intended for the IRA. The *Eksund* was apprehended at sea by French customs officers in 1987 and its crew arrested.

'Scotland Yard anti-terrorist squads have traced such deliveries of Semtex from the Irish Republic to caches in such English towns as Manchester, Liverpool, London, and elsewhere.

'The Yarmouth bomb was one of seven planned to detonate serially within the month of July. The other bombs were to be detonated along the south coast by timing devices of Taiwanese origin. The apprehension of two Irishmen in June led to the defusing and destruction of these bombs. The seventh bomb, handled by a different IRA squad, went undetected.

'Four, the Planting of the Bomb. The Yarmouth bomb was planted by a man who signed the hotel register as Jim Donnell. He took other names when abroad, such as Tom Driscoll when "shopping" in Czechoslovakia. His real name was Patrick James Cole. Cole is known to the authorities. Born Belgonnelly, County Fermanagh, in 1950. He is unmarried.

'He signed Mrs Mayer's register on the night of Friday 5 July, and was given the double bedroom overlooking the Britannia Pier and the sea on the first floor, designated Room Two. "Donnell" claimed that his wife would be joining him later. No wife appeared.

'Donnell was clearly described by both Mrs Mayer and Arold Betts. The latter saw Donnell early in the morning of the fifth from eight to eight thirty A.M., walking with another man, scrutinizing the hotel from the road outside. In Betts' words, "He 'ung round the front, then he come and 'ung round the side". What particularly drew Betts' attention was the fact that Donnell photographed the hotel from the opposite side of the street. At that time, Betts described Donnell as a ginger man in his mid-thirties, wearing a heavy suit inappropriate to the season and the place.

'Nine hours later, at five P.M., Betts saw Donnell again. This time, he was registering as a guest for one night. Betts noted that no camera was visible about his person. Mrs Mayer in Reception was asking him if he required an evening meal, which was then being served. Donnell said No. He spoke with an Irish accent. He was at that time dressed in jeans and a T-shirt bearing the legend NAPALM DEATH. The phrase forms the name of a British thrash metal group (album: "Scum") who were playing that week in Caister, outside Yarmouth.

'Mrs Mayer also noted the legend, and was unhappy about it, considering it out of keeping with her establishment. She noticed also folds in the clean T-shirt, indicating that it was new and being worn for the first time. Donnell was described as polite but "anxious" in his manner. He refused to allow Betts to take his suitcase up to the room.

'Donnell was discussed by Mrs Mayer and Betts after he retired to Room Two. Betts suggested that he was up to no good, and had probably robbed a bank in Norwich. Or alternatively, that he was a private detective sent to spy on Dominic Mayor by his ex-wife, then living in Scotland.

'Five, the Positioning of the Bomb. Although the Dianoya was badly damaged by the explosion, the Birmingham Anti-Terrorist Squad under Detective Inspector Frederick Waters has shown that Donnell installed the bomb under the toilet fitment in Room Two. This toilet fitment contains within its plastic shell a shower cubicle, washbasin, and WC bowl (unit manufactured by Brodie Originals of Oadby, Leics.).

'Detective Inspector Waters was able to show that Donnell had fitted the bomb with timer under the lip of the shower tray.

'The bomb was timed to explode at 1830 hours on Saturday 6 July. Which it did. The timer was of a type made in Taiwan.

'By that time, Donnell had left the hotel and the vicinity. He is believed to be presently in Belfast.

'Six, the Warning. At 1813 hours on 6 July, Central Yarmouth Police Station in Howard Street North received a warning of an imminent bomb explosion. The current agreed IRA code word "Shining" was given in a voice with an Irish brogue. The message was that a bomb was planted in a small hotel, unnamed, after which the caller rang off. Detective Inspector Mary Rogers, who took the call, immediately instigated an alarm system to all hotels, warning them to evacuate. Five hundred and fifty hotels, private hotels, and guest houses are registered with the Council. Before the Dianoya could be called, the bomb exploded.

'Seven, Occupants of the Hotel. The following persons were present or staying in the hotel at the time of the explosion, in the categories of residents, guests or visitors. Drinks were being served at the bar, and snacks served in the dining-room adjacent. Persons' locations at 1830 hours follow names and status.

'Residents and Staff:

Dominic Mayor	Owner	Descending from suite on top (third) floor to landing on second floor
Caroline Mayor	Owner's wife	In town with children
Daphne Mayer	Manageress	In dining-room, supervising, mixing with guests
Andrew Rawlings	Companion of manageress	In kitchens
Sally Sahir	Cook	In kitchens
Arold Betts	Servant	Location unverified
Doris Betts	Servant, wife of above	On first floor, in Room Three
Betty Obispo	Daily servant	Behind bar

'Guests on First Floor:

Percy Fletcher	Room One	Changing clothes in room
Amanda Fletcher	Wife of above	In toilet of Room One
Kieron Cranshaw	Room Two	In bar
Shirley Williamson	Friend of above	Sunning on hotel terrace
Ruby Tebbutt	Room Three	Walking on promenade outside hotel
Agnes Silcock	Mother of above	Invalid. Resting in room
Anna Weil	Room Four (single)	On beach

'Guests on Second Floor:

Samuel Jackson	Room Five	At Pleasure Beach
Beata Jackson	Wife of above	At Pleasure Beach
Bruno Lux	Room Six, brother of above	Snacks in dining-room
Hilda Lambert	Friend of above	Putting infant to bed
Benny Lambert	Infant of above	
Ray Tebbutt	Room Seven (single)	In bar
Captain Charlie Parr	Visitor	In hallway
Jennifer Tebbutt	Visitor	In bar
Jaroslav Vacek	Visitor, friend of above	In bar

'Eight, Damage. The blast caused considerable devastation. Room Two and its toilet – the site of the explosion – were completely wrecked, as was Room Three. The single room next door (Room Four) was also destroyed, and a hole blown in the external wall, causing the collapse of the ceiling above. Rooms Five and Six on the second floor were wrecked, together with landing and stairs adjoining. The floors of the private suite on the third floor fell in.

'The collapse of the floors of rooms mentioned showered furniture and debris on the bar and dining-room below. Many windows were broken. A fire broke out. Structural damage amounts to many thousands of pounds. The building itself has been declared structurally unsound.

'Slight injuries: all those persons named in Section 7 were taken to hospital and treated for minor injuries or shock, with the exception of Captain Parr. He had come to talk to Daphne Mayer and was entering the Dianoya when the detonation occurred. Parr promptly ran into the street and phoned the police from the next house. Police arrived within 4.5 minutes, ambulances within 7 minutes, two fire brigades within 7.5 minutes. Captain Parr was the first to assist the injured from the hotel after the blast.

'Serious injuries: the following were detained in hospital for more than forty-eight hours: Betty Obispo – eye injury. Amanda Fletcher – injuries to legs, thighs and back. Kieron Cranshaw – severe head injuries. Hilda and Benny Lambert – body injuries. Ray Tebbutt – two broken legs, other minor bruising. Doris Betts – leg and hip injuries, broken arm.

'Deaths: killed instantly: Dominic Mayor. Agnes Silcock. Jaroslav Vacek. Dying of brain and head injuries seventy-three hours after explosion: Jennifer Tebbutt.'

After Hengist Embry had read out these names, silence fell in the principal's room, in an instinctive token of regret.

Looking up from his paper, Embry smiled and said, 'So to the conclusions of the Embry Report.'

'Yes, yes, it's the conclusions we wish to hear,' said Stern, with a glance at his son-in-law, who sat in the shadow by the drinks cabinet.

'OK, here goes.' And Embry began to read once more, this time giving his words due emphasis.

'Our unit at AUN has investigated the circumstances which led to the four persons killed being present at that particular time and place. The question we were asking was, Why these four and not others?

'In previous times, such coincidence might be ascribed to "Fate" or "Destiny", or some such nebulous phrase, or to the Hand of God.

Our belief is that such dismissive fatalisms are inadequate for a scientific age, and should be replaced by more constructive thinking.

'We had in mind that even more recent theories, such as Kammerer's Seriality Theory or Carl Jung's Synchronicity Theory, did not fulfil requirements. It was necessary to determine whether there might be a genetic disposition in the victims towards catastrophe, or whether "bad luck" – the sense that more than ordinary ill-fortune is operative in a given system – might not predispose an individual to further increments of bad luck later in life, in what we term a "circumstance-chain"; analogously to those children who, having been deprived of love in childhood, find it difficult to establish loving relationships in adult life. Where compensation is most needed it is most lacking.

'We sought to reveal, in other words, a possible causality or linkage between mental factors and the physical world: a kind of *transpsychic reality* whose discovery and authentication would transform our understanding of human life – and link the spiritual with the physical.

'We believe we have discovered such a linkage in the case of the four deaths. The two women and two men who were killed all had histories of prior catastrophe, or else close psychic linkage with catastrophe.

'In the case of the two women killed. Jennifer Tebbutt (28) was obsessed by the fear of nuclear annihilation. As we know, fear and desire are close. Agnes Silcock (75) had lived through two World Wars, bombed out in each of them.

'In the case of the two men killed. Both had their origins in Europe. Both had suffered from the invasion of their countries by hostile forces. We obtained much of Mayor's life history from Daphne Mayer; a synopsis is appended. More data is required in the case of the Czech, Vacek, but investigation suggests he was involved with international arms smuggling. (More information is held in official sources, but emergence of Czechoslovakia from Communist domination has not led to easier accessibility of secret material in London, Prague, or Washington.)

'Both Vacek and Jennifer Tebbutt were merely visiting the Dianoya. They had occupied a room – in fact Room Two – for two days previously. They had checked out on the morning (Friday) prior to the explosion to visit Norwich, and were planning to return to London on the Sunday afternoon. Agnes Silcock was staying in the hotel on her granddaughter's (Tebbutt's) recommendation. Tebbutt and Vacek had returned briefly to the Dianoya to visit Silcock and Tebbutt's parents. Their luggage remained outside in their parked car in Dunes Drive.

'We interviewed Mrs Ruby Tebbutt, mother of the deceased girl. She had earlier had a strong premonition concerning "a death at the seaside" (she termed it "a vision"), which she had related to a second party. This is evidence for our hypothesis.

'We are researching the life histories of the surviving hotel occupants (where they can be traced) for the sake of comparison. We expect results to confirm our initial findings, which is of the existence of a transpsychic reality, perhaps already foreshadowed in the popular phrase "self-fulfilling prophecy", drawing people who have suffered sorrow towards further sorrow.

'Without anticipating final results of our survey, we believe that the four deaths will be seen to represent a kind of unhappy self-fulfilment for the persons involved.'

Silence fell. The two older men, Embry and Stern, tended to look up at the plaster strap work of the ceiling. Gordon Levine rose unbidden and poured them glasses of white wine.

Accepting his glass, Embry looked up at the young man and said earnestly, 'I expect you see all the implications of this research, Gordy. If my thesis proves correct, the world is about to change for the better. We are going to see clearly, and for the first time, what leads mankind into disastrous situations, from solitary suicide to global war. For the first time, psychic factors will take precedence over the economic, political, and nationalistic factors which flow from them.'

Beyond a curt nod of his head, Levine gave no sign of having heard this speech. Taking his glass with him, he went over to the long windows, to stand looking out at the wintry quadrangle.

'What happened to this Irish chap, Cole?' Stern asked, peering at his report.

'He got away, Sir Alastair.'

'According to your theory, should he not have perished in the explosion?'

'He may yet meet a bloody end. So one can predict.'

'"Those who live by the sword" . . .'

Both men fell silent. Stern put his elbows on his desk, supported his chin, and stared towards the television set across the room. He looked gloomy. Embry shuffled his papers and coughed.

It was Levine who broke the silence, speaking from his position at the window, arms folded, clutching his half-empty glass.

'Professor Embry, you will no doubt be able to prove your case, to show that misery attracts misery, or whatever it is, because that is what you are setting out to do. Your name will be enhanced as a result. I can see that the idea of transpsychic reality has its attractions. But whatever facts you align to support it – excuse me if I speak bluntly – I shall still regard it as poppycock.'

Embry's nostrils elongated. He sat upright in his chair. 'Facts aren't important to you. Is that what you're saying?'

'Not at all. Facts have their place.' Stern had swivelled in his chair and shook his head at his son-in-law, but Levine continued. 'Don't you insult the dead by fitting them neatly into some cock-eyed theory? I don't know who these four people were who died in the Yarmouth hotel, but they all appear to be very ordinary. You have no proof, have you, that this Czech Vacek was a dealer in arms? As for the others – well, one, Mayor, was the owner of the hotel. One was a young woman in business, with social concerns. One was an old country woman – Silcock, wasn't it? Ordinary English people. Not especially interesting. Why engineer it to look as if their deaths were in any way sought after?

'No, Professor. They were just on holiday, all except Mayor. Now they're dead, let's think of them, and the injured, simply as ordinary people. Like the rest of us, they lived out their lives as best they could. We all have to do it.'

'You're being sanctimonious, Gordy. I'm trying to be scientific.'

'That's my complaint. You're not being scientific. These four people were caught in a dreadful mischance. That's all. The workings of chance.'

'Hengist's position, surely,' interposed Stern, in his dry voice, looking from one to the other, 'is that there are laws of chance. What he calls a circumstance-chain.'

'They were caught in a dreadful mischance,' Levine repeated. 'A mischance which those who survive will remember for the rest of their lives. Let's hope the dead were at least as happy as it's possible to be in a troubled world.'

At that, Embry rose to his feet, pulling off his half-frames to wag them at Levine. 'You'll forgive me if I say that those are the words of a wimp. God, man, can't we do any better than a few pieties? Something happened. I want to find out why. Can't we academics look around us and invest good hard cash in finding a way to beat killing? This wasn't old age or cancer or a fall from a cliff. This was a bomb going off, killing innocent people. Ordinary English people, like you say. But why them exactly? I want hard understanding, not conventional condolences.'

As Embry sighed deeply, Levine started to speak, but Embry brushed his words aside. 'I need the backing of this university. It is not impossible that we can penetrate the enigma of what makes us as a species seek disaster, opt for it. I say we don't have to lie down and take what is coming to us.'

He turned to Stern, who had remained in his chair, listening gravely to the argument. 'I'm not here to be put on trial, Sir Alastair. I'm merely here to make my case – to you.'

'Quite, quite.'

'Excuse my anger, but I can't help feeling your son-in-law's attitude is all too defeatist, too European – too British.'

'You're right there,' Levine said, setting down his glass and coming forward. He had turned pale, and spoke quietly and swiftly. 'I am European, Professor. I am British. I'm also a Jew. So far, I've stayed clear of catastrophe in my life. Nevertheless, always in my conscious thought – or on the edge of it at least – is the knowledge of that appalling catastrophe, Hitler's destruction of six million Jews and other races. Many members of my family perished in those dreadful years, those dreadful events.

'If your crackpot theory holds water in any way, then those six million victims wished their deaths. Right? That's absurd and disgusting. Disgusting. I will not accept such a cruelly deceitful proposition.'

'Nevertheless—' Embry began, but Levine was in full spate.

'And I too, with that catastrophe in my bones, built into my whole world picture, should be predestined for catastrophe, if we believed your proposition. I find that idea disgusting too.

'To be honest, I prefer the old Talmudic concept of the Hand of God. God at least moves in a mysterious way. Whatever miseries He inflicts on His people, at least we are not lemmings.'

Embry thumped his fist on the principal's desk. 'I've listened to such rubbish before. "God" is simply an invention of the human mind – an invention, Levine, designed to smother the question of why we suffer. Forget it! Forget God! Think present day.

'You say we're not lemmings. We are lemmings. We go on believing the old shibboleths, or even sillier new ones. I want to cure that. We're always running to disaster, just like lemmings. Not "wished" disasters, as you keep saying. Merely *avoidable*. Avoidable in the same way so-called automobile "accidents" are ninety-nine per cent avoid-able if you cut out social factors like drink, tiredness, inattention, recklessness, and so on.

'No, let me finish! Just when things internationally seem to be looking up, wham, along comes another war or invasion or revolu-tion. That's careless existence-driving. We can't go on that way. It's time for new understanding. I have taken a substantial first step along the way. I hope you see that, Principal, even if your son-in-law doesn't?'

Embry stared at Stern. Stern stared down at his desk. Then he rose.

'Professor, I need to think this matter over. I have listened to you both, and I apologize if Gordon spoke out of turn. I respect your concern, while being unable as yet to endorse your thesis. Perhaps you would both be kind enough to leave me now, and I will study your summary.'

He rose, came round his desk, shook Embry's hand and ventured to put his other hand, frail and white, on Embry's sturdy shoulder. Embry left the room, taking care to see that Levine preceded him. The door closed behind them.

Once he was alone, Sir Alastair walked slowly up and down the old room. He had to decide whether to request the university to fund a second year of Embry's research. Deciding was one of the most difficult aspects of his position. He found it easy to set Embry's blustering but engaging personality aside and consider the possibilities of his work.

During the meeting, no stormier than many held in this room, he had left the television set switched on with its volume right down. The set stood in its mahogany case in one corner, pouring forth its images of the world. Stern crossed to his desk, picked up the zapper, and increased volume.

The day was Remembrance Sunday, Sunday 10 November. The BBC were covering the memorial ceremony at the Cenotaph. A commentator was speaking in a hushed voice as Whitehall filled with people and the service of remembrance began. Strawy yellow sunshine lit the solemn faces of the crowd.

For Sir Alastair Stern, this gathering in the heart of London was always an emotional event. His wish was that he could have been at home with his wife. Both he and Martha had lost close relations in the Second World War. Their children hated the whole idea of Remembrance Day, finding it merely ghoulish. That, he thought, was their entitlement. He had fought the Nazis in order that his children should be easy in their minds.

He stood in the middle of the room, head lowered, during the two minutes' silence. But his thoughts turned again to Embry. Gordon disliked Embry and considered him no scientist, a buffoon rather. But perhaps new lines of thought, new theories, sprang from just such minds as Embry's. The greatest of all experimental investigators into physical nature was Michael Faraday, yet Faraday was a blacksmith's son who taught himself science – and went on to make discoveries which changed the world. Something in the set of Embry's face reminded Stern of the expression on Faraday's face in a photograph he knew well. Was it not possible that his present unlicked and cranky theory might develop into something of value? Might it not be that he was on the way to discovering a kind of yardstick by which a propensity for disaster could be measured? Wasn't that an eccentricity worth pursuing?

Stern could not believe for a moment that the four people killed in the Yarmouth outrage were particularly susceptible to that fate. Yet he admired the attempt at measurement, at quantification. It was something – however superficially laughable – to set against the ever-present spectre of war and killings on an unremitting scale. In the human universe, almost everything remained to be done.

Try as he might, Sir Alastair did not understand transpsychic reality. Embry had written a book on the subject – it lay on his desk at present. He could not believe a word of it. Indeed, he thought it bunkum. However, there was something in the whole farrago to like: the connection between individual and state. It was, as Embry pointed out, too common for individuals to blame their governments for error, where governments always represented something vital in the temperaments of those governed.

Any system that aided the individual promised ultimately to improve governance. If governance improved, reciprocally ameliorating individual lives, there was a chance that war and killing might slowly atrophy. That part of Embry's argument had Stern's full support.

The two minutes' silence was over. The world came back to life. The silent masses in Whitehall began to move, sporting their scarlet poppies.

Cranky. Utopian. Absurd.

For all that, Stern wanted to give his mad American professor his head, to devise something to stand against the bloodbaths disfiguring the twentieth century. He sat down at his desk and began to think of ways in which he might approach his finance committee.

In No. 2 Clamp Lane, Ray and Ruby Tebbutt were also watching the proceedings on TV. Ruby had come in from the garden when Ray called, and was still wearing her boots.

'I'll bring us a cup of coffee,' she said.

'Let's just see this first,' Ray said, without removing his gaze from the screen.

They sat together on the sofa, watching as the Queen laid a wreath at the base of the Cenotaph, commemorating the dead of two World Wars and the wars succeeding them. Following her came the commanders of the armed services, and the heads of what remained of the British Commonwealth. Laurence Binyon's epitaph to the fallen was spoken:

> At the going down of the sun and in the morning
> We will remember them.

A military band struck up with cheerful old tunes – 'Pack Up Your Troubles', 'Goodbye Dolly Grey' – as ex-servicemen and women began the march past along Whitehall, swinging their arms as of old. The frail grey remnants of the Old Contemptibles, now few in number, came by, earning a special cheer. Everyone earned special cheers on this solemn day: the men of the Eighth Army, the Burma Star veterans, those who had fought in the Falklands and the Gulf Wars, and many more.

'Jenny hated this,' Ruby said. 'She said it was all bullshit and militarism.'

'I know,' said Ray. It was all he could manage to say through the lump in his throat. But his thoughts ran on. Of course you were right, Jenny, my love, of course. The poppies are laid for you too. You also died by an enemy bomb. But all your fierce opposition to militarism – it did no good. Perhaps it was just a premonition of how you were going to die. Perhaps your hatred of that militaristic side of England showed itself by your going off with that Czech.

No, that can't be true. My thoughts are tired of thinking about you, Jenny. What is true? Heaven help us if that bugger Mike Linwood has the truth . . . The side of England you hated was not necessarily the side I hate. But the love of country goes much deeper – and isn't so easy to express. Except in war, of course, when you can die for your country. Perhaps that's why wars are popular, fought not for hate as generally assumed, but for love . . .

When Ruby rose to go and make the coffee, Ray also stood, using his stick. He still had trouble with his injured legs; age did not improve them. He stared out across the lane at the derelict No. 1 cottage, while listening to the silver band in London playing 'Colonel Bogey'.

The poppies are for you, Jenny, my love. And for Mum and Dad, killed in the last war. The Tebbutts are a funny old lot, when you think. Death runs in the family . . . We'll never forget you, Jenny. Where you're concerned it's always Remembrance Day.

Hobbling, he followed Ruby into the kitchen.

A further change in Czechoslovakia's arms industry is signalled by the makers of Semtex – the plastic explosive – seeking Western partners. (*Guardian*, 1.2.91.) British company ICI visited the chemical works where Semtex is made at some point during 1989, 'with an eye to forming a joint venture' stated *Jane's Defence Weekly*, 16.2.91

Campaign Against the Arms Trade
April 1991 Newsletter, 50p.

Those who constantly recall their history are doomed to repeat it.

HENGIST M. EMBRY